TWO CAN KEEP A SECRET

KAREN M. McMANUS

PENGUIN BOOKS

PENGUIN BOOKS

UK | USA | Canada | Ireland | Australia
India | New Zealand | South Africa

Penguin Books is part of the Penguin Random House group of companies
whose addresses can be found at global.penguinrandomhouse.com.

www.penguin.co.uk
www.puffin.co.uk
www.ladybird.co.uk

First published in the USA by Delacorte Press,
an imprint of Random House Children's Books,
and in Great Britain by Penguin Books 2019

001

Text copyright © Karen M. McManus, 2019
Interior design by Ken Crossland

The moral right of the author has been asserted

Set in 11.16/15.25 pt Adobe Garamond Pro
Printed and bound in Great Britain by Clays Ltd, Elcograf S.p.A.

A CIP catalogue record for this book is available from the British Library

ISBN: 978–0–141–37565–6

All correspondence to:
Penguin Books
Penguin Random House Children's
80 Strand London WC2R ORL

For Gabriela, Carolina, and Erik

CHAPTER ONE

ELLERY

FRIDAY, AUGUST 30

If I believed in omens, this would be a bad one.

There's only one suitcase left on the baggage carousel. It's bright pink, covered with Hello Kitty stickers, and definitely not mine.

My brother, Ezra, watches it pass us for the fourth time, leaning on the handle of his own oversized suitcase. The crowd around the carousel is nearly gone, except for a couple arguing about who was supposed to keep track of their rental car reservation. "Maybe you should take it," Ezra suggests. "Seems like whoever owns it wasn't on our flight, and I bet they have an interesting wardrobe. A lot of polka dots, probably. And glitter." His phone chimes, and he pulls it out of his pocket. "Nana's outside."

"I can't believe this," I mutter, kicking the toe of my sneaker against the carousel's metal side. "My entire life was in that suitcase."

It's a slight exaggeration. My *actual* entire life was in La Puente, California, until about eight hours ago. Other than a few boxes shipped to Vermont last week, the suitcase contains what's left.

"I guess we should report it." Ezra scans the baggage claim area, running a hand over his close-cropped hair. He used to have thick dark curls like mine, hanging in his eyes, and I still can't get used to the cut he got over the summer. He tilts his suitcase and pivots toward the information desk. "Over here, probably."

The skinny guy behind the desk looks like he could still be in high school, with a rash of red pimples dotting his cheeks and jawline. A gold name tag pinned crookedly to his blue vest reads "Andy." Andy's thin lips twist when I tell him about my suitcase, and he cranes his neck toward the Hello Kitty bag still making carousel laps. "Flight 5624 from Los Angeles? With a layover in Charlotte?" I nod. "You sure that's not yours?"

"Positive."

"Bummer. It'll turn up, though. You just gotta fill this out." He yanks open a drawer and pulls out a form, sliding it toward me. "There's a pen around here somewhere," he mutters, pawing half-heartedly through a stack of papers.

"I have one." I unzip the front of my backpack, pulling out a book that I place on the counter while I feel around for a pen. Ezra raises his brows when he sees the battered hardcover.

"Really, Ellery?" he asks. "You brought *In Cold Blood* on the plane? Why didn't you just ship it with the rest of your books?"

2

"It's valuable," I say defensively.

Ezra rolls his eyes. "You *know* that's not Truman Capote's actual signature. Sadie got fleeced."

"Whatever. It's the thought that counts," I mutter. Our mother bought me the "signed" first edition off eBay after she landed a role as Dead Body #2 on *Law & Order* four years ago. She gave Ezra a Sex Pistols album cover with a Sid Vicious autograph that was probably just as forged. We should've gotten a car with reliable brakes instead, but Sadie's never been great at long-term planning. "Anyway, you know what they say. When in Murderland . . ." I finally extract a pen and start scratching my name across the form.

"You headed for Echo Ridge, then?" Andy asks. I pause on the second *c* of my last name and he adds, "They don't call it that anymore, you know. And you're early. It doesn't open for another week."

"I know. I didn't mean the theme park. I meant the . . ." I trail off before saying *town* and shove *In Cold Blood* into my bag. "Never mind," I say, returning my attention to the form. "How long does it usually take to get your stuff back?"

"Shouldn't be more than a day." Andy's eyes drift between Ezra and me. "You guys look a lot alike. You twins?"

I nod and keep writing. Ezra, ever polite, answers, "We are."

"I was supposed to be a twin," Andy says. "The other one got absorbed in the womb, though." Ezra lets out a surprised little snort, and I bite back a laugh. This happens to my brother all the time; people overshare the strangest things with him. We might have almost the same face, but his is the one everyone trusts. "I always thought it would've been cool to have a twin.

3

You could pretend to be one another and mess with people." I look up, and Andy is squinting at us again. "Well. I guess you guys can't do that. You aren't the right kind of twins."

"Definitely not," Ezra says with a fixed smile.

I write faster and hand the completed form to Andy, who tears off the top sheets and gives me the yellow carbon. "So somebody will get in touch, right?" I ask.

"Yep," Andy says. "You don't hear from them tomorrow, call the number at the bottom. Have fun in Echo Ridge."

Ezra exhales loudly as we head for the revolving door, and I grin at him over my shoulder. "You make the nicest friends."

He shudders. "Now I can't stop thinking about it. *Absorbed.* How does that even happen? Did he . . . No. I'm not going to speculate. I don't want to know. What a weird thing to grow up with, though, huh? Knowing how easily you could've been the wrong twin."

We push through the door into a blast of stifling, exhaust-filled air that takes me by surprise. Even on the last day of August, I'd expected Vermont to be a lot cooler than California. I pull my hair off my neck while Ezra scrolls through his phone. "Nana says she's circling because she didn't want to park in a lot," he reports.

I raise my brows at him. "Nana's texting and driving?"

"Apparently."

I haven't seen my grandmother since she visited us in California ten years ago, but from what I can remember, that seems out of character.

We wait a few minutes, wilting in the heat, until a forest-green Subaru station wagon pulls up beside us. The passenger-side window rolls down, and Nana sticks her head out. She doesn't look much different than she does over Skype, although her thick gray bangs appear freshly cut. "Go on, get in," she calls, side-eyeing the traffic cop a few feet from us. "They won't let you idle for more than a minute." She pulls her head back in as Ezra wheels his solitary suitcase toward the trunk.

When we slide into the backseat Nana turns to face us, and so does a younger woman behind the steering wheel. "Ellery, Ezra, this is Melanie Kilduff. Her family lives down the street from us. I have terrible night vision, so Melanie was kind enough to drive. She used to babysit your mother when she was young. You've probably heard the name."

Ezra and I exchange wide-eyed glances. *Yes*. Yes, we have.

Sadie left Echo Ridge when she was eighteen, and she's only been back twice. The first time was the year before we were born, when our grandfather died from a heart attack. And the second time was five years ago, for Melanie's teenage daughter's funeral.

Ezra and I watched the *Dateline* special—"Mystery at Murderland"—at home while our neighbor stayed with us. I was transfixed by the story of Lacey Kilduff, the beautiful blond homecoming queen from my mother's hometown, found strangled in a Halloween theme park. Airport Andy was right; the park's owner changed its name from Murderland to Fright Farm a few months later. I'm not sure the case would have gotten as much national attention if the park hadn't had such an on-the-nose name.

Or if Lacey hadn't been the second pretty teenager from Echo Ridge—and from the same exact street, even—to make tragic headlines.

Sadie wouldn't answer any of our questions when she got back from Lacey's funeral. "I just want to forget about it," she said whenever we asked. Which is what she's been saying about Echo Ridge our entire lives.

Ironic, I guess, that we ended up here anyway.

"Nice to meet you," Ezra says to Melanie, while I somehow manage to choke on my own saliva. He pounds me on the back, harder than necessary.

Melanie is pretty in a faded sort of way, with pale blond hair pulled into a French braid, light blue eyes, and a sprinkling of freckles. She flashes a disarming, gap-toothed smile. "You as well. Sorry we're late, but we hit a surprising amount of traffic. How was your flight?"

Before Ezra can answer, a loud rap sounds on the roof of the Subaru, making Nana jump. "You need to keep moving," the traffic cop calls.

"Burlington is the *rudest* city," Nana huffs. She presses a button on the door to close her window as Melanie eases the car behind a taxi.

I fumble with my seat belt as I stare at the back of Melanie's head. I wasn't expecting to meet her like this. I figured I would eventually, since she and Nana are neighbors, but I thought it would be more of a wave while taking out the trash, not an hour-long drive as soon as I landed in Vermont.

"I was so sorry to hear about your mother," Melanie says as she exits the airport and pulls onto a narrow highway dotted with green signs. It's almost ten o'clock at night, and a small cluster of buildings in front of us glows with lit windows. "But I'm glad she's getting the help she needs. Sadie is such a strong woman. I'm sure you'll be back with her soon, but I hope you enjoy your time in Echo Ridge. It's a lovely little town. I know Nora is looking forward to showing you around."

There. *That's* how you navigate an awkward conversation. No need to lead with *Sorry your mom drove her car into a jewelry store while she was high on opioids and had to go to rehab for four months.* Just acknowledge the elephant in the room, sidestep, and segue into smoother conversational waters.

Welcome to Echo Ridge.

I fall asleep shortly after we hit the highway and don't stir until a loud noise jolts me awake. It sounds as though the car is being pelted from every direction with dozens of rocks. I turn toward Ezra, disoriented, but he looks equally confused. Nana twists in her seat, shouting to be heard over the roar. "Hail. Not uncommon this time of year. Although these are rather large."

"I'm going to pull over and let this pass," Melanie calls. She eases the car to the side of the road and shifts into park. The hail is hitting harder than ever, and I can't help but think that she's going to have hundreds of tiny dents in her car by the time it stops. One particularly large hailstone smacks right into the middle of the windshield, startling us all.

"How is it *hailing*?" I ask. "It was hot in Burlington."

"Hail forms in the cloud layer," Nana explains, gesturing toward the sky. "Temperatures are freezing there. The stones will melt quickly on the ground, though."

Her voice isn't warm, exactly—I'm not sure warmth is possible for her—but it's more animated than it's been all night.

Nana used to be a teacher, and she's obviously a lot more comfortable in that role than that of Custodial Grandparent. Not that I blame her. She's stuck with us during Sadie's sixteen weeks of court-ordered rehab, and vice versa. The judge insisted we live with family, which severely limited our options. Our father was a one-night stand—a stuntman, or so he claimed during the whopping two hours he and Sadie spent together after meeting at an LA club. We don't have aunts, uncles, or cousins. Not a single person, except for Nana, to take us in.

We sit in silence for a few minutes, watching hailstones bounce off the car hood, until the frequency tapers and finally stops altogether. Melanie pulls back onto the road, and I glance at the clock on the dashboard. It's nearly eleven; I slept for almost an hour. I nudge Ezra and ask, "We must almost be there, right?"

"Almost," Ezra says. He lowers his voice. "Place is hopping on a Friday night. We haven't passed a building for miles."

It's pitch black outside, and even after rubbing my eyes a few times I can't see much out the window except the shadowy blur of trees. I try, though, because I want to see the place Sadie couldn't wait to leave. "It's like living in a postcard," she used to say. "Pretty, shiny, and closed in. Everyone who lives in Echo Ridge acts like you'll vanish if you venture outside the border."

The car goes over a bump, and my seat belt digs into my neck as the impact jolts me to one side. Ezra yawns so hard that his jaw cracks. I'm sure that once I crashed he felt obligated to stay awake and make conversation, even though neither of us has slept properly for days.

"We're less than a mile from home." Nana's voice from the front seat startles us both. "We just passed the 'Welcome to Echo Ridge' sign, although it's so poorly lit that I don't suppose you even noticed."

She's right. I didn't, though I'd made a mental note to look for it. The sign was one of the few things Sadie ever talked about related to Echo Ridge, usually after a few glasses of wine. "'Population 4,935.' Never changed the entire eighteen years I lived there," she'd say with a smirk. "Apparently if you're going to bring someone in, you have to take someone out first."

"Here comes the overpass, Melanie." Nana's voice has a warning edge.

"I know," Melanie says. The road curves sharply as we pass beneath an arch of gray stone, and Melanie slows to a crawl. There are no streetlights along this stretch, and Melanie switches on the high beams.

"Nana is the worst backseat driver ever," Ezra whispers.

"Really?" I whisper back. "But Melanie's so careful."

"Unless we're at a red light, we're going too fast."

I snicker, just as my grandmother hollers, "Stop!" in such a commanding voice that both Ezra and I jump. For a split second, I think she has supersonic hearing and is annoyed at our snarking. Then Melanie slams on the brakes, stopping the car so abruptly that I'm pitched forward against my seat belt.

"What the—?" Ezra and I both ask at the same time, but Melanie and Nana have already unbuckled and scrambled out of the car. We exchange confused glances and follow suit. The ground is covered with puddles of half-melted hail, and I pick my way around them toward my grandmother. Nana is standing in front of Melanie's car, her gaze fixed on the patch of road bathed in bright headlights.

And on the still figure lying right in the middle of it. Covered in blood, with his neck bent at a horribly wrong angle and his eyes wide open, staring at nothing.

CHAPTER TWO

ELLERY

SATURDAY, AUGUST 31

The sun wakes me up, burning through blinds that clearly weren't purchased for their room-darkening properties. But I stay immobile under the covers—a thin crocheted bedspread and petal-soft sheets—until a low knock sounds on the door.

"Yeah?" I sit up, futilely trying to push hair out of my eyes, as Ezra enters. The silver-plated clock on the nightstand reads 9:50, but since I'm still on West Coast time I don't feel as though I've slept nearly enough.

"Hey," Ezra says. "Nana said to wake you up. A police officer is on his way over. He wants to talk to us about last night."

Last night. We stayed with the man in the road, crouching next to him between dark pools of blood, until an ambulance came. I couldn't bring myself to look at his face at first, but once I did I couldn't look away. He was so *young*. No older than thirty,

11

dressed in athletic clothes and sneakers. Melanie, who's a nurse, performed CPR until the EMTs arrived, but more like she was praying for a miracle than because she thought it would do any good. She told us when we got back into Nana's car that he was dead before we arrived.

"Jason Bowman," she'd said in a shaking voice. "He's—he *was*—one of the science teachers at Echo Ridge High. Helped out with marching band, too. Really popular with the kids. You would have . . . you *should* have . . . met him next week."

Ezra, who's fully dressed, hair damp from a recent shower, tosses a small plastic pack onto the bed, bringing me back to the present. "Also, she said to give you these."

The unopened package has the Hanes logo on the front, along with a picture of a smiling blond woman wearing a sports bra and underpants that come halfway up her waist. "Oh no."

"Oh yes. Those are *literally* granny panties. Nana says she bought a couple sizes too small by mistake and forgot to return them. Now they're yours."

"Fantastic," I mutter, swinging my legs out of bed. I'm wearing the T-shirt I had layered under my sweater yesterday, plus a rolled-up pair of Ezra's sweatpants. When I learned I'd be moving to Echo Ridge, I went through my entire closet and ruthlessly donated anything I hadn't worn in the past few months. I pared my wardrobe down so much that everything, except for a few coats and shoes that I shipped last week, fit into a single suitcase. At the time, it felt like I was bringing order and control to at least one small part of my life.

Now, of course, all it means is that I have nothing to wear.

I pick my phone up from the nightstand, checking for a

luggage-related text or voice mail. But there's nothing. "Why are you up so early?" I ask Ezra.

He shrugs. "It's not *that* early. I've been walking around the neighborhood. It's pretty. Very leafy. I posted a couple of Insta stories. And made a playlist."

I fold my arms. "Not another Michael playlist."

"No," Ezra says defensively. "It's a musical tribute to the Northeast. You'd be surprised how many songs have a New England state in the title."

"Mm-hmm." Ezra's boyfriend, Michael, broke up with him preemptively the week before we left because, he said, "long-distance relationships don't ever work." Ezra tries to act like he doesn't care, but he's created some seriously emo playlists since it happened.

"Don't judge." Ezra's eyes drift toward the bookcase, where *In Cold Blood* is lined up neatly next to my Ann Rule collection, *Fatal Vision, Midnight in the Garden of Good and Evil,* and the rest of my true-crime books. They're the only things I unpacked last night from the boxes stacked in one corner of the room. "We all have our coping mechanisms."

He retreats to his room, and I gaze around the unfamiliar space I'll be living in for the next four months. When we arrived last night, Nana told me that I'd be sleeping in Sadie's old room. I was both eager and nervous opening the door, wondering what echoes of my mother I'd find inside. But I walked into a standard guest bedroom without a scrap of personality. The furniture is dark wood, the walls a pale eggshell. There's not much in the way of decor except for lacy curtains, a plaid area rug, and a framed print of a lighthouse. Everything smells faintly of lemon

Pledge and cedar. When I try to imagine Sadie here—fixing her hair in the cloudy mirror over the dresser or doing her homework at the old-fashioned desk—the images won't come.

Ezra's room is the same. There's no hint that a teenage girl ever lived in either of them.

I drop to the floor beside my moving boxes and root around in the nearest one until I come across plastic-wrapped picture frames. The first one I unwrap is a photo of Ezra and me standing on Santa Monica Pier last year, a perfect sunset behind us. The setting is gorgeous, but it's not a flattering picture of me. I wasn't ready for the shot, and my tense expression doesn't match Ezra's wide grin. I kept it, though, because it reminded me of another photo.

That's the second one I pull out—grainy and much older, of two identical teenage girls with long, curly hair like mine, dressed in '90s grungewear. One of them is smiling brightly, the other looks annoyed. My mother and her twin sister, Sarah. They were seventeen then, seniors at Echo Ridge High like Ezra and I are about to be. A few weeks after the photo was taken, Sarah disappeared.

It's been twenty-three years and no one knows what happened to her. Or maybe it'd be more accurate to say that if anybody does know, they're not telling.

I place the photos side by side on top of the bookcase, and think about Ezra's words in the airport last night, after Andy overshared his origin story. *What a weird thing to grow up with, though, huh? Knowing how easily you could've been the wrong twin.*

Sadie never liked talking about Sarah, no matter how hungry I was for information. There weren't any pictures of her around our apartment; I had to steal this one off the Internet. My true-crime kick started in earnest with Lacey's death, but ever since I was old enough to understand what happened to Sarah, I was obsessed with her disappearance. It was the worst thing I could imagine, to have your twin go missing and never come back.

Sadie's smile in the photo is as blinding as Ezra's. She was a star back then—the popular homecoming queen, just like Lacey. And she's been trying to be a star ever since. I don't know if Sadie would have done better than a handful of walk-on roles if she'd had her twin cheering her on. I *do* know there's no possible way she can feel complete. When you come into the world with another person, they're as much a part of you as your heartbeat.

There are lots of reasons my mother got addicted to painkillers—a strained shoulder, a bad breakup, another lost role, moving to our crappiest apartment yet on her fortieth birthday—but I can't help but think it all started with the loss of that serious-faced girl in the photo.

The doorbell rings, and I almost drop the picture. I completely forgot I was supposed to be getting ready to meet a police officer. I glance at the mirror over the dresser, wincing at my reflection. My hair looks like a wig, and all my anti-frizz products are in my missing suitcase. I pull my curls into a ponytail, then twist and turn the thick strands until I can knot the ends together into a low bun without needing an elastic. It's one of the first hair tricks Sadie ever taught me. When I was little we'd stand at the double sink in our bathroom, me watching her in the mirror so I could copy the quick, deft motion of her hands.

My eyes prick as Nana calls up the stairs. "Ellery? Ezra? Officer Rodriguez is here."

Ezra's already in the hall when I leave my room, and we head downstairs to Nana's kitchen. A dark-haired man in a blue uniform, his back to us, takes the cup of coffee Nana holds toward him. She looks like she just stepped out of an L. L. Bean catalog in khakis, clogs and a boxy oxford shirt with horizontal stripes.

"Maybe the town will finally do something about that overpass," Nana says, then catches my eye over the officer's shoulder. "There you are. Ryan, this is my granddaughter and grandson. Ellery and Ezra, meet Officer Ryan Rodriguez. He lives down the street and came by to ask us a few questions about last night."

The officer turns with a half smile that freezes as the coffee mug slips out of his hand and goes crashing to the floor. None of us react for a second, and then everybody leaps into action at once, grabbing at paper towels and picking thick pieces of ceramic mug off Nana's black-and-white tiled floor.

"I'm so sorry," Officer Rodriguez keeps repeating. He can't be more than five years older than me and Ezra, and he looks as though even he's not sure whether he's an actual adult yet. "I have no idea how that happened. I'll replace the mug."

"Oh, for goodness' sake," Nana says crisply. "Those cost two dollars at Dalton's. Sit down and I'll get you another one. You too, kids. There's juice on the table if you want some."

We all settle around the kitchen table, which is neatly set with three place mats, silverware, and glasses. Officer Rodriguez pulls a notepad from his front pocket and flips through it with a knitted brow. He has one of those hangdog faces that looks worried even now, when he's not breaking my grandmother's stuff. "Thanks for making time this morning. I just came from the Kilduffs' house, and Melanie filled me in on what happened at the Fulkerson Street overpass last night. Which, I'm sorry to say, looks like it was a hit-and-run." Nana hands him another cup of coffee before sitting down next to Ezra, and Officer Rodriguez takes a careful sip. "Thank you, Mrs. Corcoran. So it would be helpful if all of you could tell me everything you observed, even if it doesn't seem important."

I straighten in my chair, and Ezra rolls his eyes. He knows exactly what's going through my head. Even though last night was awful, I can't *not* feel a slight thrill at being part of an actual police investigation. I've been waiting for this moment half my life.

Unfortunately I'm no help, because I hardly remember anything except Melanie trying to help Mr. Bowman. Ezra's not much better. Nana is the only one who noticed little details, like the fact that there was an umbrella and a Tupperware container scattered on the street next to Mr. Bowman. And as far as investigating officers go, Ryan Rodriguez is disappointing. He keeps repeating the same questions, almost knocks over his fresh cup of coffee, and stumbles constantly over Melanie's name. By the time he thanks us and Nana walks him to the front door, I'm convinced he needs a few more years of training before they let him out on his own again.

"That was kind of disorganized," I say when Nana returns to the kitchen. "Do people take him seriously as a police officer around here?"

She takes a pan out from a cabinet next to the stove and places it on a front burner. "Ryan is perfectly capable," she says matter-of-factly, crossing to the refrigerator and pulling out the butter dish. She sets it on the counter and slices off a huge chunk, dropping it into the pan. "He may be a little out of sorts. His father died a few months ago. Cancer. They were very close. And his mother passed the year before, so it's been one thing after another for that family. Ryan is the youngest and the only one still at home. I imagine it's been lonely."

"He lived with his parents?" Ezra asks. "How old is he?" My brother is kind of judgy about adults who still live at home. He'll be one of those people, like Sadie, who moves out as soon as the ink is dry on his diploma. He has a ten-year plan that involves taking a grunt job at a radio station while deejaying on the side, until he has enough experience to host his own show. I try not to panic whenever I imagine him leaving me behind to do . . . who even knows what.

"Twenty-two, I think? Or twenty-three," Nana says. "All the Rodriguez kids lived at home during college. Ryan stayed once his father got sick." Ezra hunches his shoulders guiltily as my ears prick up.

"Twenty-three?" I repeat. "Was he in Lacey Kilduff's class?"

"I believe so," Nana says as she cracks an egg into the now-sizzling pan.

I hesitate. I barely know my grandmother. We've never talked about my missing aunt on our awkward, infrequent Skype calls, and I have no idea if Lacey's death is extra-painful for her because of what happened to Sarah. I should probably keep my mouth shut, but . . .

"Were they friends?" I blurt out. Ezra's face settles into a *here we go* expression.

"I couldn't say. They knew one another, certainly. Ryan grew up in the neighborhood and they both worked at . . . Fright

18

Farm." Her hesitation before the new name is so slight that I almost miss it. "Most kids in town did. Still do."

"When does it open?" Ezra asks. He glances at me like he's doing me a favor, but he didn't have to bother. I looked up the schedule as soon as I learned we were moving to Echo Ridge.

"Next weekend. Right before you two start school," Nana says. Echo Ridge has the latest start date of any school we've ever attended, which is one point in its favor. At La Puente, we'd already been in school two weeks by Labor Day. Nana gestures with her spatula toward the kitchen window over the sink, which looks out into the woods behind her house. "You'll hear it once it does. It's a ten-minute walk through the woods."

"It is?" Ezra looks baffled. I am too, but mostly by his utter lack of research. "So the Kilduffs still live right behind the place where their daughter . . . where somebody, um . . ." He trails off as Nana turns toward us with two plates, each holding an enormous fluffy omelet, and deposits them in front of us. Ezra and I exchange surprised glances. I can't remember the last time either of us had anything for breakfast other than coffee. But my mouth waters at the savory scent, and my stomach rumbles. I haven't eaten anything since the three Kind bars I had for dinner on last night's flight.

"Well." Nana sits down between us and pours herself a glass of orange juice from the ceramic pitcher on the table. *Pitcher*. Not a carton. I spend a few seconds trying to figure out why you'd bother emptying a carton into a pitcher before taking a sip of mine and realizing it's freshly squeezed. How are she and Sadie even related? "It's their home. The two younger girls have lots of friends in the neighborhood."

"How old are they?" I ask. Melanie wasn't just Sadie's favorite babysitter; she was almost a mentor to her in high school—and pretty much the only person from Echo Ridge my mother ever talked about. But I still know hardly anything about her except that her daughter was murdered.

"Caroline is twelve and Julia is six," Nana says. "There's quite a gap between the two of them, and between Lacey and Caroline. Melanie's always had trouble conceiving. But there's a silver lining, I suppose. The girls were so young when Lacey died, looking after them might be the only thing that kept Melanie and Dan going during such a terrible time."

Ezra cuts into the corner of his omelet and releases a small cloud of steam. "The police never had any suspects in Lacey's murder, huh?" he asks.

"No," Nana says at the same time as I say, "The boyfriend."

Nana takes a long sip of juice. "Plenty of people thought that. *Think* that," she says. "But Declan Kelly wasn't an official suspect. Questioned, yes. Multiple times. But never held."

"Does he still live in Echo Ridge?" I ask.

She shakes her head. "He left town right after graduation. Best for all involved, I'm sure. The situation took an enormous toll on his family. Declan's father moved away shortly after he did. I thought the mother and brother would be next, but . . . things worked out differently for them."

I pause with my fork in midair. "Brother?" I hadn't known Lacey's boyfriend had a brother; the news never reported much about his family.

"Declan has a younger brother, Malcolm. Around your age," Nana says. "I don't know him well, but he seems a quieter sort.

Doesn't strut around town as if he owns it, at any rate, the way his brother did."

I watch her take a careful bite of omelet, wishing I could read her better so I'd know whether Lacey and Sarah are as intertwined in her mind as they are in mine. It's been so long since Sarah disappeared; almost a quarter century with no answers. Lacey's parents lack a different kind of closure—they know *what, when,* and *how,* but not *who* or *why.* "Do you think Declan Kelly is guilty?" I ask.

Nana's brow wrinkles, as though she suddenly finds the entire conversation distasteful. "I didn't say that. There was never any hard evidence against him."

I reach for the saltshaker without responding. That might be true, but if years of reading true-crime books and watching *Dateline* have taught me anything, it's this: it's *always* the boyfriend.

CHAPTER THREE

MALCOLM
WEDNESDAY, SEPTEMBER 4

My shirt's stiff with too much starch. It practically crackles when I bend my arms to drape a tie around my neck. I watch my hands in the mirror, trying and failing to get the knot straight, and give up when it's at least the right size. The mirror looks old and expensive, like everything in the Nilssons' house. It reflects a bedroom that could fit three of my old one. And at least half of Declan's apartment.

What's it like living in that house? my brother asked last night, scraping the last of his birthday cake off a plate while Mom was in the bathroom. She'd brought a bunch of balloons that looked tiny in the Nilssons' foyer, but kept batting Declan in the head in the cramped alcove he calls a kitchen.

Fucked up, I said. Which is true. But no more fucked up than the past five years have been. Declan's spent most of them

22

living four hours away in New Hampshire, renting a basement apartment from our aunt.

A sharp knock sounds at my bedroom door, and hinges squeak as my stepsister pokes her head in without waiting for an answer. "You ready?" she asks.

"Yep," I say, picking up a blue suit coat from my bed and shrugging it on. Katrin tilts her head and frowns, ice-blond hair spilling over one shoulder. I know that look: *There's something wrong with you, and I'm about to tell you exactly what it is and how to fix it.* I've been seeing it for months now.

"Your tie's crooked," she says, heels clicking on the floor as she walks toward me, hands outstretched. A crease appears between her eyes as she tugs at the knot, then disappears when she steps back to view her work. "There," she says, patting my shoulder with a satisfied expression. "Much better." Her hand skims down to my chest and she plucks a piece of lint from my suit coat with two pale-pink fingernails and lets it drop to the floor. "You clean up all right, Mal. Who would've thought?"

Not her. Katrin Nilsson barely spoke to me until her father started dating my mother last winter. She's the queen of Echo Ridge High, and I'm the band nerd with the disreputable family. But now that we live under the same roof, Katrin has to acknowledge my existence. She copes by treating me like either a project or a nuisance, depending on her mood.

"Let's go," she says, tugging lightly at my arm. Her black dress hugs her curves but stops right above her knees. She'd almost be conservative if she weren't wearing tall, spiky heels that basically force you to look at her legs. So I do. My new stepsister might be a pain in the ass, but she's undeniably hot.

23

I follow Katrin into the hallway to the balcony staircase overlooking the massive foyer downstairs. My mother and Peter are at the bottom waiting for us, and I drop my eyes because whenever they're standing that close, his hands are usually someplace I don't want to see. Katrin and her superjock boyfriend commit less PDA than those two.

But Mom's happy, and I guess that's good.

Peter looks up and takes a break from manhandling my mom. "Don't you two look nice!" he calls out. He's in a suit too, same dark blue as mine, except he gets his tailored so they fit him perfectly. Peter's like one of those suave *GQ* watch ads come to life—square jaw, penetrating gaze, wavy blond hair with just enough gray to be distinguished. Nobody could believe he was interested in my mother when they first started dating. People were even more shocked when he married her.

He saved them. That's what the entire town thinks. Peter Nilsson, the rich and charming owner of the only law firm in town, took us from town pariahs to town royalty with one tasteful justice of the peace ceremony at Echo Ridge Lake. And maybe he did. People don't avoid my mother anymore, or whisper behind her back. She gets invited to the garden club, school committees, tonight's fund-raiser, and all that other crap.

Doesn't mean I have to like him, though.

"Nice having you back, Malcolm," he adds, almost sounding like he means it. Mom and I have been gone a week, visiting family across a few towns in New Hampshire and then finishing up at Declan's place. Peter and Katrin didn't come. Partly because he had to work, and partly because neither of them leave Echo Ridge for anyplace without room service and a spa.

"Did you have dinner with Mr. Coates while we were gone?" I ask abruptly.

Peter's nostrils flare slightly, which is the only sign of annoyance he ever shows. "I did, on Friday. He's still getting his business up and running, but when the time is right he'd be happy to talk with Declan. I'll keep checking in with him."

Ben Coates used to be mayor of Echo Ridge. After that, he left to run a political consulting business in Burlington. Declan is a few—okay, a *lot*—of credits short from finishing his poli-sci degree at community college, but he's still hoping for a recommendation. It's the only thing he's ever asked of Peter. Or of Mom, I guess, since Declan and Peter don't really talk.

Mom beams at Peter, and I let it drop. Katrin steps forward, reaching out a hand to touch the twisted beaded necklace Mom's wearing. "This is so pretty!" she exclaims. "Very bohemian. Such a nice change from all the pearls we'll see tonight."

Mom's smile fades. "I have pearls," she says nervously, looking at Peter. "Should I—"

"You're fine," he says quickly. "You look beautiful."

I could kill Katrin. Not literally. I feel like I have to add that disclaimer even in my own thoughts, given our family history. But I don't understand her constant need to make digs at Mom's expense. It's not like Mom broke up Katrin's parents; she's Peter's *third* wife. Katrin's mother was long gone to Paris with a new husband before Mom and Peter even went on their first date.

And Katrin has to know that Mom is nervous about tonight. We've never been to the Lacey Kilduff Memorial Scholarship fund-raiser before. Mostly because we've never been invited.

Or welcome.

Peter's nostrils flare again. "Let's head out, shall we? It's getting late."

He opens the front door, stepping aside to let us through while pressing a button on his key chain. His black Range Rover starts idling in the driveway, and Katrin and I climb into the back. My mother settles herself in the passenger seat and flips the radio from the Top 40 station that Katrin likes to blast to NPR. Peter gets in last, buckling his seat belt before shifting the car into gear.

The Nilssons' winding driveway is the longest part of the trip. After that, it's a few quick turns and we're in downtown Echo Ridge. So to speak. There's not much to it—a row of white-trimmed redbrick buildings on either side of Manchester Street, lined with old-fashioned, wrought iron streetlights. It's never crowded here, but it's especially dead on a Wednesday night before school's back in session. Half the town is still on vacation, and the other half is attending the fund-raiser in the Echo Ridge Cultural Center. That's where anything notable at Echo Ridge happens, unless it happens at the Nilssons' house.

Our house. Can't get used to that.

Peter parallel parks on Manchester Street and we spill out of the car and onto the sidewalk. We're right across the street from O'Neill's Funeral Home, and Katrin heaves a sigh as we pass the pale-blue Victorian. "It's too bad you were out of town for Mr. Bowman's service," she says. "It was really nice. The show choir sang 'To Sir with Love' and everybody lost it."

My gut twists. Mr. Bowman was my favorite teacher at Echo Ridge High, by a lot. He had this quiet way of noticing what you were good at, and encouraging you to get better. After Declan moved away and my dad took off, when I had a lot of pissed-off energy and nowhere to put it, he was the one who suggested I take up the drums. It makes me sick that somebody mowed him down and left him to die in the middle of the road.

"Why was he even out in a hailstorm?" I ask, because it's easier to fixate on that than to keep feeling like shit.

"They found a Tupperware container near him," Peter says. "One of the teachers at the funeral thought he might have been collecting hail for a lesson he was planning on climate change. But I guess we'll never know for sure."

And now I feel worse, because I can picture it: Mr. Bowman leaving his house late at night with his umbrella and his plastic container, all enthusiastic because he was going to *make science real.* He said that kind of thing a lot.

After a couple of blocks, a gold-rimmed wooden sign welcomes us to the cultural center. It's the most impressive of all the redbrick buildings, with a clock tower on top and wide steps leading to a carved wooden door. I reach for the door, but Peter's faster. Always. You can't out-gentleman that guy. Mom smiles gratefully at him as she steps through the entrance.

When we get inside, a woman directs us down a hallway to an open room that contains dozens of round tables. Some people are sitting down, but most of the crowd is still milling around and talking. A few turn toward us, and then, like human dominoes, they all do.

It's the moment everyone in Echo Ridge has been waiting for: for the first time in five years, the Kellys have shown up at a night honoring Lacey Kilduff.

The girl who most people in town still believe my brother killed.

"Oh, there's Theo," Katrin murmurs, slipping away into the crowd toward her boyfriend. So much for solidarity. My mother licks her lips nervously. Peter folds her arm under his and pastes on a big, bright smile. For a second, I almost like the guy.

Declan and Lacey had been fighting for weeks before she died. Which wasn't like them; Declan could be an arrogant ass a lot of the time, but not with his girlfriend. Then all of a sudden they were slamming doors, canceling dates, and sniping at each other over social media. Declan's last, angry message on Lacey's Instagram feed was the one that news stations showed over and over in the weeks after her body was found.

I'm so fucking done with you. DONE. You have no idea.

The crowd at the Echo Ridge Cultural Center is too quiet. Even Peter's smile is getting a little fixed. The Nilsson armor is supposed to be more impenetrable than this. I'm about to say or do something desperate to cut the tension when a warm voice floats our way. "Hello, Peter. And Alicia! Malcolm! It's good to see you both."

It's Lacey's mom, Melanie Kilduff, coming toward us with a big smile. She hugs my mother first, then me, and when she pulls back nobody's staring anymore.

"Thanks," I mutter. I don't know what Melanie thinks about Declan; she's never said. But after Lacey died, when it felt like the entire world hated my family, Melanie always made a point to be nice to us. *Thanks* doesn't feel like enough, but Melanie brushes my arm like it's too much before turning toward Mom and Peter.

"Please, have a seat wherever you'd like," she says, gesturing toward the dining area. "They're about to start serving dinner."

She leaves us, heading for a table with her family, her neighbor, and a couple of kids my age I've never seen before. Which is unusual enough in this town that I crane my neck for a better look. I can't get a good glimpse of the guy, but the girl is hard to miss. She's got wild curly hair that seems almost alive, and she's wearing a weird flowered dress that looks like it came out of her grandmother's closet. Maybe it's retro, I don't know. Katrin wouldn't be caught dead in it. The girl meets my eyes, and I immediately look away. One thing I've learned from being Declan's brother over the past five years: nobody likes it when a Kelly boy stares.

Peter starts toward the front of the room, but Katrin returns just then and tugs on his arm. "Can we sit at Theo's table, Dad? There's plenty of space." He hesitates—Peter likes to lead, not follow—and Katrin puts on her most wheedling voice. "Please? I haven't seen him all week, and his parents want to talk to you about that stoplight ordinance thing."

She's good. There's nothing Peter likes better than in-depth discussions about town council crap that would bore anybody else to tears. He smiles indulgently and changes course.

Katrin's boyfriend, Theo, and his parents are the only people sitting at the ten-person table when we approach. I've gone to school with Theo since kindergarten, but as usual he looks right through me as he waves to someone over my shoulder. "Yo, Kyle! Over here."

Oh hell.

Theo's best friend, Kyle, takes a seat between him and my mother, and the chair next to me scrapes as a big man with a graying blond buzz cut settles down beside me. Chad McNulty,

29

Kyle's father and the Echo Ridge police officer who investigated Lacey's murder. Because this night wasn't awkward enough already. My mother's got that deer-in-the-headlights look she always gets around the McNultys, and Peter flares his nostrils at an oblivious Theo.

"Hello, Malcolm." Officer McNulty unfolds his napkin onto his lap without looking at me. "How's your summer been?"

"Great," I manage, taking a long sip of water.

Officer McNulty never liked my brother. Declan dated his daughter, Liz, for three months and dumped her for Lacey, which got Liz so upset that she dropped out of school for a while. In return, Kyle's always been a dick to me. Standard small-town crap that got a lot worse once Declan became an unofficial murder suspect.

Waiters start moving around the room, putting plates of salad in front of everyone. Melanie steps behind a podium on the stage in front, and Officer McNulty's jaw tenses. "That woman is a tower of strength," he says, like he's daring me to disagree.

"Thank you so much for coming," Melanie says, leaning toward the microphone. "It means the world to Dan, Caroline, Julia, and me to see how much the Lacey Kilduff Memorial Scholarship fund has grown."

I tune the rest out. Not because I don't care, but because it's too hard to hear. Years of not being invited to these things means I haven't built up much resistance. After Melanie finishes her speech, she introduces a University of Vermont junior who was the first scholarship recipient. The girl talks about her medical school plans as empty salad plates are replaced with the main course. When she's done, everyone applauds and turns their attention to the food. I poke half-heartedly at my dry chicken while Peter holds court about stoplights. Is it too soon for a bathroom break?

"The thing is, it's a delicate balance between maintaining town aesthetics and accommodating changing traffic patterns," Peter says earnestly.

Nope. Not too soon. I stand, drop my napkin onto my chair, and take off.

When I've washed my hands as many times as I can stand, I exit the men's room and hesitate in the corridor between the banquet hall and the front door. The thought of returning to that table makes my head pound. Nobody's going to miss me for another few minutes.

I tug at my collar and push open the door, stepping outside into the darkness. It's still muggy, but less stifling than inside. Nights like this make me feel like I can't breathe, like everything my brother did, actual and alleged, settled over me when I was twelve years old and still weighs me down. I became *Declan Kelly's brother* before I got a chance to be anything else, and sometimes it feels like that's all I'll ever be.

I inhale deeply, and pause when a faint chemical smell hits me. It gets stronger as I descend the stairs and head toward the lawn. With my back to the lights I can't see much, and almost trip over something lying in the grass. I bend down and pick it up. It's a can of spray paint that's missing its top.

That's what I'm smelling: fresh paint. But where is it coming from? I turn back toward the cultural center. Its well-lit exterior looks the same as ever. There isn't anything else nearby that might have been recently painted, except . . .

The cultural center sign is halfway across the lawn between the building and the street. I'm practically on top of it before I can see clearly in the dim glow thrown from the nearest streetlight. Red letters cover the back of the sign from top to bottom, stark against the pale wood:

MURDERLAND
THE SEQUEL
COMING SOON

I'm not sure how long I stand there, staring, before I realize I'm not alone anymore. The girl from Melanie's table with the curly hair and the weird dress is standing a few feet away. Her eyes dart between the words on the sign and the can in my hand, which rattles when I drop my arm.

"This isn't what it looks like," I say.

CHAPTER FOUR

ELLERY
SATURDAY, SEPTEMBER 7

How's everything going?

I consider the text from my friend Lourdes. She's in California, but not La Puente. I met her in sixth grade, which was three towns before we moved there. Or maybe four. Unlike Ezra, who jumps easily into the social scene every time we switch schools, I hang on to my virtual best friend and keep the in-person stuff surface level. It's easier to move on that way. It requires fewer emo playlists, anyway.

Let's see. We've been here a week and so far the highlight is yard work.

Lourdes sends a few sad-face emojis, then adds, *It'll pick up when school starts. Have you met any cute preppy New England guys yet?*

Just one. But not preppy. And possibly a vandal.

Do tell.

I pause, not sure how to explain my run-in with the boy at Lacey Kilduff's fund-raiser, when my phone buzzes with a call from a number with a California area code. I don't recognize it, but my heart leaps and I fire off a quick text to Lourdes: *Hang on, getting a call about my luggage I hope.* I've been in Vermont a full week, and my suitcase is still missing. If it doesn't show up within the next two days, I'm going to have to start school in the clothes my grandmother bought at Echo Ridge's one and only clothing store. It's called Dalton's Emporium and also sells kitchen goods and hardware, which should tell you everything you need to know about its fashion cred. No one who's older than six or younger than sixty should shop there, ever.

"Hello?"

"Ellery, hi!" I almost drop my phone, and when I don't answer the voice doubles down on its cheerful urgency. "It's me!"

"Yeah, I know." I lower myself stiffly onto my bed, gripping the phone in my suddenly sweaty palm. "How are you calling me?"

Sadie's tone turns reproachful. "You don't sound very happy to hear from me."

"It's just— I thought we were supposed to start talking next Thursday." Those were the rules of rehab, according to Nana: Fifteen-minute Skype sessions once a week after two full weeks of treatment had been completed. Not random calls from an unknown number.

"The rules here are ridiculous," Sadie says. I can practically hear the eye roll in her voice. "One of the aides is letting me use her phone. She's a *Defender* fan." The only speaking role Sadie

34

ever had was in the first installment of what turned out to be a huge action series in the '90s, *The Defender*, about a down-on-his-luck soldier turned avenging cyborg. She played a sexy robot named Zeta Voltes, and even though she had only one line—*That does not compute*—there are still fan websites dedicated to the character. "I'm dying to see you, love. Let's switch to FaceTime."

I pause before hitting Accept, because I'm not ready for this. At all. But what am I going to do, hang up on my mother? Within seconds Sadie's face fills the screen, bright with anticipation. She looks the same as ever—nothing like me except for the hair. Sadie's eyes are bright blue, while mine are so dark they almost look black. She's sweet-faced with soft, open features, and I'm all angles and straight lines. There's only one other trait we share, and when I see the dimple in her right cheek flash with a smile, I force myself to mirror it back. "There you are!" she crows. Then a frown creases her forehead. "What's going on with your hair?"

My chest constricts. "Is that seriously the first thing you have to say to me?"

I haven't talked to Sadie since she checked into Hamilton House, the pricey rehab center Nana's paying for. Considering she demolished an entire storefront, Sadie lucked out: she didn't hurt herself or anyone else, and she wound up in front of a judge who believes in treatment instead of jail time. But she's never been particularly grateful. Everyone and everything else is at fault: the doctor who gave her too strong a prescription, bad lighting on the street, our car's ancient brakes. It didn't fully hit me until just now—sitting in a bedroom that belongs to a grandmother I barely know, listening to Sadie criticize my hair through a phone that someone could probably get fired for giving her—how *infuriating* it all is.

"Oh, El, of course not. I'm just teasing. You look beautiful. How are you?"

How am I supposed to answer that? "I'm fine."

"What's happened in your first week? Tell me everything."

I could refuse to play along, I guess. But as my eye catches the photo of Sadie and her sister on my bookcase, I already feel myself wanting to please her. To smooth things over and make her smile. I've been doing it my entire life; it's impossible to stop now. "Things are just as weird as you've always said. I've already been questioned twice by the police."

Her eyes pop. "What?"

I tell her about the hit-and-run, and the graffiti at Lacey's fund-raiser three days ago. "Declan Kelly's *brother* wrote that?" Sadie asks, looking outraged.

"He said he just found the paint canister."

She snorts. "Likely story."

"I don't know. He looked pretty shocked when I saw him."

"God, poor Melanie and Dan. That's the last thing they need."

"The police officer I talked to at the fund-raiser said he knew you. Officer McNulty? I forget his first name."

Sadie grins. "Chad McNulty! Yeah, we dated sophomore year. God, you're going to meet all my exes, aren't you? Was Vance Puckett there, by any chance? He used to be *gorgeous*." I shake my head. "Ben Coates? Peter Nilsson?"

None of those names are familiar except the last one. I met

him at the fund-raiser, right after his stepson and I reported the sign vandalism. "You dated that guy?" I ask. "Doesn't he own, like, half the town?"

"I guess so. Cute, but kind of a tight-ass. We went out twice when I was a senior, but he was in college then and we didn't really click."

"He's Malcolm's stepfather now," I tell her.

Sadie's face scrunches in confusion. "Who?"

"Malcolm Kelly. Declan Kelly's brother? The one with the spray paint?"

"Good Lord," Sadie mutters. "I cannot keep up with that place."

Some of the tenseness that's been keeping me rigid ebbs away, and I laugh as I settle back against my pillow. Sadie's superpower is making you feel as though everything's going to be fine, even when it's mostly disastrous. "Officer McNulty said his son's in our class," I tell her. "I guess he was at the fund-raiser, but I didn't meet him."

"Ugh, we're all so *old* now. Did you talk to him about the hit-and-run, too?"

"No, that officer was really young. Ryan Rodriguez?" I don't expect Sadie to recognize the name, but an odd expression flits across her face. "What? Do you know him?" I ask.

"No. How would I?" Sadie asks, a little too quickly. When she catches my dubious squint, she adds. "Well. It's just . . . now, don't go making too much of this, Ellery, because I *know* the way you think. But he fell apart at Lacey's funeral. Way more than her boyfriend did. It caught my attention, so I remembered it. That's all."

"Fell apart how?"

Sadie heaves a theatrical sigh. "I knew you'd ask that."

"You brought it up!"

"Oh, just . . . you know. He cried a lot. Almost collapsed. His friends had to carry him out of the church. And I said to Melanie, 'Wow, they must have been really close.' But she said they barely knew one another." Sadie lifts a shoulder in a half shrug. "He probably had a crush, that's all. Lacey was a beauty. What's that?" She glances off to one side, and I hear the murmur of another voice. "Oh, okay. Sorry, El, but I have to go. Tell Ezra I'll call him soon, okay? I love you, and . . ." She pauses, something like regret crossing her face for the first time. "And . . . I'm glad you're meeting people."

No apology. Saying she's sorry would mean acknowledging that something's wrong, and even when she's calling me cross-country from rehab on a contraband phone, Sadie can't do it. I don't answer, and she adds, "I hope you're doing something fun for your Saturday afternoon!"

I'm not sure if *fun* is the right word, but it's something I've been planning since I learned I was going to Echo Ridge. "Fright Farm opens for the season today, and I'm going."

Sadie shakes her head with exasperated fondness. "Of course you are," she says, and blows me a kiss before she disconnects.

Hours later, Ezra and I are walking through the woods behind Nana's house toward Fright Farm, leaves crunching beneath our feet. I'm wearing some of my new Dalton's clothes, which Ezra has been snickering at since we left the house.

"I mean," he says as we step over a fallen branch, "what would you even call those? Leisure pants?"

"Shut up," I grumble. The pants, which are some kind of synthetic stretchy material, were the most inoffensive piece of clothing I could find. At least they're black, and sort of fitted. My gray-and-white checked T-shirt is short and boxy, and has such a high neck that it's almost choking me. I'm pretty sure I've never looked worse. "First Sadie with the hair, now you with the clothes."

Ezra's smile is bright and hopeful. "She looked good, though?" he asks. He and Sadie are so similar sometimes, so blissfully optimistic, that it's impossible to say what you really think around them. When I used to try, Sadie would sigh and say, *Don't be such an Eeyore, Ellery.* Once—only once—she'd added under her breath, *You're just like Sarah.* Then pretended not to hear me when I asked her to repeat what she'd said.

"She looked great," I tell Ezra.

We hear noise from the park before we see it. Once we emerge from the woods it's impossible to miss: the entrance looms across the road in the shape of a huge, monstrous head with glowing green eyes and a mouth, wide open in a scream, that serves as the door. It looks exactly like it did in pictures from the news coverage about Lacey's murder, except for the arched sign that reads FRIGHT FARM in spiky red letters.

Ezra shades his eyes against the sun. "I'm just gonna say it: Fright Farm is a crap name. Murderland was better."

"Agreed," I say.

There's a road running between the woods and the Fright Farm entrance, and we wait for a few cars to pass before crossing it. A tall, black spire fence circles the park, enclosing clusters of tents and rides. Fright Farm opened less than an hour ago, but it's already packed. Screams fill the air as a salt-and-pepper-shaker ride flips back and forth. When we get closer to the entrance, I see that the face is covered with mottled and red-specked grayish paint so it looks like a decaying corpse. There's a row of four booths directly inside, with one cashier to a booth, and at least two dozen people waiting. Ezra and I get in line, but I break away after a few minutes to check out the information board and grab a bunch of papers stacked up beneath it.

"Maps," I tell Ezra. I hand him one, plus another sheet of paper. "And job applications."

His brow furrows. "You want to *work* here?"

"We're broke, remember? And where else would we work? I don't think there's anyplace in walking distance." Neither of us have our driver's license, and I can tell already Nana's not the chauffeuring type.

Ezra shrugs. "All right. Hand it over."

I fish a couple of pens out of my messenger bag, and we almost complete the applications before it's our turn to buy tickets. I fold Ezra's and mine together and stuff them both in the front pocket of my bag as we leave the booths. "We can drop them off before we go home."

"Where should we go first?" Ezra asks.

I unfold my map and study it. "It looks like we're in the kids' section right now," I report. "Dark Matters is to the left. That's an evil science laboratory. Bloody Big Top to the right. Probably self-explanatory. And the House of Horrors is straight ahead. That doesn't open till seven, though."

Ezra leans over my shoulder and lowers his voice. "Where did Lacey die?"

I point to a tiny picture of a Ferris wheel. "Under there. Well, that's where they found her body, anyway. Police thought she was probably meeting someone. Echo Ridge kids used to sneak into the park after hours all the time, I guess. It didn't have any security cameras back then." We both glance up at the nearest building, where a red light blinks from one corner. "Does now, obviously."

"Do you want to start there?" Ezra asks.

My throat gets dry. A group of masked kids dressed in black swoops past us, one of them knocking into my shoulder so hard that I stumble. "Maybe we should check out the games," I say, refolding the map. It was a lot easier to take ghoulish pleasure at visiting a crime scene before I met the victim's family.

We walk past snack stands and carnival games, pausing to watch a boy our age sink enough baskets in a row to win a stuffed black cat for his girlfriend. The next station has the kind of shooting gallery game where two players each try to knock over twelve targets in a box. A guy wearing a ratty hunting jacket who looks like he's forty or so pumps his fist in the air and lets out a loud guffaw. "Beat ya!" he says, punching the shoulder of the kid next to him. The man stumbles a little with the movement, and the boy recoils and backs away.

"Maybe you should give someone else a turn." The girl behind the counter is about my age and pretty, with a long brown ponytail that she winds anxiously around her fingers.

The man in the hunting jacket waves the toy gun he's holding. "Plenty of room next to me. Anybody can play if they're not too chicken." His voice is loud and he's slurring his words.

The girl crosses her arms, as if she's steeling herself to sound tough. "There are lots of other games you could play."

"You're just mad 'cause nobody can beat me. Tell you what, if any of these losers can knock down more than me I'll bow out. Who wants to try?" He turns toward the small crowd gathering around the stand, revealing a lean, scruffy face.

Ezra nudges me. "How can you resist?" he asks under his breath.

I hesitate, waiting to see if someone older or bigger might help out, but when nobody does I step forward. "I will." I meet the girl's eyes, which are hazel, heavily mascaraed, and shadowed with dark circles. She looks like she hasn't slept in a week.

The guy blinks at me a few times, then bends at the waist in an exaggerated bow. The movement almost topples him, but he rights himself. "Well, hello, madam. Challenge accepted. I'll even pay for you." He fishes two crumpled dollars out of his pocket and hands them to the girl. She takes them gingerly and drops them into a box in front of her as if they were on fire. "Never let it be said that Vance Puckett isn't a gentleman."

"Vance Puckett?" I burst out before I can stop myself. *This* is Sadie's ex? The "gorgeous" one? Either her standards were a lot lower in Echo Ridge, or he peaked in high school.

His bloodshot eyes narrow, but without a spark of recognition. Not surprising; with my hair pulled back, there's nothing Sadie-like about me. "Do I know you?"

"Ah. No. It's just . . . that's a good name," I say limply.

The ponytailed girl presses a button to reset the targets.

I move to the second station as Vance raises the gun and sets his sights. "Champions first," he says loudly, and starts firing off shots in quick succession. Even though he's clearly drunk, he manages to knock over ten of the twelve targets. He raises the gun when he's finished and kisses the barrel, causing the girl to grimace. "Still got it," Vance says, making a sweeping gesture toward me. "Your move, milady."

I raise the gun in front of me. I happen to possess what Ezra calls freakishly good aim, despite having zero athletic talent in any other capacity. My hands are slick with sweat as I close one eye. *Don't overthink it,* I remind myself. *Just point and shoot.*

I press the trigger and miss the first target, but not by much. Vance snickers beside me. I adjust my aim, and hit the second. The crowd behind me starts murmuring when I've lowered the rest of the targets in the top row, and by the time I've hit nine they're clapping. The applause spikes at number ten, and turns into whoops and cheers when I knock over the last one and finish with eleven down. Ezra raises both arms in the air like I just scored a touchdown.

Vance stares at me, slack-jawed. "You're a goddamn ringer."

"Move along, Vance," someone calls. "There's a new sheriff in town." The crowd laughs, and Vance scowls. For a few beats I think he won't budge. Then he flings his gun on the counter with a snort.

"Game's fixed, anyway," he mutters, stepping back and shoving his way through the crowd.

The girl turns toward me with a tired but grateful smile. "Thanks. He's been here for almost half an hour, freaking everyone out. I thought he was going to start firing into the crowd any minute now. They're only pellets, but still." She reaches under the counter and pulls out a Handi Wipe, swiping it thoroughly across Vance's gun. "I owe you one. Do you guys want free wristbands to the House of Horrors?"

I almost say yes, but pull out my and Ezra's job applications instead. "Actually, would you mind putting a good word in for us with your boss? Or whoever does the hiring around here?"

The girl tugs on her ponytail instead of taking the papers from me. "Thing is, they only hire kids from Echo Ridge."

"We are," I say, brightly. "We just moved here."

She blinks at us. "You did? Are you— *Ohhh*." I can almost see the puzzle pieces lock together in her mind as she glances between Ezra and me. "You must be the Corcoran twins."

It's the same reaction we've been getting all week—like all of a sudden, she knows everything about us. After spending our lives in the orbit of a city where everyone's fighting for recognition, it's weird to be so effortlessly visible. I'm not sure I like it, but I can't argue with the results when she extends her hand toward the applications with a beckoning motion. "I'm Brooke Bennett. We'll be in the same class next week. Let me see what I can do."

CHAPTER FIVE

MALCOLM
SUNDAY, SEPTEMBER 8

"You have four kinds of sparkling water," Mia reports from the depths of our refrigerator. "Not flavors. *Brands.* Perrier, San Pellegrino, LaCroix, and Polar. The last one's a little down-market, so I'm guessing it's a nod to your humble roots. Want one?"

"I want a Coke," I say without much hope. The Nilssons' housekeeper, who does all the grocery shopping, isn't a fan of refined sugar.

It's the Sunday before school starts, and Mia and I are the only ones here. Mom and Peter left for a drive after lunch, and Katrin and her friends are out back-to-school shopping. "I'm afraid that's not an option," Mia says, pulling out two bottles of lemon Polar seltzer and handing one to me. "This refrigerator contains only clear beverages."

"At least it's consistent." I set my bottle down on the kitchen island next to a stack of the college brochures that have started to arrive for Katrin on a daily basis: Brown, Amherst, Georgetown, Cornell. They seem like a stretch for her GPA, but Peter likes people to aim high.

Mia unscrews the cap from her bottle and takes a long swig, making a face. "Ew. This tastes like cleaning solution."

"We could go to your house, you know."

Mia shakes her head so violently that her red-tipped dark hair flies in her face. "No thank you. Tensions are high in the Kwon household, my friend. The Return of Daisy has everyone shook."

"I thought Daisy's coming home was temporary."

"So did we all," Mia says in her narrator voice. "And yet, she remains."

Mia and I are friends partly because, a long time ago, Declan and her sister, Daisy, were. Lacey Kilduff and Daisy Kwon had been best friends since kindergarten, so once Declan and Lacey started dating, I saw almost as much of Daisy as I did of Lacey. Daisy was my first crush; the most beautiful girl I'd ever seen in real life. I could never figure out what Declan saw in Lacey when Daisy was *right there*. Meanwhile, Mia was in love with both Lacey and Declan. We were a couple of awkward preteens trailing around after our golden siblings and their friends, lapping up whatever scraps of attention they'd throw our way.

And then it all imploded.

Lacey died. Declan left, suspected and disgraced. Daisy went to Princeton just like she was supposed to, graduated with honors, and got a great job at a consulting firm in Boston. Then, barely a month after she started, she abruptly quit and moved back home with her parents.

Nobody knows why. Not even Mia.

A key jingles in the lock, and loud giggles erupt in the foyer. Katrin comes sweeping into the kitchen with her friends Brooke and Viv, all three of them weighed down by brightly colored shopping bags.

"Hey," she says. She swings her bags onto the kitchen island, almost knocking over Mia's bottle. "Do *not* go to the Bellevue Mall today. It's a zoo. Everybody's buying their homecoming dresses already." She sighs heavily, like she wasn't doing the exact same thing. We all got a "welcome back" email from the principal last night, including a link to a new school app that lets you view your schedule and sign up for stuff online. The homecoming ballot was already posted, where theoretically you can vote anyone from our class onto the court. But in reality, everybody knows four of the six spots are already taken by Katrin, Theo, Brooke, and Kyle.

"Wasn't planning on it," Mia says drily.

Viv smirks at her. "Well, they don't have a Hot Topic, so." Katrin and Brooke giggle, although Brooke looks a little guilty while she does it.

There's a lot about my and Katrin's lives that don't blend well, and our friends top the list. Brooke's all right, I guess, but Viv's the third wheel in their friend trio, and the insecurity makes her bitchy. Or maybe that's just how she is.

Mia leans forward and rests her middle finger on her chin, but before she can speak I grab a bouquet of cellophane-wrapped flowers from the island. "We should go before it starts raining," I say. "Or hailing."

Katrin waggles her brows at the flowers. "Who are *those* for?"

"Mr. Bowman," I say, and her teasing grin drops. Brooke makes a strangled sound, her eyes filling with tears. Even Viv shuts up. Katrin sighs and leans against the counter.

"School's not going to be the same without him," she says.

Mia hops off her stool. "Sucks how people in this town keep getting away with murder, doesn't it?"

Viv snorts, pushing a strand of red hair behind one ear. "A hit-and-run is an *accident*."

"Not in my book," Mia says. "The hitting part, maybe. Not the running. Mr. Bowman might still be alive if whoever did it stopped to call for help."

Katrin puts an arm around Brooke, who's started to cry, silently. It's been like that all week whenever I run into people from school; they're fine one minute and sobbing the next. Which does kind of bring back memories of Lacey's death. Minus all the news cameras. "How are you getting to the cemetery?" Katrin asks me.

"Mom's car," I say.

"I blocked her in. Just take mine," she says, reaching into her bag for the keys.

Fine by me. Katrin has a BMW X6, which is fun to drive. She doesn't offer it up often, but I jump at the chance when she does. I grab the keys and make a hasty exit before she can change her mind.

"How can you stand living with her?" Mia grumbles as we walk out the front door. Then she turns and walks backward, gazing up at the Nilssons' enormous house. "Well, I guess the perks aren't bad, are they?"

I open the X6's door and slide into the car's buttery leather interior. Sometimes, I still can't believe this is my life. "Could be worse," I say.

It's a quick trip to Echo Ridge Cemetery, and Mia spends most of it flipping rapidly through all of Katrin's preprogrammed radio stations. "Nope. Nope. Nope. Nope," she keeps muttering, right up until we pull through the wrought iron gates.

Echo Ridge has one of those historic cemeteries with graves that date back to the 1600s. The trees surrounding it are ancient, and so huge that their branches act like a canopy above us. Tall, twisting bushes line gravel paths, and the whole space is enclosed within stone walls. The gravestones are all shapes and sizes: tiny stumps barely visible in the grass; tall slabs with names carved across the front in block letters; a few statues of angels or children.

Mr. Bowman's grave is in the newer section. We spot it right away; the grass in front is covered with flowers, stuffed animals, and notes. The simple gray stone is carved with his name, the years of his life, and an inscription:

Tell me and I forget
Teach me and I may remember
Involve me and I learn

I unwrap our bouquet and silently add it to the pile. I thought there'd be something I'd want to say when I got here, but my throat closes as a wave of nausea hits me.

Mom and I were still visiting family in New Hampshire when Mr. Bowman died, so we missed his funeral. Part of me was sorry, but another part was relieved. I haven't been to a funeral since I went to Lacey's five years ago. She was buried in her homecoming dress, and all her friends wore theirs to her funeral, splashes of bright colors in the sea of black. It was hot for October, and I remember sweating in my itchy suit beside my father. The stares and whispers about Declan had already started. My brother stood apart from us, still as a statue, while my father pulled at the collar of his shirt like the scrutiny was choking him.

My parents lasted about six months after Lacey was killed. Things weren't great before then. On the surface their arguments were always about money—utility bills and car repairs and the second job Mom thought Dad should get when they cut his hours at the warehouse. But really, it was about the fact that at some point over the years, they'd stopped liking one another. They never yelled, just walked around with so much simmering resentment that it spread through the entire house like poisonous gas.

At first I was glad when he left. Then, when he moved in with a woman half his age and kept forgetting to send support checks, I got angry. But I couldn't show it, because *angry* had become something people said about Declan in hushed, accusing tones.

Mia's wobbly voice brings me back into the present. "It sucks that you're gone, Mr. Bowman. Thanks for always being so nice and never comparing me to Daisy, unlike every other teacher in the history of the world. Thanks for making science almost interesting. I hope karma smacks whoever did this in the ass and they get exactly what they deserve."

My eyes sting. I blink and look away, catching an unexpected glimpse of red in the distance. I blink again, then squint. "What's that?"

Mia shades her eyes and follows my gaze. "What's what?"

It's impossible to tell from where we're standing. We start picking our way across the grass, through a section of squat, Colonial-era graves carved with winged skulls. *Here lyeth the Body of Mrs. Samuel White* reads the last one we pass. Mia, momentarily distracted, aims a pretend kick at the stone. "She had her own name, asshole," she says. Then we're finally close enough to make out what caught our eye back at Mr. Bowman's grave, and stop in our tracks.

This time, it's not just graffiti. Three dolls hang from the top of a mausoleum, nooses around their necks. They're all wearing crowns and long, glittering dresses drenched in red paint. And just like at the cultural center, red letters drip like blood across the white stone beneath them:

I'M BACK
PICK YOUR QUEEN, ECHO RIDGE
HAPPY HOMECOMING

A garish, red-spattered corsage decorates a grave next to the mausoleum, and my stomach twists when I recognize this section of the cemetery. I stood almost exactly where I'm standing now when Lacey was buried. Mia chokes out a furious gasp as she makes the same connection, and lunges forward like she's about to sweep the bloody-looking corsage off the top of Lacey's grave. I catch her arm before she can.

"Don't. We shouldn't touch anything." And then my disgust takes a brief backseat to another unwelcome thought. "Shit. I have to be the one to report this *again.*"

I got lucky last week, sort of. The new girl, Ellery, believed me enough that when we went inside to tell an adult, she didn't mention she'd found me holding the can. But the whispers started buzzing through the cultural center anyway, and they've been following me around ever since. Twice in one week isn't great. Not in line with the *Keep Your Head Down Till You Can Get Out* strategy I've been working on ever since Declan left town.

"Maybe somebody else already has and the police just haven't gotten here yet?" Mia says, looking around. "It's the middle of the day. People are in and out of here all the time."

"You'd think we'd have heard, though." Echo Ridge gossip channels are fast and foolproof. Even Mia and I are in the loop now that Katrin has my cell number.

Mia bites her lip. "We could take off and let somebody else make the call. Except . . . we told Katrin we were coming here, didn't we? So that won't work. It'd actually look worse if you *didn't* say something. Plus it's just . . . mega creepy." She digs the toe of her Doc Marten into the thick, bright-green grass. "I mean, do you think this is a *warning* or something? Like what happened to Lacey is going to happen again?"

"Seems like the impression they're going for." I keep my voice casual while my brain spins, trying to make sense of what's in front of us. Mia pulls out her phone and starts taking pictures, circling the mausoleum so she can capture every angle. She's nearly done when a loud, rustling noise makes us both jump. My heart thuds against my chest until a familiar figure bursts through a pair of bushes near the back of the cemetery. It's Vance Puckett. He lives behind the cemetery and probably cuts through here every day on his way to . . . wherever he goes. I'd say the liquor store, but it's not open on Sunday.

Vance starts weaving down the path toward the main entrance. He's only a few feet away when he finally notices us, flicking a bored glance our way that turns into a startled double take when he sees the mausoleum. He stops so short that he almost falls over. "What the hell?"

Vance Puckett is the only person in Echo Ridge who's had a worse post–high school descent than my brother. He used to run a contracting business until he got sued over faulty wiring in a house that burned down in Solsbury. It's been one long slide into the bottom of a whiskey bottle ever since. There were a rash of petty break-ins in the Nilssons' neighborhood right around the same time that Vance installed a satellite dish on Peter's roof, so everyone assumes he's found a new strategy for paying his bills. He's never been caught at anything, though.

"We just found this," I say. I don't know why I feel the need to explain myself to Vance Puckett, but here we are.

He shuffles closer, his hands jammed into the pockets of his olive-green hunting jacket, and circles the mausoleum, letting out a low whistle when he finishes his examination. He smells faintly of booze like always. "Pretty girls make graves," he says finally. "You know that song?"

"Huh?" I ask, but Mia replies, "The Smiths." You can't stump her on anything music-related.

Vance nods. "Fits this town, doesn't it? Echo Ridge keeps losing its homecoming queens. Or their sisters." His eyes roam across the three dolls. "Somebody got creative."

"It's not *creative*," Mia says coldly. "It's horrible."

"Never said it wasn't." Vance sniffs loudly and makes a shooing motion with one hand. "Why are you still here? Run along and tell the powers that be."

I don't like getting ordered around by Vance Puckett, but I don't want to stay here, either. "We were just about to."

I start toward Katrin's car with Mia at my side, but Vance's sharp "Hey!" makes us turn. He points toward me with an unsteady finger. "You might want to tell that sister of yours to lie low for a change. Doesn't seem like a great year to be homecoming queen, does it?"

CHAPTER SIX

"It's like *Children of the Corn* around here," Ezra mutters, scanning the hallway.

He's not wrong. We've been here only fifteen minutes, but there are already more blond-haired, blue-eyed people than I've ever seen gathered in one place. Even the building Echo Ridge High is housed in has a certain Puritan charm—it's old, with wide pine floors, high arched windows, and dramatic sloped ceilings. We're heading from the guidance counselor's office to our new homeroom, and we might as well be leading a parade for all the stares we're getting. At least I'm in my airplane wardrobe, washed last night in preparation for the first day of school, instead of a Dalton's special.

We pass a bulletin board covered with colorful flyers, and Ezra pauses. "It's not too late to join the 4-H Club," he tells me.

"What's that?"

He peers closer. "Agriculture, I think? There seem to be cows involved."

"No thanks."

He sighs, running his eyes over the rest of the board. "Something tells me they don't have a particularly active LGBTQ-Straight Alliance here. I wonder if there's even another out kid."

Normally I'd say there must be, but Echo Ridge is pretty small. There are less than a hundred kids in our grade, and only a few hundred total in the school.

We turn from the board as a cute Asian girl in a Strokes T-shirt and stack-heeled Doc Martens passes by, her hair buzzed short on one side and streaked red on the other. "Hey, Mia, you forgot to cut the other half!" a boy calls out, making the two football-jacketed boys on either side of him snicker. The girl lifts her middle finger and shoves it in their faces without breaking stride.

Ezra gazes after her with rapt attention. "Hello, new friend."

The crowd in front of us parts suddenly, as three girls stride down the hallway in almost perfect lockstep—one blonde, one brunette, and one redhead. They're so obviously Somebodies at Echo Ridge High that it takes me a second to realize that one of them is Brooke Bennett from the Fright Farm shooting range. She stops short when she sees us and offers a tentative smile.

"Oh, hi. Did Murph ever call you?"

"Yeah, he did," I say. "We have interviews this weekend. Thanks a lot."

The blond girl steps forward with the air of someone who's used to taking charge. She's wearing a sexy-preppy outfit: collared shirt under a tight sweater, plaid miniskirt, and high-heeled boo-ties. "Hi. You're the Corcoran twins, aren't you?"

Ezra and I nod. We've gotten used to our sudden notoriety. Yesterday, while I was grocery shopping with Nana, a cashier I'd never seen before said, "Hello, Nora . . . and Ellery," as we were checking out. Then she asked me questions about California the entire time she was bagging our groceries.

Now, the blond girl tilts her head at us. "We've heard all about you." She stops there, but the tone of her voice says: *And when I say* all, *I mean the one-night-stand father, the failed acting career, the jewelry store accident, the rehab. All of it.* It's kind of impressive, how much subtext she manages to pack into one tiny word. "I'm Katrin Nilsson. I guess you've met Brooke, and this is Viv." She points to the red-haired girl on her left.

I should have known. I've heard the Nilsson name con-stantly since I got to Echo Ridge, and this girl has *town royalty* written all over her. She's not as pretty as Brooke, but somehow she's much more striking, with crystal-blue eyes that remind me of a Siamese cat's.

We all murmur hellos, and it feels like some sort of uncom-fortable audition. Probably because of the assessing look Katrin keeps giving Ezra and me, as though she's weighing whether we're worth her continued time and attention. Most of the hall-way is only pretending to be busy with their lockers while they wait for her verdict. Then the bell rings, and she smiles.

"Come find us at lunch. We sit at the back table next to the biggest window." She turns away without waiting for an answer, blond hair sweeping across her shoulders.

Ezra watches them leave with a bemused expression, then

turns to me. "I have a really strong feeling that on Wednesdays, they wear pink."

Ezra and I have most of the same classes that morning, except for right before lunch, when I head to AP calculus and Ezra goes to geometry. Math isn't his strong suit. So I end up going to the cafeteria on my own. I make my way through the food line assuming that he'll join me at any minute, but when I exit with a full tray, he's still nowhere in sight.

I hesitate in front of the rows of rectangular tables, searching the sea of unfamiliar faces, when my name rings out in a clear, commanding voice. "Ellery!" I look up, and spot Katrin with her arm in the air. Her hand makes a beckoning motion.

I'm being summoned.

It feels as though the entire room is watching me make my way to the back of the cafeteria. Probably because they are. There's a giant poster on the wall beside Katrin's window table, which I can read when I'm less than halfway there:

SAVE THE DATE

Homecoming is October 5!!!

Vote now for your King and Queen!

When I reach Katrin and her friends, the redheaded girl, Viv, shifts to make room on the bench. I put my tray down and slide in next to her, across from Katrin.

"Hi," Katrin says, her blue cat's eyes scanning me up and down. If I have to dress in clothes from Dalton's tomorrow, she's definitely going to notice. "Where's your brother?"

"I seem to have misplaced him," I say. "But he always turns up eventually."

"I'll keep an eye out for him," Katrin says. She digs one pale-pink nail into an orange and tears off a chunk of the peel, adding, "So, we're all *super* curious about you guys. We haven't had a new kid since . . ." She scrunches her face. "I don't know. Seventh grade, maybe?"

Viv straightens her shoulders. She's small and sharp-featured, wearing bright-red lipstick that goes surprisingly well with her hair. "Yes. That was me."

"Was it? Oh, right. Such a happy day." Katrin smiles distractedly, still focused on me. "But moving in middle school is one thing. Senior year is rough. Especially when everything is so . . . new. How do you like living with your grandmother?"

At least she didn't ask, like the grocery store cashier yesterday, if I'd left a "Hollywood hottie" behind. The answer to that is no, by the way. I haven't had a date in eight months. Not that I'm counting. "It's all right," I tell Katrin, sliding my eyes toward Brooke. Other than a muted hello when I sat down, she's been totally silent. "A little quiet, though. What do you guys do around here for fun?"

I'm hoping to draw Brooke into the conversation, but it's Katrin who answers. "Well, we're cheerleaders," she says, waving a hand between her and Brooke. "That takes up a lot of time in the fall. And our boyfriends play football." Her eyes drift a few tables away, where a blond boy is setting down his tray. The entire table is a sea of purple-and-white athletic jackets. The boy catches her eye and winks, and Katrin blows him a kiss. "That's my boyfriend, Theo. He and Brooke's boyfriend, Kyle, are co-captains of the team."

Of course they are. She doesn't mention a boyfriend for Viv. I feel a small surge of solidarity—*single girls unite!*—but when

I flash a smile at Viv she meets it with a cool stare. I get the feeling, suddenly, that I've stumbled onto territory she'd rather not share. "That sounds fun," I say limply. I've never been part of the football-and-cheerleading crowd, although I appreciate the athleticism of both.

Viv narrows her eyes. "Echo Ridge might not be Hollywood, but it's not *boring*."

I don't bother correcting Viv that La Puente is twenty-five miles outside Hollywood. Everyone in Echo Ridge just assumes we lived in the middle of a movie set, and nothing I say will convince them otherwise. Besides, that's not our main issue right now. "I didn't say it was," I protest. "I mean, I can tell already there's a lot going on around here."

Viv looks unconvinced, but it's Brooke who finally speaks up. "None of it good," she says flatly. Her eyes are shiny as she turns toward me, and she looks like she's in desperate need of a full night's sleep. "You—your grandmother found Mr. Bowman, didn't she?" I nod, and tears begin to spill down her pale cheeks.

Katrin swallows a piece of orange and pats Brooke's arm. "You have to stop talking about it, Brooke. You keep getting worked up."

Viv heaves a dramatic sigh. "It's been an awful week. First Mr. Bowman, then all that vandalism cropping up around town." Her tone is concerned, but her eyes are almost eager as she adds, "It's going to be our first feature of the year for the school paper. A summary of what's been going on all week, juxtaposed with this year's seniors talking about where they were five years ago. It's the kind of story that might even get picked up by the local news." She looks at me with slightly more warmth. "I should interview you. You found the graffiti at the cultural center, didn't you? You and Malcolm."

"Yeah," I say. "It was awful, but not nearly as awful as the cemetery." That made me sick when I heard about it, especially when I tried to imagine how the Kilduffs must feel.

"The whole thing is *horrible*," Viv agrees, turning toward Katrin and Brooke. "I hope nothing bad happens when you guys are announced next Thursday."

"Announced?" I ask.

"They're going to announce the homecoming court at assembly next Thursday morning," Viv explains, gesturing toward the homecoming poster over Brooke's shoulder. "Everyone's voting between now and then. Did you download the Echo Ridge High app? Homecoming votes are on the main menu."

I shake my head. "No, not yet."

Viv makes a tsking noise. "Better hurry. Voting closes next Wednesday. Although most of the court is already a done deal. Katrin and Brooke are total shoo-ins."

"You might get nominated too, Viv," Katrin says graciously. Even though I just met her, I can tell she doesn't actually believe there's a chance in hell of that happening.

Viv shudders delicately. "No thank you. I don't want to be on the radar of some murderous creep who's decided to strike again."

"Do you really think that's what this is about?" I ask, curious. Viv nods, and I lean forward eagerly. I've been thinking about the vandalism almost nonstop for the past couple of days, and I'm dying to share theories. Even with Viv. "Interesting. Maybe. I mean, it's definitely what the person who's doing it *wants* us to think. And that's disturbing on its own. But I keep wondering—even if you were brazen enough to get away with murder and then brag about doing it again five years later, the MO's are completely different."

Katrin's face is a total blank. "MO?" she asks.

"Modus operandi," I say, warming to the topic. It's one where I'm perfectly confident. "You know, the method somebody uses to commit a crime? Lacey was strangled. That's a very personal and violent way to kill someone, and not likely to be premeditated. But these threats are public, and they require planning. Plus they're much less, well, *direct.* To me, it feels more like a copycat. Which isn't to say that person isn't dangerous. But maybe they're dangerous in a different way."

There's a moment of silence at the table, until Katrin says, "Huh," and bites into an orange slice. She chews carefully, her eyes fixed on a spot somewhere over my shoulder. *There it is,* I think. She just mentally dismissed me from the popular crowd. That didn't take long.

If Ezra's told me once, he's told me a hundred times. *Nobody wants to hear your murder theories, Ellery.* Too bad he bailed on me for lunch.

Then a new expression crosses Katrin's face, one that's sort of irritated and indulgent at the same time. "You're going to get kicked out of school one day for wearing that shirt," she calls to someone.

I turn to see Malcolm Kelly in a faded gray T-shirt with "KCUF" written across the front in block letters. "Hasn't happened yet," he replies. In the bright fluorescent lights of the Echo Ridge High cafeteria, I get a much better look at him than

I did at the cultural center. He's wearing a backward baseball cap over unruly brown hair, framing an angular face and wide-set eyes. They meet mine and flicker with recognition. He waves, and the movement jars his tray enough that he almost drops the whole thing. It's totally awkward and also, weirdly, kind of cute.

"I'm sorry," Viv says as Malcolm turns away, in the least apologetic tone I've ever heard. "But I find it *super sketch* that the first person to see both threats is Declan Kelly's weirdo brother." She shakes her head emphatically. "Uh-uh. Something's off there."

"Oh, Viv," Katrin sighs, like they've had some variation on this conversation at least a dozen times before. "Malcolm's all right. Kind of nerdy, but all right."

"I don't think he's a nerd." Brooke's been quiet for so long that her sudden pronouncement startles everyone. "Maybe he used to be, but he's gotten cute lately. Not as cute as Declan, but still." Then she drops her head again and starts playing listlessly with her spoon, as if contributing to the conversation sapped whatever small reserves of energy she had.

Katrin gives her a speculative look. "Didn't realize you'd noticed, Brooke."

My head swivels, looking for Malcolm, and I spot him sitting with that girl Mia from the hallway, and my brother. I'm not surprised; Ezra has a knack for inserting himself into whatever social group he's decided to join. At least I'll have another lunch option when I don't get invited back to Katrin's table.

Viv snorts. "Cute, my ass," she says flatly. "Declan should be in jail."

"You think he killed Lacey Kilduff?" I ask, and she nods.

Katrin cocks her head, confused. "But weren't you just saying that whoever killed Lacey is leaving those threats around town?" she asks. "Declan lives in another state."

Viv leans an elbow on the table, staring at her friend, eyes wide. "You live with the Kellys and you seriously don't know?"

Katrin frowns. "Know what?"

Viv waits a few beats for maximum impact, then smirks. "Declan Kelly is back in town."

CHAPTER SEVEN

MALCOLM
MONDAY, SEPTEMBER 9

Echo Ridge has one bar, which technically is only half in town because it sits right on the border of neighboring Solsbury. Unlike most Echo Ridge businesses, Bukowski's Tavern has a reputation for leaving people alone. They won't serve minors, but they don't card at the door. So that's where I meet Declan on Monday afternoon, after spending the first day back at school pretending that *yeah, sure, I knew my brother was around.*

Bukowski's doesn't look like it belongs in Echo Ridge. It's small and dark, with a long bar at the front, a few scarred tables scattered around the room, and a dartboard and pool table in the back. The only thing on the walls is a neon Budweiser sign with a flickering *w.* There's nothing cute or quaint about it.

"You couldn't give me a heads-up you were in town?" I ask when I slide into a seat across from Declan. I mean to say it like a joke, but it doesn't come out that way.

"Hello to you too, little brother," Declan says. I saw him less than a week ago, but he looks bigger here than he did in Aunt Lynne's basement apartment. Maybe because Declan was always larger than life in Echo Ridge. Not that the two of us ever hung out at Bukowski's before. Or anywhere, really. Back in grade school, when my dad was trying to make me and football happen, Declan would occasionally deign to play with me. He'd get bored fast, though, and the more I missed, the harder he'd throw. After a while I'd give up trying to catch the ball and just put my hands up to protect my head. *What's your problem?* he'd complain. *I'm not trying to hit you. Trust me, would you?*

He'd say that as if he'd ever done anything to earn it.

"You want something to drink?" Declan asks.

"Coke, I guess."

Declan raises his hand to an elderly waitress in a faded red T-shirt cleaning beer taps behind the bar. "Two Cokes, please," he says when she arrives at our table. She nods without much interest.

I wait until she leaves to ask, "What are you doing here?"

A muscle twitches in Declan's jaw. "You say it like I'm violating some kind of restraining order. It's a free country."

"Yeah, but . . ." I trail off as the waitress returns, placing cocktail napkins and tall glasses of Coke with ice in front of us. My phone exploded during lunch once word got out that Declan was in Echo Ridge. And he *knows* that. He knows exactly the kind of reaction this would get.

Declan leans forward, resting his forearms on the table. They're almost twice the size of mine. He works construction jobs when he's not taking classes, and it keeps him in better shape than football did in high school. He lowers his voice, even though the only other people in Bukowski's are two old guys wearing baseball caps at the end of the bar. "I'm sick of being treated like a criminal, Mal. *I didn't do anything.* Remember?" He rubs a hand over his face. "Or do you not believe that anymore? Did you ever?"

"Of course I did. Do." I stab at the ice in my drink with my straw. "But why now? First Daisy's back and now you. What's going on?"

The ghost of a frown flits across Declan's face when I mention Daisy, so quick I almost miss it. "I'm not *back,* Mal. I still live in New Hampshire. I'm here to see someone, that's all."

"Who? Daisy?"

Declan heaves an exasperated sigh. "Why are you so hung up on Daisy? Do you still have a thing for her?"

"No. I'm just trying to figure this out. I saw you *last week,* and you never said you were coming." Declan shrugs and takes a sip of Coke, avoiding my eyes. "And it's kind of shitty timing, you know. With all the crap going on around town."

"What does that have to do with me?" He breaks into a scowl when I don't respond right away. "Wait. Are you kidding me? People think I had something to do with that? What's next? Am I responsible for global warming now, too? Fucking hell, Mal." One of the old guys at the bar looks over his shoulder, and Declan slumps back against the chair, glowering. "For the record. Just so we're clear. I didn't come here to write creepy-ass slogans on signs and walls or whatever."

"Graves," I correct.

"*Whatever,*" Declan grits out, low and dangerous.

I believe him. There's no possible universe in which my hot-headed, testosterone-fueled brother dresses a trio of dolls up like homecoming queens and ties them to a mausoleum. It's easier to imagine him placing his hands around Lacey's throat and squeezing the life out of her.

Jesus. My hand shakes as I pick up my glass, rattling the ice in it. I can't believe I just thought that. I take a sip and swallow hard. "Then why *did* you come? And how long are you staying?"

Declan drains his Coke and signals for the waitress. "Jack and Coke this time," he says when she arrives.

Her lips thin as she glances between us. "ID first."

Declan reaches for his wallet, then hesitates. "You know what? Forget it. Just another Coke." She shrugs and walks away. Declan shakes his head like he's disgusted with himself. "See what I did there? Decided not to get a drink, even though I wanted one, because I don't feel like showing my name to some woman I don't even know. That's my fucking life."

"Even in New Hampshire?" I ask. One of the old guys at the bar keeps glancing our way. I can't tell whether it's because I'm so obviously underage or . . . because.

"Everywhere," Declan says. He goes silent again as the wait-ress brings a Coke, then raises the glass to me in a toast. "You know, you and Mom have a good thing going here, Mal. Peter likes to pretend I don't exist, but he's solid with you guys. You might even get college out of the deal."

He's right. I might. Which makes me feel guilty, so I say, "Peter says he's talking to Mr. Coates about a job for you." Since Ben Coates was the mayor of Echo Ridge when Lacey died, he got interviewed a few times about what he thought might have happened. *A tragic, random act of violence,* he always said. *Some depraved individual passing through.*

Declan laughs darkly. "I guarantee you that's bullshit."

"No, they got together Labor Day weekend, and—"

"I'm sure they did. And they might even have mentioned me. Probably along the lines of how it'd be career suicide to hire me. It is what it is, Mal, and I won't be a pain in Peter's ass about it. I'm not trying to drive a wedge between him and Mom. Or you. I'll stay out of your way."

"I don't want you to stay out of my way. I just want to know why you're here."

Declan doesn't answer right away. When he does, he sounds less angry and more tired. "You know what happened with me and Lacey, before she died? We outgrew each other. But we didn't know that, because we were a couple of dumb kids who'd been together forever and thought we were supposed to stay that way. If we were regular people, we would've eventually figured out how to break up and that would have been that. We'd have moved on. Wound up with someone else." His voice dips lower. "That's how things should've ended."

The guy at the bar who's been staring at us gets up and starts moving our way. When he's crossed half the room I realize he's not as old as I thought he was: early fifties, maybe, with thick arms and a barrel chest. Declan doesn't turn around, but gets up abruptly and pulls out his wallet. "I gotta go," he says, dropping a ten on the table. "Don't worry, all right? Everything's fine."

He brushes past the guy, who half turns to call after him, "Hey. You Declan Kelly?" Declan continues toward the door, and the guy raises his voice. "*Hey.* I'm talking to you."

Declan grasps the doorknob and leans against the door, shouldering it open. "I'm nobody," he says, and disappears outside.

I'm not sure what the guy's going to do—keep coming toward me, maybe, or follow Declan outside—but he just shrugs and heads for the bar, settling himself back onto his stool. His friend leans toward him, muttering something, and they both laugh.

It hits me, as I finish my Coke in silence, that Declan's life is a lot shittier up close than it seems from a state away.

Half an hour later I'm dragging my ass home, because it didn't occur to my brother before making his dramatic exit to ask if I might need a ride. I'm rounding the bend toward Lacey's old house when I spot someone a few feet ahead of me on the road, wheeling an oversized suitcase behind her.

"Hey," I call when I get close enough to tell who it is. "Leaving town already?"

Ellery Corcoran turns just as her suitcase wheels hit a rock on the ground, almost jerking the luggage out of her hand. She pauses and balances it carefully next to her. While she's waiting for me to catch up, she pulls her hair back and knots it into some kind of twist, so quickly I barely see her hands move. It's kind of mesmerizing. "The airline lost my luggage more than a week ago, and they just delivered it." She rolls her eyes. "To our *neighbors*."

"That sucks. At least it showed up, though." I gesture to the suitcase. "You need help with that?"

"No thanks. It's easy to roll. And my grandmother's house is right there."

A breeze stirs, sending stray tendrils of hair across Ellery's face. She's so pale, with sharp cheekbones and a stubborn chin, that she'd look severe if it weren't for her eyes. They're inky black, huge and a little bit tilted at the edges, with eyelashes so long they look fake. I don't realize I'm staring until she says, "What?"

I shove my hands into my pockets. "I'm glad I ran into you. I've been meaning to thank you for the other night. At the fundraiser? For not, you know, assuming I was the . . . perpetrator."

A smile tugs at the corners of her mouth. "I don't know a lot of vandals, but I have to imagine most of them don't look quite so horrified by their own handiwork."

"Yeah. Well. It would be easy to assume. Most people here do. And that would've been . . . not great for me."

"Because your brother was a suspect in Lacey's murder," she says. Matter-of-factly, like we're talking about the weather.

"Right." We start walking again, and I have this weird impulse to tell her about my meeting with Declan. I've been out of sorts about it since I left Bukowski's Tavern. But that would be oversharing, to say the least. Instead, I clear my throat and say, "I, um, met your mother. When she came back for Lacey's funeral. She was . . . really nice."

Nice isn't the right word. Sadie Corcoran was like this bolt of energy that swept through town and electrified everybody, even in the middle of mourning. I got the sense that she considered Echo Ridge one big stage, but I didn't mind watching the performance. We all needed the distraction.

Ellery squints into the distance. "It's funny how everyone

remembers Sadie here. I'm pretty sure I could visit every town I've ever lived in and nobody would notice."

"I doubt that." I shoot her a sideways glance. "You call your mom by her first name?"

"Yeah. She used to have us pretend she was our older sister when she went on auditions, and it stuck," Ellery says in that same matter-of-fact tone. She shrugs when I raise my brows. "Mothers of preschoolers aren't considered particularly sexy in Hollywood."

An engine roars behind us—faintly at first, then so loud that we both turn. Headlights flash, coming way too fast, and I grab Ellery's arm to yank her out of the road. She loses her grip on the suitcase and yelps as it topples into the path of the oncoming car. Brakes squeal, and the bright-red BMW's wheels stop inches in front of the handle.

The driver's side window lowers, and Katrin pokes her head out. She's in her purple Echo Ridge cheerleading jacket; Brooke is in the passenger seat. Katrin's eyes drop to the suitcase as I grab it off the ground and haul it back to safety. "Are you going somewhere?" she asks.

"Christ, Katrin. You almost ran us over!"

"I did not," she scoffs. She arches a brow as Ellery takes the suitcase handle from me. "Is that yours, Ellery? You're not moving again, are you?"

"No. Long story." Ellery starts rolling the oversized suitcase toward the grassy knoll in front of her grandmother's house. "I'm almost home, so . . . I'll catch you guys later."

"See you tomorrow," I say, as Katrin waves and utters a lazy "Byeeeee." Then she raps her palm against the car door and narrows her eyes at me. "You've been keeping secrets. You didn't tell me Declan was back in town."

"I had no idea until today," I say.

Katrin shoots me a look of pure skepticism. Brooke leans forward in her seat, pulling the sleeves of her purple cheerleading jacket over her hands as if she's cold. Her eyes dart between Katrin and me as Katrin asks, "You expect me to believe that?"

I feel my temper flare. "I don't care if you believe it or not. It's the truth."

My stepsister and my brother have nothing to do with one another. Declan didn't come to our mom's wedding to Peter and doesn't visit. Katrin hasn't mentioned his name once in the entire four months we've been living together.

She looks unconvinced, but jerks her head toward the backseat. "Come on, we'll give you a ride." She turns toward Brooke and adds, just loud enough for me to hear, "You're welcome."

Brooke lets out an irritated little huff. I don't know what that's about, and I'm not tempted to ask. Katrin's in peak pain-in-the-ass mode right now, but I'm tired of walking. I climb into the backseat, and barely have a chance to close the door before Katrin floors the gas again. "So what's Declan doing here, anyway?" she asks.

"I don't know," I say, and then I realize what's been bothering me about my half-hour conversation with Declan ever since I left Bukowski's. It's not just that I didn't know he was here.

It's that he avoided every single one of my questions.

CHAPTER EIGHT

ELLERY
MONDAY, SEPTEMBER 9

As soon as I close the door behind me in Nana's hallway, I drop to my knees beside my suitcase and reach for the zipper. Inside is a jumbled mess of clothes and toiletries, but it's all so beautifully familiar that I gather as much as I can hold in my arms and hug it to my chest for a few seconds.

Nana appears in the doorway between the kitchen and the hall. "I take it everything's there?" she asks.

"Looks like it," I say, holding up my favorite sweater like a trophy.

Nana heads upstairs without another word, and I spy a flash of red against my dark clothes: the small velvet pouch that holds my jewelry. I scatter its contents on the floor, picking a necklace out of the pile. The thin chain holds an intricate silver charm that looks like a flower until you examine it closely enough to realize it's a dagger. "For my favorite murder addict," Sadie said when she gave it to me for my birthday two years ago.

I used to wish she'd ask me why I was so drawn to stuff like that, and then maybe we could have a real conversation about Sarah. But I guess it was easier to just accessorize.

I'm fastening the dagger around my neck when Nana comes down the stairs with a shopping tote dangling from one arm. "You can bring your things upstairs later. I want to make a trip to Dalton's before dinnertime." At my questioning look, she lifts the bag on her arm. "We may as well return the clothes I bought you last week. It hasn't escaped my notice that you've been borrowing from your brother instead of wearing them."

My cheeks heat as I scramble to my feet. "Oh. Well. I just hadn't gotten around to—"

"It's fine," Nana says drily, plucking her keys from a board on the wall. "I harbor no illusions about my familiarity with teen fashion. But there's no reason to let these go to waste when someone else can use them."

I peer hopefully behind her. "Is Ezra coming with us?"

"He's out for a walk. Hurry up, I need to get back and make dinner."

After ten days with my grandmother, there are a few things I know. She'll drive fifteen miles under the speed limit the entire way to Dalton's. We'll get home at least forty minutes before six o'clock, because that's when we eat and Nana doesn't like to rush when she cooks. We'll have a protein, a starch, and a vegetable. And Nana expects us to be in our rooms by ten o'clock. Which we don't protest, since we have nothing better to do.

It's weird. I thought I'd chafe under the structure, but there's something almost soothing about Nana's routine. Especially in contrast to the past six months with Sadie, after she found a doctor who'd keep refilling her Vicodin prescription and went from distracted and disorganized to full-on erratic. I used to wander around our apartment when she stayed out late, eating microwave mac and cheese and wondering what would happen to us if she didn't come home.

And then finally one night, she didn't.

The Subaru crawls to Dalton's, giving me plenty of time to stare out the window at the slender trees lining the road, gold leaves starting to mix with the green. "I didn't know leaves changed color this early," I say. It's September ninth, a week after Labor Day, and the temperature is still warm and almost summery.

"Those are green ash trees," Nana says in her teacher voice. "They change early. We're having good weather for peak foliage this year: warm days and cool nights. You'll see reds and oranges popping up in a few weeks."

Echo Ridge is by far the prettiest place I've ever lived. Nearly every house is spacious and well maintained, with interesting architecture: stately Victorians, gray-shingled Capes, historic Colonials. The lawns are freshly mowed, the flower beds neat and orderly. All the buildings in the town center are red brick and white-windowed, with tasteful signs. There's not a chain-link fence, a dumpster, or a 7-Eleven in sight. Even the gas station is cute and almost retro-looking.

I can see why Sadie felt hemmed in here, though, and why Mia stalks through school like she's searching for an escape hatch. Anything different stands out a mile.

My phone buzzes with a text from Lourdes, checking on the luggage situation. When I update her about my newly recovered suitcase, she texts back so many celebratory GIFs that I almost miss my grandmother's next words. "Your guidance counselor called."

I stiffen in my seat, trying to imagine what I could've done wrong on the first day of school when Nana adds, "She's been reviewing your transcript and says your grades are excellent, but that there's no record of you taking the SATs."

"Oh. Well. That's because I didn't."

"You'll need to take them this fall, then. Have you prepped?"

"No. I didn't think . . . I mean . . ." I trail off. Sadie doesn't have a college degree. She's gotten by on a small inheritance from our grandfather, plus temp work and the occasional acting job. While she's never discouraged Ezra and me from applying to college, she's always made it clear that we'd be on our own if we did. Last year I took one look at tuition for the school closest to home, and immediately bounced off their website. I might as well plan a trip to Mars. "I'm not sure I'm going to college."

Nana brakes well in advance of a stop sign, then inches toward the white line. "No? And here I thought you were a future lawyer."

Her eyes are fixed firmly on the road, so she doesn't catch my startled look. Somehow, she managed to land on my one and only career interest—the one I stopped mentioning at home because Sadie would groan *ugh, lawyers* every time I did. "Why would you think that?"

"Well, you're interested in criminal justice, aren't you? You're analytical and well spoken. Seems like a good fit." Something light and warm starts spreading through my chest, then stops when I glance down at the wallet sticking out of my messenger bag. Empty, just like my bank account. When I don't answer right away, Nana adds, "I'll help you and your brother out, of course. With tuition. As long as you keep your grades up."

"You *will*?" I turn and stare at her, the spark of warmth returning and zipping through my veins.

"Yes. I mentioned it to your mother a few months ago, but—well, she wasn't in the best frame of mind at the time."

"No. She wasn't." My mood deflates, but only for a second. "You'd really do that? You can, um, afford it?" Nana's house is nice and all, but it's not exactly a mansion. And she clips coupons, although I have the feeling it's more of a game with her than a necessity. She was really pleased with herself over the weekend when she scored six free rolls of paper towels.

"State school," she says crisply. "But you have to take the SATs first. And you need time to prepare, so you should probably sign up for the December session."

"All right." My head's in a whirl, and it takes a minute for me to finish the sentence properly. "Thank you, Nana. That's seriously awesome of you."

"Well. It would be nice to have another college graduate in the family."

I tug at the silver dagger around my neck. I feel . . . not *close* to my grandmother, exactly, but like maybe she won't shoot me down if I ask the question I've been holding in since I arrived in Echo Ridge. "Nana," I say abruptly, before I lose my nerve. "What was Sarah like?"

I can feel my aunt's absence in this town, even more than

my mother's. When Ezra and I are out running errands with Nana, people have no problem talking to us as though they've known us their entire lives. Everyone skirts around Sadie's rehab, but they have plenty of other things to say; they'll quote her *Defender* line, joke about how Sadie must not miss Vermont winters, or marvel at how similar my hair is to hers. But they never mention Sarah—not a memory, an anecdote, or even an acknowledgment. Every once in a while I think I see the flicker of an impulse, but they always pause or look away before changing the subject.

Nana is silent for so long that I wish I'd kept my mouth shut. Maybe we can both spend the next four months pretending I did. But when she finally speaks, her tone is calm and even. "Why do you ask?"

"Sa—my mom doesn't talk about her." Nana's never said anything when we call our mother by her first name, but I can tell she doesn't like it. Now isn't the time to annoy her. "I've always wondered."

A light rain starts to fall, and Nana switches on windshield wipers that squeak with every pass. "Sarah was my thinker," she says finally. "She read constantly, and questioned everything. People thought she was quiet, but she had the sort of dry humor that snuck up on you. She loved Rob Reiner movies—you know, *Spinal Tap, The Princess Bride*?" I nod, even though I've never seen the first one. I make a mental note to look it up on Netflix when we get home. "Sarah could quote them all by heart. Very smart girl, especially in math and science. She liked astronomy and used to talk about working for NASA when she grew up."

I absorb the words like a thirsty sponge, amazed that Nana

told me so much in one fell swoop. And all I had to do was *ask*. What a concept. "Did she and my mom get along?" I ask. They sound so different, even more so than I'd imagined.

"Oh yes. Thick as thieves. Finished each other's sentences, like you and your brother do. They were very distinct personalities, but could mimic one another like you wouldn't believe. Used to fool people all the time."

"Airport Andy would be jealous," I say, before forgetting that I never told Nana the absorbed-twin story.

Nana frowns. "What?"

"Nothing. Just a joke." I swallow the small lump that's formed in my throat. "Sarah sounds great."

"She was marvelous." There's a warmth to Nana's voice I've never heard before, not even when she talks about her former students. *Definitely* not when she talks about my mother. Maybe that was another thing about Echo Ridge that Sadie couldn't stand.

"Do you think— Could she still . . . be somewhere?" I fumble over the words, my fingers twisting the chain at my neck. "I mean, like she ran away or something?" I regret it as soon as I say it, like I'm accusing Nana of something, but she just shakes her head decisively.

"Sarah would never." Her voice drops a little, like the words hold too much weight.

"I wish I could have met her."

Nana pulls into a parking spot in front of Dalton's and shifts the Subaru into park. "So do I." I sneak a glance at her, afraid I'll see tears, but her eyes are dry and her face relaxed. She doesn't seem to mind talking about Sarah at all. Maybe she's been waiting for someone to ask. "Could you grab the bag from the backseat please, Ellery?"

"Okay," I say. My thoughts are a tangled whirl, and I nearly drop the plastic bag into the rain-soaked gutter next to the sidewalk when I get out of the car. I wrap the bag's handles around my wrist to keep it secure, and follow Nana inside Dalton's Emporium.

The cashier greets Nana like an old friend, and graciously takes the pile of clothes without asking the reason for the return. She's scanning tags I never removed when a high, sweet voice floats through the store. "I want to see myself in the big window, Mommy!" Seconds later a girl in a gauzy blue dress appears, and I recognize Melanie Kilduff's daughter. It's the little one, about six years old, and she stops short when she sees us.

"Hello, Julia," Nana says. "You look very nice."

Julia catches the hem of her dress in one hand and fans it out. She's like a tiny version of Melanie, right down to the gap between her front teeth. "It's for my dance recital."

Melanie appears behind her, trailed by a pretty preteen with crossed arms and a sulky expression. "Oh, hi," Melanie says with a rueful smile as Julia runs for a raised dais surrounded by mirrors near the front of the store. "Julia wants to see herself *onstage,* as she calls it."

"Well, of course she does," the clerk says indulgently. "That dress was made to be seen." A phone rings behind her, and she disappears into a back room to answer it. Nana lifts her purse off the counter as Julia hops onto the dais and spins, the dress's skirt floating around her.

"I look like a princess!" she crows. "Come look, Caroline!"

Melanie follows and fusses with the bow on the back of the dress, but the older daughter hangs behind, her mouth pulling downward.

"A princess," she mutters under her breath, staring at the rack of homecoming dresses to our right. "What a stupid thing to want to be."

Maybe Caroline isn't thinking about Lacey, or the dolls at the cemetery with their red-spattered gowns. Maybe she's just being a moody almost teenager, annoyed at getting dragged along for her little sister's shopping expedition. Or maybe it's more than that.

As Julia twirls again, a bolt of hot, white anger pulses through me. It's not a normal reaction to such an innocent moment—but the common thread running through this store isn't normal, either. We've all lost our version of a princess, and none of us know why. I'm sick of being tangled up in Echo Ridge's secrets, and of the questions that never end. I want answers. I want to help this little girl and her sister, and Melanie, and Nana. And my mother.

I want to do *something*. For the missing girls, and the ones left behind.

CHAPTER NINE

MALCOLM
THURSDAY, SEPTEMBER 19

"What's up, loser?" I tense a split second before Kyle McNulty's shoulder rams into mine, so I stumble but don't crash against the locker bay. "Your dickhead brother still in town?"

"Fuck you, McNulty." It's my standard response to Kyle, no matter the situation, and it's never not applicable.

Kyle's jaw twitches as Theo smirks beside him. I used to play football with both of them in elementary school, back when my father was still hoping I'd turn into Declan 2.0. We weren't friends then, but we didn't actively hate one another. That started in middle school. "He'd better stay the hell away from my sister," Kyle spits.

"Declan couldn't care less about your sister," I say. It's true, and ninety percent of the reason Kyle can't stand me. He scowls, edging closer, and I curl my right hand into a fist.

"Malcolm, hey." A voice sounds behind me as a hand tugs

at my sleeve. I turn to see Ellery leaning against a locker, her head tilted, holding one of those Echo Ridge High *Month-at-a-Glance* calendars that most people recycle instantly. Her expression is preoccupied, and I'd almost believe she didn't notice she was interrupting a near fight if her eyes didn't linger on Kyle a few seconds too long. "Do you mind showing me where the auditorium is? I know we have assembly now, but I can't remember where to go."

"I can give you a hint," Kyle sneers. "Away from this loser."

I flush with anger, but Ellery just gives him a distracted nod. "Oh, hi, Kyle. Did you know your zipper's down?"

Kyle's eyes drop automatically to his pants. "No it's not," he complains, adjusting it anyway as Theo snorts out a laugh.

"Move along, boys." Coach Gagnon comes up behind us, clapping Kyle and Theo on the shoulder. "You don't want to be late for assembly." First period is canceled today, so the entire school can be herded into the auditorium for rah-rah speeches about football season and the homecoming court announcements. In other words, it's the Kyle-and-Theo Show.

They follow Coach Gagnon down the hall. I turn toward Ellery, who's absorbed in her calendar again. I'm both impressed that she stopped Kyle in his tracks so easily and embarrassed that she thought she had to. Her eyes flick up, such a deep brown they're almost black, framed by thick lashes. When a pink tinge works its way into her cheeks, I realize I'm staring. Again. "You didn't need to do that," I say. "I can handle those guys."

God, I sound like some puffed-up little kid trying to act tough. Kyle's right. I *am* a loser.

Ellery does me the favor of acting like she didn't hear. "Every time I see Kyle, he's being an ass to someone," she says, stuffing the calendar into her bag and hoisting it higher over her shoulder. "I don't understand why he's such a big deal around here. What does Brooke even see in him?"

It's an obvious change of subject, but a fair question. "Hell if I know."

We enter the stream of students heading down the hallway toward the auditorium. "What was he saying about his sister?" Ellery asks. "Does she go here?"

"No, she's older. Liz was in Declan's class. They went out for, like, three months when they were sophomores, and she was kind of obsessed with him. He broke up with her for Lacey."

"Ah." Ellery nods. "I'm guessing she didn't take that well?"

"That's an understatement." We push through the auditorium's double doors, and I lead Ellery toward the farthest corner of the stands, where Mia and I always sit. Ellery and Ezra have been eating lunch with us since last week, and we've been doing the standard getting-to-know-you stuff: talking about music, movies, and the differences between California and Vermont. This is the first time I've been alone with Ellery since I saw her with her suitcase—and just like then, we've skipped past being polite and gone straight for the dark stuff. I'm not sure why, but I tell her, "Liz stopped going to school for a while, and ended up having to repeat. It took her two extra years to graduate."

Ellery's eyes widen. "Wow, seriously? Just because a guy broke up with her?"

I drop into a seat at the top of the bleachers. Ellery settles in beside me, lifting her bag over her head and placing it at her feet. Her hair is a lot more under control now than it was the

85

first time I met her. I kind of miss the old look. "Well, she wasn't great at school to start with," I say. "But the McNultys blamed Declan. So Kyle hates me by association."

Ellery gazes up at the rafters. They're filled with banners from Echo Ridge sports teams throughout the years: a couple dozen in football, basketball, and hockey. For such a small school, Echo Ridge brings home a lot of championships. "That's not fair. You shouldn't be blamed for whatever's going on with your brother."

I have the feeling we're not talking about Liz McNulty anymore. "Welcome to life in a small town. You're only as good as the best thing your family's done. Or the worst."

"Or the worst thing that's been done *to* them," Ellery says in a musing way.

It hits me, then, why talking to her feels so familiar sometimes: because we're two sides of the same coin. Both of us are stuck in one of Echo Ridge's unsolved mysteries, except her family lost a victim and mine has a suspect. I should say something comforting about her aunt, or at least acknowledge that I know what she's talking about. But I'm still trying to figure out the right words when a loud "Heyyyy!" rings out from our right.

Mia clomps toward us with Ezra in tow. They're both wearing black-and-white Fright Farm staff T-shirts, and when I raise my brows at them Mia crosses her arms defensively over her chest. "We didn't plan this," she says, dropping onto the bench beside me. "Purely a coincidence."

"Mind meld," Ezra says with a shrug.

I forgot the twins started working at Fright Farm this week. Half the school does; I'm one of the few kids at Echo Ridge High who's never even applied there. Even if it hadn't scared the crap out of me when I was younger, there's too much of a connection to Lacey. "How's that going?" I ask, turning toward Ellery.

"Not bad," she says. "We're checking wristbands at the House of Horrors."

"Primo job," Mia says enviously. "Brooke hooked you guys up. *So* much better than serving slushies to toddlers." Mia's not a fan of anyone under the age of twelve, but she's been stuck working in the kids' section of Fright Farm since her first season. Every time she angles for a transfer, her boss shuts her down.

Mia sighs and props her chin in her hands. "Well, here we go. At long last, the mystery of who's going to come in a distant third for homecoming queen will be answered." The bleacher rows closer to the floor start filling up, and Coach Gagnon heads toward the podium at the front of the room.

"Viv Cantrell?" Ezra guesses. "She's been posting pictures of her dress on Instagram."

Mia makes a face at him. "You follow Viv on Instagram?"

He shrugs. "You know how it is. She followed me, I followed back in a moment of weakness. She posts about homecoming a *lot*." His expression turns thoughtful. "Although, I don't think she has a date yet."

"You should unfollow," Mia advises. "That's way more information about Viv than any one person needs to have. Anyway, she doesn't have a shot at homecoming court. Maybe Kristi Kapoor, though." At Ezra's questioning glance, she adds, "She's on student council, and people like her. Plus she's one of, like, three other students of color in our class, so everybody can feel progressive when they vote for her."

"Who are the others?" Ezra asks.

"Besides me? Jen Bishop and Troy Latkins," Mia says, then glances between him and Ellery. "And maybe you guys? Are you Latinx?"

Ezra shrugs. "Could be. We don't know our dad. But Sadie did say his name was either José or Jorge, so chances are good."

"Your mom is legendary," Mia says admiringly. "She was homecoming queen too, wasn't she?"

Ezra nods as I blink at Mia. "How would you even know that?" I ask.

Mia shrugs. "Daisy. She's super into Echo Ridge homecoming history. Maybe because she was runner-up." At Ellery's curious look she adds, "My sister. Graduated five years ago. Always the bridesmaid and never the bride, if by bride you mean homecoming queen."

Ellery leans forward, looking interested. "Was she jealous?"

"If she was, you'd never know," Mia says. "Daisy is sugar and spice and everything nice. The perfect Korean daughter. Until recently."

The podium microphone screeches as Coach Gagnon taps on it. "Is this thing on?" he yells. Half the room laughs dutifully and the other half ignores him. I join the second group and tune him out, surreptitiously pulling out my phone. I haven't heard from Declan since I met him at Bukowski's Tavern. *You still around?* I text.

Delivered. Read. No response. Same story all week.

"Good morning, Echo Ridge High! Are you ready to meet your court?" I look up at the change in voice, and suppress a groan at the sight of Percy Gilpin at the podium. Percy is senior class president, and everything about him makes me tired:

his energy, his springy hair, his relentless pursuit of Echo Ridge High elective offices, and the purple blazer he's worn to every school event since we were freshmen. He's also friendly with Viv Cantrell, which is probably all that anybody needs to know about him.

"Let's kick things off with the gentlemen!" Percy rips open an envelope with a flourish, like he's about to announce an Oscar winner. "You'll be choosing your king from one of these three fine fellows. Congratulations to Theo Coolidge, Kyle McNulty, and Troy Latkins!"

Ezra watches, perplexed, as Percy raises his arms amid hoots and cheers. "What is *with* that guy? He's like one of those old-school game show hosts in a teenager's body."

"You nailed it." Mia yawns and twirls her thumb ring. "That went exactly as expected. Good for Troy, I guess. He's not a total dick. Won't win, though."

Percy lets the backslapping and high fives subside, then opens another envelope. "And now it's time for the ladies, who may be last but are definitely not least. Echo Ridge High, let's give it up for Katrin Nilsson, Brooke Bennett, and—"

He pauses, looks up, and looks down at the paper in his hand again. "Um." Another beat passes, and people start shifting in their seats. A few clap and whistle, like they think maybe he's done. Percy clears his throat too close to the microphone, and the resulting screech of feedback makes everyone wince.

Mia leans forward, her face scrunched in confusion. "Wait. Is Percy Gilpin *speechless*? That's a beautiful but unprecedented sight."

Percy turns toward Coach Gagnon, who gestures impatiently

at him to go on. "Sorry," Percy says, clearing his throat again. "Lost my place for a second. Um, so, congratulations to Ellery Corcoran!"

Ellery goes still, her eyes round with shock. "What the hell?" she says, her cheeks staining red as scattered applause ripples through the auditorium. "How did that happen? It doesn't make sense. Nobody here even knows me!"

"Sure they do," Mia says, just as somebody yells out, "Who?" to muted laughter. Mia's right, though; everybody knows who the Corcoran twins are. Not because they're high profile at school, but because Sadie Corcoran, who *almost* made it in Hollywood, is larger than life around here.

And because Sarah Corcoran is Echo Ridge's original lost girl.

"High five, princess!" Ezra says. When Ellery doesn't respond, he lifts her hand and slaps it against his own. "Don't look so glum. This is a nice thing."

"It doesn't make sense," Ellery repeats. Percy is still at the podium, talking about next week's pep rally, and the attention of the room has already started to wander. "I mean, did *you* vote for me?"

"No," Ezra says. "But don't take it personally. I didn't vote for anyone."

"Did you guys?" Ellery asks, looking at Mia and me.

"No," we both say, and I shrug apologetically. "Nonvoters over here, too."

Ellery twists her hair over one shoulder. "I've been at school less than two weeks. I've hardly talked to anybody except you three. If you guys didn't vote for me—and believe me, I'm not insulted, because I didn't vote either—then why would anyone else?"

"To welcome you to town?" I say half-heartedly.

She rolls her eyes, and I can't blame her. Even after less than two weeks here, she has to know Echo Ridge High isn't that kind of place.

Katrin's in a mood Friday morning.

Her driving is worse than ever—stop signs optional, the entire way to school. When we arrive she parks crookedly between two spots, crowding out another kid who was headed our way. He honks as she flounces out of the car, slamming her door and taking off for the entrance without a backward look.

It's one of those days when she's pretending I don't exist.

I take my time entering the building and as soon as I get to the hallway, I know something's off. There's a weird buzzing energy, and the snippets of conversation I catch don't sound like the usual gossip and insults.

"Must have broken in—"

"Somebody hates them—"

"Maybe it's not a joke after all—"

"It's not like anybody did that to Lacey, though—"

Everyone's grouped in clusters, heads bent together. The biggest crowd of people is around Katrin's locker. There's a smaller knot around Brooke's. My stomach starts to twist, and I spot Ezra and Ellery standing next to hers. Ellery's back is to me, but Ezra is turned my way, and his face stops me in my tracks. His laid-back, California-guy vibe is gone, and he looks like he wants to stab somebody.

When I get closer, I see why.

Ellery's dingy gray locker is splashed with bright-red paint.

A red-spattered, twisted doll dangles from the handle, just like the ones in the cemetery. I crane my neck to look down the hallway, and see enough to know Katrin's and Brooke's lockers got the same treatment. Thick black letters are scrawled across the red on Ellery's:

REMEMBER MURDERLAND, PRINCESS?
I DO

Ezra catches my eye. "This is messed up," he seethes as Ellery turns. Her face is composed but pale, a humorless smile at the corners of her mouth.

"So much for welcoming me to town," she says.

CHAPTER TEN

"What are we looking for?" Ezra asks.

"I don't know," I admit, placing a stack of yearbooks on the desk in front of him. We're at the Echo Ridge library on Saturday morning, armed with jumbo cups of take-out coffee from Bartley's diner. I wasn't sure we'd get them past the librarian, but she's well into her eighties and asleep in her chair. "Anything weird, I guess."

Ezra snorts. "El, we've been here three weeks. So far we've reported a dead body, gotten jobs at a murder site, and been targeted by a homecoming stalker. Although that last one was all you." He takes a sip of coffee. "You're gonna have to be more specific."

I drop into a seat across from him and slide a book from the middle of the pile. It has *Echo Ridge Eagles* on its spine, date-stamped from six years ago. Lacey's junior year, one year before she died. "I want to check out Lacey's class. It's strange, isn't it, how these people who were part of her inner circle when she died are suddenly back in town? Right when all this other stuff starts happening?"

"What, you think Malcolm's brother had something to do with that? Or Mia's sister?" Ezra raises a brow. "Maybe we should've invited them along for coffee and crime solving."

"You know what you always say, Ezra," I say, opening the yearbook. "Nobody wants to hear my murder theories. Especially when it involves their siblings. That's the kind of thing you need to ease into."

We're snarking, because that's what we do. A lifetime of living with Sadie provided a master class in pretending everything's fine. But I've barely eaten since yesterday and even Ezra—who usually inhales Nana's cooking like he's trying to make up for seventeen years of frozen dinners—refused breakfast before we left.

Now, he runs his eyes over the remaining yearbooks. "What should I do? Look at their senior year?" He sucks in his cheeks. "It's probably pretty grim. *In memoriam* for Lacey, that kind of thing."

"Sure. That or . . ." My eyes drop to the bottom of the pile. "Sadie's yearbook is in there, too. If you're curious."

Ezra stills. "About what?"

"What she was like in high school. What *they* were like. Her and Sarah."

His jaw ticks. "What does that have to do with anything?"

I lean forward and glance around the small room. Besides

the sleeping librarian, there's no one here except a mother reading quietly to her toddler. "Haven't you ever wondered why we've never been to Echo Ridge before? Like, ever? Or why Sadie never talks about her sister? I mean, if *you* suddenly . . . disappeared"—I swallow hard against the bile in my throat—"I wouldn't move across the country and act like you'd never existed."

"You don't know what you'd do," Ezra objects. "You don't know what Sadie's really thinking."

"No, I don't. And neither do you. That's my *point*." The little boy's mother turns our way, and I lower my voice. I reach up and squeeze the dagger on my necklace. "We never have. We just got jerked from one town to the next while Sadie ran away from her problems. Except she finally landed in trouble she can't make disappear, and here we are. Back where it all started."

Ezra regards me steadily, his dark eyes somber. "We can't fix her, El."

I flush and look down at the pages in front of me—rows and rows of kids our age, all smiling for the camera. Ezra and I don't have any yearbooks; we've never felt connected enough to any of our schools to bother with a keepsake. "I'm not trying to *fix* her. I just want to understand. Plus, Sarah's part of this, somehow. She has to be." I rest my chin in my hands and say what I've been thinking since yesterday. "Ezra, nobody in that school voted me onto homecoming court. You know they didn't. Someone rigged the votes, I'm sure of it. Because I'm connected to Sarah."

My locker was cleaned and repainted by lunchtime on Friday, like nothing ever happened. But I've felt exposed ever since, the back of my neck prickling when I think about the fact that someone, somewhere went to a lot of trouble to add my name to that court. I told Viv that I didn't think the vandal and Lacey's murderer are the same person, and objectively, that still makes sense. Subjectively, though, the whole thing makes me sick.

Ezra looks dubious. "How does somebody rig votes?"

"By hacking the app. It wouldn't be hard."

He cocks his head, considering. "That seems extreme."

"Oh, and bloody Barbie dolls are restrained?"

"Touché." Ezra drums his fingers on the table. "So what, then? You think Lacey and Sarah are connected, too?"

"I don't know. It seems unlikely, doesn't it? They happened almost twenty years apart. But somebody's threading all these things together, and there has to be a reason why."

Ezra doesn't say anything else, but takes Sadie's yearbook from the bottom of the pile and opens it. I pull Lacey's closer to me and flip through the junior class pictures until I reach the *K*s. They're all there, the names I've been hearing since I got to Echo Ridge: Declan Kelly, Lacey Kilduff, and Daisy Kwon.

I've seen Lacey before in news stories, but not Daisy. She shares a few features with Mia, but she's much more conventionally pretty. Preppy, even, with a headband holding back her shiny, pin-straight hair. Declan Kelly reminds me of Malcolm on steroids; he's almost aggressively handsome, with piercing, dark-fringed eyes and a cleft in his chin. All three of them look like the kind of teenagers you'd find on a CW show—too beautiful to be real.

The *R* section is a lot less glam. Officer Ryan Rodriguez's high-school-junior self is an unfortunate combination of prominent Adam's apple, acne, and bad haircut. He's improved since then, though, so good for him. I turn the yearbook around to show Ezra. "Here's our neighbor."

Ezra glances at Officer Rodriguez's photo without much interest. "Nana mentioned him this morning. She's got some cardboard boxes she wants us to bring over. She says he sold the house? Or he's going to sell the house. Anyway, he's packing stuff up."

I straighten in my chair. "He's leaving town?"

He shrugs. "She didn't say that. Just that the house was too big for one person, now that his dad's dead. Maybe he's getting an apartment nearby or something."

I turn the yearbook back toward me and flip the page. The club and candid photo section comes after class pictures. Lacey was part of almost everything—soccer, tennis, student council, and choir, to name just a few. Declan mostly played football, it looks like, and was a good-enough quarterback that the team won a state championship that year. The last photo in the junior section is of the entire class, posing in front of Echo Ridge Lake during their year-end picnic.

I pick Lacey out right away—she's dead center, laughing, her hair blowing in the wind. Declan's behind her with his arms wrapped around her waist, his head tucked into her shoulder. Daisy stands beside them looking startled, as though she wasn't ready for the shot. And on the far edge of the group is gangly Ryan Rodriguez, standing stiffly apart from everyone else. It's not his awkward pose that catches my eye, though. The camera caught him staring straight at Lacey—with an expression of such intense longing that he almost looks angry.

He probably had a crush, Sadie said. *Lacey was a beauty.*

I study the three faces: Declan, Daisy, and Ryan. One who never left—until now, maybe—and two who returned. Malcolm doesn't know where Declan is staying, but Mia's mentioned more than once that her sister is back in her old room. What had Mia said about Daisy during Thursday's assembly, again? *Always a bridesmaid, never a bride.*

Ezra spins the yearbook he's been studying around so that it's facing me, and slides it across the table. "Is this what you wanted to see?"

A girl with a cloud of curly dark hair is at the top of the page, her smile so bright it's almost blinding. My mother, twenty-three years ago. Except the name under the picture reads *Sarah Corcoran.* I blink at it a couple of times; in my mind, Sarah's always been the serious, almost somber twin. I don't recognize this version. I flip to the previous page and see Sadie's picture at the bottom. It's identical, right down to the head tilt and the smile. The only difference is the color of their sweaters.

The pictures were taken their senior year, probably in September. A few weeks later, shortly after Sadie was crowned homecoming queen, Sarah was gone.

I close the book as a wave of exhaustion hits me. "I don't know," I admit, stretching and turning toward a row of tiny windows on the far wall that sends squares of sunlight across the hardwood floor. "When do we have to be at work, again?"

Ezra glances at his phone. "In about an hour."

"Should we stop by Mia's and see if she's working today?"

"She's not," Ezra says.

"Should we stop by Mia's and see if she's working today?" I repeat.

Ezra blinks in confusion, then shakes his head like he's just waking up. "Oh, sorry. Are you suggesting a reconnaissance mission?"

"I wouldn't mind meeting the mysterious Daisy," I tell him.

"Roger that," Ezra says. He gestures to the stack of yearbooks between us. "Are you gonna check any of these out?"

"No, I'm just— Hang on." I pull out my phone and snap a few photos of the yearbook pictures we've just been looking at. Ezra watches me with a bemused expression.

"What are you going to do with those?" he asks.

"Documenting our research," I say. I don't know if this morning will turn out to be worth anything, but at least it *feels* productive.

When I finish, we each take an armful of yearbooks and return them to the Reference section. I throw our empty coffee cups into a recycling bin, which makes a much louder noise than I expected. The sleeping librarian startles and blinks at us with watery, unfocused eyes as we pass her desk.

"Can I help you?" she yawns, feeling around for the glasses looped on a chain around her neck.

"No thanks, all set," I say, nudging Ezra to walk faster so we can exit before she recognizes us and we have to spend fifteen minutes making polite conversation about California. We push through the library's front door into bright sunshine, and descend wide steps to the sidewalk.

Ezra and I walked home from school with Mia a couple of days ago, and she's only a block from the library. The Kwons' house is unusual for Echo Ridge: a modern, boxy construction set on a large expanse of lawn. A stone path connects from the sidewalk to the front stairs, and we're halfway across it when a gray Nissan pulls into the driveway.

The driver's side window is half down, framing a girl with long dark hair who's gripping the steering wheel like it's a life preserver. Oversized sunglasses cover half her face, but I can see enough to tell that it's Daisy. Ezra raises his hand, about to call a greeting, then lowers it as Daisy lifts a phone to her ear.

"I don't think she sees us," I say, glancing between the car and the front door. "Maybe we should just ring the bell."

Before we can move, Daisy drops her phone, crosses her arms over the steering wheel, and lowers her head onto them. Her shoulders start to shake, and Ezra and I exchange uneasy glances. We stand there for what feels like ten minutes, although it's probably less than one, before Ezra take a tentative step forward. "Do you think we should, um . . ."

He trails off as Daisy suddenly raises her head with a strangled little scream and slams her hands, hard, on either side of the steering wheel. She whips off her sunglasses and runs her hands over her eyes like she's trying to erase any trace of tears, then shoves the glasses back on. She throws the car into reverse and starts to back up, stopping when she looks out the window and catches sight of us.

Ezra offers the sheepish half wave of someone who knows he just accidentally observed a private moment. Daisy's only indication that she sees him is to roll up her window before she backs out of the driveway and leaves in the direction she came from.

"Well, you wanted to meet the mysterious Daisy," Ezra says, watching her taillights disappear around a bend. "There she goes."

CHAPTER ELEVEN

MALCOLM
THURSDAY, SEPTEMBER 26

When I poke my head into Mia's room, she's wedged in against a small mountain of pillows on her bed, her MacBook propped on her lap. She has her earbuds in, nodding along to whatever's playing, and I have to rap on the door twice before she hears me. "Hey," she says too loudly before unplugging. "Practice over already?"

"It's past four." My one and only activity at Echo Ridge High—which is one more than Mia's ever signed up for—is band. Mr. Bowman got me into it in ninth grade when he suggested I take drum lessons, and I've been doing it ever since.

It's not the same without him. The woman who took over isn't half as funny as he was, and she's got us doing the same old crap from last year. I'm not sure I'll stick it out. But tomorrow night we're playing at a pep rally, and I have a solo that nobody else knows.

Mia stretches her arms over her head. "I didn't notice. I was just about to text you, though." She shuts her laptop and puts it aside, swinging her legs off the bed and onto the floor. "Freaking Viv's most cherished dream has come true. The *Burlington Free Press* picked up her story about the vandalism, and now they're covering it along with a five-year anniversary piece on Lacey. A reporter called a little while ago, trying to get hold of Daisy."

My stomach flops like a dying fish. "Shit."

I shouldn't be surprised. The Homecoming Stalker—so named by the *Echo Ridge Eagle* student newspaper—has been busy. He, or she, left a bloody mess of raw meat on the hood of Brooke's car Monday, which made her gag when she saw it. Ellery got off comparatively easy a day later, with a spray paint job on the side of Armstrong's Auto Repair that reads CORCO-RANS MAKE KILLER QUEENS.

Yesterday was Katrin's turn. On the street where Mr. Bowman died, in the corner that's turned into a makeshift memorial with flowers and stuffed animals, someone added an oversized print of Katrin's class picture with the eyes gouged out and an RIP date of October 5—next weekend's homecoming dance. When Peter found out about it, he got as close to losing his shit as I've ever seen him. He wanted homecoming canceled, and Katrin barely talked him out of calling Principal Slate. This morning, we got a homeroom announcement reminding us to report anything suspicious to a teacher. But so far, homecoming is still on.

Mia grabs a black studded sweatshirt from the back of her desk chair. "You didn't hear anything from Declan about it? I figured the reporter must have tried to reach him, too."

"No." Declan finally answered my texts over the weekend to tell me he was back in New Hampshire. Other than that, we haven't spoken since we met in Bukowski's Tavern. I still don't know what he was doing here, or where he was staying.

"Daisy's been holed up in her room ever since the call came in," Mia says, yanking the sweatshirt over her head. The fabric muffles her voice as she adds, "Not that there's anything unusual about *that*."

"You still want to go to Bartley's for dinner?" I ask. Dr. and Mr. Kwon both work late on Thursdays, and Peter and my mother have *date night,* so Mia and I are heading for Echo Ridge's only restaurant. "I have Mom's car, so we don't have to walk."

"Yeah, definitely. I need to get out of this house. Also, I invited the twins, so they're expecting us. I told them five, though. We can hang out and have coffee till then." She stuffs her keys into her pocket and heads for the door, hesitating as she reaches the hallway. "I'm just gonna check . . ." She backtracks a few steps to a closed door across from her bedroom, and raps on the frame. "Daisy?" No answer, so Mia knocks harder. "Daze?"

"What?" comes a quiet voice.

"Me and Malcolm are getting dinner at Bartley's. Do you want to come?"

"No thanks. I have a headache."

"You might feel better after you have some food."

Daisy's tone hardens. "I said *no,* Mia. I'm in for the night."

Mia's lip quivers a little before she scowls. "Fine," she mutters, turning away. "I don't know why I bother. Let the parents worry about her." She stalks down the stairs like she can't wait to get out of the house. Mia and I both think the other has it better, homewise: I like how the Kwons' place is bright and modern, and her parents talk to us like we actually have a clue what's going on in the world; she likes the fact that Peter and my mother barely pay attention to anything I do. The Kwons always wanted Mia to be more like Daisy—sweet, studious, and popular. The kind of person who can be counted on to say and do all the right things. Until, all of a sudden, she didn't.

"What *do* your parents think?" I ask Mia as we step outside and into the driveway.

Mia kicks a stray rock. "Who knows. In front of me they just say, *Oh, your sister was working too hard, she needed a break.* But they're having all these tense conversations in their room with the door closed."

We get into my mother's car and buckle in. "Tense how?" I ask.

"I don't know," Mia admits. "I try to listen, but I can't catch anything except tone."

I back out of the Kwons' driveway and into the road, but haven't gone far when my phone vibrates in my pocket. "Hang on," I say, pulling off to the side. "I want to make sure that's not Declan." I shift the car into park and extract my phone, grimacing when I see the name. "Never mind. It's Katrin."

"What does *she* want?"

I frown at the screen. "She says she has a favor to ask."

Mia grabs my arm in mock horror, eyes popping. "Don't answer, Mal. Whatever it is, you don't want any part of it."

I haven't replied, but Katrin's still typing. Gray dots linger for so long that I wonder if she put her phone down and forgot to finish the message. Then it finally appears. *Brooke just broke up with Kyle. I don't know why, but homecoming's next weekend and she needs a date. I was thinking you could ask her. She seems to like you. Probably just as a friend but whatever. You weren't going to go anyway, were you? Hang on, I'll send her number.*

I show the message to Mia, who snorts. "Christ, the entitlement of that girl!" She mimics Katrin's clipped, breezy tone. *"You weren't going to go anyway, were you?"*

Another text appears from Katrin, with contact information for Brooke, and I save it automatically. Then I shrug and put my phone away. "Well, she has a point. I wasn't." Mia chews her lip without responding, and I raise my brows at her. "What— were *you?*"

"Maybe. If they still have it," she says, and glares when I start to laugh. "Don't give me attitude, Mal. I can go to a dance if I want to."

"I know you can. I'm just surprised at the 'want to' part. You have the least school spirit of anyone I've ever met. I thought that was, like, a badge of honor with you."

Mia makes a face. "Ugh, I don't know. One of Daisy's old friends called to say that a bunch of them are going to be chaperones for the dance, and asked if she wanted to go too. I think she was considering it, which would be the first thing she's done besides hide in her bedroom since she came home, but then she said, *Well, Mia's not even going.* So I said, *Yeah I am,* and now I guess I have to, and you can wipe that stupid smirk off your face anytime."

I swallow my grin. "You're a good sister, you know that?"

"Whatever." She picks at the peeling black polish on her

thumbnail. "Anyway, I was thinking about asking that hot girl who works at Café Luna. If she says no, Ezra is my friend backup."

I frown. "*Ezra* is your friend backup? You've known him for two weeks!"

"We've bonded. We like all the same music. And you have no idea how nice it is to finally have a queer friend at school."

I can't fault her for that, I guess. Mia's taken shit for years from guys like Kyle and Theo who think *bisexual* equals *threesome*. "You should just go with Ezra, then," I say. "Forget the Café Luna girl. She's pretentious."

Mia tilts her head, considering. "Maybe. And *you* should go with Ellery." She shoots me a shrewd look. "You like her, don't you?"

"Of course I like her," I say, aiming for a casual tone. I fail.

"Oh my God," Mia snorts. "We're not in fourth grade, Mal. Don't make me ask if you *like* like her." She props her boots against the glove compartment. "I don't know what you're waiting for. I think she likes you, too." A lock of hair falls into her eye, and she peers into the rearview mirror to readjust the clip holding it back. Then she goes rigid, twisting in her seat to look out the back window. "What the hell?"

I'm not sure if I'm relieved or disappointed that something distracted her. "What?"

Mia's still staring out the window, scowling. "Where's she going? I thought she was *in for the night*." I turn to see Daisy's gray Nissan backing out of the Kwons' driveway, heading in the opposite direction from us. "Follow her," Mia says abruptly. She pokes me in the arm when I don't move right away. "Come on,

Mal, please? I want to see what she's up to. She's such a freaking vault lately."

"She's probably going to buy Tylenol," I say, but execute a three-point turn to get behind Daisy's rapidly disappearing taillights. I'm curious, too.

We follow her through the center of town and past Echo Ridge Cemetery. Mia sits up straighter in her seat when the Nissan slows, but Daisy doesn't stop. I wonder if she thought about visiting Lacey's grave, and then couldn't bring herself to do it.

Daisy leaves Echo Ridge and winds her way through two neighboring towns. I start copying her turns like I'm on autopilot without paying much attention to where we are. It's almost four-thirty, nearly past the point when we'll be able to get to Bartley's in time to meet the twins, when she finally pulls into the driveway of a white Victorian building. I brake and ease onto the shoulder of the road, shifting into park as we wait for Daisy to get out of the car. She's wearing shades even though the sun is low on the horizon, and walks quickly toward the building's side door. When she disappears inside, I ease the car forward so Mia and I can read the sign out front.

Northstar Counseling
Deborah Creighton, PsyD

"Huh," I say, feeling oddly deflated. I'd thought whatever Daisy was up to would be more surprising. "Well, I guess that's that."

Mia scrunches up her forehead. "Daisy's seeing a psychologist? Why wouldn't she just say so? What's with all the sneaking around?"

I drive past Deborah Creighton's office, looking for a good spot to turn the car around. When I reach the empty driveway of a darkened house, I pull halfway in and then reverse out so we can go back the way we came. "Maybe she wants privacy."

"All she *has* is privacy," Mia complains. "It's so weird, Mal. She always had a million friends and now she doesn't have any. Or at least, she never sees them."

"Do you think she's depressed? Because she lost her job?"

"She *quit* her job," Mia corrects. "And she doesn't seem depressed. Just . . . withdrawn. But I don't know, really. I hardly know who she is anymore." She slumps down into her seat and turns up the radio, too loud for us to keep talking.

We drive in silence until we pass the "Welcome to Echo Ridge" sign and make our way to Manchester Street, stopping at the light in front of the common. Mia snaps off the radio and looks to our left. "They're repainting Armstrong's."

"Guess they had to." There must be only one coat of paint on Armstrong Auto Repair's wall so far, because you can still see the faint outline of CORCORANS MAKE KILLER QUEENS beneath it. A ladder leans against the wall, and we watch as a man slowly makes his way to the bottom. "Is that Vance Puckett?" I ask. "Somebody actually let that guy use a ladder? And trusted him to paint in straight lines?" Echo Ridge's town drunk and alleged petty criminal isn't usually the go-to guy for odd jobs. Armstrong Auto Repair must have been desperate to get the job done fast.

"That's a worker's comp claim waiting to happen," Mia says. She cranes her neck and squints. "Hold up. Is that your future homecoming date heading his way?"

For a second I think she means Ellery, until Brooke Bennett

gets out of a car parked across the street. The light turns green, but there's no one behind me, so I stay put. Brooke slams the car door shut and walks quickly toward Vance. Almost as though she'd been waiting for him to finish. She tugs on his sleeve as he steps off the ladder, and he puts a can of paint on the ground before facing her.

"What the hell?" Mia pulls out her phone to zoom the camera in on them. "What could those two possibly be talking about?"

"Can you see anything?"

"Not really," Mia grumbles. "My zoom sucks. But her hand gestures seem sort of . . . agitated, don't you think?" She flaps one hand in a piss-poor imitation of Brooke.

The light turns red again and a car pulls up behind us. Brooke starts backing away from Vance, and I keep an eye on him in case he's about to try anything weird with her. But he doesn't move, and she doesn't seem as though she's trying to get away from him. When she turns toward the street, I glimpse her face just before the light changes. She doesn't look scared or upset, or in tears like she has been for the past couple of weeks.

She looks determined.

CHAPTER TWELVE

ELLERY
FRIDAY, SEPTEMBER 27

This time it's Ezra's phone that buzzes with the California number.

He holds it up to me. "Sadie?" he asks.

"Probably," I say, glancing instinctively at the doorway. We're in the living room killing time watching Netflix after dinner, and Nana's in the basement doing laundry. She irons everything, including our T-shirts, so she's got at least another half hour down there. Still, Ezra gets to his feet and I follow him to the staircase.

"Hello?" he answers halfway up. "Yeah, hey. We thought it was you. Hang on, we're in transit." We get ourselves settled in his room with the door closed—Ezra at his desk and me in the window seat beside it—before he props up his phone and switches to FaceTime.

"There you are!" Sadie exclaims. Her hair's pulled back into a low, loose ponytail with tendrils escaping everywhere. It makes her look younger. I search her face for clues for how she's doing, because our "official" calls over Skype don't tell me anything. And neither does Nana. But Sadie is wearing the same cheerful, determined expression she's had every time I've glimpsed her over the past few weeks. The one that says, *Everything is fine and I have nothing to explain or apologize for.* "What are you two doing at home on a Friday night?"

"Waiting for our ride," Ezra says. "We're going to a pep rally. At Fright Farm."

Sadie scratches her cheek. "A pep rally *where*?"

"Fright Farm," I say. "Apparently they do school stuff there sometimes. We get a bunch of free passes so people can hang out after."

"Oh, fun! Who are you going with?"

We both pause. "Friends," Ezra says.

It's mostly true. We're meeting Mia and Malcolm there. But our actual ride is Officer Rodriguez, because Nana wasn't going to let us leave the house until she ran into him downtown and he offered to take us. We can't tell Sadie that, though, without falling down a rabbit hole of everything we're *not* telling her.

Before we started our weekly Skype calls with Sadie, Hamilton House Rehabilitation Facility sent a three-page *Resident Interactions Guide* that opened with "Positive, uplifting communication between residents and their loved ones is a cornerstone of the recovery process." In other words: *skim the surface.* Even now, when we're having a decidedly unofficial call, we play by the rules. Needing a police escort after getting targeted by an anonymous stalker isn't on the list of rehab-approved topics.

"Anyone special?" Sadie asks, batting her eyelashes.

My temper flares, because Ezra *had* somebody special back home. She knows perfectly well he's not the type to move on a month later. "Just people from school," I say. "It's getting busy around here. We have the pep rally tonight, and homecoming next Saturday."

If Sadie notices the coolness in my voice, she doesn't react. "Oh my gosh, is it homecoming already? Are you two going to the dance?"

"I am," Ezra says. "With Mia." His glance shifts toward me, and I read in his eyes what he doesn't say: *Unless it gets canceled.*

"So fun! She sounds great. What about you, El?" Sadie asks.

I pick at a frayed seam on my jeans. When Ezra told me last night that Mia asked him to homecoming, it hit me that I'm a "princess" without a date. Even though I'm positive the votes were a setup, something about that still rankles. Maybe because, until last night, I assumed our new friends weren't the school-dance types. Now, I guess it's just Malcolm who isn't. With me, anyway.

But Sadie doesn't know about any of that. "Undecided," I say.

"You should go!" she urges. "Take the cute vandal." She winks. "I sensed a little attraction the last time we spoke, amirite?"

Ezra turns toward me with a grin. "The what, now? Is she talking about Mal?"

My skin prickles with resentment. Sadie doesn't get to do this; she doesn't get to embarrass me about something I haven't sorted out my own feelings about, when she never tells us anything that matters about herself. I straighten my shoulders and incline my head, like we're playing chess and I just figured out

113

my next move. "Homecoming is such a big deal around here, isn't it?" I say. "People are *obsessed* with the court. They even remember how you were queen, like, twenty years ago."

Sadie's smile changes into something that looks fixed, unnatural, and I lean in closer to the phone. She's uncomfortable, and I'm glad. I want her to be. I'm tired of it always being me. "You've never really talked about that," I add. "Must have been a fun night."

Her laugh is as light as spun sugar, and just as brittle. "As fun as a small-town dance can be, I guess. I hardly remember it."

"You don't remember being homecoming queen?" I press. "That's weird." Ezra tenses beside me, and even though I don't look away from Sadie, I can feel his eyes on me. We don't do this; we don't dig for information that Sadie doesn't want to give. We follow her conversational lead. Always.

Sadie licks her lips. "It wasn't that big of a deal. Probably more of an event now that kids can document the whole thing on social media." She shifts her eyes toward Ezra. "Speaking of which, I'm loving your Instagram stories, Ez. You make the town look so pretty, I almost miss living there."

Ezra opens his mouth, about to answer, but I speak first. "Who did you go to homecoming with?" I ask. My voice is challenging, daring her to try to change the subject again. I can tell she wants to, so badly that I almost backtrack and do it myself. But I can't stop thinking about what Caroline Kilduff said in Dalton's Emporium. *A princess. What a stupid thing to want to be.* Sadie was one—my extroverted, attention-loving mother hit the absolute pinnacle of high school popularity—and she never, ever talks about it.

I need her to talk about it.

At first, I don't think she'll answer. When the words spring past her lips she looks as surprised as I am. "Vance Puckett," she says. I'm not prepared for that, and my jaw drops before I can stop it. Ezra inhales sharply beside me. A crease appears between Sadie's eyes, and her voice pitches upward as she looks between us. "What? Have you met him?"

"Briefly," Ezra says, at the same time I ask, "Were you serious with him?"

"I wasn't serious about anyone back then." Sadie tugs on one of her earrings. It's her nervous tell. I twist a strand of hair around my finger, which is mine. If Sadie dislikes this line of questioning, she's going to *hate* the next one.

"Who did Sarah go with?" I ask.

It's like I took an eraser and wiped the expression right off her face. I haven't asked about Sarah in years; Sadie trained me not to bother. Ezra cracks his knuckles, which is *his* nervous tell. We're all wildly uncomfortable and I can see, all of a sudden, why Hamilton House counsels "uplifting communication."

"Excuse me?" Sadie asks.

"Who was Sarah's homecoming date? Was it someone from Echo Ridge?"

"No," Sadie says, glancing over her shoulder. "What's that? Oh, okay." She turns back to the camera with an expression of forced brightness. "Sorry, but I need to go. I wasn't supposed to use this phone for more than a couple of minutes. Love you both! Have fun tonight! Talk soon!" She makes a kissy face at us and disconnects.

Ezra stares at the newly blank screen. "There wasn't anybody behind her, was there?"

"Nope," I say as the doorbell rings.

"What was that about?" he asks quietly.

I don't answer. I can't explain it; the urge I had to make Sadie tell us something—*anything*—that was true about her time in Echo Ridge. We sit in silence until Nana's voice floats up the stairs.

"Ellery, Ezra. Your ride is here."

Ezra pockets his phone and gets to his feet, and I follow him into the hallway. I feel restless and unanchored, and have a sudden urge to grab my brother's hand the way I used to when we were little. Sadie likes to say we were born holding hands, and while I'm pretty sure that's physically impossible, she has dozens of pictures of us clutching one another's tiny fingers in our crib. I don't know if Sadie used to do that with Sarah, because—*surprise*—she's never said.

When we get downstairs, Officer Rodriguez is waiting in Nana's foyer in full uniform, his hands clasped stiffly in front of him. I can see his Adam's apple rise and fall as he swallows. "How's it going, guys?"

"Great," Ezra says. "Thanks for the ride."

"No problem. I don't blame your grandmother for being concerned, but we're working with Fright Farm staff and school administrators to make sure the pep rally is a safe environment for every student."

He sounds like he's reading from a script, and I can see the gawky teenager peeking out from beneath his new-cop veneer. I'd mentioned to Nana how Sadie had described him during our first call in Echo Ridge—broken-hearted and falling apart at Lacey's funeral—but she just made the *pshhh* noise I've come to associate with conversations about Sadie. "I don't remember that," Nana huffed. "Your mother is being dramatic."

It's her standard response to Sadie, and I guess I can't blame her. But I keep looking at the photo of Lacey's junior class picnic that I snapped on my phone. When I zoom in on sixteen-year-old Ryan Rodriguez, I can see it. I can imagine that lovesick-looking boy breaking down over losing her. What I can't tell, though, is whether he'd do it because he was sad, or because he was angry.

Nana folds her arms and glares at Officer Rodriguez as Ezra and I grab our coats. "Every student, yes. But you need to be especially vigilant about the three girls involved." Her mouth puckers. "I'd be happier if they canceled homecoming altogether. Why give whoever is behind this more ammunition?"

"Well, the opposite side of that argument is, why give them more power?" Officer Rodriguez says. I blink at him in surprise, because that actually made sense. "If anything, we feel there's safety in numbers," he continues. "Fright Farm is always packed on a Friday. Whoever we're dealing with likes to operate behind the scenes, so I'm optimistic they'll stay away entirely tonight." He pulls out his keys and almost drops them, saving them at the last second with an awkward lunge. So much for that brief flash of competence. "You guys ready?"

"As we'll ever be," Ezra says.

We follow Officer Rodriguez out the door to his squad car waiting in the driveway, and I take the front seat while Ezra slides into the back. I'm still rattled by my conversation with Sadie, but I don't want to miss the opportunity to observe Officer Rodriguez at close range. "So this will be in the Bloody Big Top area, right?" I ask as I clip my seat belt.

"Yep. Same stage where they have the Dead Man's Party show," Officer Rodriguez says.

I meet Ezra's eyes in the rearview mirror. For a town so obsessed with its own tragic past, Echo Ridge is strangely laissez-faire about holding a high school pep rally at a murder site. "Would you be going if you weren't working?" I ask.

Officer Rodriguez backs out of our driveway. "To the pep rally? No," he says, sounding amused. "These things are for you guys. Not the adults in town."

"But you didn't graduate all that long ago," I say. "I thought maybe it was the sort of thing people would meet up at when they're back in town? Like, my friend Mia might be bringing her sister." That's a total lie. As far as I know, Daisy's still shut up in her room. "She graduated a while ago. Daisy Kwon? Did you know her?"

"Sure. Everyone knows Daisy."

Her name didn't evoke a reaction; his voice is calm and he seems a little preoccupied as he turns onto the main road. So I push a different button. "And Declan Kelly's back too, huh? Malcolm wasn't sure if he'd be here tonight." Ezra kicks lightly at my seat, telegraphing a question with the movement: *What are you up to?* I ignore it and add, "Do you think he will be?"

A muscle in Officer Rodriguez's jaw twitches. "I wouldn't know."

"I'm so curious about Declan," I say. "Were you friends with him in high school?"

His lips press into a thin line. "Hardly."

"Were you friends with Lacey Kilduff?" Ezra pipes up from the backseat. He's finally gotten with the program. Better late than never.

It doesn't help, though. Officer Rodriguez reaches out an

arm and flips a knob on the dashboard, filling the car with static and low voices. "I need to check for updates from the station. Can you keep it down for a sec?"

Ezra shifts in the backseat, leaning forward so he can mutter close to my ear, "Oh-for-two."

CHAPTER THIRTEEN

ELLERY
FRIDAY, SEPTEMBER 27

Officer Rodriguez walks with us to the far end of the park, past the Demon Rollercoaster with its blood-red waterfall and the entrance to the Dark Witch Maze. Two girls giggle nervously as a masked attendant hands them each a flashlight. "You'll need these to navigate the pitch-black lair you're about to experience," he intones. "But be careful along your journey. Fear awaits the further you go."

One of the girls examines her flashlight, then shines it on the thatched wall of the maze. "These are going to shut off right when we need them, aren't they?" she asks.

"Fear awaits the further you go," the attendant repeats, stepping to one side. A clawed hand shoots out of the wall and makes a grab for the nearest girl, who shrieks and falls back against her friend.

"Gets them every time," Officer Rodriguez says, lifting the flap to one of the Bloody Big Top tents. "Here's where I leave you guys. Good luck finding seats."

The bleachers ringing a circular stage are packed, but as Ezra and I scan the crowd we spot Mia waving energetically. "About time!" she says when we reach her. "It's been hell holding these seats." She stands, picking her coat up from the bench beside her, and Ezra glances down at a small concession stand set up to the left of the stage.

"I'm going to get a drink. You guys want anything?"

"No, I'm good," I say, and Mia shakes her head. Ezra thuds down the stairs as I squeeze past Mia in the too-small space. It's not until I sit down that I notice the flash of red hair beside me.

"You certainly like to cut it close," Viv says. She's in a green corduroy jacket and jeans, a gauzy yellow scarf looped around her neck. Two other girls sit beside her, each holding steaming Styrofoam cups.

I look at her and then at the stage, where Katrin, Brooke, and the other cheerleaders are lining up. "I thought you were a cheerleader," I say, confused.

Mia fake-coughs, *"Sore point,"* as Viv stiffens.

"I don't have time for cheerleading. I run the school paper." A note of pride creeps into her voice as she gestures toward the aisle in front of the stage, where a man is setting up an oversized camera. "Channel 5 in Burlington is covering the vandalism story based on *my* article. They're getting local color."

I lean forward, intrigued despite myself. "The school's letting them?"

"You can't stop the free press," Viv says smugly. She points toward a striking, dark-haired woman standing next to the camera, microphone dangling from one hand. "That's Meli Dinglasa. She graduated from Echo Ridge ten years ago and went to Columbia's journalism school." She says it almost reverently, twisting her scarf until it's even more artfully draped. Her outfit would look incredible on TV, which I'm starting to think is the point. "I'm applying there early decision. I'm hoping she'll give me a reference."

On my other side, Mia plucks at my sleeve. "Band's about to start," she says. Ezra returns just in time, a bottled water in one hand.

I tear my eyes away from the reporter as dozens of students holding instruments file through the back entrance and array themselves across the stage. I'd been expecting traditional marching band uniforms, but they're all in black athletic pants and purple T-shirts that read "Echo Ridge High" across the front in white lettering. Malcolm's in the first row, a set of snare drums draped around his neck.

Percy Gilpin jogs onto the stage in the same purple blazer he wore to the assembly last week, and bounds up to a makeshift podium. He adjusts the microphone and raises both hands in the air as people in the stands start to clap. "Good evening, Echo Ridge! You ready for some serious fall fun? We've got a big night planned to support the Echo Ridge Eagles, who are *undefeated* heading into tomorrow's game against Solsbury High!"

More cheers from the crowd, as Mia executes a slow clap beside me. "Yay."

"Let's get this party started!" Percy yells. The cheerleaders take center stage in a V-formation, their purple-and-white pom-poms planted firmly on their hips. A small girl steps out from the band's brass section, squinting against the bright overhead lights. Percy blows a whistle and the girl brings a trombone to her lips.

When the first few notes of "Paradise City" blare out, Ezra and I lean across Mia to exchange surprised grins. Sadie is a Guns N' Roses fanatic, and we grew up with this song blasting through whatever apartment we were living in. An LED screen at the back of the stage starts flashing football game highlights, and within seconds the entire crowd is on its feet.

About halfway through, as everything's building to a crescendo, the other drummers stop and Malcolm launches into this fantastic, frenetic solo. His drumsticks move impossibly fast, the muscles in his arms tense with effort, and my hand half lifts to fan myself before I realize what I'm doing. The cheerleaders are in perfect rhythm with the beat, executing a crisp, high-energy routine that ends with Brooke being tossed into the air, ponytail flying, caught by waiting hands just as the song ends and the entire band takes a bow as one.

I'm clapping so hard my palms hurt as Mia catches my eye and grins. "I know, right?" she says. "I lose all my cynicism when the band performs. It's Echo Ridge's uniting force."

I accidentally knock into Viv when I sit back down, and she shifts away with a grimace. "There's not enough room on this bench," she says sharply, turning to her friends. "I think we might see better farther down."

"Bonus," Mia murmurs as the three of them file out of our row. "We scared Viv away."

A few minutes later, a shadow falls across Viv's vacated seat.

I glance up to see Malcolm in his purple Echo Ridge High T-shirt, minus the drums. "Hey," he says. "Room for one more?" His hair is tousled and his cheeks flushed, and he looks really, really cute.

"Yeah, of course." I shift closer to Mia. "You were great," I add, and he smiles. One of his front teeth is slightly crooked, and it softens the moody look he usually has. I gesture toward the stage, where Coach Gagnon is talking passionately about tradition and giving your all. Photos are still looping on the LED screen behind him. "Will you play an encore?"

"Nah, we're done for the night. It's football talk time."

We listen for a few minutes to the coach's speech. It's getting repetitive. "What happened six years ago?" I ask. "He keeps bringing it up."

"State championship," Malcolm says. "Echo Ridge won when Declan was a junior." And then I remember the yearbook from the library, filled with pictures of the team's huge, come-from-behind victory against a much bigger school. And Declan Kelly, being carried on his teammates' shoulders afterward.

"Oh, that's right," I say. "Your brother threw a Hail Mary touchdown with seconds left in the game, didn't he?" It's a little weird, maybe, how perfectly I remember a game I never attended, but Malcolm just nods. "That must have been amazing."

Something like reluctant pride flits across Malcolm's face. "I guess. Declan was bragging for weeks that he was going to win that game. People laughed, but he backed it up." He runs a hand through his sweat-dampened hair. It shouldn't be attractive, the way his hair spikes up afterward in uneven tufts, but it is. "He always did."

I can't tell if it's just my own nagging suspicions of Declan that make Malcolm's words sound ominous. "Were you guys close?" I ask. As soon as the words are out of my mouth, I realize I've made it sound as though Declan is dead. "*Are* you close?" I amend.

"No," Malcolm says, leaning forward with his elbows on his knees. His voice is quiet, his eyes on the stage. "Not then, and not now."

Every once in a while, it feels like Malcolm and I are having some kind of sub-conversation that we don't acknowledge. We're talking about football and his brother, supposedly, but we're also talking about *before and after*. It's how I think about Sadie—that she was one way before the kind of loss that rips your world apart, and a different version of herself afterward. Even though I didn't know her until Sarah was long gone, I'm sure it's true.

I want to ask Malcolm more, but before I can Mia reaches across me and punches him in the arm. "Hey," she says. "Did you do the thing?"

"No," Malcolm says, avoiding Mia's gaze. She glances between us and smirks, and I get the distinct feeling that I'm missing something.

"And let's not forget, after we defeat Solsbury tomorrow—and we *will*—we've got our biggest test of the season with the homecoming game next week," Coach Gagnon says. Between his perfectly bald head and the shadows cast by the Big Top's stadium lighting, he looks like an exceptionally enthusiastic alien. "We're up against Lutheran, our only defeat last year. But that's not going to happen this time around! Because *this* time—"

A loud popping noise fills my ears, making me jump. The

bright lights snap off and the LED screen goes black, then flashes to life again. Static fills the screen, followed by a photo of Lacey in her homecoming crown, smiling at the camera. The crowd gasps, and Malcolm goes rigid beside me.

Then Lacey's picture rips in two, replaced by three others: Brooke, Katrin, and me. Theirs are class photos, but mine is a candid, with my face half turned from the camera. A chill inches up my spine as I recognize the hoodie I wore yesterday when Ezra and I walked downtown to meet Malcolm and Mia at Bartley's.

Somebody was watching us. *Following* us.

Horror-movie laughter starts spilling from the speakers, literal *mua-ha-ha*s that echo through the tent as what looks like thick red liquid drips down the screen, followed by jagged white letters: SOON. When it fades away, the Bloody Big Top is utterly silent. Everyone is frozen, with one exception: Meli Dinglasa from Channel 5. She strides purposefully onto the stage toward Coach Gagnon, with her microphone outstretched and a cameraman at her heels.

CHAPTER FOURTEEN

MALCOLM
SATURDAY, SEPTEMBER 28

The text from Declan comes as I'm walking against the departing crowds at Fright Farm Saturday night: *In town for a few hours. Don't freak out.*

I almost text back *I'm at the scene of your alleged crime. Don't freak out,* but manage to restrain myself to a simple *What for?* Which he ignores. I stuff the phone back in my pocket. If Declan's been paying attention to the local news, he knows about last night's pep rally turned stalker sideshow. I hope he was in New Hampshire surrounded by people when all that went down, or he's only going to make the speculation worse.

Not my problem. Tonight I'm just the chauffeur, collecting Ellery and Ezra after work. There was no way their grandmother was letting them walk through the woods after what happened last night. To be honest, I'm a little surprised she agreed to let me pick them up, but Ellery says closing is two hours past Mrs. Corcoran's usual bedtime.

I expect the House of Horrors to be empty, but music and laughter spill out toward me as I approach the building. The entire park was built around this house, an old Victorian at the edge of what used to be another wooded area. I've seen pictures of it before it became a theme park attraction, and it was always stately but worn-looking—as if its turrets were about to crumble, or the steps leading up to the wide porch would collapse if you stepped on them wrong. It still looks like that, but now it's all part of the atmosphere.

I haven't been here since I was ten, when Declan and his friends brought me. They took off when we were halfway through, like the assholes they were, and I had to go through the rest of the house on my own. Every single room freaked me out. I had nightmares for weeks about a guy in a bloody bathtub with stumps for legs.

My brother laughed when I finally stumbled out of the House of Horrors, snotty-nosed and terrified. *Don't be such a wuss, Mal. None of it's real.*

The music gets louder as I climb the steps and turn the doorknob. It doesn't budge, and there's no bell. I knock a few times, which feels weird, like, who do I expect to answer the door at a haunted house, exactly? Nobody does, so I head back down the stairs and edge around to the back. When I turn the corner, I see concrete steps leading down to a door that's wedged open with a piece of wood. I descend the stairs and push the door open.

I'm in a basement room that looks like it's part dressing room, part staff room. The space is large, dimly lit, and cluttered with shelves and clothes racks. A vanity with an oversized bulb mirror is shoved to one side, its surface covered with jars and bottles. Two cracked leather couches line the walls, with a glass-topped end table between them. There's a closet-sized bathroom to the left, and a half-open door in front of me that leads into a small office.

I'm hovering a few steps inside, searching for a way upstairs, when a hand pushes open a frayed velvet curtain on the opposite end of the room. The sudden movement makes me gasp like a scared kid, and the girl who steps through the curtain laughs. She's almost as tall as I am, dressed in a tight black tank top that shows off intricate tattoos against brown skin. She looks like she could be a few years older than me. "Boo," she says, then crosses her arms and cocks her head. "Party crasher?"

I blink, confused. "What?"

She tsks. "Don't play innocent with me. I'm the makeup artist. I know everybody, and *you* are trespassing." I half open my mouth to protest, then close it as her stern look dissolves into a wide smile. "I'm just messing with you. Go upstairs, find your friends." She crosses over to a minifridge next to the vanity and pulls out a couple bottles of water, pointing one toward me like a warning. "But this is a dry party, understand? Whole thing'll get shut down if we gotta deal with a bunch of drunk teenagers. Especially after what happened last night."

"Sure. Right," I say, trying to sound like I know what she's talking about. Ellery and Ezra didn't say anything about a party. The tall girl sweeps aside the velvet curtain to let me through.

I climb a set of stairs into another hallway that opens into a dungeon-like room. I recognize the room immediately from my last visit inside, with Declan, but it looks a lot less sinister filled with party guests. A few people are still partly in costume, with masks off or pushed up on their foreheads. One guy's holding a rubber head under his arm while he talks to a girl in a witch's dress.

A hand tugs at my sleeve. I look down to see short, bright-red nails and follow them up to a face. It's Viv and she's talking, but I can't hear what she's saying over the music. I cup a hand to my ear, and she raises her voice. "I didn't know you worked at Fright Farm."

"I don't," I say back.

Viv frowns. She's drenched in some kind of strawberry perfume that doesn't smell bad, exactly, but reminds me of something a little kid would wear. "Then why did you come to the staff party?"

"I didn't know there was a party," I answer. "I'm just picking up Ellery and Ezra."

"Well, good timing. I've been wanting to talk to you." I eye her warily. I've seen Viv almost every week since I moved into the Nilssons', but we've barely exchanged a dozen words the entire time. Our whole relationship, if you can call it that, is based on *not* wanting to talk to one another. "Can I interview you for my next article?" she asks.

I don't know what she's angling for, but it can't be good. "Why?"

"I'm doing this 'Where Are They Now?' series on Lacey's murder. I thought it would be interesting to get the perspective of someone who was on the sidelines when it happened, what with your brother being a person of interest and all. We could—"

"Are you out of your mind?" I cut her off. "No."

Viv lifts her chin. "I'm going to write it anyway. Don't you want to give your side? It might make people more sympathetic to Declan, to hear from his brother."

I turn away without answering. Last night, Viv was front and center in the local news coverage of the pep rally stunt, getting interviewed like some kind of Echo Ridge crime expert. She's been in Katrin's shadow for so long, there's no way she's letting her moment in the spotlight go. But I don't have to help extend her fifteen minutes of fame.

I shoulder through the crowd and finally spot Ellery. She's hard to miss—her hair is teased into a black cloud around her head and her eyes are so heavily made up that they seem to take up half her face. She looks like some kind of goth anime character. I'm not sure what it says about me that I'm kind of into it.

She catches my eye and waves me over. She's standing with a guy a few years older than us with a man-bun, a goatee, and a tight henley shirt with the buttons undone. The whole look screams *college guy trolling for high school girls,* and I hate him instantly. "Hey," Ellery says when I reach them. "So apparently there's a party tonight."

"I noticed," I say with a glare toward Man Bun.

He's not fazed. "House of Horrors tradition," he explains. "It's always on the Saturday closest to the owner's birthday. I can't stay, though. Got a toddler at home that never sleeps. I have to give my wife a break." He swipes at his face and turns to Ellery. "Is all the blood off?"

Ellery peers at him. "Yeah, you're good."

"Thanks. See ya later," the guy says, and starts pushing his way through the crowd.

"So long," I say, watching him leave with a lot less venom now that I know he wasn't hitting on Ellery. "The blood he's referring to is makeup, right?"

Ellery laughs. "Yeah. Darren spends all night in a bloody bathtub. Some people don't bother washing their makeup off till they get home, but he tried that once and *terrified* his child. Poor kid might be scarred for life."

I shudder. "I was scarred for life going through that room, and I was ten."

Ellery's giant anime eyes get even wider. "Who brought you here when you were *ten*?"

"My brother," I say.

"Ah." Ellery looks thoughtful. Like she can see into the secret corner of my brain that I try not to visit often, because it's where my questions about what really happened between Declan and Lacey live. That corner makes me equal parts horrified and ashamed, because every once in a while, it imagines my brother losing control of his hair-trigger temper at exactly the wrong moment.

I swallow hard and push the thought aside. "I'm kind of surprised they'd have this after what happened last night."

Ellery gazes around us. "I know, right? But hey, everyone here works in a Halloween theme park. They don't scare easy."

"Do you want to stay for a while?"

She looks regretful. "Better not. Nana didn't even want us to work tonight. She's pretty freaked out."

"Are you?" I ask.

"I . . ." She hesitates, pulling on a strand of teased hair and winding it around her finger. "I want to say no, because I hate the fact that some anonymous creep can rattle me. But yeah. I am. It's just too . . . close, you know?" She shivers as someone squeezes past her in a *Scream* mask. "I keep having these conversations with my mother where she has no idea what's going on, and all I can think is—no wonder she never wanted to bring us here. Her twin sister disappears, her favorite babysitter's daughter is murdered, and now this? It's enough to make you feel like the whole town is cursed."

"Your mother doesn't know about—anything?" I ask.

"No. We're only supposed to have *uplifting communication* with her." She releases her hair. "You know she's in rehab, right? I figured the entire town knows."

"They do," I admit. She snort-laughs, but the sadness behind it tugs at my chest. "I'm sorry you're dealing with that. And I'm sorry about your aunt. I've been meaning to tell you that. I know it all happened way before we were born, but . . . that sucks. In a massively stating-the-obvious sort of way."

Ellery drops her eyes. "I'm pretty sure it's why we wound up here. I don't think Sadie's ever dealt with it. No closure, no nothing. I didn't connect the dots when Lacey died, but that's when things started going downhill. Must've brought bad memories too close to the surface. So it's sort of ironic that she's in the dark now, but—what can you do?" She raises her water bottle in a mock salute. "Three cheers to *uplifting communication*. Anyway. We should probably find Ezra, huh? He said he was going downstairs to get some water."

We make our way out of the crowded dungeon and take

the staircase down to the staff room, but there's no sign of Ezra there. It's cooler than it was upstairs, but I'm still overheated and a little thirsty. I cross over to the minifridge and take out two bottles of water, putting one on the vanity and offering the other to Ellery.

"Thanks." She reaches out a hand, but our timing's off; I let go before she's grasped it fully, and it falls to the floor between us. When we both reach for it, we almost knock heads. Ellery laughs and puts a hand on my chest.

"I have it," she says, and picks it up. She straightens, and even in the dim lighting I can see how red her cheeks are. "We're so graceful, aren't we?"

"That was my fault," I say. The whole exchange has left us standing closer than we need to be, but neither of us moves away. "Bad handoff. You can see why I never made it as a football player." She smiles and tilts her head up and, holy hell, her eyes are pretty.

"Thanks," she murmurs, getting redder.

Oh. I said that out loud.

She moves a little closer, brushing against my hip, and an electric charge runs through me. Are we . . . should I . . .

Don't be such a wuss, Mal.

God. Of all times to hear my brother's stupid voice.

I reach out a hand and trace my thumb along Ellery's jaw. Her skin is just as soft as I thought it would be. Her lips part, I swallow hard, and just then there's a loud scratching noise behind us and somebody says, "Damn it!" in a frustrated tone.

Ellery and I break apart, and she twists to face the office. She's across the room in a second, easing open the cracked door.

Brooke Bennett is slumped on the floor, wedged between the desk and some kind of giant recycling bin. Ellery goes to her and crouches down.

"Brooke? Are you okay?" she asks.

Brooke's hair hangs in her face, and when she pushes it aside she nearly stabs herself in the eye with something small and silvery. Ellery reaches over and takes it. I can see from the doorway that it's a paper clip, pulled open and unfurled so its edges are exposed. Another one just like it rests on the floor next to her.

"This is harder than he said it would be," Brooke says, her voice slurring.

"Who said?" Ellery asks, setting both paper clips on the desk. "What's hard?"

Brooke snickers. "That's what *she* said."

It looks like nobody gave Brooke the heads-up about tonight being a dry party. "Do you want some water?" I ask, holding out my untouched bottle.

Brooke takes it from me and unscrews the cap. She swallows a greedy gulp, spilling some water down her front, before handing it back. "Thanks, Malcolm. You're so nice. The nicest person in your entire house. By a *lot*." She wipes her mouth on her sleeve and focuses on Ellery. "You look different. Are those your real eyes?"

Ellery and I glance at each other and we both suppress a laugh. Drunk Brooke is kind of entertaining. "What are you doing down here?" Ellery asks. "Do you want to come upstairs?"

"No." Brooke shakes her head vehemently. "I need to get it back. I shouldn't have . . . I just shouldn't have. I have to show them. It's not right, it's not okay."

"Show them what?" I ask. "What happened?"

Sudden tears spring into her eyes. "That's the million-dollar question, isn't it? *What happened?*" She puts a finger to her lips and shushes loudly. "Wouldn't you like to know?"

"Is this about the pep rally?" Ellery asks.

"No." Brooke hiccups and holds her stomach. "Ugh. I don't feel so good."

I grab a nearby wastebasket and hold it out. "Do you need this?"

Brooke takes it, but just stares listlessly at the bottom. "I want to go home."

"Do you want us to find Kyle?"

"Kyle and I are *over*," Brooke says, waving her hand as though she just made him disappear. "And he's not here anyway." She sighs. "Viv drove me, but I don't want to see her right now. She'll just lecture me."

"I can give you a ride," I offer.

"Thanks," Brooke slurs.

Ellery stands and plucks at my sleeve. "I'm going to find Ezra. Be right back."

I crouch next to Brooke after Ellery leaves. "You want some more water?" I ask. Brooke waves me away, and for the life of me I can't think of what to say next. Even after living with Katrin for four months, I'm still not comfortable around girls like Brooke. Too pretty, too popular. Too much like Lacey.

Minutes crawl by, until Brooke draws her knees up to her chest and lifts her eyes toward mine. They're unfocused and ringed with dark circles. "Have you ever made a really bad mistake?" she asks quietly.

I pause, trying to figure out what's going on with her so I can frame a good answer. "Well, yeah. Most days."

"No." She shakes her head, then burrows her face in her arms. "I don't mean regular stuff," she says, her voice muffled. "I mean something you can't take back."

I'm lost. I don't know how to be helpful. "Like what?"

Her head is still down, and I have to edge closer to hear what she's saying. "I wish I had different friends. I wish everything was different."

Footsteps approach, and I stand up as Ellery and Ezra poke their heads into the office. "Hey, Mal," Ezra says, and then his gaze drops to Brooke. "Everything okay in here?"

"I want to go home," Brooke repeats, and I offer a hand to help her to her feet.

She revives a little when we get outside, and only needs occasional steadying as we make our way toward my mother's Volvo. It's the nicest car we've ever owned, courtesy of Peter, and I really hope Brooke doesn't throw up in it. She seems to be thinking the same thing, and rolls down the window as soon as Ezra helps her into the passenger seat.

"What's your address?" I ask as I climb in behind the wheel.

"Seventeen Briar Lane," Brooke says. The far edge of town.

The twins slam the back doors and I turn to face them as they buckle themselves in. "You guys are right around the corner from here. I'll drop you off first so your grandmother doesn't worry."

"That'd be great, thanks," Ellery says.

I back the Volvo out of its spot and head for the exit. "Sorry you had to leave the party," Brooke says, scrunching down in her seat. "I shouldn't have had anything to drink. Can't hold it. That's what Katrin always says."

"Yeah, well. Katrin doesn't know everything." It seems like the thing to say, even if she was right in this particular case.

"Hope not," Brooke says in a low tone.

I glance at her before pulling onto the main road, but it's too dark to read her expression. It sounds like she and Katrin are fighting, which is weird. I've never seen them on the outs, maybe because Brooke lets Katrin take the lead in everything. "We weren't planning on staying anyway," I reassure her.

It's a quick trip to the Corcorans' house, which is dark except for a single light blazing on the front porch.

"Looks like Nana's asleep," Ezra says, pulling a set of keys from his pocket. "I was worried she'd be waiting up. Thanks for the ride, Mal."

"Any time."

Ezra opens the car door and gets out, waiting in the driveway for his sister. "Yeah, thanks Malcolm," Ellery says, slinging her bag over one shoulder. "Talk to you soon."

"Tomorrow, maybe?" I blurt out, turning to face her. She pauses, her eyes questioning, and I freeze for a second. Did I imagine that I almost kissed her in the basement, or that it seemed like she wanted me to? Then I plow ahead anyway. "I mean—I could call you, or something. If you want to, you know, talk."

God. Real smooth.

But she gives me a full smile, dimple and all. "Yeah, definitely. That sounds good. Let's talk." Brooke clears her throat, and Ellery blinks. Like she'd forgotten for a few seconds that

Brooke was in the car. I know I did. "Bye, Brooke," Ellery says, climbing out the door that Ezra just exited.

"Bye," Brooke says.

Ellery shuts the car door and turns to follow her brother up the drive. She passes Brooke's open window just as Brooke sighs deeply and rubs a listless hand across her face. Ellery pauses and asks, "Are you going to be okay?"

Brooke shifts to face her. She doesn't speak for so long that Ellery frowns, darting concerned eyes toward me. Then Brooke lifts her shoulders in a shrug.

"Why wouldn't I be?" she says.

CHAPTER FIFTEEN

ELLERY
SUNDAY, SEPTEMBER 29

The photo albums are more than twenty years old, dusty and brown at the edges. Even so, seventeen-year-old Sadie practically jumps off the page in her daring black homecoming dress, all wild hair and red lips. She's entirely recognizable as the younger version of her present-day self, which is more than I can say for her date.

"Wow," Ezra says, inching closer toward me on Nana's living room rug. After much trial and error with her stiff furniture, we've decided it's the most comfortable seat in the room. "Sadie wasn't kidding. Vance was hot back then."

"Yeah," I say, studying Vance's high cheekbones and lazy smirk. Then I glance at the clock over Nana's fireplace, for about the fifth time since we've been sitting here. Ezra catches the movement and laughs.

"Still only eight-thirty. Has been for an entire minute. In other words: too early for Malcolm to call you." Ezra didn't miss my moment with Malcolm in the car last night, and he wouldn't let me go to sleep until I told him about our near kiss in the Fright Farm staff room.

"Shut up," I grumble, but my stomach flutters as I fight off a smile.

Nana works her way into the living room with a can of lemon Pledge and a dustcloth. It's her usual Sunday-morning ritual: seven o'clock Mass, then housework. In about fifteen minutes she's going to send Ezra and me outside to rake the lawn. "What are you two looking at?" she asks.

"Sadie's homecoming pictures," Ezra says.

I expect her to frown, but she just aims a spray of Pledge at the mahogany table in front of the bay window. "Did you like Vance, Nana?" I ask as she wipes the surface clean. "When he and Sadie were dating?"

"Not particularly," Nana sniffs. "But I knew he wouldn't last. They never did."

I flip through the next couple of pages in the album. "Did Sarah go to homecoming?"

"No, Sarah was a late bloomer. The only boys she ever talked to were the ones Sadie went out with." Nana stops dusting and puts the can down, pushing the bay window curtain aside and peering out. "Now, what's he doing here this early on a Sunday?"

"Who?" Ezra asks.

"Ryan Rodriguez."

I close the photo album as Nana heads for the front door

and pulls it open. "Hello, Ryan," she says, but before she can say anything more he interrupts her.

"Is Ellery here?" he asks. He sounds hurried, urgent.

"Of course—"

He doesn't wait for her to finish. He pushes past her, eyes searching the room until they land on me. He's in a faded Echo Ridge High sweatshirt and jeans, faint dark stubble tracing his jaw. He looks even younger without his uniform on, and also like he just woke up. "Ellery. Thank God. Have you been here all night?"

"Ryan, what on earth?" Nana shuts the door and folds her arms tightly across her chest. "Is this about the homecoming threats? Did something new happen?"

"Yes, but it's not . . . it's a different . . ." He runs a hand through his hair and takes a deep breath. "Brooke Bennett didn't come home last night. Her parents aren't sure where she is."

I don't even realize I've gotten to my feet until I hear a loud thud—the photo album has slipped from my hand to the floor. Ezra rises more slowly, his face pale and his eyes darting between me and Officer Rodriguez. But before either of us can say anything, Nana lets out a strangled cry. Every drop of color drains from her face, and for a second I think she might faint. "Oh, dear God." She walks unsteadily to a chair and collapses into it, clutching at the armrests. "It happened. It happened again, right in front of your faces, and you didn't do a thing to stop it!"

"We don't know what happened. We're trying to—" Officer Rodriguez starts, but Nana doesn't let him finish.

"A girl is *missing*. A girl who was threatened in front of the entire town two days ago. Just like my granddaughter." I've never seen Nana like this; it's as if every emotion she's been suppressing for the past twenty years just flooded to the surface. Her face is red, her eyes watery, and her entire body trembles as she speaks. The sight of my calm, no-nonsense grandmother this upset makes my heart pound even harder. "No one on the police force did anything of substance to protect Ellery *or* Brooke. *You let this happen.*"

Officer Rodriguez flinches, as startled as if she'd slapped him. "We didn't— Look, I know how upsetting this is. We're all concerned, that's why I'm here. But we don't know Brooke's missing. She might very well be with a friend. We have several officers looking into that. It's too early to assume the worst."

Nana folds her hands in her lap, her fingers threaded so tightly together that her knuckles are white. "Missing girls don't come home in Echo Ridge, Ryan," she says in a hollow voice. "You know that."

Neither of them are paying any attention to Ezra or me. "El," my brother says in a low voice, and I know what's coming next. *We have to tell them.* And we do, of course. From what Officer Rodriguez has said so far, it doesn't sound as though he has any idea that Brooke left Fright Farm with us. Or that Malcolm was the one who ultimately took her home. Alone.

Last night, slumped in the passenger seat as Malcolm dropped us off, Brooke had looked so tired and defeated that I couldn't help but check in with her one last time.

Are you going to be okay?

Why wouldn't I be?

Nana and Officer Rodriguez are still talking, but I can only process scraps of what they're saying. My chest shakes when

I take a breath. I know I have to speak up. I know I have to tell Officer Rodriguez and my grandmother that our friend—*Declan Kelly's brother*—was very likely the last person to see an Echo Ridge homecoming princess before she went missing.

And I know exactly how that's going to look.

CHAPTER SIXTEEN

MALCOLM

SUNDAY, SEPTEMBER 29

I don't realize it's déjà vu until I'm in the middle of it.

When I wander into the kitchen Sunday morning, it doesn't strike me as strange at first that Officer McNulty is sitting at our kitchen island. He and Peter are both on the town council, so I figure they're probably talking stoplights again. Even though it's barely eight-thirty in the morning, and even though Officer McNulty is listening with a surprising amount of interest to Katrin's long-winded description of her date with Theo last night.

My mother is fluttering around the kitchen, trying to fill cups of coffee that people haven't emptied yet. Officer McNulty lets her top his off, then asks, "So you didn't see Brooke at all last night? She didn't call you or text you at any point in the evening?"

"She texted to see if I was coming to the party. But I wasn't."

"And what time was that?"

Katrin scrunches her face up, thinking. "Around . . . ten, maybe?"

"Could I see your phone, please."

The official tone of the request makes my skin prickle. I've heard it before. "Is something going on with Brooke?" I ask.

Peter rubs a hand over his unshaven jaw. "Apparently she wasn't in her room this morning, and it looks as though her bed wasn't slept in. Her parents haven't seen her since she left for work last night, and she's not answering her phone."

My throat closes and my palms start to sweat. "She's not?"

Officer McNulty hands Katrin's phone back to her just as it buzzes. She looks down, reads the message that's popped up on her screen, and pales. "It's from Viv," she says, her voice suddenly shaky. "She says she lost track of Brooke at the party and hasn't talked to her since." Katrin bites her lower lip and shoves the phone at Officer McNulty, like maybe he can make the text say something different. "I really thought they'd be together. Brooke stays over after work sometimes because Viv's house is closer."

Dread starts inching up my spine. *No. This can't be happening.*

Mom sets down the coffeepot and turns toward me. "Malcolm, you didn't happen to see Brooke when you picked the twins up, did you?"

Officer McNulty looks up. "You were at Fright Farm last night, Malcolm?"

Shit. Shit. Shit.

"Just to give the Corcoran twins a ride home," Mom says quickly. But not as though she's really worried that I'm going to get into trouble.

146

My stomach twists. She has *no* idea.

Officer McNulty rests his forearms on the kitchen island's shiny, swirling black marble. "Did you happen to see Brooke while you were there?" His tone is interested, but not intense like it was when he interrogated Declan.

Not yet.

Five years ago we were in a different kitchen: our tiny ranch, two miles from here. My dad glowered in a corner and my mother twisted her hands together while Declan sat at the table across from Officer McNulty and repeated the same things over and over again. *I hadn't seen Lacey in two days. I don't know what she was doing that night. I was out driving.*

Driving where?

Just driving. I do that sometimes.

Was anybody with you?

No.

Did you call anybody? Text anybody?

No.

So you just drove by yourself for—what? Two, three hours?

Yeah.

Lacey was dead by then. Not just missing. Workers found her body in the park before her parents even knew she hadn't come home. I sat in the living room while Officer McNulty fired questions at Declan, my eyes glued to a television program I wasn't watching. I never went into the kitchen. Never said a word. Because none of it involved me, not really, except for the part where it became this slowly burning fuse that eventually blew my family apart.

"I . . ." I'm taking too long to answer. I scan the faces around me like they'll give me some clue how to respond, but all I can see are the same expressions they always wear whenever I start to talk: Mom looks attentive, Katrin exasperated, and Peter is all patient forbearance marred only by a slight nostril flare. Officer McNulty scratches a note on the pad in front of him, then flicks his eyes toward me in a cursory, almost lazy way. Until he sees something in my face that makes him tense, like he's a cat batting at a toy that suddenly came to life. He leans forward, his blue-gray eyes locked on mine.

"Do you have something to tell us, Malcolm?" he asks.

CHAPTER SEVENTEEN

ELLERY

SUNDAY, SEPTEMBER 29

This time, unlike after the hit-and-run with Mr. Bowman, I'm a good witness. I remember everything.

I remember taking the paper clip from Brooke's hand, and picking up a second one from the floor. "Paper clips?" Officer Rodriguez asks. He went directly into questioning mode as soon as Ezra told him we'd left Fright Farm with Brooke. We moved into the kitchen, and Nana made cocoa for everyone. I grasp the still-warm mug gratefully as I explain what happened before Ezra joined Malcolm and me.

"Yeah. They were pulled apart, you know, so they were almost straight. People do that kind of thing sometimes, like a nervous habit?" I do, anyway. I've never met a paper clip I didn't immediately twist out of its preexisting shape.

I remember Brooke being sort of goofy and funny and

rambling at first. "She made a *that's what she said* joke," I tell Officer Rodriguez.

His face is a total blank. "That's what she said?"

"Yeah, you know, from *The Office*? The TV show?" I tilt my head at him, waiting for it to click, but his brow stays knit in confusion. How can anyone in his twenties not get that reference? "It's something the lead character used to say as, like, a punch line after a double entendre. Like when someone says something is hard, they could be referring to a difficult situation or, you know. To a penis."

Ezra spits out his cocoa as Officer Rodriguez turns bright red. "For heaven's sake, Ellery," Nana snaps. "That's hardly pertinent to the conversation at hand."

"I thought it was," I say, shrugging. It's never *not* interesting observing Officer Rodriguez's reactions to things he doesn't expect.

He clears his throat and avoids my eyes. "And what happened after the . . . joke?"

"She drank some water. I asked her what she was doing in the basement. Then she started seeming more upset." I remember Brooke's words like she'd just spoken them five minutes ago: *I shouldn't have. I have to show them. It's not right, it's not okay. What happened? Wouldn't you like to know?*

My stomach squeezes. Those are the sort of things that seem like nonsense when a drunk girl is babbling at a party, but ominous when she's missing. Brooke is *missing*. I don't think that's really sunk in yet. I keep thinking Officer Rodriguez is going to get a call any second telling him she met up with friends after she got home. "She got a little teary when she said all that," I say. "I asked her if it was about the pep rally, but she said no."

"Did you press her?" Officer Rodriguez asks.

"No. She said she wanted to go home. I offered to get Kyle and she said they'd broken up. And that he wasn't there anyway. So Malcolm offered her a ride home, and she said okay. That's when I left to get Ezra. Driving Brooke home was . . ." I pause, weighing what to say next. "It wasn't planned. At all. It just happened."

Officer Rodriguez's forehead creases in a quizzical frown. "What do you mean?"

Good question. What *do* I mean? My brain has been whirring since Officer Rodriguez said Brooke was missing. We don't know what it means yet, but I do know this: if she doesn't show up soon people will expect the worst, and they'll start pointing fingers at the most obvious suspect. Which would be the person who saw her last.

It's the cliché moment of every *Dateline* special: the friend or neighbor or colleague who says, *He's always been such a nice guy, nobody ever would have believed he could be capable of this.* I can't think everything through clearly yet, but I do know this: there was no master plan to get Brooke alone. I never got the sense that Malcolm was doing anything except trying to help her out. "I mean, it was just random chance that Malcolm ended up giving Brooke a ride," I say. "We didn't even know she was in the office at first."

"Okay," Officer Rodriguez says, his expression neutral. "So you left to find Ezra, and Malcolm was alone with Brooke for . . . how long?"

I look at Ezra, who shrugs. "Five minutes, maybe?" I say.

"Was Brooke's demeanor any different when you returned?"

"No. She was still sad."

"But you said she wasn't sad earlier. That she was joking."

"She was joking and *then* she was sad," I remind him.

"Right. So, describe the walk to the car for me, please. Both of you."

It goes on like that for another ten minutes until we finally, painstakingly get to the moment in our driveway when I asked Brooke if she was going to be okay. I gloss over the part where Malcolm asked if he could call me, which doesn't seem important right now. Ezra doesn't bring it up, either.

"She said, *Why wouldn't I be*?" Officer Rodriguez repeats.

"Yeah."

"And did you answer?"

"No." I didn't. It hits me with a sharp stab of regret, now, that I should have.

"All right." Officer Rodriguez snaps the notebook shut. "Thank you. This has been helpful. I'll let you know if I have any follow-up questions."

I unclench my hands, realizing I've been knotting them in my lap. They're covered with a thin sheen of sweat. "And if you find Brooke? Will you let us know she's all right?"

"Of course. I'm heading to the station now. Maybe she's already home, getting a talking-to from her parents. Most of the time that's—" He stops suddenly, his neck going red as he darts a glance at Nana. "That's what we hope for."

I know what he was about to say. *Most of the time that's*

how these things turn out. It's the sort of thing police officers are trained to tell worried people so they won't spiral into panic when somebody goes missing. But it's not comforting in Echo Ridge.

Because Nana's right. It's never been true.

CHAPTER EIGHTEEN

MALCOLM
SUNDAY, SEPTEMBER 29

"You're an important witness here, Malcolm. Take your time."

Officer McNulty is still resting his forearms on the kitchen island. His sleeves are rolled up, and his watch reads 9:15. Brooke has been missing for almost ten hours. It's not that much time, but it feels like forever when you start imagining all the things that could happen to a person while the rest of the world is sleeping.

I'm sitting on the stool beside him. There are only a couple of feet between us, which doesn't feel like enough. Officer McNulty's eyes are still on me, cold and flat. He said *witness,* not *suspect,* but that isn't how he's looking at me. "That's it," I say. "That's everything I remember."

"So the Corcoran twins can corroborate your story right up until you dropped them off at their house?"

Jesus. *Corroborate your story.* My stomach tightens. I should've brought Brooke home first. Everything would look a lot different if I had. "Yeah," I say.

What the hell must Ellery be thinking right now? Does she even know?

Who am I kidding? This is Echo Ridge. Officer McNulty has been at our house for more than an hour. *Everyone* knows.

"All right," Officer McNulty says. "Let's go back a little while, before last night. Did you notice anything unusual about Brooke in the past few weeks? Anything that concerned or surprised you?"

I slide my eyes toward Katrin. She's leaning against the counter, but stiffly, like she's a mannequin somebody propped there. "I don't really know Brooke," I say. "I don't see her much."

"She's here a lot though, isn't she?" Officer McNulty asks.

It feels like he's after something, but I don't know what. Officer McNulty's eyes drop from my face to my knee, and I realize it's jiggling nervously. I press a fist onto my leg to stop the movement. "Yeah, but not to hang out with me."

"She thought you were cute," Katrin says abruptly.

What the hell? My throat closes, and I couldn't answer even if I knew what to say.

Everyone turns toward Katrin. "She's been saying that for a while," she continues. Her voice is low, but every word is perfectly clear and precise. "Last weekend, when she was sleeping over, I woke up and she wasn't in the room. I waited for, like, twenty minutes before I fell asleep again, but she didn't come back. I thought maybe she was visiting *you*. Especially since she broke up with Kyle a couple of days later."

The words hit me like a punch to the gut as all the heads in the room swivel to me. Jesus Christ, why would Katrin say something like that? She has to know how it would make me look. Even more suspicious than I already do. "She wasn't," I manage to say.

"Malcolm doesn't have a girlfriend," my mother says quickly. In the space of a half hour she's aged a year: her cheeks are hollow, her hair's straggling out of its neat bun, and there's a deep line etched between her brows. I know she's been traveling down the same memory lane that I have. "He's not like . . . he's always spent more time with his friends than with girls."

He's not like Declan. That's what she was about to say.

Officer McNulty's eyes bore into mine. "If there was anything going on with you and Brooke, Malcolm, now is the time to mention it. Doesn't mean you're in trouble." His jaw twitches, betraying the lie. "Just another piece of this puzzle we're trying to figure out."

"There wasn't," I say, meeting Katrin's cool stare. She edges closer to Peter. He's been silent all this time, arms folded, an expression of deep concern on his face. "The only time I ever see Brooke is when she's with Katrin. Except . . ." A thought hits me, and I look at Officer McNulty again. He's fully alert, leaning forward. "I did see her a few days ago. I was in the car with Mia," I add hastily. "We saw Brooke downtown, talking with Vance Puckett."

Officer McNulty blinks. Frowns. Whatever he was expecting me to say, that wasn't it. "Vance Puckett?"

"Yeah. He was painting over the graffiti on Armstrong's Auto Repair, and Brooke walked up to him. They were talking sort of . . . intensely. You asked about anything unusual, and that was, um, unusual." Even as the words spill out of me, I know how they sound.

Like a guy with something to hide who's trying to deflect attention.

"Interesting." Officer McNulty nods. "Vance Puckett was in the drunk tank last night, and in fact"—he glances at his watch—"is most likely still there. Thank you for the information, though. We'll be sure to follow up with him." He sits back and crosses his arms. He's wearing a dress shirt, and nicely pressed pants. I realize he was probably getting ready for church when all this happened. "Is there anything else you think would be good for us to know?"

My phone sits heavy in my pocket. It hasn't been buzzing, which means Mia probably isn't even awake yet. The last text I have was the one Declan sent before I entered the House of Horrors to pick up the twins.

In town for a few hours. Don't freak out.

Why was he here? Why was my brother here, *again,* when a girl goes missing?

If I showed that text to Officer McNulty now, everything would change. Katrin would stop looking daggers at me. Officer McNulty wouldn't keep asking the same question a dozen different ways. His suspicion would shift away from me, and go back to where it's been ever since Lacey died. To Declan.

I swallow hard and keep my phone where it is. "No. There's nothing."

CHAPTER NINETEEN

ELLERY

SUNDAY, SEPTEMBER 29

I can't sit still.

I pace through Nana's house all afternoon, picking things up and then putting them down. The bookshelves in her living room are full of those porcelain figures she likes—Hummels, Nana calls them. Little boys and girls with blond hair and apple cheeks, climbing trees and carrying baskets and hugging one another. Nana told me, when I picked one up a couple of days ago, that Sadie had broken it when she was ten.

"Knocked that one on the ground so its head split in two," Nana said. "She glued the pieces back together. I didn't notice for weeks."

Once you know to look for it, though, it's obvious. I held the porcelain girl in my hand and stared at the jagged white line running down one side of her face. "Were you mad?" I'd asked Nana.

"Furious," she said. "Those are collector's items. The girls weren't supposed to touch them. But Sadie couldn't keep her hands off them. I knew it was her, even when Sarah told me *she'd* done it."

"Sarah did? Why?"

"She didn't want her sister to get punished," Nana said. For the first time when talking about Sarah, a spasm of grief crossed her face. "I was always a little harder on Sadie, I suppose. Because she was usually the one causing trouble."

It didn't occur to me, until just now, that some of that sadness might have been for my mother. For another cracked girl, broken and pieced clumsily back together. Still standing, but not the same.

There's only one family photo in the living room: it's of Nana and my grandfather, looking like they're in their late thirties, and Sadie and Sarah around twelve years old. I pick it up and study their faces. All I can think is: *they had no idea.*

Just like Brooke's family had no idea. Or maybe they did. Maybe they've been worried since Brooke's locker was vandalized and the bloody meat was thrown on her car, wondering if there was something they should be doing. Maybe they're sick about it now. Because it's almost one o'clock, and nobody's heard a word from her.

My phone buzzes, and I put the photo down to pull it from my pocket. My pulse jumps when I see a text from Malcolm: *Can we talk?*

I hesitate. I'd thought about texting him after Officer Rodriguez left, but I didn't know what to say. I still don't. Gray dots appear, and I forget to breathe while I watch them.

I understand if you don't want to.

The thing is, I do.

I text back, *Okay. Where?*

Wherever you want. I could come by?

That's a good idea, because there's no way Nana's letting me out of the house today. I'm surprised she even went to the basement to do laundry. *When?* I ask.

Ten minutes?

Okay.

I go upstairs and knock on Ezra's bedroom door. He doesn't answer, probably because he's blasting music with his headphones on. It's his go-to escape whenever he's worried. I twist the knob and push open the door and sure enough, he's at his desk with a pair of Bose clamped firmly over his ears, staring at his laptop. He jumps when I tap his shoulder.

"Malcolm's coming over," I say once he's pulled off the headphones.

"He is? Why?"

"Um. He didn't say, exactly. But I assume . . . you know. He wants to talk about Brooke and maybe . . ." I think about his second message. *I understand if you don't want to.* "Maybe explain what happened after he dropped us off."

"We know what happened," Ezra says. We already heard a version of it from Nana, who heard it from Melanie, who probably heard it from Peter Nilsson. Or one of those other people in Echo Ridge who seem to know everything as soon as it happens. "Malcolm dropped Brooke off and she went inside." He frowns when I don't answer. "What, do you not believe that? Ellery, come on. He's our *friend.*"

"Who we've known a month," I say. "And the first time I met

him, he was holding a can of spray paint at Lacey's fund-raiser."
Ezra's mouth opens, but I plow ahead before he can interrupt.
"Look, all I'm saying is that it's not unreasonable to question
him right now."

"*Do* you question him?" Ezra asks.

I hesitate. I don't want to. I've never seen Malcolm be anything but kind, even when he was frustrated. Not to mention,
he's spent the past five years in the shadow of *Declan Kelly—
murder suspect*. Even if he was the sort of person who wanted
to hurt Brooke, he's not an idiot. He wouldn't put himself in a
Declan-like situation before doing it.

Unless it wasn't premeditated.

God. It's exhausting, thinking this way. Ezra is lucky he hasn't
read as many true-crime books as I have. I can't shut them out.

He shakes his head at me, looking disappointed but not
particularly surprised. "This is exactly what we don't need right
now, El. Wild theories that distract people from what's really
going on."

"Which is?"

He rubs a hand over his face. "Hell if I know. But I don't
think it involves our friend just because he was in the wrong
place at the wrong time."

I twist my hands and tap my foot. I still can't stop moving.
"I'm going to wait outside. You coming?"

"Yeah," Ezra says, pulling his headphones from around his
neck and dropping them on the cluttered desk. He's done more
to personalize his room than I have, covering the walls with pictures from our last school and posters of his favorite bands. It
looks like a teenager's room, while mine still looks like a guest

room. I don't know what I'm waiting for. Some feeling like I belong here, maybe.

We go downstairs and outside to Nana's front porch, settling ourselves on the bench beside the door. We haven't been there more than a couple of minutes when Mrs. Nilsson's car pulls into our driveway. Malcolm gets out and lifts his hand in an anemic wave, then makes his way up the lawn to us. There's room for one more on our bench, but Malcolm doesn't sit there. He leans against the porch railing, facing us, and shoves his hands into his pockets. I don't know where to look, so I pick a spot over his shoulder. "Hey, guys," he says quietly.

"How are you holding up, Mal?" Ezra asks.

I steal a glance at Malcolm as the tense lines of his face briefly relax. It means the world to him, I realize, that Ezra greeted him like normal.

"Been better," he says. "I just wanted to tell you"—he's looking at me, as if he knows Ezra never had a second's doubt—"I wanted you to hear from me what I told Officer McNulty, that I saw Brooke get home safely. I watched her go inside and close the door. And then I drove home, and that's all I knew about anything until this morning."

"We know. Wrong place, wrong time," Ezra says, echoing what he said upstairs. "People can't hold that against you."

"Well." Malcolm slouches lower against the railing. "The thing is— Katrin is saying stuff." He swallows hard. "She thinks Brooke and I were hooking up."

I go rigid as Ezra inhales sharply. "What?" he asks. "Why?"

Malcolm shrugs helplessly. "I don't know. She asked me last week if I'd take Brooke to homecoming. Since she'd just broken up with Kyle and didn't have a date." He darts a glance at me, which I catch out of the corner of my eye because I'm staring over his shoulder again. "I didn't ask her, and Katrin never brought it up again. But that's the only time she's ever talked about Brooke and me. Even then, she said we'd just go as friends."

I look down and watch a ladybug crawl across one of the porch floorboards until it slips through a crack. "I thought you and Katrin got along," I say.

"I thought so, too," Malcolm says, his voice heavy. "I honestly don't know where this is coming from. I'm sick about it. I'm worried out of my mind about Brooke. But it isn't true. At all. So I wanted you to know that, too."

I finally meet his eyes full-on. They're sad and scared and, yes, kind. In that moment, I choose to believe he's not *a Kelly boy with a temper,* or *someone with opportunity and motive,* or *the quiet kind you'd never suspect.* I choose to believe he's the person he's always shown himself to be.

I choose to trust him.

"We believe you," I say, and he sags visibly with relief.

CHAPTER TWENTY

MALCOLM
MONDAY, SEPTEMBER 30

Brooke is still missing at lunchtime. And I'm getting a firsthand look at what my brother went through five years ago.

The entire Echo Ridge High student body has been staring at me all morning. Everybody's whispering behind my back, except the few who get right in my face. Like Kyle McNulty. He and his sister, Liz, were away all weekend visiting her friends at the University of Vermont, so nobody's interrogating *him*. Almost as soon as I walked into the hallway this morning, he grabbed my arm and slammed me against the locker bay. "If you did anything to Brooke, I will *end* you," he growled.

I broke away and shoved him back. "Fuck you, McNulty." He probably would've hit me then if a teacher hadn't stepped between us.

Now Mia and I are headed for the cafeteria, passing a

homecoming poster along the way. During morning announcements, Principal Slate said that while they hadn't decided whether to cancel Saturday's dance, it was being "significantly scaled back," with no homecoming court. He ended with a reminder to report anything or anyone suspicious.

Which, for most of the student body, is me.

If I weren't so sick to my stomach, I might laugh at how fiercely Mia glares at everyone we pass in the hallway. "Go ahead and try it," she mutters, as a couple of Kyle's teammates who are twice her size give me the once-over. "I hope you do."

In the cafeteria we grab trays. I pile food on mine that I know I won't be able to eat and then we make our way to our usual table. By unspoken agreement we both sit with our backs against the wall, facing the cafeteria. If anybody's coming for me, I'd rather see them do it.

Mia sends a look of pure loathing toward Katrin's table, where Viv is gesturing dramatically. "Already working on her next story, I'll bet. This is exactly the plot twist she was waiting for."

I force down a sip of water. "Jesus, Mia. They're friends."

"Stop thinking the best of people, Mal," Mia says. "Nobody's doing it for you. We should . . ." She trails off as the noise level in the cafeteria grows louder. The Corcoran twins have emerged from the food line, trays in hand. I haven't talked to them yet today, and every time I've spotted one of them they were surrounded by knots of students. The whole school knows they were the second-to-last people to see Brooke before she disappeared, and everybody wants their take on Saturday night. I don't have to be within earshot to know what kind of questions they're getting: *Have you guys heard that Brooke and Malcolm were hooking up? Did they act weird around each other? Were they fighting?*

Do you think he did something to her?

I could tell yesterday that Ezra is exactly like Mia: it never even occurred to him that I might've done anything except drop Brooke off. Ellery's mind doesn't work that way, though. She's naturally suspicious. I get it, but . . . it stung. And even though it seemed like she came around eventually, I'm not sure it's going to last when half the school is whispering in her ear.

Mia watches the two of them like she's having the exact same thought. Ezra's eyes light on us at almost the same time Katrin's hand shoots into the air. "Ellery!" Katrin calls. "Over here!" She doesn't include Ezra, and I feel pathetically grateful when he starts toward us. Even though I know it's probably just because he wasn't invited anywhere else.

Ellery hesitates, and it feels as though the entire cafeteria is watching her. Her curly hair is long and loose today, and when she looks toward Katrin it obscures half her face. My heart jackhammers in my chest as I try to tell myself it doesn't matter what she does. It won't change anything. Brooke will still be missing, and half the town will still hate me because I'm a Kelly.

Ellery lifts her hand and waves at Katrin, then turns away from her and follows Ezra to our table. I exhale for what feels like the first time all day, relieved, but the buzz in the cafeteria only gets louder. Ezra reaches us first, pulling out two chairs with a noisy scrape and lowering himself into one of them. "Hey," he says quietly. Ellery puts her tray next to his and slips into the remaining chair, offering me a tentative smile.

Just like that, we're all outsiders together.

• • •

It's not right, it's not okay.

That's the part of what Brooke said in the Fright Farm office that sticks with me the most. With Ellery, too. "The one time I sat with her and Katrin at lunch, she looked worn down," she says. "Something was definitely bothering her."

We're at Mia's house after school, scattered around her living room. I'm keeping a constant eye on social media, hoping for some kind of positive update on Brooke, but all I see are posts about organizing a search. The police don't want people doing anything on their own, so they're recruiting volunteers for a co-ordinated effort.

Daisy is holed up in her bedroom as usual, and Mia's parents aren't home. Thank God. I'd like to think Dr. and Mr. Kwon wouldn't treat me any different from how they always have, but I'm not ready to find out.

"Maybe that's why she was talking to Vance," Mia says. She's still seething that nobody took me seriously about that. "She could've been asking for help."

Ezra looks dubious. "I don't know. I've only met the guy once, but he didn't strike me as the helpful type."

"He was Sadie's homecoming date," Ellery says. "That means nothing, I guess, but . . . it's weird how he keeps popping up, isn't it?"

"Yeah," I agree. "But he was locked up all night."

"According to Officer McNulty," Ellery says darkly.

I blink at her. "What, you—you think he was making that up?" At least she's equal opportunity with her conspiracy theories.

"I don't think the Echo Ridge police are very competent, do

you?" she asks. "Somebody basically drew them a map that was all, *hey, hello, here's my next victim.* And she disappeared anyway."

She half swallows the last word, hunching down in the Kwons' oversized leather armchair. I blink, surprised at how lost she suddenly looks, and then I could kick myself for being so caught up in my own problems that I didn't make the connection sooner. "You're scared," I say, because *of course* she is. She was on that list too.

Ezra leans forward on the couch. "Nothing's going to happen to you, El," he says. Like he can make it true through sheer force of will. Mia nods vigorously beside him.

"I know." Ellery hugs her knees to her chest and rests her chin on them. "That's not how this works, right? It's always one girl. There's no reason to worry about me right now, or Katrin. Just Brooke."

There's no way in hell I'm going to remind her that we don't have a clue how any of this works. "We can worry about all of you. But it'll be all right, Ellery. We'll make sure of it." It's the worst reassurance ever, coming from the guy who thought he got Brooke home safely. But it's all I've got.

Light footsteps sound on the stairs, and Daisy appears on the landing. She's wearing giant sunglasses and an oversized sweater, clutching her bag like a shield. "I'm going out for a little while," she says, heading for the Kwons' front door and pulling a jacket off their coatrack. She moves so quickly, she looks as though she's gliding across the floor.

"'Kay," Mia says, scrolling through her phone like she's barely listening. But as soon as the door closes behind Daisy, Mia's head snaps up. "Let's follow her," she says in a loud whisper, springing to her feet.

Ezra and Ellery lift their brows in almost comical unison. "We already know where she goes," I object, my face getting hot as the twins exchange surprised glances. Great. Nothing like outing yourself as a stalker in front of your only friends.

"But we don't know why," Mia says, peering through the blinds of the window next to the door. "Daisy's seeing a psychologist and she never told me," she adds over her shoulder to the twins. "It's all very mysterious and I, for one, am sick of mysteries around here. At least we can do something about this one if we're quick enough. Okay, she just pulled out. Let's go."

"Mia, this is ridiculous," I protest, but to my surprise Ellery's already halfway to the door, with Ezra right behind her. Neither of them seems concerned about the fact that Mia's spying on her own sister with my help. So we pile into my mother's Volvo, and head down the same road Daisy took last Thursday. We catch up to her pretty quickly, and keep a few car lengths behind her.

"Don't lose her," Mia says, her eyes on the road. "We need answers."

"What are you going to do? Try to listen in on her session?" Ezra sounds both confused and disturbed. I'm with him; even if that wasn't a massive violation of Daisy's privacy and probably illegal, I don't see how you could do it.

"I don't know," Mia says with a shrug. Typical Mia: all action, no planning. "She's going twice in one week. That seems like a lot, doesn't it?"

"Beats me," I say, getting into the left lane in preparation for a turn that Daisy will be making at the next intersection. Except she doesn't. I swerve to stay straight and the car behind me blares its horn as I run a yellow light.

"Smooth," Ezra notes. "This is going well. Very stealthy."

Mia frowns. "*Now* where's she going?"

"Gym?" I guess, starting to feel foolish. "Shopping?"

But Daisy doesn't head downtown, or toward the highway that would take us to the nearest mall. She sticks to back roads until we pass Bukowski's Tavern and enter Solsbury, the next town over. The houses are smaller and closer together here than they are in Echo Ridge, and the lawns look like they get mowed a lot less. Daisy's blinker comes on after we pass a liquor store, and she turns in front of a sign that reads "Pine Crest Estates."

That's an optimistic name, I think. It's an apartment complex, full of the kind of cheap, boxy places you can't find in Echo Ridge but that are all over Solsbury. Mom and I checked out someplace similar right before she and Peter got together. If they hadn't, we weren't going to be able to hang on to our house for much longer. Even if it *was* the smallest, crappiest house in all of Echo Ridge.

"Is she moving out?" Mia wonders. Daisy inches through the parking lot, angling the gray Nissan in front of number 9. There's a blue car to her right, and I pull into an empty spot next to that. We all scrunch down in our seats as she gets out of the car, like that'll keep us incognito. All Daisy would have to do is turn her head to catch sight of my mother's Volvo. But she doesn't look around as she gets out, just strides forward and knocks on the door.

Once, twice, and then a third time.

Daisy pulls off her sunglasses, stuffs them into her bag, and knocks again. "Maybe we should leave before she gives up. I don't think they're ho—" I stop talking when the door to number 9 opens. Somebody wraps his arms around Daisy and swings her halfway around, kissing her so deeply that Mia lets out a gasp beside me.

"Oh my God, Daisy has a boyfriend," she says, scrambling out of her seat belt and leaning so far left that she's practically in my lap. "And here she's been so Mopey McMoperson since she moved home! I did *not* see that coming." We're all craning our necks for a better view, but it's not until Daisy breaks away that I catch sight of who she's with—along with something I haven't seen in years.

My brother grinning like his face is about to break, before he pulls Daisy inside and shuts the door behind her.

CHAPTER TWENTY-ONE

ELLERY

MONDAY, SEPTEMBER 30

"So," Malcolm says, plugging tokens into one end of a foosball table. "That was interesting."

After leaving Declan's apartment, we stopped at the first place we came to that we were pretty sure he and Daisy wouldn't show up on a date. It happened to be a Chuck E. Cheese's. I haven't been to one in years, so I've forgotten what a sensory assault they are: flashing lights, beeping games, tinny music, and screaming children.

The guy letting people in at the door wasn't sure about us at first. "You're supposed to come with kids," he said, glancing behind us at the empty hallway.

"We *are* kids," Mia pointed out, extending her hand for a stamp.

Turns out, Chuck E. Cheese's is the perfect location for a clandestine debrief. Every adult in the place is too busy either chasing after or hiding from their children to pay us any attention. I feel weirdly calm after our trip to Pine Crest Estates, the dread that came over me at Mia's house almost entirely gone. There's something satisfying about unlocking another piece of the Echo Ridge puzzle, even if I'm not yet sure where it fits.

"So," Mia echoes, gripping a handle on the other end of the foosball table. Ezra is next to her, and I'm beside Malcolm. A ball pops out of one side, and Mia spins a bar furiously, missing the ball completely. "Your brother and my sister. How long do you think that's been going on?"

Malcolm maneuvers one of his players carefully before smacking the ball, and would have scored if Ezra hadn't blocked it. "Damned if I know. Since they both came back, maybe? But that still doesn't explain what they're doing here. Couldn't they hook up in New Hampshire? Or Boston?" He passes the ball to one of his own men, then backward to me, and I rocket a shot across the field into the open goal. Malcolm gives me a surprised, disarmed grin that dissolves the tense set of his jaw. "Not bad."

I want to smile back, but I can't. There's something I've been thinking ever since we pulled away from Pine Crest Estates, and I keep weighing how—or whether—to bring it up.

"I don't think they can hook up *anywhere*," Mia says. "Can you imagine if one of the reporters who've been prowling around Echo Ridge got wind of this? Lacey Kilduff's boyfriend and best friend, together five years later? While somebody's making a mockery of her death by writing bullshit all around town and another girl's just gone missing?" She shudders, managing to nick the ball with the edge of one of her men. "People would *hate* them."

"What if it's not five years later?" The words pop out of me,

173

and Malcolm goes still. The foosball rolls unchallenged down the length of the table and settles into a corner. "I mean," I add, almost apologetically, "they might've been together for a while."

Mia shakes her head. "Daisy's had other boyfriends. She almost got engaged to the guy she was dating at Princeton."

"Okay, so not all five years," I say. "But maybe . . . at some point in high school?"

Malcolm's jaw has gone tense again. He braces his forearms on the table and fastens his green eyes on me. Both are disconcerting at close range, if I'm being honest. "Like when?"

Like while Declan was still dating Lacey. It'd be the classic deadly love triangle. I have to bite the inside of my cheeks to keep from saying it out loud. What if Declan and Daisy fell in love years ago and wanted to be together, but Lacey wouldn't let him go? Or threatened to do something to Daisy in retaliation? And it infuriated Declan so much that he lost control one night and killed her? Then Daisy broke things off with him, obviously, and tried to forget him, but couldn't. I'm itching to expand on my theory, but one look at Malcolm's frozen face tells me I shouldn't. "I don't know," I hedge, dropping my eyes. "Just throwing out ideas."

It's like I told Ezra in the library: You can't spring a *your-siblings-might-be-murderers* theory onto people all at once.

Mia doesn't notice the subtext of my back-and-forth with Malcolm. She's too busy savagely jerking her rod of blue players without ever touching the ball. "It wouldn't be an issue if Daisy would just *talk* to me. Or to anyone in our family."

"Maybe you need to pull a little-sister power play," Ezra suggests.

"Such as?"

He shrugs. "She tells you what's going on, or you tell your parents what you just saw."

Mia goggles at him. "That's straight-up *evil*."

"But effective, I'll bet," Ezra says. He glances at Malcolm. "I'd suggest the same thing to you, but I just saw your brother, so."

"Oh yeah." Malcolm grimaces. "He'd kill me. Not literally," he adds hastily, with a sideways glance at me. "But also, he knows I'd never do it. Our father wouldn't care, but our mom would lose it. Especially now."

Mia's eyes gleam as she lines one of her men up for a shot. "I have no such concerns."

We play for a few minutes without speaking. My mind keeps racing along the Declan-Daisy theory that I didn't say, testing it for holes. There are a few, admittedly. But it's such a true-crime staple when girls go missing or are harmed: *it's always the boyfriend*. Or a frustrated wannabe. Because when you're seventeen, and beautiful, and you're found murdered in a place known for hookups, what could it possibly be except a crime of passion?

So that leaves Declan. The only other person I'm even remotely suspicious of is the guy Lacey never noticed—Officer Ryan Rodriguez. I can't forget his photo in the yearbook, or Sadie's description of him breaking down at Lacey's funeral. Still, Officer Rodriguez doesn't *fit* like Declan does—he makes perfect sense, especially now that we know about him and Daisy.

I don't believe for one second that they're a new thing. The only question in my mind is whether Malcolm's willing to admit it.

I steal a glance at Malcolm as he twists his handles, fully concentrating on the game. Brow furrowed, green eyes crinkling when he makes a good shot, lean arms flexing. He has absolutely no idea how attractive he is, and it's kind of a problem. He's so used to living in his brother's shadow that he doesn't believe he's the kind of guy who could've snagged the attention of a girl like Brooke. Anybody else can see it from a mile away.

He looks up and meets my eyes. *Busted.* I feel myself go red as his mouth lifts in a half smile. Then he glances down again, pulling his phone from his pocket and unlocking the screen. His face changes in an instant. Mia sees it too and stops spinning her handles. "Any news?" she asks.

"A text from my mom. Nothing about Brooke," Malcolm says, and we all relax. Because from the look on his face, it wouldn't have been good. "Except there's a search party tomorrow. During the day, so Echo Ridge students aren't supposed to go. And there's an article in the *Boston Globe.*" He sighs heavily. "My mom's freaking out. She gets traumatized any time the news mentions Lacey."

"Can I see?" I ask. He hands the phone to me, and I read the section framed within the screen:

> The small town was already on edge after a series of vandalism incidents beginning in early September. Buildings and signs were defaced with messages written as though they were from Lacey Kilduff's killer. The anonymous threats promised another attack on one of the girls elected to homecoming court—a short list that included Brooke Bennett. But those who've been following the story closely don't see any real connection.

"Even if someone was unhinged enough to get away with murder and brag about it five years later, the MO's are completely different," says Vivian Cantrell, a senior at Echo Ridge High who has covered the story for her school paper. "Strangulation is a brutal crime of passion. The threats are public, and they require planning. I don't think there's any relation at all to what happened to Lacey, or what's going on with Brooke."

I grip the phone more tightly. That's almost exactly what I said two weeks ago at lunch. Viv basically stole my entire spiel and used it to replace her original point of view. Before this, she'd been telling everybody that Lacey's death and the anonymous threats *had* to be related.

Why did Viv suddenly change her tune?

CHAPTER TWENTY-TWO

ELLERY
WEDNESDAY, OCTOBER 2

It's the first week in October, and starting to get dark earlier. But even if it weren't, Nana would insist on driving Ezra and me to our shift at Fright Farm after dinner.

I don't bother reminding her that it's only a ten-minute walk as she plucks her keys from a hook next to her wall-mounted phone. Brooke has been missing for four days, and the entire town is on edge. Search parties all day, and candlelight vigils at night. After two days of heated debate at school, homecoming is still on for Saturday—but without a court. I'm no longer technically a princess. Which is fine, I guess, since I still don't have a date.

The same few theories keep circulating: that Brooke ran away, that she's the victim of the Murderland killer, that one of the Kelly boys did something to her. Everything in Echo Ridge feels like a thick, bubbling mess that's about to boil over.

Nana is silent on the ride over, clutching the steering wheel and driving fifteen miles below the speed limit until we near the entrance. Then she pulls to the side of the road and says, "The House of Horrors closes at eleven, right?"

"Right."

"I'll be outside the gates at eleven-oh-five."

That's two hours past her bedtime, but we don't argue. I told her earlier that Malcolm could give us a ride, and she insisted on picking us up anyway. I don't think she believes he's involved in Brooke's disappearance—she hasn't told us to stop hanging out with him—but she's not taking any chances, and I can't blame her. I'm a little surprised she's still letting us go to work.

Ezra and I climb out of the car and watch its taillights recede so slowly that a bicycle passes it. We're halfway through the gates when my phone rings with a familiar California number.

I hold it up to Ezra. "Sadie must've heard."

It was only a matter of time. Brooke's disappearance has become national news, and Nana's been hanging up all week on reporters angling for a "One Town, Three Missing Girls" story. Hamilton House Rehabilitation Facility allegedly bans Internet access, but since Sadie's already used her borrowed cell phone to check out Ezra's Instagram before FaceTiming us, she's obviously flouting that rule, too.

I slide to answer and press the phone to my ear. "Hi, Sadie."

"Ellery, thank God you picked up." Her agitated voice crackles across the line. "I just read about what's happening there. Are you and Ezra all right?"

"We're fine. Just worried about Brooke."

"Oh my God, of course you are. That poor girl. Her poor family." She pauses for a beat, her breath harsh in my ear. "So

179

the article . . . it said there were *threats* beforehand? Toward three girls, and that one of them was someone who . . . who was related to . . . Was it you, Ellery?"

"It was me," I confirm. Ezra gestures like he wants me to FaceTime, but I wave him off. It's too crowded here.

"Why didn't you *tell* me?"

The bitter laugh springs out of me without warning. "Why would I?"

Silence on the other end, so complete that I think she's disconnected. I'm about to pull the phone away from my ear to check when Sadie says, "Because I'm your mother and I have a right to know."

It's exactly the wrong thing to say. Resentment floods my veins, and I have to grip the phone extra tight to stop myself from hurling it to the ground. "Oh, really? You have a *right to know*? That's rich coming from somebody who's never told us anything that matters."

"What are you talking about?"

"Our father? We're not allowed to ask questions about him! Our grandmother? We barely knew her until we had to live with her! Our aunt? You had a twin sister, as close as me and Ezra are, and you never, *ever* talk about her. Now we're stuck here watching the same horrible story unfold *again* and everybody's talking about the first girl who went missing. Except us. We don't know anything about Sarah because you won't even say her name!"

I'm breathing hard, my heart pounding as I stalk through the park. I don't know whether I'm relieved or horrified to finally be saying these things to Sadie. All I know is that I can't stop.

"You're not okay, Sadie. I mean, you get that, right? You're not in rehab because of some freak accident that'll be a funny

180

story to tell at parties when you get out. You weren't taking those pills to *relax*. I've spent years waiting for something like this to happen, and I thought . . . I was afraid . . ." Tears blur my vision and slide down my face. "This whole year I've been expecting *that* phone call. The one Nana got, and Melanie got. The one that says you're never coming home."

She's been silent during my entire tirade, but this time, before I can check to see whether she's hung up on me, I hear a choked sob. "I . . . *can't*," Sadie says in a ragged voice that I'd never recognize if I didn't know it was her. "I can't talk about her. It *kills* me."

I've wandered near the games section, and I have to plug my free ear against the noise of the park. Ezra stands a short distance away, his arms folded and his face grave. "It's killing you not to," I say. She doesn't answer, and I squeeze my eyelids shut. I can't look at my brother right now. "Sadie, I *know*, okay? I know exactly how you must feel. Me and Ezra both do. It's horrible what happened to Sarah. It sucks and it's not fair and I'm so, so sorry. For you and for Nana and for her." My mother's sobs on the other end of the line pierce me like a knife to the heart. "And I'm sorry I yelled at you. I didn't mean to. It's just . . . I feel like we're going to be stuck like this forever if we can't talk about it."

I open my eyes while I wait for her to answer. It's almost dark now, and the park lights glow against the deep blue sky. Screams and catcalls fill the air and little kids chase one another with their parents a safe distance behind. All of Fright Farm's success is based on how much people love to be scared in a controlled environment. There's something deeply, fundamentally satisfying about confronting a monster and escaping unscathed.

Real monsters aren't anything like that. They don't let go.

"Do you know what I was doing the night Sarah disappeared?" Sadie asks in the same hoarse voice.

My reply is barely a whisper. "No."

"Losing my virginity to my homecoming date." She lets out a hysterical half laugh, half sob. "I was supposed to be with Sarah. But I blew her off. For *that*."

"Oh, Sadie." I don't even realize I've sunk to the ground until my free hand touches grass. "It's not your fault."

"Of course it's my fault! If I'd been with her she'd still be here!"

"You don't know that. You can't— You were just living your life. Being *normal*. You didn't do anything wrong. None of this is your fault."

"Would you feel that way? If something happened to Ezra when you were supposed to be with him?" I don't answer right away, and she cries harder. "I can't look at my mother. I couldn't look at my father. I didn't speak to him for almost a year before he died and then I drank my way through the entire funeral. You and your brother are the only thing I've ever done right since Sarah disappeared. And now I've ruined that too."

"You didn't ruin anything." I say it automatically to comfort her, but as soon as the words are out of my mouth, I realize they're true. Ezra and I might not have had the most stable childhood, but we never had any doubt that our mother loved us. She never put a job or a boyfriend ahead of us, and it wasn't until the pills took hold that her haphazard parenting turned into actual neglect. Sadie's made mistakes, but they're not the kind that leave you feeling like you don't matter. "We're fine and we love you and please don't do this to yourself. Don't blame yourself for something so awful that you never could've seen coming." I'm babbling now, my words tripping over themselves, and Sadie lets out a teary laugh.

"Listen to us. You wanted to talk, huh? Be careful what you wish for."

There's so much I want to say, but all I can manage is, "I'm glad we're talking."

"Me too." She takes a deep, shuddering breath. "There's more I should tell you. Not about Sarah, but about— Oh hell. I have to go, Ellery, I'm sorry. Please be careful there, and I'll call again when I can." Then she's gone. I drop the phone from my ear and get to my feet as Ezra strides toward me, looking ready to burst.

"What's going on? I heard some of it, but—"

Movement over his shoulder catches my eye, and I put a hand on his arm. "Hang on. I have a *lot* to tell you, but . . . there's somebody I want to talk to first." I wipe my eyes and glance at my phone. We're already late for work, but oh well.

An older woman is manning the shooting gallery where Brooke used to work, yawning as she makes change and pulls levers. Vance Puckett stands with a toy gun mounted on his shoulder, methodically knocking over targets. Malcolm told us at lunch that he was interrogated again last night by Officer Mc-Nulty, who said the police interviewed Vance about his conversation with Brooke downtown. According to Vance, Brooke just asked him what time it was. Malcolm was frustrated, but Mia threw up her hands in resignation. "Of course. Why should he help out? There's nothing in it for him, and he doesn't care about anybody in this town."

Maybe she's right. Or maybe he's just broken in his own way.

Vance fishes in his pockets for change to play another round. I sidle past a trio of preteens and plunk two dollars on the counter. "My treat this time," I say.

He turns and squints, tapping his forefinger to his chin. It takes a few seconds for him to recognize me. "Shooter girl. You got lucky that last game."

"Maybe," I say. "I have six bucks on me. Should we play best two out of three?" He nods, and I gesture toward the targets. "Champions first."

Vance gets off to a shaky start, only hitting eight out of twelve targets. It kills my competitive spirit to miss five when it's my turn, but all this will be pointless if he stalks off in a huff again when we're done.

"You lost your touch." Vance smirks when I lower my gun. Ezra, who's watching us with his hands on his hips, looks like he's physically biting his tongue.

"I was just warming up," I lie.

I keep it close in the next couple of rounds, losing by one each time. Vance is pumped up by the end, preening and chuckling, going so far as to slap me on the back when I miss my final shot. "Nice try, kid. You almost pulled one out."

"I guess I did get lucky last time," I say with a theatrical sigh. I don't have Sadie's talent, which is obvious from Ezra's grimace as we move to one side so the people waiting behind us can play. But I'm hoping it's good enough for a drunk guy. "My mother told me it probably wouldn't happen again."

Vance adjusts his cap over oily hair. "Your mother?"

"Sadie Corcoran," I say. "You're Vance, right? She said you

184

guys went to homecoming together and that I should introduce myself. I'm Ellery."

It's weird holding out my hand after what Sadie just told me. But he takes it, looking genuinely flummoxed.

"She said that? Wouldn't have thought she even remembers me."

She talks about you all the time, I almost say, but decide to keep things believable. "She does. It's not easy for her to talk about Echo Ridge after what happened to her sister, but— She's always spoken well of you."

It's close enough to true, I guess. And I'm feeling pretty charitable toward him myself, since he's the only person in Echo Ridge who has an alibi for both Sarah's and Brooke's disappearances. Suddenly, Vance Puckett is the most trustworthy man in town.

He spits on the ground, close to my sneakers. Somehow, I manage not to flinch. "Damn shame what happened."

"I know. She's never gotten over it. And now my friend is missing. . . ." I glance at the new woman behind the counter. "I guess you knew Brooke, huh? Since you play here all the time."

"Nice kid," he says gruffly. He shuffles his feet, looking antsy and ready to move on. Ezra taps his watch and raises his brows at me. *Get to the point.*

"The worst thing is, I know something was bothering her before she disappeared," I say. "We were supposed to get together on Sunday so she could tell me what was going on, but we never got the chance. And it's killing me." Tears spring into my eyes, still close to the surface from my conversation with Sadie, and spill down my cheeks. I'm playing a part, but Sadie's always said the best acting happens when you're emotionally connected to the scene. I'm torn up enough about what happened to Brooke to pull it off. "I just— I wish I knew what she needed."

Vance rubs his jaw. Rocks back on his heels, twists to look at the crowd over his shoulder. "I don't like getting involved," he mumbles. "Not with people in this town, and especially not with the police."

"Me either," I say quickly. "We're total outsiders here. Brooke was—*is*—one of my only friends." I fish around in my bag for a Kleenex and blow my nose.

"She asked me a strange question last week." Vance speaks quietly, in a rush, and my heart leaps into my throat. "Wanted to know how to pick a lock." A shifty expression crosses his face. "Not sure why she'd think *I'd* know. I told her to Google it, or watch a YouTube video or something. Or just use a couple of paper clips."

"Paper clips?" I ask.

Vance swats at a hovering bug. "Those work sometimes. So I'm told. Anyway . . ." He meets my gaze, and I see a glimmer of something like kindness in his bloodshot eyes. "That's a thing that was on her mind. So now you know."

"Thanks," I say, feeling a pinprick of shame for manipulating him. "You have no idea how much that helps."

"Well. You tell your mother I said hello." He tips his baseball cap and shuffles past Ezra, who brings his hands together in a slow clap once Vance is out of hearing range.

"Well played, El. Although that guy's never gonna let you live down the loss."

"I know," I sigh, digging for another Kleenex to dry my still-damp cheeks. As I watch Vance melt into the crowd, a prickle of excitement works its way up my spine. "Did you hear what he said, though? He told Brooke to pick a lock with *paper clips*."

"Yeah. So?"

"So that's what she was holding in the House of Horrors office, remember? A straightened paper clip. I took it from her. She said something like, *This is harder than he said it would be*." My voice climbs with anticipation, and I force it back down. "She was trying to pick a lock right then and there. And we interrupted her."

"The desk, maybe?" Ezra wonders.

I shake my head. "I get stuff out of that desk all the time. It isn't locked. But—" Heat floods my face as I remember where Brooke was sitting. "But I think I know what is."

CHAPTER TWENTY-THREE

MALCOLM
THURSDAY, OCTOBER 3

By Thursday, search parties for Brooke aren't limited to school hours anymore. There's one this afternoon, covering the woods behind the Nilssons' house. Peter's a volunteer captain, and when I get home from band practice he's loading a cardboard box filled with flyers, bottled water, and flashlights into the back of his Range Rover.

"Hello, Malcolm." He doesn't look at me as I get out of Mom's Volvo. Just brushes his palms together as though they're dusty. I'm sure they aren't. Peter's car is as pristine as everything else the Nilssons own. "How was school?"

"Same." In other words: *not good.* "When are we leaving?"

Peter crosses his arms, displaying razor-sharp creases in the sleeves of his shirt. "*We* are leaving in ten minutes," he says. The emphasis is clear, but when I don't respond he adds, "I don't think it's a good idea for you to come, Malcolm."

My heart sinks. "Why?" It's a pointless question. I know why. Officer McNulty has been back twice already to ask me follow-up questions.

Peter's nostrils flare. "Emotions are running high right now. You'd be a distraction. I'm sorry. I know that's hard to hear, but it's the truth, and our first priority is finding Brooke."

My temper spikes. "I *know*. I want to help."

"The best way you can help is to stay here," Peter says, and my palms itch with an almost irresistible desire to punch the smug look off his face. I'm sure he's genuinely concerned, and he might even be right. But he gets off on being the hero, too. Always has.

He claps a hand on my shoulder, quickly, like he's killing a bug. "Why don't you go inside and see if there's any more water in the fridge? That would be helpful."

A vein above my eye starts to throb. "Sure," I say, swallowing my anger because getting into a pissing match with Peter isn't going to help Brooke.

When I get inside, I hear the staircase in the foyer creak. I'm hoping for my mother, but it's Katrin with a heap of red fabric hanging over her arm, followed by Viv. Katrin freezes when she sees me, and Viv almost bumps into her. Both of their faces harden into the mask of dislike I've been seeing everywhere since Sunday.

I make an effort to act like I normally would. "What's that?" I ask, gesturing toward Katrin's arm.

"My homecoming dress," she snaps.

I eye the dress with a feeling of mild dread. I've been trying to block out the fact that homecoming is Saturday. "It's weird they're still having that." Katrin doesn't reply, and I add, "What are you doing with your dress?"

"Your mom's going to have it pressed." She gives me a wide

berth as she makes her way into the kitchen, carefully draping the dress over the back of a chair. It's nice, I guess, that my mom does stuff like that for Katrin. Peter says Katrin's own mother hasn't responded to any of his calls all week, other than to text something about bad cell reception in the South of France. There's always some excuse.

When she's finished arranging the dress, Katrin stares at me with glacial blue eyes. "I'd better not see you there."

Somehow, Katrin doesn't make me angry like Peter does. Maybe because I know she's barely eaten or slept since Brooke went missing. Her cheeks are hollow, her lips chapped, her hair in a messy ponytail. "Katrin, come on," I say, my palms spread wide. The universal gesture of a guy who has nothing to hide. "Can we talk about this? What have I ever done to make you think I'd be capable of hurting Brooke?"

She presses her lips together, nostrils flaring slightly. For a second she looks exactly like Peter. "You were involved with her and you didn't tell anyone."

"Jesus." I rake a hand through my hair, feeling a tug in my chest. "Why do you keep *saying* that? Because you lost track of her during a sleepover? She was probably in the bathroom." Katrin and I were never friends, exactly, but I thought she knew me better than this.

"My room *has* a bathroom," Katrin points out. "She wasn't there."

"So she went for a walk."

"She's afraid of the dark."

I give up. She's latched onto this for some reason, and there's no talking her out of it. I guess whatever bond I thought we had was just in my head. Or something that amused her when she had nothing better to do. "Your dad's getting ready to leave," I say instead.

"I know. I need a phone charger. Wait here, Viv," she instructs. She stalks down the hallway leading to the study, leaving Viv and me to eye one another warily. I half expect her to follow Katrin, but she's a good minion. She stays put.

"Still writing that article?" I ask.

Viv flushes. "No. I'm much too upset about Brooke to even think about that." Her eyes are dry, though. Have been all week. "Anyway, I already told the media what I think, so . . . as far as I'm concerned, it's done."

"Good," I say. I turn away from her and open the double doors of the refrigerator. There are two six-packs of bottled water on the middle shelf, and I tuck them under my arm before heading outside.

The back of Peter's Range Rover is still open. I push aside a cardboard box and drop the water beside it. The flash of a familiar face catches my eye, and I pull out a flyer from the box. Brooke's class picture is plastered next to the word MISSING, her hair tumbling loose around her shoulders and her smile bright. It startles me, because I can't remember the last time I saw Brooke looking that happy. I scan the rest of the flyer:

Name: Brooke Adrienne Bennett

Age: 17

Eyes: Hazel

Hair: Brown

Height: 5'4"

Weight: 110 pounds

Last seen wearing: Olive blazer, white T-shirt, black jeans, leopard-print flats

Somebody else must have told them that last part; I was no help when Officer McNulty asked me to describe Brooke's clothes. *She looked nice,* I said.

"I think that's everything." Peter's voice startles me, and I drop the flyer back into the box. He opens the driver's side door and glances at his watch with a small frown. "Could you ask Katrin and Viv to come to the car, please?"

"Okay." My phone buzzes as I head back inside, and when I get into the kitchen I pull it out, to a series of texts from Mia.

Hey.

You should come over.

This just popped up online and it's already everywhere.

The last message links to a *Burlington Free Press* article titled "A Tragic Past—and a Common Thread." My stomach drops as I start to read.

Echo Ridge is reeling.

This picturesque town, nestled near the Canadian border and boasting the highest per capita income in the county, experienced its first tragic loss in 1996 when high school senior Sarah Corcoran vanished while walking home from the library. Then, five years ago, homecoming queen Lacey Kilduff was found dead in the aptly named (and since renamed) Murderland Halloween park.

Now another beautiful and popular teenager, seventeen-year-old Brooke Bennett, is missing. Though Brooke and Lacey are close in age, there seems to be little connection between the two young women, except an odd coincidence: the high school senior who dropped Bennett off at home the night she disappeared is the younger brother of Lacey Kilduff's former boyfriend, Declan Kelly.

Kelly, who was questioned repeatedly after Lacey Kilduff's death but never arrested, moved out of state four years ago and has maintained a low profile since. So it came as a surprise to many in this close-knit community that Kelly relocated to the neighboring town of Solsbury shortly before Brooke Bennett's disappearance.

Shit. Viv might not be writing any more articles, but someone else sure is. Suddenly, Peter looks like a genius. If I weren't going to cause drama during the search for Brooke before, I sure as hell would now.

Katrin enters the kitchen gripping her phone. Her cheeks are bright red, and I brace myself for another tirade. She probably just read the same article. "Peter wants you guys outside," I say, hoping to cut off whatever lecture she has planned.

She nods mechanically without speaking, looking first at Viv and then at me. Her face is weirdly immobile, like she's wearing a Katrin mask. Her hands shake as she shoves her phone into her pocket.

"He's not letting me come," I add. "He says I'll be a distraction."

I'm testing her, waiting for the expected *Well, you would be* or *Distraction doesn't cover it, asshole.* But all she says is, "Okay."

She swallows hard once, then twice. "Okay," she repeats, like she's trying to convince herself of something. She meets my eyes and looks down quickly, but not before I catch how huge her pupils are.

She doesn't look mad anymore. She looks afraid.

CHAPTER TWENTY-FOUR

I get to Mia's house half an hour later and I hear shouting as soon as I step onto the driveway. It's too early for her parents to be home, and anyway, they're not yellers. Mia's the only Kwon who ever raises her voice. But it's not her making all that noise.

Nobody answers the doorbell, so I push the door open and step into the Kwons' living room. The first thing I see is Ellery, sitting cross-legged in an armchair, her eyes wide as she surveys the scene in front of us. Mia stands barefoot next to the fireplace, hands on her hips, looking defiant but tiny without the height her boots give her. Daisy is across from her, a candlestick gripped in one hand and an expression of pure rage distorting her usually serene features.

"I'm going to *kill you*," Daisy shrieks, drawing her arm back threateningly.

"Stop being so dramatic," Mia says, but her eyes don't leave the candlestick.

"What the hell?" I ask, and they both turn toward me.

Daisy's furious expression briefly recedes, then comes roaring back like a tidal wave. "Oh, him too? You've got the entire Scooby Gang here while you lay this bullshit on me?"

I blink. I've never heard Daisy swear before. "What bullshit?"

Mia speaks before Daisy can. "I told her I know all about Declan, and I'm going to tell Mom and Dad if she doesn't explain why they're both back in Echo Ridge." She takes an involuntary step back as Daisy fastens her with a withering stare. "It's going a little worse than I expected."

"You have some nerve—" Daisy brandishes the candlestick for emphasis, but stops in slack-jawed horror when she loses her grip and sends it flying directly toward Mia's head. Mia is too startled to move out of the way, and when it clocks her in the temple she drops like a stone.

Daisy's hands fly to her mouth. "Oh my God. Oh my God, Mia. Are you all right?" She falls to her knees and scrambles toward her sister, but Ellery—who I never even saw move—is already there.

"Malcolm, can you get a wet towel?" she asks.

I stare down at Mia. Her eyes are open, her face pale, and a stream of blood runs down one side of her head. "Oh no, oh no," Daisy moans, her hands covering her face now. "I'm sorry. I'm so, so sorry." I fast-track it to the bathroom and grab a hand towel, then run it under the faucet and jam back to the living room.

Mia is sitting up now, looking dazed. I hand Ellery the towel and she gently pats up and down the side of Mia's head until the blood is cleared away. "Is she going to need stitches?" Daisy asks in a shaking voice.

Ellery presses the towel to Mia's temple for a few seconds, then pulls it away and peers at the cut. "I don't think so. I mean, I'm no expert, but it's actually tiny. Looks like one of those shallow scrapes that just happens to bleed a lot. It'll probably leave a bruise, but it should be fine with a Band-Aid."

"I'll get it," I volunteer, returning to the Kwons' bathroom. Dr. Kwon is an obstetrician and her medicine cabinet is so perfectly organized, I find what I need within seconds. When I return this time, some of the color is back in Mia's face.

"God, Daze," she says reproachfully as Ellery positions the Band-Aid on her temple and presses down. "I didn't realize you *literally* wanted to kill me."

Daisy slumps back, her legs tucked to one side. "It was an accident," she says, skimming her fingers across the hardwood floor. She looks up, her mouth half twisted in a wry grin. "I'm sorry for drawing blood. But you sort of deserved it."

Mia brushes an index finger across her bandage. "I just want to know what's going on."

"So you ambush me while your friend is here?" Daisy's voice starts to rise again, but she checks herself and lowers it. "Seriously, Mia? Not cool."

"I needed the moral support," Mia grumbles. "And the protection, apparently. But come on, Daisy. You can't keep on like this. People know where Declan lives now. Stuff is gonna come out. You need someone on your side." She gestures toward me as I lower myself onto the edge of the Kwons' stone fireplace. "We're all on Mal's side. We can be on yours too."

I glance at Ellery, who doesn't look convinced. I don't think Mia picked up on what Ellery was hinting at in Chuck E. Cheese's—that Daisy and Declan could have been involved with one another while Lacey was still alive. That kind of thing would fly right over Mia's head, because even though she complains about Daisy, she also trusts her completely. I've never been able to say the same thing about Declan.

Daisy turns toward me, her dark eyes brimming with sympathy. "Oh, Malcolm. I haven't even told you how sorry I am about what's been going on. The way people are . . . whispering. Accusing you without any proof. It all brings back so many memories."

"Daisy." Mia interrupts before I can answer. Her voice is calm and quiet, nothing like her usual strident tone. "Why did you leave your job after you'd barely started it?"

Daisy heaves a deep sigh. She lifts a hunk of shiny dark hair and spills it over her shoulder. "I had a nervous breakdown." She purses her lips as Mia's brows shoot up. "Not expecting that one?"

Mia, wisely, doesn't mention trailing Daisy to her psychologist. "What, were you, like . . . in the hospital or something?"

"Briefly." Daisy lowers her eyes. "The thing is, I never really dealt with Lacey's death, you know? It was so horrible. So twisted and awful and painful that I pushed it down and forced myself to forget about it." She gives a strangled little laugh. "Great plan, right? Totally worked. It was okay while I was at school, I guess. But when I moved to Boston and had so many new responsibilities, I couldn't function. I started having nightmares, then panic attacks. At one point I called an ambulance because I thought I was dying of a heart attack."

"You went through a horrible loss," Mia says comfortingly.

Daisy's lashes flicker. "Yes. But I wasn't just sad. I was guilty."

Out of the corner of my eye, I see Ellery tense. "About what?" Mia asks.

Daisy pauses. "Circle of trust, right? This can't leave the room. Not yet." She glances toward me, then Ellery, and bites her lip.

Mia reads her mind. "Ellery's totally trustworthy."

"I can leave," Ellery volunteers. "I understand. We don't know one another."

Daisy hesitates, then shakes her head. "It's all right. You've heard this much, you might as well hear the rest. My psychologist keeps telling me I have to stop being ashamed. It's starting to sink in, although I still feel like a terrible friend." She turns toward Mia. "I was in love with Declan all through high school. I never said a word. It was just this . . . thing I lived with. And then the summer before senior year, he started treating me differently. Like he *saw* me." She gives an embarrassed little laugh. "God, I sound like an eighth grader. But it gave me this, I don't know, *hope,* I guess, that things could be different someday. Then one night he told me he was in love with me, too."

Daisy's whole face glows, and I remember why I used to have such a crush on her. Mia is sitting as still as I've ever seen her, like she's afraid the slightest movement will end the conversation. "I told him we couldn't do anything about it," Daisy continues. "I wasn't *that* bad of a friend. He said he thought Lacey had found someone else, anyway. She was acting distant. But when he asked her, she wouldn't admit it. They started fighting. It got really messy and ugly and— I just sort of withdrew. I didn't want to be the cause of that."

Daisy's eyes get shiny as she continues. "Then Lacey died and the whole world fell apart. I couldn't *stand* myself. Couldn't deal with knowing I'd been keeping this secret that I'd never get to explain to her." Tears spill down her cheeks and she lets out a choked little sob. "And I *missed* her. I still miss her, so much."

I steal a glance at Ellery, who's wiping her own eyes. I get the feeling that she just took Daisy off her mental list of suspects in Lacey's murder. If Daisy feels guilty about anything other than liking her best friend's boyfriend, she's one hell of an actress.

Mia grabs Daisy's hand in both of her own as Daisy continues. "I told Declan we couldn't talk anymore, and I got out of Echo Ridge as soon as I could. I thought it was the right thing to do for both of us. We'd been wrong not to be open with Lacey from the start, and there wasn't a way to fix that anymore." She drops her head. "Plus, there's this whole other layer when you're one of the only minority families in town. You can't make a mistake, you know? We've always had to be so perfect."

Mia regards her sister thoughtfully. "I thought you liked being perfect," she says in a small voice.

Daisy sniffs. "It's fucking *exhausting*."

Mia lets out a surprised snort of laughter. "Well, if *you* can't handle it, there's no hope for me in this town." She's still holding Daisy's hand, and shakes it like she's trying to knock some sense into her sister. "Your psychologist is right, Daze. You didn't do anything wrong. You liked a guy. You stayed away from him, even when he liked you back. That's being a good friend."

Daisy dabs at her eyes with her free hand. "I wasn't, though. I couldn't stand to think about the investigation, and I shut down anytime I was near the police. It wasn't until years later that I started thinking about things that might actually be helpful."

"What do you mean?" I ask. Ellery leans forward like a puppet that just got its strings yanked.

"I remembered something," Daisy says. "A bracelet Lacey started wearing right before she died. It was really unusual—a bangle that almost looked like antlers twisted together." She shrugs at Mia's dubious expression. "Sounds weird, I know, but it was gorgeous. She was really coy about where she got it, too. Said it wasn't from Declan, or her parents. When I was in the hospital in Boston, trying to figure out how my life had gotten so far off track, I started wondering who'd given it to her and whether it was somebody who, well . . ." She trails off. "You know. I wondered."

"So you came back here to investigate?" Ellery looks like she approves.

"I came back here to *recover*," Daisy corrects. "But I also asked Lacey's mom if I could have the bracelet, as a keepsake. She didn't mind. I started Googling it, trying to find something similar. And I did." A note of pride creeps into her voice. "There's a local artist who makes them. I wanted to check her out, but I didn't feel quite strong enough to do it on my own." Her voice dips a little. "Declan used to text me occasionally. The first time he did after all this happened, I asked him to visit the jeweler with me."

And there you have it, I think. An actual, rational explanation for what Declan has been doing in Echo Ridge. Would've been nice if he'd ever told me any of this himself.

Mia raises her brows. "Was that the first time you'd seen him since you left for Princeton? I'll bet you two had a lot to talk about. Or, you know, *not* talk about."

Daisy's entire face goes red. "We were mostly focused on the bracelet."

"*Sure* you were." Mia smirks.

This conversation is going off the rails. "You guys have any luck?" I ask, trying to get it back on track.

Daisy sighs. "No. I thought maybe the jeweler would look through her sale records when I told her why I was there, but she wasn't at all helpful. I handed the bracelet off to the police, hoping she'd take it more seriously if they followed up with her, but I haven't heard anything since." She lets go of Mia's hand and rolls her shoulders like she just finished an exhausting workout. "And that's the whole sordid tale. Except for the part where Declan and I finally got together. I love him." She shrugs helplessly. "I always have."

Mia leans back on her haunches. "That's quite a story."

"You *cannot* tell Mom and Dad," Daisy says, and Mia mimes zipping her lips.

"I have a question," Ellery pipes up. She starts doing that twisty thing with her hair again as Daisy turns to face her. "I was just wondering who you gave the bracelet to? What police officer, I mean. Was it someone in Echo Ridge?"

Daisy nods. "Ryan Rodriguez. He graduated from Echo Ridge High the same year I did. Do you know him?"

Ellery nods. "Yeah. Were you guys friends at school?" She looks like she's back in investigative mode, which I'm starting to realize is her default setting.

"No." Daisy looks amused at the idea. "He was really quiet

back then. I barely knew him. But he was on duty when I got to the station, so . . ." She shrugs. "I gave it to him."

"Do you, um, think he was the best person to handle something like this?" Ellery asks.

Daisy crinkles her brow. "I don't know. I guess. Why not?"

"Well. I'm just wondering." Ellery leans forward, elbows on her knees. "Did it ever occur to you that *he* might've given the bracelet to Lacey?"

CHAPTER TWENTY-FIVE

ELLERY
FRIDAY, OCTOBER 4

When I knock on the cellar door, I'm not sure anyone will answer. It's four o'clock on Friday afternoon, three hours before the House of Horrors is supposed to open. I'm not working tonight, and no one's expecting me. Unless you count my grandmother, who's *expecting me* to be in my room and is going to be furious if she realizes I've left and walked through the woods on my own. Even in the middle of the afternoon.

Brooke's been missing almost a week now, and nobody in Echo Ridge is supposed to walk anywhere alone.

I knock louder. The park is noisy and crowded, a blend of music, laughter, and shrieks as a roller coaster rattles nearby. The door cracks just enough for an eye to peer out. It's deep brown and winged with expertly applied liner. I flutter my fingers. "Hi, Shauna."

"Ellery?" The Fright Farm makeup artist swings the door open with one tattooed arm. "What are you doing here?"

I step inside and look around for any sign of Murph, my boss. He's a stickler for rules. Shauna is a lot more laid-back. I can't believe my luck that she's here and he isn't, although I half expect him to come barreling through the velvet curtain with a clipboard any second. "Are you here alone?" I ask.

Shauna raises a brow at me. "That's an ominous question." She doesn't look worried, though. Shauna has at least six inches on me, and is all slender muscle and perfectly toned arms. Plus her spiky heels would make lethal weapons in a pinch.

"Heh. Sorry. But I have a favor to ask, and I didn't want to ask Murph."

Shauna leans against the doorframe. "Well, now you've got my attention. What's up?"

I channel Sadie again, twisting my hands with fake nerves. "My grandmother gave me an envelope to deposit at the bank the other day, and I can't find it. I was trying to figure out where it went, and I remembered that I tossed a bunch of stuff into the recycling bin the last time I was here." I bite my lip and look at the ground. "I'm pretty sure the envelope went with it."

"Ooh, sorry." Shauna grimaces. "Can she write another check?"

I'm ready for that objection. "It wasn't a check. It was cash." I tug at my dagger necklace, running my thumb over the sharp point at the bottom. "Almost five hundred dollars."

Shauna's eyes widen. "Who the hell carries around that much cash?"

Gah. Maybe she noticed I lifted my entire excuse from *It's a*

Wonderful Life. "My grandmother," I say as innocently as I can. "She doesn't trust checks. Or credit cards. Or ATMs."

"But she trusts you?" Shauna looks as though she'd like to give Nana a detailed explanation of why that's a terrible idea.

"She won't when she finds out. Shauna, is there any chance . . . do you think I could get the keys to the recycling bin? Do you know where they are?" She hesitates, and I put my hands together in a praying gesture. "Please? Just this once, to save me from having to hand every cent I've earned over to my grandmother? I'll owe you big-time."

Shauna chuckles. "Look, you don't have to beg. I'd open the damn thing if I had a key, but I don't. No idea where it is. You'll have to ask Murph." She gives my arm a sympathetic pat. "He'll understand. Five hundred dollars is a lot of money."

He would, probably. He'd also stand over me the entire time. "Okay," I sigh.

Shauna goes to the vanity and plucks a few makeup brushes from a can, dropping them into a half-open leather bag resting on the chair. "I have to get a move on. You caught me on the way out. The evil clowns need touching up at Bloody Big Top." She zips the bag closed and slings it over her shoulder, crossing to the door and pulling it open. "You wanna come with? Murph might be there."

"Sure." I make as if to follow her, then wince and put a hand on my belly. "Ugh. Do you mind if I use the bathroom first? I've had kind of a stomach virus all day. I thought it was better, but—"

Shauna waves me away. "Just meet me there. Make sure the door locks behind you."

"Thanks." I dash toward the tiny restroom for effect, but

she's already out the door. As soon as I hear it click, I pull two paper clips out of my pocket and head for the office.

I've never tried to pick a lock before. But I took Vance's advice, and I've watched a lot of YouTube videos in the past twenty-four hours.

"You took it *all*?" Ezra stares at me as I empty a trash bag's worth of paper onto Mia's bedroom floor.

"Well, how was I supposed to know what's important and what isn't? I couldn't sit there on the floor and sift through it. Anybody might've walked in."

Malcolm eyes the pile. "At least we know they haven't emptied it in a while."

Mia plops down cross-legged on the floor and scoops up a handful of paper. "What are we even looking for?" she mutters. "This is some kind of invoice. This looks like an envelope for an electric bill." She makes a face. "We're gonna be here for a while."

The four of us sit in a circle around the pile and start sifting through its contents. My pulse has slowed since I left the House of Horrors, but it's still jumping. I checked the office thoroughly and didn't see any security cameras, but I know they're all over the park. It's entirely possible that someone's staring at footage of me hauling a garbage bag through Fright Farm right now. Which, okay, could easily be the sort of thing an employee would do in the normal course of business. But it could also look weird, and I wasn't exactly subtle about it. I didn't even wear a baseball cap or pull my hair back.

So I hope it's worth it.

We're silent for almost fifteen minutes until Malcolm, who's sprawled next to me, clears his throat. "The police want to look at my phone."

Mia freezes, a scrap of paper dangling from her fingers. "*What?*"

We're all staring at him, but he doesn't meet anyone's eyes. "Officer McNulty said that with Brooke still missing, they need to dig a little deeper. I didn't know what to do. Peter was . . . kind of great, actually. He managed to get across the point that they shouldn't be asking for access to my personal stuff without a warrant while still sounding totally helpful. Officer McNulty ended up apologizing to *him*."

"So they didn't do it?" I ask, placing another invoice on our reject pile. That's all we've found so far: invoices for food, maintenance, supplies, and the like. I guess I shouldn't be surprised that it takes a huge amount of fake blood to keep a Halloween theme park running.

"Not yet," Malcolm says grimly. He finally looks up, and I'm struck by how dull his eyes are. "They won't find anything about Brooke if they do. Other than that text from Katrin telling me I should invite her to homecoming, which could go either way. But there are a bunch of texts between me and Declan and . . . I don't know. After that article yesterday, I'd rather not get scrutinized like that." He tosses aside a sheet of paper with a frustrated grunt. "Everything looks bad when you examine it too closely, right?"

Thursday's *Burlington Free Press* article rehashed the past five years of Declan's life, from the time Lacey died to his recent move to Solsbury, sprinkled with occasional references to the unnamed younger brother who was a key witness in

Brooke's disappearance. It was the sort of article Viv might have written—no actual news, but lots of speculation and innuendo.

Last night, I sat in my room in front of my bookshelf full of true-crime novels and made a timeline of everything I could think of related to the three missing girls and Echo Ridge:

October 1996: Sadie & Vance are crowned homecoming queen/king

October 1996: Sarah disappears while Sadie is with Vance

June 1997: Sadie leaves Echo Ridge

August 2001: Sadie returns for Grandpa's funeral

June 2014: Lacey's junior class picnic with Declan, Daisy & Ryan

August 2014: Declan and Daisy get together—Lacey has a secret boyfriend?

October 2014: Lacey and Declan are crowned homecoming queen/king

October 2014: Lacey is killed at Murderland (Fright Farm)

October 2014: Sadie returns for Lacey's funeral

June 2015: Daisy & Declan graduate, leave Echo Ridge (separately?)

July 2019: Daisy returns to Echo Ridge

August 2019: Daisy gives Lacey's bracelet to Ryan Rodriguez

August 30, 2019: Ellery & Ezra move to Echo Ridge

September (or August??) 2019: Declan returns to Echo Ridge

September 4, 2019: *Anonymous homecoming threats start*

September 28, 2019: *Brooke disappears*

Then I hung it on my wall and stared at it for over an hour, hoping I'd see some kind of pattern emerge. I didn't, but when Ezra came in, he noticed something I hadn't. "Look at this," he said, tapping a finger on *August 2001*.

"What about it?"

"Sadie came back to Echo Ridge in August 2001."

"I know. I wrote it. So?"

"So we were born in May 2002." I stared at him blankly and he added, "Nine. Months. Later," enunciating each word slowly.

I gaped at him, blindsided. Of all the mysteries in Echo Ridge, our paternity has been the last one on my mind. "*Oh* no. No, no, no," I said, leaping backward as though the timeline had caught fire. "No way. That's not what this is for, Ezra!"

He shrugged. "Sadie said she had something more to tell us, didn't she? That stuntman story has always been kind of sketchy. Maybe she looked up an old flame while she was—"

"Get out!" I yelled before he could finish. I yanked *In Cold Blood* out of the bookcase and threw it at him. "And don't come back unless you have something useful, or at least not *horrifying*, to contribute."

I've been trying to put what Ezra said out of my mind ever since. Whatever it could mean is totally separate from the missing girls, and anyway, I'm sure the timing's just a coincidence. I would've brought it up with Sadie last night at our weekly Skype call if she hadn't skipped it. Her counselor told Nana she was "exhausted."

One step forward, one step back.

"Huh." Ezra's voice brings me back to the present. "This is different." He separates a thin yellow sheet from everything else, smoothing a wrinkled corner.

I scoot closer to him. "What is it?"

"Car repair," he says. "For somebody named Amy Nelson. A place called Dailey's Auto in . . ." He squints at the sheet of paper. "Bellingham, New Hampshire."

We both turn instinctively toward Malcolm. The only thing I know about New Hampshire is that his brother lives there. *Used* to live there.

Malcolm's expression tightens. "I've never heard of it."

Ezra keeps reading. *"Front of vehicle damage due to unknown impact. Remove and replace front bumper, repair hood, repaint vehicle. Rush charges, forty-eight hours."* His brows rise. "Yikes. The bill's more than two grand. Paid in cash. For a . . ." He pauses, his eyes scanning the bill. "A 2016 BMW X6. Red."

Malcolm shifts beside me. "Can I see?" Ezra hands him the receipt, and a deep crease appears between Malcolm's brows as he studies it. "This is Katrin's car," he says finally, looking up. "It's her make and model. And her license plate."

Mia grabs the thin yellow paper out of his hand. "Really? Are you sure?"

"Positive," Malcolm says. "She drives me to school most days. And I park next to that car every time I drive my mom's."

"Who's Amy Nelson?" Ezra asks.

Malcolm shakes his head. "No idea."

"There's a phone number for her," Mia says, holding the paper in front of Malcolm. "Is that Katrin's number?"

"I don't know her number off the top of my head. Let me

check." Malcolm pulls his phone out and presses a few keys. "It's not hers. But hang on, that number's in my phone. It's . . ." He sucks in a breath and turns to Mia. "You remember how Katrin sent me that text, asking me to invite Brooke to homecoming?" Mia nods. "She sent Brooke's phone number, too. I saved it to Contacts. This is it."

"Wait, what?" Ezra asks. "Brooke's number is on a repair receipt for Katrin's car?"

While Malcolm was scrolling, I was on my phone looking up Bellingham, New Hampshire. "The repair shop is three hours away," I report.

"So Brooke . . ." Mia studies the receipt. "So Brooke helped Katrin fix her car, I guess. But they didn't take it to Armstrong's Auto—or even anyplace in Vermont. And they used a fake name. Why would they do that?"

"What did Katrin say about her car being wrecked?" I ask, looking at Malcolm.

Malcolm knits his brow. "Nothing. It wasn't." I blink at him, confused, and he adds, "It wasn't wrecked, I mean. It's fine. Maybe there's some kind of mistake. Unless . . . wait." He turns back to Mia, who's still staring at the receipt. "When was the car fixed?"

"Um . . ." Mia's eyes flick to the top of the paper. "It was brought in August thirty-first, and 'Amy' picked it up on September second. Oh, right." She looks at Malcolm. "You and your mom were on vacation then, weren't you? When did you get back?"

"September fourth," Malcolm says. "The day of Lacey's fund-raiser."

"So you wouldn't have known the car was gone," Mia says. "But wouldn't Mr. Nilsson have said something?"

"Maybe not. Katrin spent days at a time at Brooke's house over the summer." Malcolm taps an unconscious beat on his knee with one fist, his expression thoughtful. "So maybe that's why Brooke got involved. She was Katrin's cover while the car was getting fixed. Peter's always telling her she needs to drive more carefully. She was probably afraid he'd take it away if he knew."

"Okay," Ezra says. "That all makes sense, I guess. The fake name is kind of dumb—I mean, all anybody would have to do is look up the license plate number to know who the car really belongs to. But they probably figured it wouldn't come to that." He pauses, frowning. "The only thing I don't understand is, if that's what happened, why was Brooke so desperate to get the receipt back? Assuming this is what she was looking for, but"—he gestures at the pile of invoices we've already discarded—"nothing else seems relevant. If you've gone through the trouble of having an undercover car repair and disposing of the evidence, wouldn't you just leave it to be shredded? Mission accomplished, right?"

I think back to Brooke's words in the Fright Farm office. *That's the million-dollar question, isn't it? What happened? Wouldn't you like to know?* My heart rate starts rising. "Mia," I say, turning toward her. "What date was the car brought in, again?"

"August thirty-first," she says.

"August thirty-first." I repeat. My skin prickles, every nerve twitching.

Ezra tilts his head. "Why do you look like you just swallowed a grenade?"

"Because we came in from LA the night before that. August thirtieth, remember? The hailstorm. The night Mr. Bowman was killed in a hit-and-run." Nobody says anything for a second, and I tap the paper Mia is holding. *Front of vehicle damage due to unknown impact?*"

Mia's entire body goes rigid. Ezra says "Holy shit," at the same time Malcolm says, "No." He turns toward me, his eyes pained. "Mr. Bowman? Katrin wouldn't . . ." He trails off when Mia drops the repair receipt in his lap.

"I hate to say it," she says with surprising gentleness. "But it's starting to look an awful lot like she did."

CHAPTER TWENTY-SIX

MALCOLM
SATURDAY, OCTOBER 5

"You look absolutely beautiful, Katrin."

I turn from the refrigerator at the sound of my mother's voice, grasping a too-warm seltzer and stepping closer to the foyer so I have a clear view of the staircase. Katrin's descending it like royalty in a red dress, her hair pulled back in some kind of complicated twist. She looks better than she has all week, but she still doesn't have her usual sparkle. There's something brittle about her face.

The neckline on her dress dips low, displaying a lot more cleavage than Katrin usually shows. It should be distracting, but even that doesn't derail the train of thought that's been running through my brain since yesterday afternoon.

What do you know? What did you do?

"Whoa." Katrin's boyfriend, Theo, doesn't have the same

problem. His eyes zero in on her chest until he remembers that her dad's in the room. "You look amazing."

I can't see Peter, but his voice is full of forced heartiness. "Let's get some pictures of the four of you."

That's my cue to leave. Katrin and Theo are doubling to homecoming with two of my least favorite people at Echo Ridge High: Kyle McNulty and Viv Cantrell. It's not a date, Katrin explained to my mother. Just two people who are worried about Brooke, coming together while the town tries to hang on to some kind of normal. From the glimpse I saw of Kyle when they arrived, he looks as though he got talked into it and already regrets saying yes.

All the money raised from selling homecoming tickets is going toward a reward fund for information leading to Brooke's safe return. Most of the businesses in town are giving matching donations, and Peter's law firm is doubling theirs.

I retreat into the study while everyone poses. Mia's still going with Ezra, and she was texting me until an hour ago trying to convince me to ask Ellery. Under different circumstances I probably would have. But I couldn't get Katrin's words out of my head: *I'd better not see you there.* She's backed off on treating me like a criminal, but I know that's what everyone at school is thinking. I don't care enough about a pointless dance to deal with three hours of getting whispered about and judged.

Besides, I'm not sure I can act normal around my stepsister right now.

I haven't told anyone what we found yesterday. Despite the wild theories, all it really amounts to is a receipt with questionable contact information. Still, it's been eating at me all day, making it almost impossible to look at Katrin without the words bursting out of me: *What do you know? What did you do?*

The murmur of voices in the foyer grows louder as Katrin and her friends get ready to leave for the dance. Pretty soon, only Peter and Mom will be home. Suddenly, the last thing in the world I want to do is spend a Saturday night alone with my thoughts. Before I second-guess myself too much, I fire off a text to Ellery. *Do you want to hang out tonight? Watch a movie or something?*

I don't know if she'll be up for it, or if her grandmother will even let her. But Ellery replies within a few minutes, and the vise gripping my chest loosens a little when I read her response.

Yeah, sure.

Turns out, if you invite a girl over on homecoming night, your mother *will* read into it.

Mom flutters around Ellery with zero chill after her grandmother drops her off at our house. "Do you two want popcorn? I can make some. Are you going to be in the den, or the living room? The den is more comfortable, probably, but I don't think that television has Netflix. Maybe we could set it up real quick, Peter?"

Peter puts a hand on her shoulder, like that'll stop her from spinning out. "I'm sure Malcolm will let us know if he has any pressing technological requirements." He gives Ellery the full Peter Nilsson smile experience as she unwinds a scarf from around her neck and stuffs it into her bag. "Very nice to see you again, Ellery. I didn't get a chance to tell you at Lacey's fund-raiser, but your mother was one of my favorite people in town while she was here." He gives a self-deprecating laugh. "I even took her to the movies a couple of times, although I think I bored her to tears. I hope she's doing well, and that you're enjoying your time in Echo Ridge, even though . . ." A shadow passes over his face. "We're not at our best right now."

I keep my expression neutral to hide how much I wish he'd shut up. Way to remind everyone that half the town thinks I did something to Brooke. Which I guess is the other reason I didn't ask Ellery to homecoming. I'm not sure she'd say yes.

"I know," Ellery says. "We moved here at a strange time. Everyone's been really nice, though." She smiles at me, and my bad mood lifts. Her hair is long and loose around her shoulders, the way I like it. I didn't realize till now that I had a preference, but it turns out I do.

"Can I get you something to drink?" Mom asks. "We have seltzer, or juice, or—" She looks ready to document the entire contents of our refrigerator, but Peter starts gently steering her toward the balcony staircase before Ellery can reply. Thank God.

"Malcolm knows where everything is, Alicia. Why don't we finish up the Burns documentary upstairs?" He favors me with a smile almost as warm as the one he gave Ellery. It doesn't reach his eyes, but points for trying, I guess. "Give us a shout if you need anything."

"Sorry," I say when the sound of their footsteps on the stairs has faded. "Mom's a little rusty at the meeting-new-friends thing. You want some popcorn?"

"Sure," she says, and grins. Her dimple flashes, and I'm happy I texted her.

I lead her into the kitchen, where she hops onto a stool

in front of the island. I open the cabinet next to the sink and root around until I find a box of microwave popcorn. "And don't worry, your mom's cool. Your stepfather, too." She sounds surprised as she says it, as if she wasn't expecting that from Katrin's dad.

"He's all right," I say grudgingly, extracting a bag of popcorn and tossing it into the microwave.

Ellery winds a curl around her finger. "You don't talk about your dad much. Do you see him, or . . . ?" She hesitates, like she's not one hundred percent sure he's even still alive.

The sound of popping kernels fills the air. "Not really. He lives in southern Vermont now, near Massachusetts. I spent a week there over the summer. Mostly he emails sports-related articles under the mistaken assumption that I'll find them interesting. Peter tries a little harder than that." When I say it, it surprises me to realize it's true. "He talks a lot about college, what I want to do after, stuff like that."

"What *do* you want to do?" Ellery asks.

The popping sounds slow. I pull the bag from the microwave and tear it open, releasing a cloud of buttery steam. "I don't have a clue," I admit. "What about you?"

"I'm not sure. I have this idea that I'd like to be a lawyer, but— I don't know if it's realistic. I didn't even think till this year that college was a thing that might happen. Sadie never could have sent us. But my grandmother keeps talking about it like she will."

"Same for me, with Peter," I say. "You know he's a lawyer, right? I'm sure he'd be happy to talk to you about it. Fair warning, though—ninety percent of his job sounds really boring. Although maybe that's just him."

She laughs. "Noted. I might take you up on that." My back is to her as I hunt in a cabinet for a popcorn bowl, and when she speaks again her voice is much quieter. "It's weird, but for the longest time I almost couldn't . . . *see* myself in the future," she says. "I'd think about what happened to my aunt and imagine that one of us, out of me and my brother, might not make it all the way through high school. Like only one Corcoran twin gets to move on. And Ezra's so much more like my mom than I am, so . . ." I turn to see her staring out our kitchen window into the darkness, her expression reflective. Then she shivers, and flashes me an apologetic grimace. "Sorry. That got morbid fast."

"We have screwed-up family histories," I tell her. "Morbid comes with the territory."

I lead her into the Nilssons' living room and lower myself into one corner of the sofa, the bowl of popcorn next to me. She curls up beside it and hands me my drink. "What do you want to watch?" I ask, flicking on the remote and scrolling through the channel guide.

"I don't care," Ellery says. She plucks a small handful of popcorn from the bowl between us. "I'm just glad to be out of my house for the night."

My channel-hopping lands us on the first *Defender* movie. It's past the part where Sadie appears, but I keep it there in her honor anyway. "Yeah, I get it. I keep thinking how it was almost exactly a week ago that I dropped Brooke off." I unscrew the top of my seltzer. "I've been meaning to thank you, by the way. For, you know. Believing me."

Ellery's liquid dark eyes hold mine. "It's been an awful week for you, hasn't it?"

"I saw what Declan went through, remember?" Images of a futuristic city with dark, rain-slicked streets flash across the screen in front of us. The hero is on the ground, cowering as a couple of muscle-bound, leather-clad guys loom over him. He's not half cyborg yet, so he's about to get his ass kicked. "This was better."

Ellery shifts beside me. "But he had a whole history with Lacey. It's not like you were Brooke's boyfriend, or . . ." She hesitates briefly. "Her best friend."

We managed to go almost fifteen minutes without poking the elephant in the room. Good for us, I guess.

"Do you think we should show the police what we found?" I ask.

Ellery chews her lip. "I don't know. I'm kind of worried about how I got it, to be honest. And it might look sketchy to have you involved. Plus I still don't trust Ryan Rodriguez." She frowns at the television screen. "Something's off with that guy."

"There are other police officers," I say. But Officer McNulty is the lead on this case, and the thought of talking to him again makes my stomach churn.

"The thing is . . . I've been wondering about something." Ellery picks up the remote like she's about to change the channel, but juggles it meditatively in her hand instead. "Assuming our leap of logic is right and Katrin actually"—she lowers her voice to a near whisper—"ran over Mr. Bowman. Do you think, um, that's *all* she did?"

I try to swallow a piece of popcorn, but I can't. My throat is too dry. I take a deep gulp of my drink before answering Ellery, and while I do, I think about Katrin gliding down our stairs today with that masklike expression. The way she'd thrown me under the bus when I was first questioned. The scared look in her eyes the day of Peter's search party. "What do you mean?"

"Well." Ellery says the word slowly, reluctantly, like someone's prying it out of her. "I should probably preface this by saying . . . I think about crime a lot. Like, an abnormal amount. I get that. It's sort of a problem. So you have to take what I say with a grain of salt, because I'm just this . . . naturally suspicious person, I guess."

"You suspected me, right? For a while." Ellery freezes, eyes wide. Shit, I didn't mean to come out with that. I almost apologize and change the subject. But I don't, because now that I've said it, I want to hear her response.

"I . . . I honestly hate that I'm like this, Mal." I think that might be the first time she's ever called me by my nickname, but before I can process that momentous occasion, I'm horrified to see her eyes water. "It's just— I grew up never knowing what happened to my aunt. Nobody would tell me anything, so I'd read terrible crime stories to try to understand. But all that did was make me more confused and paranoid. Now I'm at the point where I feel like I can't trust anybody who's not my literal twin." A tear slips down her cheek. She drops the remote onto the couch to swipe angrily at her cheek, leaving a red mark on her pale skin. "I don't know how to relate to people. Like, I pretty much only ever had one friend before I moved here. Then I met you and Mia, and you guys were so great, but all this happened and . . . I'm sorry. I didn't really think *that* about you, but I did . . . think about it. If that makes sense. It probably doesn't."

A knot releases in my chest. "It does. It's okay. Look, I get

222

it." I gesture around the room. "Check out my big homecoming night. Not sure if you noticed, but I only have one friend, too. I said it in the kitchen, right? We have screwed-up family histories. It's crap most of the time, but it does mean I understand you. And I . . . like you."

I move the popcorn bowl onto the coffee table and put a tentative arm around her. She sighs and leans into me. I mean it as a friendly hug, mostly, but her hair's tumbling across one eye, so I push it back, and before I know it both my hands are cupping her cheeks. Which feels really good. Ellery's eyes are steady on mine, her lips curved in a small, questioning smile. I draw her face closer and before I can overthink it, I kiss her.

Her mouth is soft and warm and just a little bit buttery. Heat spreads through me slowly as she slides her hand up my chest and around the back of my neck. Then she nips lightly at my bottom lip, and the heat turns into an electric jolt. I wrap my arms around her and pull her half on my lap, kissing her lips and the skin between her jaw and her collarbone. She pushes me back against the pillows and molds her body to mine and, holy hell, this night is going a *lot* better than I expected.

A loud, clattering noise makes both of us freeze. Somehow we dislodged the remote and sent it flying across the floor. Ellery sits up just as my mother's voice, which is much too close for someone who's supposed to be upstairs, calls, "Malcolm? Is everything all right?"

Crap. She's in the kitchen. Ellery and I disentangle as I call, "Fine. We just dropped the remote." We put a foot between us on the couch, both of us red-faced with sheepish grins, waiting for my mother's response.

"Oh, okay. I'm making hot chocolate, do you want some?"

"No thanks," I say, as Ellery tries to get her curls under control. My hands are itching to mess them up again.

"What about you, Ellery?" Mom asks.

"I'm all set, thanks." Ellery says, biting her lip.

"All right." I wait an endless minute for my mother to go back upstairs, but before it's up Ellery has scooted all the way to the other end of the couch.

"It's probably good we were interrupted," she says, going even redder. "I feel like maybe I should tell you my theory before . . . anything."

My brain isn't working all that well right now. "Tell me your what?"

"My criminal theory."

"Your— Oh. Yeah, that." I suck in a breath for composure and adjust my position on the couch. "It's not about me, though, right?"

"Definitely not," she says. "But it *is* about Katrin. And how I think that if we're right about Mr. Bowman, maybe that was just the beginning of, um, things." She winds a strand of hair around her finger, which I'm starting to realize is never a good sign. I still can't wrap my brain around Katrin possibly running over Mr. Bowman; I'm not sure I'm ready for more *things*. But I've spent the past five years avoiding conversations about Lacey and Declan, and that never solved anything.

"What do you mean?" I ask.

"Well. If we go back to the receipt, we're pretty sure Brooke knew about the accident, right? She was either in the car when it happened, or Katrin told her after." Ellery releases her hair

224

to start pulling on her necklace. "Katrin must've been terrified about people finding out. It's one thing to have an accident, but to leave afterward without stopping to help . . . she'd be a pariah at school, plus it'd ruin her dad's standing in town. Not to mention the criminal charges. So she decided to cover it up. And Brooke agreed to help, but I think she must have regretted that. She always looked so worried and sad. Ever since I met her, which was *right* after Mr. Bowman died. Unless she was always like that?"

"No," I say, my stomach twisting as I think of Brooke's smiling class picture on the MISSING poster. "She wasn't."

"And then in the Fright Farm office, she kept saying things like, *I shouldn't have, I have to tell them, it's not okay.* Which makes me think she felt guilty."

Pressure clamps down on my skull. "She asked me if I'd ever made a really bad mistake."

Ellery's eyes widen. "She did? When?"

"In the office. While you were looking for Ezra. She said . . ." I search my memory, but the exact words won't come. "Something about making a mistake that wasn't, like, a regular mistake. And that she wished she had different friends."

Ellery nods seriously. "That fits," she says.

I'm pretty sure I don't want to know, but I ask anyway. "With what?"

"Lots of things. Starting with the vandalism," Ellery says. I blink at her, startled. "The messages didn't appear until after Katrin repaired her car. She got it back on September second, and Lacey's fund-raiser was September fourth, right?" I nod, and Ellery continues, "I kept thinking about what it must've

225

been like for Katrin then, with the whole town mourning Mr. Bowman and looking for answers. She was probably walking on eggshells, terrified of getting found out or giving herself away. So I thought, what if *Katrin* was the one who started the vandalism?"

"Why would she do that?" I can't keep the disbelieving edge out of my voice.

Ellery runs a fingernail along the floral pattern of the couch, refusing to look at me. "As a distraction," she says quietly. "The whole town started focusing on the threats instead of what happened to Mr. Bowman."

I feel a stab of nausea, because she's not wrong. The Homecoming Stalker made Mr. Bowman's hit-and-run fade into the background a lot faster than should have been possible for such a popular teacher. "But why pull *you* into it?" I ask. "And herself, and Brooke?"

"Well, Katrin and Brooke make sense because if they're targets, nobody would think they're involved. Me, I don't know." Ellery keeps tracing the pattern, her eyes trained on her hand like if she loses concentration for even a second, the entire couch will disappear. "Maybe I was just a way to . . . thicken the intrigue, or something. Because my family is loosely tied to tragic homecomings, too, even though Sadie was the queen and not Sarah."

"How would Katrin even do it, though? She was in the cultural center when the sign got vandalized," I point out. "And onstage with the rest of the cheerleaders when the screen started flashing all that stuff at Fright Farm."

"The screen could've been set up beforehand. But for the

rest . . . she'd have needed help, I guess. Brooke was already pulled in, and Viv and Theo would do anything Katrin says, wouldn't they? Or was there a time at the cultural center when you lost sight of her?"

"I mean . . . yeah." I think of Katrin slipping away as soon as all eyes turned toward my mother and me. *Oh, there's Theo.* How long was she gone? I rub a hand across my temple like that'll help me remember. It doesn't. The more Ellery and I talk, the more agitated I feel. "Maybe. But if I'm being honest, it's kind of a stretch, Ellery. And it still doesn't explain what happened to Brooke."

"That's what I'm worried about," Ellery says in the same low voice. "I keep thinking that while Katrin was distracting the town, Brooke was working up the courage to tell people what happened. And she wanted to get the proof back. What if Katrin knew that and . . . did something to keep her quiet?"

A chill settles over me. "Like what?"

"I don't know. And I really, really hope I'm wrong." Ellery speaks quickly, in a rush, like she hates what she's saying but needs to get it out anyway. "But Katrin had motive. She had opportunity. That's two out of the three things you need to commit a crime."

My stomach feels like lead. "What's the third?"

"You have to be the kind of person who would do something like that." Ellery finally looks up, her expression pensive.

"Katrin wouldn't." The words spring out of me without thought.

"Even if she thought she'd lose everything?" I'm not as quick to speak this time, and Ellery presses on, "It might explain why she threw out that random accusation about you and Brooke, right? Anything to deflect."

"But, Ellery . . . Christ, what are you even talking about here?" My voice drops to a tense whisper. "Kidnapping? Worse? I can get on board with the rest of it, sort of. The hit-and-run, even planting all those messages around town. That's extreme, but I can imagine someone doing it under pressure. Making Brooke actually . . . *go missing* is a whole other level."

"I know," Ellery says. "Katrin would either have to be so desperate that she lost all sense of right or wrong, or be a cold-blooded criminal." She's back to tracing patterns on the sofa again. "You've lived with her for a few months. Do you see a possibility for either of those?"

"No way. Katrin leads a charmed life." But even as I say it, I know it's not entirely true. Peter might dote on Katrin, but in the four months I've lived here I've barely heard anything about the first Mrs. Nilsson. Katrin doesn't just not talk *to* her mother, she doesn't talk *about* her. It's almost like she has only one parent. It's one of the few things we have in common. It sucks, but it doesn't mean you're warped for life. Probably.

Ellery and I are silent for a few minutes, watching the robotically enhanced Defender mow down his former nemesis. That's what made this series so popular, I think: that a regular guy who's constantly beaten down could suddenly become special and powerful. In Hollywood, no plotline is impossible. Maybe Ellery's spent too much time in that world.

Or maybe I don't know my stepsister at all.

"If any of it's true, you'd think she'd make another move with the anonymous threats, wouldn't you?" I finally ask. "They stopped when Brooke disappeared. If you wanted to distract people, now would be the time." The TV screen flickers as the Defender extinguishes all the lights on a city block. "*Right* now, actually. At homecoming."

Ellery sends me a cautious look. "You know, I was thinking that, but . . . I didn't want to say anything. I kind of feel like I've already said too much."

"I don't like hearing it," I admit. "But . . . there's a lot about Katrin lately that doesn't fit. Maybe we should pay more attention to what she's up to. And where she is."

Ellery raises her brows. "Do you think we should go to homecoming?"

"We could." I glance at the clock on the wall. "It's been going on for less than an hour. Still plenty of time for her to make a move, if she's going to."

Ellery gestures at her black shirt and jeans. "I'm not exactly dressed for it."

"Do you have anything at home that could work? We could stop there first."

"Nothing super formal, but . . . I guess so." She looks uncertain. "Are you sure, though? I feel like I kind of sprang a lot on you at once. Maybe you should let it sink in for a while."

I give her a half grin. "Are you trying to get out of going to homecoming with me?"

She flushes. "No! I just . . . it's, um . . . huh." I've never seen her at a loss for words before. It's cute. Ellery might be a walking *Forensic Files* episode, but there's still something about her that I can't stop thinking about. Lots of things.

It's not just that, though. Earlier today it seemed like a

no-brainer to stay home. All I wanted was to keep my head down and avoid conflict. Except now I'm stuck here watching a bad '90s movie like I have something to be ashamed of, while Katrin—who at the very least has been shady about her car—put on a bright-red dress and went to a party.

I'm tired of watching my life turn into Declan Part Two. And I'm tired of doing nothing while my friends try to figure out how to dig me out of trouble I shouldn't even be in.

"Then let's go," I say.

CHAPTER TWENTY-SEVEN

ELLERY
SATURDAY, OCTOBER 5

Nana is, to put it mildly, not pleased with this turn of events.

"You said you were going to watch a movie," she says from the other side of my closed bedroom door as I yank a dress over my head. It's black and sleeveless, with a flared A-line skirt that ends just above my knees. The material is casual jersey, but I put on a few long, glittering necklaces to dress it up. With my one and only pair of heels, it can pass for semiformal.

"We changed our minds," I say, reaching for a bottle of curl enhancer and squeezing a small amount into my palm. I already spent more time than I'd like to admit on my hair before leaving for Malcolm's, but the battle against frizz never ends.

"I don't like the idea of you going to this dance, Ellery. Not after everything that's happened over the past few weeks."

"You let Ezra go," I point out, slipping into my shoes.

"Ezra wasn't targeted like you were. One of the girls who was on the homecoming court with you is *missing*, for God's sake. It could be dangerous."

"But, Nana, there's not even a court anymore. Now the whole thing is more of a fund-raiser. There'll be kids and teachers everywhere. Brooke didn't disappear when she was in the middle of a crowd like that. She was at home with her parents." I run my hands through my hair, brush mascara across my lashes, and coat my lips with sheer red gloss. Done.

Nana doesn't have a good response for that. When I open my door, she's standing there with her arms folded, and she frowns as she looks me up and down. "Since when do you wear makeup?" she asks.

"It's a dance." I wait for her to move, but she doesn't.

"Is this a date?"

I get full-body butterflies as I think about kissing Malcolm on his couch, but blink at Nana like it's the first time I'd ever considered her question. "What? No! We're going as friends, like Mia and Ezra. We got bored and decided to meet up with them. That's all."

I can feel my cheeks flame. I do not, as Sadie would put it, have the appropriate emotional connection to this scene. Nana looks entirely unconvinced. We regard one another in silence for a few seconds until she sags against the doorway. "I could forbid you, I suppose, though that never worked with your mother. She'd just go behind my back. But I want you to call when you get there, and I want you to come straight home after. With your *brother*. Daisy Kwon is a chaperone. She brought him and Mia, and she can take you home, too."

"Okay, Nana." I try to sound grateful, because I know this

isn't easy for her. Plus if I'm going to be annoyed with anyone it should be me, for somehow managing to turn my first kiss with Malcolm into a stakeout. Maybe I need to work out a system with Ezra so he can text *Nobody wants to hear your murder theories* the next time I get the urge to ruin my own night.

I follow her downstairs, where my seriously cute not-date is waiting. The side benefit to me forcing us off the couch is getting to see Malcolm in a suit again. "Hi, Mrs. Corcoran," he says, and then his eyes go satisfyingly wide when he catches sight of me. "Wow. You look great."

"Thanks. So do you," I say, even though I already told him that at his house. We smile at one another in a way that's not helping the *we're just friends* argument.

"Ellery needs to be back by ten-thirty," Nana interjects, throwing out an arbitrary time that we did *not* agree to upstairs. "She'll be coming home with Ezra."

"No problem, Mrs. Corcoran," Malcolm says before I can reply. "Thanks for letting her go with me."

I'm not positive, but I think Nana's expression might soften a little as she opens the door for us. "Have a good time. And a *safe* time."

We cross the lawn to the Volvo, and Malcolm opens the passenger door for me. I tip my head back to look up at him. I'm about to make a joke—something to ease the tension caused by my grandmother's obvious nerves—but my eyes wander to his lips and the slope of his neck where it meets his crisp white shirt collar, and I forget what I was about to say.

His knuckles brush against my arm, raising goose bumps. "Do you want to get a coat? It's cold out."

"No, that's okay." I tear my eyes away from his weirdly

enticing collar and fold myself into the seat. We veer away from the heavy topics of the night while we drive, talking about a comic-book series we both like and a spin-off movie that neither of us has seen.

The school parking lot is packed, and Malcolm grabs one of the last open spots at the far end. I immediately regret my decision not to bring a coat, but when I start shivering Malcolm pulls his suit jacket off and settles it over my shoulders. It smells like him, a clean mix of shampoo and laundry detergent. I try not to inhale too obviously while we walk.

"Here goes nothing," he says, opening the front doors.

I pull out my phone and call Nana to let her know we've arrived safely, then disconnect as we turn the corner that leads to the auditorium. The first thing we see is a purple-draped table, staffed by a blond woman in a flowered dress. Her bangs are teased higher than average for the decade we're in. "Oh no," Malcolm mutters, halting his steps.

"What?" I ask, putting my phone into the pocket of my dress. I slip Malcolm's jacket off my shoulders and hand it back to him.

Malcolm takes his time putting it back on before he starts moving again. "That's Liz McNulty. Kyle's sister. She *hates* me. Looks like she's a chaperone."

"That woman?" I peer at her. "The one Declan broke up with for Lacey?" Malcolm nods. "I thought she was your brother's age."

"She is."

"She looks forty!"

I'm whispering, but he still shushes me as we approach the table. "Hi, Liz," Malcolm says in a resigned tone.

The woman glances up from her phone, and her expression immediately settles into a look of deep dislike. "Tickets," she growls without returning the greeting.

"We don't have them yet," Malcolm says. "Can I get two, please?"

Liz looks positively triumphant when she tells him, "We're not selling them at the door."

Malcolm pauses in the act of reaching for his wallet. "That's kind of a flawed system."

"You're supposed to buy them ahead of time," Liz sniffs.

"Hey, guys," a melodic voice calls behind us. I turn to see Daisy coming out of the gym, looking pretty in a formfitting blue dress and high heels. A blast of loud music accompanies her until she closes the door.

"Hi," I say, relieved to see a friendly face. "You look nice."

"Gotta dress up for chaperone duty, right, Liz?" Daisy says. Liz smooths the front of her frumpy dress, and I feel a pang of sympathy for her. Daisy flicks her eyes between Malcolm and me. "I'm surprised to see you two here. Mia said you weren't coming."

"We changed our minds. But we didn't know you needed tickets ahead of time," I add, giving Liz my most ingratiating smile.

Liz crosses her arms over her chest, ready to argue until Daisy puts a placating hand on her arm. "Oh, I'm sure it's okay now that the dance is more than half over. Right, Liz?" No response, but Daisy presses on. "Principal Slate wouldn't want to turn any-one away. Not on a night like this, when the school is trying to bring people together. And we need every penny we can get for the reward fund." She flashes the kind of sweet, winning smile that probably got her elected to student council all four years at Echo Ridge High. Liz continues to glower, but with less certainty. I guess Daisy's secret relationship with Declan is still under wraps, or Liz would probably be a lot less charitable.

"We'd really appreciate it," I say. Malcolm, wisely, keeps his mouth shut.

Liz holds out her palm with an annoyed snort. "Fine. Five dollars. *Each.*"

Malcolm hands over a ten and we walk with Daisy into the gymnasium. Loud, thumping music hits us again, and I blink as my eyes adjust to the dim lighting. Purple streamers and silver balloons are everywhere and the room is packed with dancing students. "Should we look for Mia and Ezra?" Malcolm asks, raising his voice to be heard over the thumping noise. I nod and he turns toward the center of the room, but Daisy pulls at my arm before I can follow.

"Can I ask you something?" she shouts.

I hesitate as Malcolm disappears into the crowd without realizing I'm not behind him. "Um, okay," I say, not sure what to expect.

Daisy puts her head close to mine so she doesn't have to yell. "I've been thinking about what you said. About Ryan Rodriguez and the bracelet?" I nod. We hadn't gotten much chance to discuss that on Thursday, once Mia and Daisy's parents came home and started hyperventilating over Mia's head injury. She told them she tripped headfirst into the fireplace mantel. "It's been worrying me. Why do you think he might have given it to Lacey? Do you know something?"

"No," I admit. I don't want to catalog all my vague suspicions to Daisy, especially after what she'd said that day: *There's this whole other layer when you're one of the only minority families in town.* Sometimes I forget how . . . *not* diverse Echo Ridge is. But when I look around at the crowded gym, I remember. And it feels less harmless to toss speculation around about someone whose last name is Rodriguez.

Besides, even though I crossed Daisy off my suspect list after getting to know her better, I still think Declan is sketchy. Malcolm might not talk to him much, but I'm sure Daisy does.

"It's just because he knew her," I say instead.

Daisy's brow creases. "But . . . it's not like they were friends."

"He was so devastated when she died, though."

She straightens up in surprise, her pretty eyes wide. "Says who?"

"My mother." Daisy still looks confused, so I add, "She saw him at the funeral. When he got hysterical and had to be carried out?"

"*Ryan Rodriguez* did?" Daisy's tone is incredulous, and she shakes her head decisively. "That didn't happen."

"Maybe you missed it?" I suggest.

"No. Our class was small, we were all on one side of the church. I would've noticed." Daisy's mouth curves in an indulgent smile. "Your mom was probably being dramatic. Hollywood, right?"

I pause. Daisy's response is almost exactly what Nana said when I brought it up a couple of weeks ago. *That didn't happen.* Then, I thought Nana was being dismissive. But that was before I'd fully experienced how odd Sadie can be when it comes to talking about Echo Ridge. "Yeah, I guess," I say slowly.

I don't think Daisy has any reason to lie about Ryan's behavior at Lacey's funeral. But does Sadie?

"Sorry, I separated you from your date, didn't I?" Daisy says as we spy Malcolm emerging from a crowd in the middle of the room. "I better circulate and make myself useful. Have fun." She waves and heads for the sidelines, pirouetting to avoid a couple of theater kids starting a dramatic waltz as the music slows down.

"What happened to you?" Malcolm asks when he reaches me. He looks more disheveled than he did when we got here, like someone who found himself at the edge of a mosh pit but didn't go all in: jacket unbuttoned, tie loosened, hair mussed.

"Sorry. Daisy wanted to ask me something. Did you find them?"

"No. I got intercepted by Viv." His shoulders twitch in an irritated shudder. "She's already lost Kyle and she's not happy about it. And she's mad at Theo because he brought a flask and Katrin's half drunk."

I scan the gym until I spot a bright-red dress. "Speaking of," I say, nodding toward the dance floor. Katrin and Theo are slow-dancing in the middle of the room, her arms wrapped around his neck like she's trying to keep from drowning. "There she is."

Malcolm follows my gaze. "Yep. Doesn't look much like a killer, does she?"

Something in me deflates. "You think I'm ridiculous, don't you?"

"What? No," Malcolm says quickly. "I just meant— Whatever might happen isn't happening right this second, so . . . maybe we could dance?" He slides a finger beneath his tie and tugs to loosen it further. "Since we're here and all."

My stomach starts doing that fluttering thing again. "Well. We do need to blend," I say, and accept the hand he holds out to me.

My arms circle his neck and his hands graze my waist. It's the classic awkward slow-dance position, but after a couple of offbeat sways he pulls me closer and then, suddenly, we fit. I relax against him, my head on his chest. For a few minutes I just enjoy how solid he feels, and the steady beat of his heart beneath my cheek.

Malcolm leans toward my ear. "Can I ask you something?" I lift my head, hoping he's going to ask if he can kiss me again, and almost say yes preemptively before he adds, "Are you afraid of clowns?"

Huh. That was a letdown.

I lean back and stare into his eyes, which look steely gray instead of green beneath the dim lights. "Um. What?"

"Are you afraid of clowns?" he asks patiently, like it's a perfectly normal conversation starter.

So I go with it. "No. I've never understood the whole clown phobia, to be honest." I shake my head, and a stray curl grazes my lips and sticks to the gloss. Reminding me, once again, why I don't wear makeup. Before I can figure out a graceful way to extricate it, Malcolm does it for me, tucking the curl behind my ear and letting his hand settle briefly on my neck before it returns to my waist.

A jolt of energy shoots down my spine. *Oh.* All right. Maybe lip gloss has its uses.

"Me either," he says. "I feel like clowns get kind of a bad rap, you know? They just want to entertain."

"Are you, like, their spokesperson?" I ask, and he grins.

"No. But there's this clown museum in Solsbury— Well, calling it a museum is kind of a stretch. It's this old woman's house that's crammed full of antique clown stuff. She gives anybody who shows up a giant box of popcorn and she has, like, six dogs that just hang out there in the middle of all the clown memorabilia. And sometimes she plays movies against one of the walls, but they don't always have clowns in them. Or usually, even. Last time I went the movie was *Legally Blonde*."

I laugh. "Sounds delightful."

"It's weird," Malcolm admits. "But I like it. It's funny and sort of interesting, as long as you're not afraid of clowns." His hands tighten on my waist, just a little. "I thought maybe you'd like to go sometime."

I have a lot of questions, starting with *Only me, or me and my brother plus Mia?* and *Will it be a date, or is it just a strange thing you like that nobody else will do?* and *Should we get you one hundred percent cleared of any felonies first?* But I bite them back and respond with, "I'd like that."

Because I would.

"Okay. Good," Malcolm says with a crooked smile. Suddenly, whatever rhythm we've managed to find vanishes; he steps on my foot, I clock him with my elbow, my hair sticks to my face for reasons I can't even comprehend. It's all going to hell very quickly, until he freezes and says, "Do you see Katrin?"

I look toward the center of the gym where we'd seen her last, but she's gone. "Theo's still there," I say, tilting my chin in his direction. He's doing a terrible job of trying to look casual while pouring the contents of a flask into his Solo cup. "But I don't see her."

The music switches to a fast song and Malcolm motions for me to follow him. We wind our way off the dance floor, weaving in and out of the crowd, and circle the perimeter of the auditorium. I catch a couple of people staring at Malcolm, and before I can think too much about it I grab hold of his hand. I spot Mia and Ezra within a bigger group, dancing frenetically. Daisy is off to the side with a couple of chaperones, standing slightly apart from them with a preoccupied expression. It makes me wonder what homecoming was like for her five years ago, watching the boy she loved and her best friend get crowned king and queen. Whether she was jealous—or unconcerned, thinking her turn would come soon enough.

And I wonder what it was like for Sadie more than twenty years ago, there without her sister, dancing with a boy she must have liked at least a little bit. A perfect night turned into a cruel memory.

"She's not here," Malcolm says, but just then, I see a flash of bright red where I wasn't expecting it to be.

The far corner of the gym has an exit next to the bleachers that's been covered with balloons and streamers in an attempt to make it look inaccessible. Katrin emerges from beneath the stands and, without checking to see whether a chaperone's in sight, pushes the door open and slips outside.

Malcolm and I exchange glances. The straight path to the door is strewn with dancing classmates and chaperones, so we stick to the edge of the gym until we come to the opposite side. We slip underneath the bleachers and make our way along the wall toward the door, encountering only one couple making out. When we emerge on the other side, we look around more carefully than Katrin did before following her out the door.

It's cool and quiet outside, the moon full and bright above us. Katrin's nowhere in sight. The football field is to our left, the front of the building to our right. By unspoken agreement, we both go right.

When we turn the corner nearest the school entrance, Katrin is standing frozen near the Echo Ridge High sign. Malcolm tugs me back into the shadows as she half turns, and I spy a clutch in her hands. My eyes strain and my breath catches as I watch her fumble with the clasp. Even though the sensible part of my brain wonders what she could possibly manage to fit in there other than keys and a tube of lip gloss, I pull out my cell phone and set it to Video.

But before Katrin can take anything out of the bag, she drops it. My phone frames her in almost cinematic moonlight as she freezes, bends at the waist, and vomits loudly into the grass.

CHAPTER TWENTY-EIGHT

Post-homecoming Echo Ridge seems tired on Sunday, as though the entire town is hung over. Church is emptier than usual, and we hardly see anyone while we run errands with Nana after. Even Melanie Kilduff, who usually jogs past at some point while we're doing yard work, is nowhere in sight when Ezra and I pull weeds from the side lawn.

"So how did you end things with Malcolm?" Ezra asks.

I yank on a dandelion and accidentally behead it instead of pulling it out by the roots. "I mean, you saw," I say, annoyed. The dance ended promptly at ten o'clock last night, and we all got herded out of the auditorium like cattle with a strict curfew. Daisy beat Nana's deadline by fifteen minutes. Nana stayed up unusually late, hovering around Ezra and me, and I ended up texting him an update of my night instead of describing it in person. "We said good night."

243

"Yeah, but you must've made plans, right?"

I extract the rest of the dandelion and toss it into the plastic bucket between us. "I think we might go to a clown museum."

Ezra frowns. "A what now?"

"A clown museum. That's kind of beside the point, though, isn't it?" I sit back on my haunches, frustrated. "I really thought something else would happen last night. With Katrin, I mean. But all we did was catch her in the dastardly act of throwing up."

Ezra shrugs. "It wasn't a bad idea. She's pretty central to everything that's been going on around here, but . . ." He trails off and wipes his brow, leaving a faint smear of dirt on his forehead. "But maybe we should let the experts handle it. Give the receipt to the police. You don't have to tell them how you got it. Malcolm could say he found it."

"But then it doesn't make any sense. The only reason the receipt is meaningful is because Brooke was trying to get it back."

"Oh. Right."

The faint roar of a car engine approaches, and I turn to see Officer Rodriguez's police cruiser pass our house and turn into his driveway a few doors down. "Too bad our local officer is so sketchy," I mutter.

"Haven't you given that up yet?" Ezra asks. "Daisy told you last night that Officer Rodriguez didn't make a scene at Lacey's funeral. Nana said the same thing. I don't know why Sadie would say he did if it wasn't true, but at the very least, whatever she thinks she saw is open to interpretation. Other than that, what has the guy done? Taken a bad yearbook photo? Maybe you should give him a chance."

I get to my feet and brush off my jeans. "Maybe you're right. Come on."

"Huh?" Ezra squints up at me. "I didn't mean *now*."

"Why not? Nana's been after us to bring over those moving boxes, right? So he can pack up his house before he tries to sell it? Let's do it now. Maybe we can feel him out about what's happening with the investigation."

We leave our yard tools where they are and head inside. Nana is upstairs dusting when we gather a couple dozen flattened cardboard boxes from the basement. When we shout up to her what we're doing, she doesn't protest.

Ezra takes the lion's share of the boxes and I grab the rest, following him outside onto the wide dirt road that leads to the Rodriguezes' house. It's a dark-brown Cape, smaller than the rest of the neighborhood homes and set back from the street. I've never seen it up close before. The front windows have bright blue flower boxes, but everything inside them looks like it's been dead for months.

Officer Rodriguez answers within a few seconds of Ezra pressing the bell. He's out of uniform in a blue T-shirt and sweatpants, and his hair looks overdue for a trim. "Oh, hey," he says, pulling the door open wide. "Nora mentioned she'd be sending those over. Great timing. I'm taking some things out of the living room now."

He didn't invite us in, exactly, but I step into the hallway anyway. "You're moving?" I ask, hoping to keep the conversation going. Now that I'm inside the Rodriguezes' house, I'm more curious about him than ever.

Officer Rodriguez takes the boxes from us and props them against the wall. "Eventually. Now that my dad's gone it's too much house for one person, you know? But there's no rush. Gotta figure out where to go first." He lifts an arm to scratch the back of his head. "You guys want something to drink? Water, maybe?"

"Do you have any coffee?" Ezra asks.

Officer Rodriguez looks doubtful. "Are you allowed to drink that?"

"We're, like, five years younger than you," Ezra points out. "And it's *coffee*. I'm not asking you for meth." I snicker, even as I realize that Ezra must have a decent comfort level with Officer Rodriguez to give him a hard time like that. He doesn't usually openly challenge authority figures, even as a joke.

Officer Rodriguez smiles sheepishly. "Well, your grandmother's kind of strict. But yeah, I just made some." He turns, and we trail him into a kitchen with mustard-colored appliances and old-fashioned flowered wallpaper. Officer Rodriguez pulls a couple of mismatched mugs out of a cabinet and roots around in a drawer for spoons.

I lean against the counter. "We were wondering, um, how things are going with the investigation about Brooke," I say, feeling a familiar tightening in my chest. Some days, like yesterday, I'm almost busy enough to forget how every passing hour makes it less and less likely that Brooke is going to come home safely. "Any news?"

"Nothing I can share," Officer Rodriguez says, his tone turning more businesslike. "I'm sorry. I know it's hard on you guys, having seen her right before she disappeared."

He looks like he means it. And right now, as he fills a snowman mug with steaming coffee and hands it to me, he seems so nice and normal and decidedly non-murder-y that I wish I'd brought the car repair receipt with me.

Except I still don't know much about him. Not really.

"How is her family doing?" Ezra asks, settling into a kitchen chair. There's a stray penny on the table in front of him, and he starts spinning it across the surface.

"About as you'd expect. They're worried sick. But they appreciate everything the town is doing," Officer Rodriguez says. He crosses to the refrigerator and opens it, pushing around the contents. "Do you guys take milk? Or half-and-half?"

"Either," Ezra says, catching the penny midspin between two fingers.

I peer into the attached living room, where an oversized picture of three little kids hangs over the mantel. "Is that you when you were little?" I ask. Since I have so few of my own, family photos are like catnip to me. I always feel like they must say a lot about the person they belong to, which is probably why Sadie hates them. She doesn't like giving anything away.

Officer Rodriguez is still looking through the refrigerator, his back toward me. "What?"

"That picture over your fireplace." I set my mug down on the counter and go out to the living room for a closer look. The top of the mantel is crowded with more pictures, and I gravitate toward a triple-frame one with what looks like graduation photos.

"You shouldn't—" Officer Rodriguez calls, and there's a crashing noise behind me. As I turn to see him tripping over an ottoman, my gaze skims past a picture of Ezra.

Wait. No. That can't be right.

My eyes lock on the framed photo of a young man in military fatigues, leaning against a helicopter and smiling into the camera. Everything about him—the dark hair and eyes, the sharp planes of his face, even the slightly lopsided grin—looks exactly like my brother.

And me.

I draw in a sharp breath, my fingers closing around the frame seconds before Officer Rodriguez tries to snatch it off the mantel. I stumble backward, both hands gripping the picture as something that feels a lot like panic zips through my bloodstream. My skin is hot and my vision is clouding up. But I can still see that face with perfect clarity in my mind's eye. It could be my brother dressed up as a soldier for Halloween, but it's not.

"Who is this?" I ask. My tongue feels thick, like it's been shot through with Novocain.

Officer Rodriguez's face is beet red. He looks as though he'd rather do anything other than answer me, but he finally does. "My dad, right after he served in Desert Storm."

"Your *dad*?" The word comes out as a shriek.

"Ellery? What the hell?" Ezra's puzzled tone sounds miles away.

"Shit." Officer Rodriguez runs both hands through his hair. "This is . . . okay. This is not how I wanted things to go. I was going to, I don't know, talk to your grandmother or something. Except I had no idea what to say, so I just kept putting it off and . . . I mean, I don't even know." I meet his eyes, and he swallows hard. "It might be a coincidence."

My legs have turned into rubber bands. I drop into an armchair, still clutching the picture frame. "It's not a coincidence."

Impatience edges into Ezra's voice. "What are you talking about?"

Officer Rodriguez doesn't look anything like his father. If he did, I might've been as startled as he was the first time we met. Suddenly it all makes sense—the dropped coffee mug in Nana's kitchen, the nervous stuttering and bumbling every time he saw us. I'd taken it for ineptitude at first, then guilt about Lacey. Never, not once, did it occur to me that Ryan Rodriguez looked like a deer in perpetual headlights because he was trying to process the fact that we're probably related.

Probably? I scan the photo in my hands. I've never looked anything like Sadie except for the hair and dimple. But those near-black, upturned eyes, the sharp chin, the smile—it's what I see in the mirror every day.

Officer Rodriguez clasps his hands in front of him like he's getting ready to pray. "Maybe we should get your grandmother."

I shake my head emphatically. I don't know much right now, but I *do* know that Nana's presence wouldn't do anything except up the awkward quotient by a thousandfold. Instead, I hold the frame out to Ezra. "You need to see this."

I feel as though all seventeen years of my life flash in front of me as my brother crosses the room. My brain races at the same pace, trying to come up with some explanation for all the parts that now seem like a lie. Like, maybe Sadie really did meet up with someone named Jorge or José at a nightclub, and genuinely believed everything she'd ever told us about our father. Maybe she didn't even remember what now seems like a pretty obvious precursor to that—a fling with a married guy while she was in town for her father's funeral.

Except. I remember her expression when I'd first mentioned Officer Rodriguez's name—how something uncomfortable and almost shifty crossed her face. When I'd asked her about it, she'd told me that story about him falling apart at Lacey's funeral. Something that I'd built an entire criminal theory around until two people told me it didn't happen.

Ezra sucks in a sharp breath. "Holy shit."

I can't bring myself to look at his face, so I dart a glance at Officer Rodriguez instead. A muscle twitches in his cheek. "I'm sorry," he says. "I should have— Well, I don't know what I should've done, to be honest. We could . . . get a test or something, I guess, to make sure. . . ." He trails off and crosses his arms. "I don't think he knew. Maybe I'm wrong, but I think he would've said something if he had."

Would've. Past tense. Since his father—and ours, I guess—has been dead for three months.

It's too much to take in. Voices buzz around me, and I should probably listen because I'm sure they're saying something important and meaningful, but I can't hear the words clearly. Everything is white noise. My palms are sweating, my knees shaking. My lungs feel like they've shrunk and can only hold spoonfuls of air at a time. I'm getting so dizzy that I'm afraid I'm going to pass out in the middle of the Rodriguezes' living room.

And maybe the worst thing about it all is this: how horribly, childishly, and desperately I want my mom right now.

CHAPTER TWENTY-NINE

MALCOLM

SUNDAY, OCTOBER 6

It's one of those dreams that's really a memory.

Mia and I are on her couch, our eyes glued to her television as we watch coverage of Lacey's funeral from the day before. We'd been there, of course, but we couldn't tear ourselves away from reliving it on-screen.

Meli Dinglasa, an Echo Ridge High grad who'd been toiling in obscurity at a local news station until someone got the brilliant idea to put her in front of the camera for this story, stands on the church steps clutching a microphone. "Yesterday, this shattered New England town came together at Lacey Kilduff's funeral, mourning the loss of such a promising young woman. But amidst the sorrow, questions continue to whirl around those who knew the teen victim best."

The camera cuts to video of Declan leaving the church in

a badly fitting suit, tight-lipped and scowling. If he's trying to look the part of "Disreputable Ex with a Chip on His Shoulder," he's doing a great job.

Mia clears her throat and leans forward, clutching a pillow. "Do you think whoever did it was at the funeral yesterday?" She catches sight of my face and hastily adds, "I don't mean any of her friends. Obviously. I just mean— I wonder if it's somebody we know. Right there with us, in the middle of the crowd."

"They wouldn't show up," I say, with more certainty than I feel.

"You don't think?" Mia chews her bottom lip, eyes flicking over the screen. "They should give everybody there the killer test."

"The what?"

"I heard about it at school," Mia says. "It's a riddle about a girl. She's at her mother's funeral, and she sees some guy she doesn't know. She falls in love with him and decides he's her dream guy. A few days later, she kills her sister. Why'd she do it?"

"Nobody would do that," I scoff.

"It's a riddle. You have to answer. They say murderers always give the same answer."

"Because she . . ." I pause, trying to think of the most twisted answer possible. I feel comfortable about doing that with Mia, in a way I wouldn't with anybody else right now. She's one of the only people in Echo Ridge who's not staring accusingly at Declan—and at me, like I must be a bad seed by association. "Because the sister was the man's girlfriend and she wanted him for herself?"

"No. Because she thought the man might go to her sister's funeral, too."

I snort. "That doesn't even make sense."

"Do you have a better way to tell who's a cold-blooded killer?"

I scan the crowd on-screen, looking for an obvious sign that somebody's not right. Something twisted lurking among all the sad faces. "They're the most messed-up person in the room."

Mia curls deeper into her corner of the couch, pressing the pillow tight against her chest. "That's the problem, though, isn't it? They are, but you can't tell."

I startle awake so violently that I almost fall out of bed. My pulse is racing and my mouth is cottony dry. I haven't thought about that day in years—Mia and I sneak-watching news coverage of Lacey's funeral while I hid at her house because mine was already bubbling over with angry tension. I don't know why I'd dream about it now, except . . .

Katrin would either have to be so desperate that she lost all sense of right or wrong, or be a cold-blooded criminal. Even after catching Katrin doing nothing worse than looking for a quiet place to puke, I can't get Ellery's words out of my head.

I run a hand through sweat-dampened hair and flip over, trying to sink back into sleep. No good. My eyes keep popping open, so I roll over to check the time on my phone. Just past three a.m., so it's surprising to see a text from Ellery that's time-stamped ten minutes ago.

Sorry I didn't reply sooner. Stuff happened.

It only took her fifteen hours to get back to my *I had fun last night* text. Which was making me paranoid for a different reason.

I prop myself up on one elbow, feeling a twinge of worry. I don't like the sound of *stuff,* or the fact that Ellery's awake at three a.m. I'm about to message her back when a sound outside my door makes me pause. The light tread of footsteps is almost imperceptible, except for a tiny creak from the loose floorboard in front of my room. But now that my ears are straining, I hear someone going downstairs and opening the front door.

I push my sheets aside, climb out of bed, and cross to my window. The moon's just bright enough that I can make out a figure with a backpack walking quickly down our driveway. Not Peter-sized, and the confident stride doesn't look anything like my mother's. Which leaves Katrin.

Katrin would either have to be so desperate that she lost all sense of right or wrong, or be a cold-blooded criminal. God. Ellery's words are like my brain's very own Fright Farm Demon Rollercoaster, circling in an endless, horrifying loop. And now, watching the figure below me disappear into darkness, all I can think is that it's pretty reckless to wander around Echo Ridge at three in the morning with Brooke still missing.

Unless you know there's nothing to be afraid of.

Unless *you're* what people should be afraid of.

I root around on my floor for sneakers. Holding them in one hand, I grab my phone with the other and slip out my bedroom door into the darkened hallway. I make my way downstairs as silently as I can, although with Peter's loud snoring I probably don't need to bother. When I reach the foyer, I jam my feet into my sneakers and slowly open the front door. I don't see Katrin anywhere, and all I hear are crickets and rustling leaves.

I look both ways when I reach the end of the driveway. There are no streetlights on our stretch of road, and I can't see anything except the shadowy shapes of trees. School is toward the left, and downtown is right. *School,* I think. Where homecoming was last night. I turn left and stay at the edge of the road, walking close to the tall bushes that line our nearest neighbor's property. Our street feeds into a bigger one that's more well lit, and when I turn onto it I can make out Katrin a few blocks ahead of me.

I lift my phone and text Ellery. *I'm following Katrin.*

I don't expect a response, but she answers within seconds. *WHAT???*

Why are you up?

Long story. Why are you following Katrin?

Because she left the house at 3am & I want to know why.

Solid reason. Where's she headed?

Idk. School, maybe?

It's a good twenty-minute walk to Echo Ridge High from our house, even with both Katrin and me moving at a quick pace. My phone vibrates in my hand a couple of times as I walk, but I keep my eyes on Katrin. In the hazy moonlight there's something almost insubstantial about her, like she might disappear if I stop paying attention. I keep thinking about our parents' wedding reception last spring, when my new stepsister wore a brittle smile and a short white dress like some kind of bride in training. While Peter and Mom circled the floor for their first dance, she grabbed a couple of champagne glasses from a passing waiter's tray and handed one to me.

"We're stuck with one another now, aren't we, Mal?" she asked before downing half of hers in one gulp. She clinked her glass against mine. "Might as well get used to it. Cheers."

I liked her better than I thought I would that night. And since. So I would really fucking hate for Ellery to be right about any of this.

Katrin stops a few hundred feet short of Echo Ridge High, at a stone wall that divides the school from neighboring property. The streetlights in front of the school throw off a yellowish glow, enough for me to see her put the backpack down and crouch beside it. I kneel behind a bush, my heart beating uncomfortably fast. While I wait for Katrin to rise again, I look down at the last text I received from Ellery: *What's she up to?*

About to find out. Hang on.

I open my camera and flip it to Video, hit Zoom, and train it on Katrin as she pulls something square and white out of the backpack. She unfolds it like a map and steps toward the stone wall. I watch as she fastens one corner of what she's holding to the top of the wall with duct tape, then repeats the process until a sign with red lettering is prominently displayed.

NOW PLAYING

MURDERLAND, PART 2

TOLD YOU SO

My heart skips a beat and I almost drop my phone. Katrin puts the duct tape back in her backpack and zips it up, then slings it over her shoulder, turning and striding back the way she came. She's wearing a hoodie with her hair tucked up beneath it, but when she passes within a few feet of me I get a clear shot of her face.

When I can't hear her footsteps any longer, I move forward so

I can record the sign up close. The bright-red letters are splashed against the white background, but there's nothing else—no dolls, no pictures, none of the creepy gleefulness of her previous work. I text the video to Ellery and write, *This is what she's up to.* Then I wait, but not for long.

Oh my God.

My fingers feel numb as I type. *You called it.*

We have to give this to the police, Ellery replies. *The receipt, too. I shouldn't have hung on to it for this long.*

My stomach rolls. Jesus, what's my mother going to think? Will part of her be relieved that it takes the focus off Declan and me, or is it just the same shit show, different channel? And Peter—my brain seizes trying to imagine how he'll react to Katrin being mixed up in something like this. Especially if I'm the one bringing it to light.

But I have to. There's too much piling up, and all of it points to my stepsister.

I start walking and texting at the same time. *I know. I'm going to make sure she's headed home & not someplace else. Should we go to the station tomorrow morning?*

I'd rather show Officer Rodriguez first. Do you want to come by my house around six & we can go together?

I blink at the screen. Ellery has spent weeks telling anyone who'd listen—which, granted, is mostly Ezra, Mia, and me—that she thinks Officer Rodriguez is sketchy. Now she wants to go to his house at the crack of dawn, handing over stuff we're not supposed to have? I glance away from my phone and see that I'm gaining a little too quickly on Katrin; if I keep up my pace I'll walk right past her. I slow down and text, *Why him?*

It takes a few minutes for Ellery's message to appear. She's either writing a novel, or taking her time figuring out what to say. When her text finally comes through, it's not what I was expecting.

Let's just say he owes me one.

"So you got this receipt how, again?"

Officer Rodriguez hands me a cup of coffee in his kitchen. Early-morning sun streams through the window over the sink, striping the table with gold. I'm so tired that the effect reminds me of a pillow, and all I want to do is lay my head down and shut my eyes. I left a note for Mom and Peter saying I was going to the gym, which is only slightly more believable than what I'm actually doing.

"The recycling bin was unlocked," Ellery says, twisting a curl around her finger.

"Unlocked?" Officer Rodriguez's eyes are ringed with dark circles. Considering what Ellery told me on the way over about the picture of his father, I doubt he slept much last night either.

"Yeah."

"But everything was still inside?"

She meets his gaze without blinking. "Yeah."

"Okay." He rubs a hand over his face. "Let's go with that. Regardless of whether the bin was locked or unlocked, its contents weren't your property to take."

"I didn't think discarded items were anyone's property," Ellery says. She sounds like she really, really hopes she's right.

Officer Rodriguez leans back in his chair and regards her

258

in silence for a few seconds. He and Ellery don't resemble one another much. But now that I know there's a chance they're related, the stubborn set of their jaws looks exactly the same. "I'm going to treat this as an anonymous tip," he finally says, and Ellery visibly exhales. "I'll look into the car situation. Given Brooke's state of mind when you saw her at Fright Farm, it's an interesting thread to follow."

Ellery crosses her legs and jiggles one foot. She's been full of nervous energy since she got here, constantly shifting and fidgeting. Unlike Officer Rodriguez and me, she seems wide awake. "Are you going to arrest Katrin?"

Officer Rodriguez holds up a palm. "Whoa. Not so fast. There's no evidence that she's committed a crime."

She blinks, startled. "What about the video?"

"It's of interest, sure. But there's no destruction of property involved. Trespassing, maybe. Depends on who owns the wall."

"But what about all the other times?" I ask.

He shrugs. "We don't know she was involved with those. All we know is what you saw this morning."

I grip my mug. The coffee is already cold, but I drink it anyway. "So everything we gave you is useless."

"*Nothing* is useless when someone goes missing," Officer Rodriguez says. "All I'm saying is that it's premature to draw conclusions based on what you've shared. That's my job, okay? Not yours." He leans forward and raps his knuckles on the table for emphasis. "Listen up. I appreciate you guys coming to me, I really do. But you need to stay out of this from now on. Not only for your safety, but because if you *are* circling around someone who played a role in Brooke's disappearance, you don't want to tip them off. Okay?" We both nod, and he crosses his arms. "I'm going to need a verbal confirmation."

"You're better at this than I thought," Ellery says under her breath.

Officer Rodriguez frowns. "What?"

She raises her voice. "I said, okay."

He juts his chin toward me, and I nod. "Yeah, all right."

"And please keep this between us." Officer Rodriguez levels his gaze at Ellery. "I know you're close to your brother, but I'd prefer you not share what we've discussed outside this room."

I doubt she's planning to honor that request, but she nods. "Okay."

Officer Rodriguez glances at the clock on his microwave. It's almost six-thirty. "Does your grandmother know you're here?"

"No," Ellery says. "She doesn't know *anything*." Officer Rodriguez's eyes flick toward me at the emphasis, and I keep my face carefully blank. It's a little surprising, maybe, that nobody in Echo Ridge made the connection between his father and the twins before now. But Mr. Rodriguez was one of those private family guys that nobody saw much of. Even when you did, he didn't resemble the photo Ellery showed me on her phone. He'd been wearing thick glasses as long as I could remember, and had gotten a lot heavier. And balder. Ezra better enjoy his hair while he can.

"You should get home, then. She'll worry if she wakes up and you're not there. You too, Malcolm."

"Okay," Ellery says, but she doesn't move. She jiggles her foot again and adds, "I was wondering something. About you and Lacey."

Officer Rodriguez cocks his head. "What about me and Lacey?"

"I asked you once if you were friends, and you wouldn't answer me."

"I wouldn't?" His mouth twists in a wry smile. "Probably because it's none of your business."

"Did you . . ." She pauses. "Did you ever want to, you know, ask her out or anything?"

He huffs out a small laugh. "Sure. Me and most of the guys in our class. Lacey was beautiful, but . . . she wasn't just that. She cared about people. Even if you were nobody at school, she made you feel like you mattered." His expression darkens. "It still tears me up, what happened to her. I think that's half the reason I became a cop."

Ellery's eyes search his, and whatever she sees there relaxes the tense set of her shoulders. "Are you still looking into her murder?"

Officer Rodriguez shoots her an amused glance as his phone buzzes. "Give it a rest, Ellery. And go home." He glances at the screen, and all the color drains from his face. He pushes his chair back with a loud scrape and gets to his feet.

"What?" Ellery and I ask at the same time.

He reaches for a set of keys on the counter. "Go home," he says again, but this time not like it's a joke. "And stay there."

CHAPTER THIRTY

ELLERY

MONDAY, OCTOBER 7

I'm sitting on Nana's front steps, phone in hand. Malcolm left a few minutes ago, and Officer Rodriguez is long gone. Or maybe I should start calling him Ryan. I don't know the protocol for addressing probable half brothers who, until recently, were on your short list of cold-case murder suspects.

Anyway, I'm alone. Something's obviously going on with *Ryan,* but I have no idea what. All I know is that I'm sick to death of watching lies pile up on top of one another like the world's worst Jenga game. I pull up the photo I snapped of Mr. Rodriguez's army picture, studying the familiar lines of his face. When Ezra noticed the August 2001 date on my timeline I was afraid that maybe—*maybe*—we were dealing with a potential Vance Puckett paternity situation. I never imagined this.

I can't call Sadie. I don't know whose phone she's been using, and anyway, it's the middle of the night in California. Instead, I send the photo to her Gmail with the subject line *We need to talk*. Maybe she'll read her email when she borrows the aide's phone again.

I check the time; it's barely six-thirty. Nana won't be up for another half hour. I'm antsy and don't feel like going back inside, so I head for the woods behind the house instead. Now that pieces are falling into place about Katrin's involvement in Brooke's disappearance, I'm not scared about walking through the woods on my own. I follow the familiar path to Fright Farm, trying to empty my brain of thought and just enjoy the crisp fall air.

I emerge from the woods across the street from Fright Farm, and pause. I'd never noticed how different the gaping mouth of the entrance looks when the park is closed: less kitschy and more forbidding. I suck in a breath and let it out, then cross the deserted street, my eyes on the still, silent Ferris wheel cutting into the pale-blue sky.

When I reach the entrance, I put my hand on the mottled paint of the wooden mouth, trying to imagine what Lacey was feeling when she snuck into the park after hours five years ago. Was she excited? Upset? Scared? And who was she with, or who was she meeting? Without Daisy or Ryan on my list of suspects, it's back to who it's always been—Declan Kelly. Unless I'm missing someone.

"Do you have a reason for being here?"

The voice sends my heart into my throat. I whirl around to see an older man in a police uniform, one hand on the radio at his hip. It takes me a few seconds to recognize him—Officer

McNulty, the one who's been interrogating Malcolm all week. Liz and Kyle's father. He and Kyle look alike, both tall and broad with light hair, square jaws, and eyes that are just a little too close together. "I . . . was, um, taking a walk." An unexpected rush of nerves makes my voice wobble.

I don't know why I'm spooked, suddenly, by a middle-aged police officer. Maybe it's those flat, blue-gray eyes that remind me too much of his asshole son's. There's something cold and almost methodical about how thoroughly Kyle hates Malcolm. It was a stroke of good luck that we didn't run into him at homecoming the other night.

Officer McNulty eyes me carefully. "We don't recommend kids walking alone in town just now." He rubs his chin and squints. "Does your grandmother know you're here?"

"Yeah," I lie, wiping my damp palms on my pants. His radio crackles with static, and I think of how Ryan rushed out of his house this morning. I flop a hand toward the radio. "Is, um, something going on? With Brooke, or . . ."

I trail off as Officer McNulty's face hardens. "Excuse me?" he asks tersely.

"Sorry." Five weeks of Ryan's superhuman patience made me forget that most cops don't like getting pestered with questions from teenagers. "I'm just worried."

"Worry at home," he says, in the most *conversation-closed* voice I've ever heard.

I take the hint and mumble a good-bye, hightailing it across the street and back into the woods. I've never appreciated Ryan more—or at all, I guess, if I'm being truthful—and I feel sorry for Malcolm having to answer Officer McNulty's questions day after day.

The damp of the early-morning dew is seeping through my sneakers as the leaves on the ground get thicker. The discomfort increases my annoyance with Officer McNulty. No wonder his kids are sour enough to hold a five-years-long grudge about a bad breakup. I realize I don't know the whole story, and maybe Declan was a jerk to Liz. But she should leave Malcolm out of it, and Kyle should just mind his own business entirely. He's obviously not the kind of guy who knows how to let things go. He'd probably even hate Lacey if she were still around, for being the girl Declan chose over his sister. And Brooke for breaking up with him, and . . .

I slow down as it hits me, and blood rushes to my head so quickly that I grab a nearby branch for support. It never occurred to me, until right now, that the only person in Echo Ridge with a grudge against every single person involved in Lacey's death, and Brooke's disappearance, is Kyle McNulty.

But that doesn't make sense. Kyle was only twelve when Lacey died. And he has an alibi for the night Brooke disappeared: he was out of town with Liz.

The sister Declan had dumped for Lacey.

My heart squeezes in my chest as I start connecting dots. I've always thought that Lacey died because of *someone's* jealous passion. I just never considered that person might be Liz McNulty. Declan broke up with Liz, and Lacey died. Five years later, Brooke breaks up with Kyle, who's friends with Katrin, and . . . *God.* What if they teamed up to take care of a mutual problem?

I barely register that I'm in Nana's backyard as I yank my phone out of my pocket with shaking hands. Ryan gave me his phone number yesterday, after the photo fiasco in his house.

I need to call him, right now. Then movement catches my eye, and I see Nana racing toward me in her plaid bathrobe and slippers, her gray hair wild. "Hi, Nana—" I start, but she doesn't let me finish.

"What in God's name are you doing out here?" she shouts, her face stricken. "Your bed wasn't slept in last night! Your brother had no idea where you were! I thought you had *disappeared*." Her voice cracks on the last word, sending a stab of guilt through me. I hadn't even considered that she might wake up and find me gone—and what that would be like for her.

She's still barreling my way, and then suddenly she's hugging me for the first time ever. Very tightly, and somewhat painfully.

"I'm sorry," I manage. It's a little hard to breathe.

"What were you thinking? How could you? I was about to call the police!"

"Nana, I can't . . . you're kind of crushing me."

She drops her arms, and I almost stumble. "Don't you *ever* do that again. I was worried sick. Especially . . ." She swallows visibly. "Especially now."

The back of my neck prickles. "Why now?"

"Come inside and I'll tell you." She turns and waits for me to follow, but I'm rooted to the spot. For the first time since I've been outside all morning, I realize my hands are numb with cold. I pull the sleeves of my sweater over them and wrap my arms around my body.

"Just tell me now. Please."

Nana's eyes are red around the rims. "There's a rumor going around that the police found a body in the woods near the Canadian border. And that it's Brooke's."

CHAPTER THIRTY-ONE

MALCOLM
MONDAY, OCTOBER 7

Somehow, we're supposed to still go to school.

"There's nothing you can do," Mom keeps repeating on Monday morning. She puts an overfull bowl of Cheerios in front of me on the kitchen island, even though I never eat cereal. "Nothing is confirmed about Brooke. We have to think positive and act normally."

The message might go over better if she didn't pour coffee into my Cheerios while she's saying it. She doesn't notice, and when she turns I grab milk off the island and top off the bowl. It's not the worst thing I've ever eaten. Plus I got back from Officer Rodriguez's an hour ago and didn't bother trying to sleep. I could use the caffeine.

"I'm not going," Katrin says flatly.

Mom eyes her nervously. Peter's gone, already left for work, and she's never been good at standing up to Katrin. "Your father would—"

"Understand," Katrin says in the same monotone. She's in the hoodie and athletic pants she wore last night, her hair pulled back into a low, messy ponytail. There's a plate of strawberries in front of her, and she keeps cutting one into smaller and smaller pieces without putting any of it into her mouth. "Anyway, I'm sick. I threw up this morning."

"Oh, well, if you're *sick.*" My mother looks relieved at the excuse, and turns toward me with more confidence. "You, on the other hand, need to go."

"Fine by me." I'm good with being anywhere Katrin's not. If she hadn't played sick, I would have. There's no way I can sit in a car with her this morning. Especially not *her* car. More and more, it's sinking in that if Katrin did half the things we think she might have, chances are good she ran down Mr. Bowman and left him to die in the street. And that's just for starters. I grip my cereal spoon more tightly as I watch her methodically start cutting up a second strawberry, and it's all I can do not to reach out and smash everything on her plate into a pulp.

All this waiting is a nightmare. Especially when you know you're going to hate whatever answer comes.

Mom smooths a hand over her bathrobe. "I'm going to take a shower, unless either of you need anything?"

"Can I take your car?" I ask.

She smiles distractedly on her way to the stairs. "Yes, of course." And then she's gone, leaving Katrin and me alone in the kitchen. There's no sound except the clink of my spoon against the bowl and the loud ticking of the wall clock.

I can't handle it for even five minutes. "I'm leaving early," I say, getting up and dumping my half-finished coffee cereal in the garbage disposal. When I turn, Katrin is staring straight at me, and I'm struck silent by the cold blankness in her eyes.

"Why don't you just walk to school?" she asks. "You like walking, don't you?"

Fuck. She knows I followed her last night. I got too close on the way home.

"Who doesn't," I say tersely. I reach for Mom's keys on the kitchen island, but before I can pick them up Katrin lays a hand over them. She regards me with the same cool stare.

"You're not as smart as you think you are."

"And you're not sick." *To your stomach, anyway.* I pull the keys from beneath her hand and grab my backpack off the floor. I don't want her to see how rattled I am, so I look away, even though I'd like one last chance to read her expression.

What do you know? What did you do?

I drive to school in a haze, almost missing the entrance. It's so early that I have my pick of spots in the parking lot. I cut the engine but keep the radio on, searching for a news station. NPR is talking politics and all the local shows are breaking down the Patriots' come-from-behind win yesterday, so I pull out my phone and search the *Burlington Free Press* site. There's a blurb at the bottom of the Metro section: *Police investigate human remains found on an abandoned property in upper Huntsburg.*

Human remains. My stomach turns, and for a second I'm positive I'll puke up every single coffee-soaked Cheerio that I was stupid enough to eat this morning. But it passes, and I recline my seat and close my eyes. I just want to rest for a few minutes, but the lack of sleep catches up with me and I'm dozing when a loud rap on my window startles me awake. I look groggily at the car clock—it's two minutes past the final bell—then out the window.

Kyle and Theo are standing there, and they don't look like they're about to give me a friendly warning about being late. Viv is a few yards behind them, her arms crossed, a look of smug anticipation on her face. Like a kid at a birthday party who's about to get that pony she's always wanted.

I could drive away, I guess, but I don't want to give them the satisfaction of chasing me off. So I get out of the car.

"You're gonna be la—" is all I get out before Kyle drives his fist into my stomach. I fold in half, and my vision goes white from the pain. He follows up with another punch, to my jaw, that sends me reeling against the car. My mouth fills with the coppery taste of blood as Kyle leans forward, his face inches from mine.

"You're going down for this, Kelly," he spits, and pulls back for another punch.

Somehow I manage to duck and land a blow to Kyle's face before Theo steps in and pins my arms behind my back. I stomp on Theo's foot, but I'm off balance and he only lets out a slight grunt before tightening his grip. Sharp pain shoots through my ribs, and the entire left side of my face feels like it's on fire. Kyle wipes a trickle of blood from his mouth with a grim smile. "I should have done this years ago," he says, and hauls his fist back for a punch that'll break my face.

It doesn't come, though. A bigger fist closes over his and yanks him backward. For a few seconds I don't know what the hell is going on, until Declan steps forward and looms over

Theo. "Let him go," he says in a low, threatening tone. When Theo doesn't, Declan wrenches one of his arms so hard that Theo squeals in pain and backs off, hands up. Once I'm released I see Kyle sprawled on the ground a few feet away, motionless.

"Is he gonna get up?" I ask, rubbing my aching jaw.

"Eventually," Declan says. Theo doesn't even check on Kyle, just sprints past him on his way to the back entrance. Viv is nowhere in sight. "Fucking cowards, going two on one." Declan reaches for the Volvo's door and pulls it open. "Come on, let's get out of here. No point in you going to school today. I'll drive."

I slump in the passenger seat, nauseated and dizzy. I haven't been punched since ninth grade, and it wasn't anywhere near that hard. "Why are you here?" I ask.

Declan turns the keys I left in the ignition. "I was waiting for you."

"Why?"

His jaw sets in a hard line. "I remember the first day of school after . . . news like this."

I suck in a breath and wince. I wonder if my ribs are cracked. "What, you knew something like this was gonna happen?"

"It happened to me," he says.

"I didn't know that." I didn't know much back then, I guess. Too busy trying to pretend none of it was going on.

We drive in silence for a minute until we near a corner store, and Declan suddenly swerves into the parking lot. "Hang on a sec," he says, before shifting into park and disappearing inside. When he comes out a couple of minutes later, he's holding something square and white in one hand. He tosses it to me as he opens the door. "Put those on your face."

271

Frozen peas. I do as he says, almost groaning in relief as the cool seeps into my burning skin. "Thanks. For these and . . . you know. Saving my ass."

Out of the corner of my eye, I see him shake his head. "Can't believe you got out of the car. Amateur."

I'd laugh, but it hurts too much. I sit still, with the peas on my face as we leave Echo Ridge for Solsbury, tracing the path I took to his apartment last week. Declan must be thinking the same thing, because he says, "You're a little bitch for following Daisy." He looks like he's seriously considering turning the car around and leaving me in the parking lot with Kyle.

"I tried asking you what you were doing in town," I remind him. "Didn't work." He doesn't answer, just sort of grunts, which I decide means *point taken.* "When did you move here?"

"Last month," he says. "Daisy needs to be around her parents. And me. So . . . here I am."

"You could've told me about her, you know."

Declan snorts. "Really, little brother?" He turns into Pine Crest Estates and pulls into the parking spot in front of number 9. "You couldn't wait to get me out of Echo Ridge. The last thing you'd want to hear is that I'd moved one town over. No, wait, that's the second-last. The *last* thing is me being with Lacey's best friend. I mean, hell, what would the Nilssons say, right?"

"I hate the Nilssons." It slips out without thinking.

Declan raises his brows as he opens his door. "Trouble in paradise?"

I hesitate, trying to figure out how to explain, when my stomach seizes. I barely make it out of the car before I bend in half and vomit my breakfast all over the asphalt. Thank God it's quick, because the movement makes my ribs feel like someone

272

just ripped them out. My eyes water as I clutch the side of the car for support, gasping.

"Delayed reaction," Declan says, reaching into the car for the discarded peas. "Happens sometimes." He lets me limp to the apartment on my own, unlocks the door, and points me toward the couch. "Lie down. I'll find an ice pack for your hand."

Declan's apartment is the most cliché bachelor pad ever. There's nothing in it except a couch and two armchairs, a giant television, and a bunch of milk crates for shelves. The couch is comfortable, though, and I sink into it while Declan roots around in his freezer. Something plastic digs into my back, and I pull out a remote. I aim it at the television and press the power button. A golf green with the ESPN logo in one corner fills the screen, and I click away, scrolling mindlessly through channels until the word *Huntsburg* catches my eye. I stop surfing as a man in a police uniform standing in front of a lectern says, ". . . have been able to make a positive identification."

"Declan." My throat hurts and my voice cracks, but when he doesn't answer, I rasp louder. *"Declan."*

His head emerges from the kitchen. "What? I can't find the—" He stops at the sight of my face, and comes into the living room just as the officer on-screen takes a deep breath.

"The body is that of a young woman who's been missing from Echo Ridge since last Saturday: seventeen-year-old Brooke Bennett. The Huntsburg police department would like to extend our condolences to Miss Bennett's family and friends, and our support to her hometown police department. At this time, the investigation into cause of death is ongoing and no further details will be released."

CHAPTER THIRTY-TWO

ELLERY
MONDAY, OCTOBER 7

I know the script. I've read it in countless books, and seen it play out dozens of times on television. All week, in the back of my mind, I knew how it would probably end.

What I didn't understand was how mind-numbingly awful it would feel.

At least I'm not alone. Ezra and Malcolm are in the living room with me Monday afternoon, six hours after the Huntsburg police found Brooke. None of us went to school today, although Malcolm's day was more eventful than ours. He showed up an hour ago, bruised and battered, and Nana has been handing him fresh ice packs every fifteen minutes.

We're arranged stiffly on her uncomfortable furniture, watching Channel 5 news coverage scroll across the screen. Meli Dinglasa is standing on Echo Ridge Common, her dark hair whipping across her face as the leafy branches behind her sway in the wind.

She's been talking nonstop since we turned the TV on, but only a few phrases sink in: . . . *dead for more than a week . . . foul play suspected but not confirmed . . . yet another taunting message found this morning near Echo Ridge High School . . .*

"Great timing, Katrin," Ezra mutters.

Malcolm's sitting next to me on the couch. One side of his jaw is bruised and swollen, the knuckles on his right hand are scraped raw, and he winces every time he moves. "Someone needs to pay this time," he says in a low, angry voice. I reach for his uninjured hand. His skin is warm, and his fingers wrap around mine without hesitation. For a couple of seconds I feel better, until I remember that Brooke is dead and everything is horrible.

Every time I close my eyes, I see her. Working the shooting range at Fright Farm, trying to stand up to Vance. Wandering the halls at Echo Ridge High looking sad and worried. Swaying and rambling her way out of the Fright Farm office on the night she disappeared. I should have pushed her harder to tell us what was wrong. I had a chance to change the course of that night, and I blew it.

When my phone rings with the familiar California number, I almost don't answer it. Then I figure, what the hell. The day can't possibly get any worse.

"Hi, Sadie," I say tonelessly.

"Oh, Ellery. I saw the news. I'm so, so sorry about your friend. And I saw—" She pauses, her voice wavering. "I saw your email. I wasn't sure what I was looking at until I zoomed in on the uniform and saw . . . his name."

"Did you think it was Ezra at first? Because I sure did." I'm surprised to find that beneath the heavy misery of Brooke's death, I can still manage to spare an undercurrent of anger for my mother. "How could you not tell us? How could you let us live a lie for seventeen years and think our father was *José the freaking stuntman*?" I don't bother keeping my voice down. It's not like anyone in the room doesn't know what's going on.

"It wasn't a total lie," Sadie says. "I wasn't *sure,* Ellery. The stuntman happened. And, well . . . Gabriel Rodriguez also happened, a little while afterward." Her voice drops. "Sleeping with a married man was a huge mistake. I never should have gone there."

"Yeah, well, he shouldn't have either." I don't have any empathy to spare for the man in that photograph. He doesn't feel like my father. He doesn't feel like anything. Besides, keeping the marital vows was *his* job. "But why did you?"

"I wasn't thinking straight. My father was gone, memories of Sarah were everywhere, and I just— I made a bad choice. Then the timing of the pregnancy fit better with the, um . . . other situation, and I wanted that to be true, and so . . . I convinced myself that it was."

"How?" I look at Ezra, who's staring at the floor with no indication that he's hearing any of this. "How did you convince yourself of that when—what was his name again? *Gabriel?*— looked exactly like Ezra?"

"I didn't remember what he looked like," Sadie says, and I snort out a disbelieving laugh. "I'm not kidding. I told you before, I drank my way through the entire funeral."

"Okay. But you remembered enough that you knew he was

a possibility, right? That's why you were so shifty the first time I mentioned Officer Rodriguez."

"I— Well, yes. It rattled me," she admits.

"So you lied to cover it up. You made up a story about Officer Rodriguez at Lacey's funeral, and you made me suspicious of him."

"What?" Sadie sounds bewildered. "Why would that make you suspicious of him? Suspicious about what?"

"That's not the point!" I snap. "The point is it *did*, and then I didn't ask him for help when I could have, and now Brooke is dead and maybe—" I stop, all the anger suddenly drained out of me, remembering how I hadn't told anyone what we'd found in the Fright Farm recycling bin for an entire weekend. Keeping secrets that weren't mine to hold. Like mother, like daughter. "Maybe I made everything worse."

"Made what worse? Ellery, I'm sure you didn't do anything wrong. You can't blame yourself for—"

"Ellery." Nana sticks her head into the living room. "Officer Rodriguez is here. He says you called him?" Her eyes fasten on the phone at my ear. "Who are you talking to?"

"Just someone from school," I answer Nana, then turn back to the phone. "I have to go," I tell Sadie, but before I can disconnect, Ezra extends his hand.

"Let me talk," he says, and his voice holds the same dull fury that mine did. It takes a lot to make the two of us mad, especially at Sadie. But she managed.

I hand Ezra the phone and tug Malcolm to his feet. We head for the hallway as Nana returns to the kitchen. Ryan is standing in front of the front door, his face sad and haggard. I don't know how I ever thought he looked young for his age. "Hey, guys," he says. "I was just heading home when I got your message. What's so urgent?" He catches sight of Malcolm's swollen jaw, and his eyes widen. "What happened to you?"

"Kyle McNulty," Malcolm says shortly.

"You want to press charges?" Ryan asks.

Malcolm grimaces. "No."

"Maybe you can convince him to change his mind," I say. "In the meantime, I have this kind of . . . theory about Kyle. That's why I called you." I lick my lips, trying to get my thoughts in order. "I ran into Officer McNulty this morning, and—"

Ryan frowns. "Where did you run into Officer McNulty?"

I wave my hand dismissively. "That part's not important." I don't want to get sidetracked with a lecture about not going home when Ryan told me to. "But it got me thinking about Kyle, and how connected he is to everything that's been happening around here. Declan broke up with his sister, Liz, and that was a whole big thing while you guys were in school, right?" Ryan nods warily, like he has no idea where I'm headed and isn't sure he wants to find out. Malcolm looks the same. I haven't shared any of this with him yet. I wasn't sure I'd have the energy to do it more than once.

"Then Lacey dies and Declan's basically run out of town," I continue. "And now, five years later, Brooke breaks up with Kyle. And Brooke disappears. And Kyle and Katrin are friends, and we already know Katrin is involved in the homecoming threats, so . . ." I steal a glance at Ryan to see how he's taking all this. He doesn't look as impressed as I'd hoped. "Basically, I think they're all in it together. Liz, Kyle, and Katrin."

"That's your new theory?" Ryan asks. I don't appreciate the somewhat sardonic emphasis he puts on the word *new*. Malcolm just sags against the wall, like he's too exhausted to get into any of this right now.

"Yes," I say.

Ryan folds his arms. "It doesn't concern you that Liz and Kyle have alibis?"

"They're each other's alibi!" I say. It only makes me more sure I'm on to something.

"So you think . . . what? We just took their word for it?"

"Well. No." A trickle of doubt seeps in. "Did somebody else see them?"

Ryan rakes a hand through his hair. "I shouldn't tell you this, it's not your business. But maybe it'll get you to stop trying to do my job and trust me. For once." He lowers his voice. "An entire *fraternity* saw them. There are pictures. And video. Time-stamped and posted on social media."

"Oh," I say in a small voice, embarrassment warming my cheeks.

He makes a frustrated noise in his throat. "Will you knock it off now? Please? I appreciate you coming to me this morning, but like I told you, at this point, you're more likely to hurt the investigation than help if you keep talking about it. In fact . . ." He shoves his hands into his pockets and slides his eyes toward Malcolm. "I was just telling your mother, Malcolm, that it might not be a bad idea to stay with friends for a day or two."

Malcolm goes stiff. "Why? Is something happening with Katrin? Was it the video, or—"

"I'm not talking about anything specific. But tensions are

running high, and I . . ." Ryan pauses, like he's searching for exactly the right words. "I wouldn't want you to accidentally say something to her that could . . . interfere."

"Interfere how?" Malcolm asks.

"It's just a suggestion. Tell your mother to consider it, all right?"

"Should I be worried about Katrin?" Malcolm asks. "Doing something, I mean?" Ryan doesn't answer, and Malcolm glowers. "It's bullshit that she's just walking around like nothing happened. You have proof she's shady and you're not doing anything with it."

"You have no idea what we're doing." Ryan's face doesn't change, but his tone gets steely. "I'm asking you to lie low. That's it. All right?" We nod, and he clears his throat. "How is, ah, everything else, Ellery? With your mom and . . . you know?"

"Horrible," I say. "But who really cares, right?"

He heaves a sigh that sounds as bone-deep exhausted as I feel. "Right."

CHAPTER THIRTY-THREE

MALCOLM
THURSDAY, OCTOBER 10

Turns out I didn't need to leave the house. Katrin did.

Her aunt swooped in two days after Brooke's body was found. She wanted to take Katrin to New York, but the Echo Ridge police asked her not to leave the state while the investigation is pending. So they're at some five-star hotel in Topnotch, instead. Which pisses me off every time I think about it. Of all the possible scenarios I thought might happen once I turned over that video of Katrin, her taking a spa vacation wasn't one of them.

"So much for keeping the key witnesses nearby," Declan snorts when I tell him. "We were all told we had to stay in Echo Ridge after Lacey died. Money talks, I guess."

I'm at his apartment, having dinner with him and Daisy. It's weird for a few reasons. One, I've never seen my brother cook before. Two, he's surprisingly good at it. And three, I can't get used to seeing him with Daisy. My brain keeps wanting to replace her with Lacey, and it's kind of unnerving.

He doesn't know about the car repair receipt, or the video I took of Katrin. I'm keeping my promise to Officer Rodriguez to stay quiet. It's not hard with Declan. We might be getting along better than usual, but he still talks a lot more than he listens.

"Peter didn't want her to go," I say, shifting in my chair and wincing at the pain in my ribs. Turns out they're only bruised, not cracked, but they still hurt like hell. "Katrin's aunt insisted."

"Getting away isn't a bad idea, though," Daisy says. She and Declan are washing dishes while I sit at the kitchen table, and she keeps brushing against him even though there's plenty of room for two in front of the double sink. "It's so horrible, those first few days after. All you can think about is what you could have done differently. At least a new environment is a distraction." She sighs and flips the towel she's holding over her shoulder, leaning into Declan. "I feel for Katrin, honestly. This brings back such awful memories of Lacey."

Declan kisses the top of her head, and the next thing I know they're whispering, nuzzling, and about ten seconds away from a full-on make-out session. It's uncomfortable, not to mention crap timing after what we've just been talking about. I realize they've been suppressing their big forbidden love for years, but I could've used another half hour. Minimum.

When the doorbell rings, I'm relieved at the interruption. "I'll get it," I volunteer, springing up as fast as my bruised ribs will let me.

Too fast, as it turns out. Even though Declan's front door is only steps away from the kitchen, I'm still wincing when I open it. Officer Ryan Rodriguez is standing on Declan's stoop, wearing his full police uniform. He blinks in surprise when he sees me. "Oh, hey, Malcolm. I wasn't expecting to see you here."

"Um. Same," I say. "Are you . . ." I try to think of a reason why he might be here, and can't come up with one. "What's up?"

"Is your brother around?"

"Yeah, come on in," I say, and he steps through the door.

Declan and Daisy have managed to separate by the time we enter the kitchen. "Hey, Declan," Officer Rodriguez says, folding his arms in front of him like a shield. I know that stance; it's the one I get around Kyle McNulty. I don't remember much about Ryan from when he was in high school, since he and Declan didn't hang out, but I do know this: if you weren't part of Declan's crew, chances are he would've treated you like shit at some point. Not slamming you into lockers, necessarily, but acting like your existence annoyed him. Or pretending you didn't exist at all.

"And . . . Daisy," Officer Rodriguez adds.

Crap. I swallow nervously and look at Declan. I forgot nobody's supposed to know those two are together. My brother doesn't acknowledge me, but I can see the muscles in his jaw tighten as he steps slightly in front of Daisy.

At least they aren't shoving their tongues down one another's throats anymore.

"Ryan, hi!" Daisy says, with the kind of forced cheerfulness I've noticed she uses whenever she's stressed. Unlike Mia, who just glares extra hard. "Nice to see you again."

Declan, on the other hand, cuts to the chase. "What are you doing here?"

Officer Rodriguez clears his throat. "I have a few questions for you."

Everybody goes still. We've heard that before.

"Sure," Declan says, a little too casually. We're all still standing in his cramped little kitchen, and he gestures to the table. "Have a seat."

Officer Rodriguez hesitates, his eyes flicking toward me. "I could, or . . . do you want to step outside for a minute? Not sure if you want Daisy and your brother here, or—" He rocks back and forth on his heels, and suddenly I can see all the nervous bumbling Ellery was talking about. It's like the guy is regressing by the minute in Declan's and Daisy's presence.

"No," Declan says shortly. "This is fine."

Officer Rodriguez shrugs and lowers himself into the nearest chair, folding his hands on the table while he waits for Declan to sit across from him. Daisy drops beside Declan, and since I can't think of anything else to do and nobody's asked me to leave, I take the last chair. Once we're all seated, Officer Rodriguez focuses his gaze on Declan and says, "Could you tell me your whereabouts the Saturday before last? September twenty-eighth?"

I feel almost exactly like I did the morning that Brooke disappeared, when I realized I'd have to tell Officer McNulty that I was the last person to see her. *This can't be happening.*

Shit. Shit. Shit.

Declan doesn't answer right away, and Officer Rodriguez clarifies, "The night Brooke Bennett disappeared."

Panic starts worming its way into my chest as Declan's voice rises. "Are you fucking kidding me?" he asks. Daisy puts a hand on his arm.

284

Officer Rodriguez's voice is mild, but firm. "No. I am not kidding you."

"You want to know where I was the night a girl disappeared. Why?"

"Are you refusing to answer the question?"

"*Should* I?"

"He was with me," Daisy says quickly.

I study her, trying to get a read on whether she's telling the truth. Her pretty face is suddenly all hard lines and angles, so maybe she's lying. Or maybe she's just scared.

Some emotion flits across Officer Rodriguez's face, but it's gone before I can figure out what it is. "Okay. And may I ask where you two were?"

"No," Declan says, at the same time Daisy replies, "Here."

I still can't tell if she's lying.

It goes on like that for a few minutes. Daisy smiles like her teeth hurt the whole time. A dull red flush creeps up Declan's neck, but Officer Rodriguez seems to be getting progressively at ease.

"All right," he says finally. "If I could switch gears for a minute. Have you ever been to Huntsburg?"

Daisy's eyes widen as Declan goes rigid. "Huntsburg," he repeats. This time he doesn't state the obvious: *You're asking me if I've ever been to the town where Brooke's body was discovered?*

"Right," Officer Rodriguez says.

"No," Declan growls.

"Never?"

"Never."

"Okay. One last thing." Officer Rodriguez digs into his pocket and pulls out something in a sealed plastic bag that glints under the cheap track lighting in Declan's kitchen. "This was found in Huntsburg, in the same general area as Brooke's body. Does it look familiar to you?"

My blood turns to ice. It does to me.

The ring is big and gold with the words "Echo Ridge High" etched around a square purple stone. The number 13 is on one side, and the initials "DK" on another. Declan's class ring, although he never wore it. He gave it to Lacey junior year, and she kept it on a chain around her neck. I haven't seen it in years. Not since before she died.

It never occurred to me, until just now, to wonder where it went.

Daisy pales. Declan pushes back from the table, his face expressionless. "I think we're done talking," he says.

It's not enough to make an arrest, I guess, because Officer Rodriguez leaves after Declan stops answering his questions. Then Declan, Daisy, and I sit silently in the kitchen for the longest minute of my life. My thoughts blur together, and I can't look at either of them.

When Declan finally speaks up, his voice is stilted. "I haven't seen that ring since before Lacey died. We argued about it. We'd been fighting all week. All I wanted to do was break things off, but . . . I didn't have the guts to come right out and say it. So I asked her for my ring back. She wouldn't give it to me. That was the last time I ever saw it. Or her." His hands are clenched into tight fists. "I have no clue how it ended up in Huntsburg."

Daisy's chair is angled toward him. Her hand is on his arm again. "I know," she murmurs.

Damn it all to hell, I *still* can't tell if she's lying. I can't tell if anyone's lying.

Declan hasn't ever told that story before. Maybe he didn't remember the ring till just now, either. Maybe he didn't want to remind anyone of how much he and Lacey had been fighting before she died.

Or maybe it didn't happen.

It's been creeping up on me for weeks now how little I know my brother. When I was really young he was like a superhero to me. Later, he was more like a bully. After Lacey died, he turned into a ghost. He's helped me out since Brooke's body was discovered—but until then, all he'd done was lie and sneak around.

And now I can't shut off that corner of my brain that keeps asking, *What if?*

"Fuck you, Mal." Declan's voice makes me jump. His neck is still brick red, his expression thunderous. "You think I can't tell what's running through your head right now? It's written all over your face. You think I did it, don't you? You always have." I open my mouth to protest, but no words come. His face darkens even further. "Get the hell out of here. Just leave."

So I do. Because the answer isn't *yes*, but it's not *no*, either.

CHAPTER THIRTY-FOUR

ELLERY

"But none of it makes any sense."

I'm at Malcolm's house, curled up on his couch like on homecoming night. He has the *Defender* movie on again, but neither of us are watching it. He texted me half an hour ago: *I need your true-crime brain.*

I'm not sure why he trusts me after my Kyle-Liz theory imploded so spectacularly. But here I am. I don't think I'm helping, though. Declan being Lacey's killer has always made sense to me. But being Brooke's? Never even crossed my mind.

"What connection is there between Declan and Brooke?" I ask.

Malcolm's eyes flash. "None that I know of. Except that he was in town the night she disappeared. If the police had ever looked at my phone, they'd have seen his text." He takes out his phone and unlocks it, then swipes for a minute. He holds the phone out to me and I'm looking at a message. *In town for a few hours. Don't freak out.*

I read it twice, and when I look back up at Malcolm, his face is the picture of misery. "I thought that . . . I was trying to help Declan out by not, you know. Telling the police," he says haltingly. "I thought it was just bad timing. But what if . . . Christ, Ellery." He slumps back against the couch, rubbing a hand so hard across his bruised face that it has to hurt. "What if it was more than that?"

I study Declan's text again, wondering why I don't find it more disturbing. After all, I've had him at the top of my suspect list for weeks, and this puts him at the scene of the crime. Problem is, it's not the *right* crime. "Okay, but . . . Declan was in the process of moving then, right? Or he had moved? So he had a perfectly good reason for being here," I say, handing the phone back to Malcolm. "And why would he send you that text if he was planning something? You'd think he'd be more subtle."

"Subtle isn't how Declan rolls. I get what you're saying, though." Malcolm brightens a little, then jiggles his phone as though he's weighing it. "I should let my mother know what's up. But she's having dinner with a friend, and she's hardly done that kind of thing since she and Peter got married. I feel like I should let her have a few hours of peace before everything goes to hell again."

I think back to my one lunch at Echo Ridge High with Brooke, when she'd said that Malcolm was cute but couldn't compare to Declan. "Do you think— Could Declan and Brooke have been secretly dating or something?"

"What, while he was *also* secretly dating Daisy?"

"I'm just trying to figure out how the ring could've gotten there. Would he have given it to Brooke?"

Malcolm's voice is ragged. "Maybe? I mean, you'd think somebody would've noticed him sneaking around with a high school girl, but maybe not." He runs a hand through his hair. "I shouldn't have left Declan's place. Me and him—I don't know. It's always been complicated. We're not close. Sometimes I've almost hated him. But he's not a . . . serial killer." He almost chokes on the words.

"Do you think Daisy knows more than she's saying?"

"Do *you*?" Malcolm asks.

I'd had Daisy in mind as a potential accomplice right up to the day she clocked Mia in the head with a candlestick, then spilled her guts after. She'd seemed so sincere and heartbroken that I couldn't picture it anymore. "No," I say slowly. "I mean, why would she go through the trouble of looking for Lacey's bracelet if she were? The case was ice cold at that point. If she were involved, the last thing she'd want to do is get the police thinking about it again. And Declan helped her, didn't he? Although . . . well, I guess he's not the one who gave the bracelet to Lacey, right? Daisy said as much. So maybe he figured it didn't matter."

Malcolm rubs his temple and sighs, deep and weary. "I want to believe him. So much."

I'm a little surprised to realize that I do too. "I have to say . . . look, I guess you know I've always had questions about your brother." I rest my chin in my hand, thinking. "But a dropped ring at a murder site is a little too convenient, isn't it? And none of it fits with Katrin's anonymous messages, or what we think might've happened with Brooke and her car."

"Too many puzzle pieces," Malcolm says moodily.

We lapse into silence for a few minutes, watching *The Defender* until a light knock on the doorframe startles us both. It's Peter Nilsson, looking casually handsome in a polo shirt and khakis. He has a crystal tumbler in one hand, filled with ice and amber liquid. "You two all right? Need anything?"

Malcolm is silent, so I speak up. "No, thank you. We're fine." Mr. Nilsson doesn't leave immediately, so I feel like I should make more conversation. Plus, I'm curious. "How is Katrin doing, Mr. Nilsson? We miss her at school."

"Ah. Well." He leans against the door with a sigh. "She's devastated, of course. It's good for her to have some time away with her aunt."

"Is that her mother's sister, or yours?" I ask.

"Mine," Peter says. "Eleanor and her husband live in Brooklyn. We don't see them as often as we'd like, but she and Katrin had a nice visit last month."

Malcolm stirs beside me on the couch. "They did?"

"Sure. Katrin went to New York, did some shopping." Peter's brow creases slightly. "That was my interpretation, anyway, by the number of bags she brought home."

"I don't remember that," Malcolm says.

"You and your mother were on vacation," Peter says. "It was a last-minute thing. Eleanor's husband was out of town for business so she flew Katrin down for the weekend. Although she almost didn't make it. That was the night of that hailstorm, remember? The plane was delayed for hours." He chuckles and sips his drink. "Katrin kept texting me complaints from the run-way. She has no patience."

I'm sitting close enough to Malcolm that our arms are brushing, and I can feel him tense at the same time I do. My entire body goes numb and my pulse starts to race, but I manage to speak. "Oh, that's so frustrating. I'm glad she made it there eventually."

Mr. Nilsson's eyes wander to the screen. "*The Defender,* huh? That's your mother's movie, isn't it?"

"Yeah. She only had one line, though." I don't know how I'm still talking normally when a million thoughts are zipping through my head. "'That does not compute.'"

"At least it's a memorable one. Well, I won't keep you from it. You sure I can't get you anything?"

Malcolm mutely shakes his head, and Mr. Nilsson turns and retreats back into the dark hallway. We sit in silence, my heart hammering so loudly that I can hear it in my ears. I'm sure Malcolm's is doing the same. "Fuck," he finally breathes.

I keep my voice to the lowest whisper possible. "Katrin wasn't here on Labor Day weekend. You and your mom weren't here. There's only one person in your house who could've driven Katrin's car that night."

"Fuck," Malcolm says again. "But he—he wasn't here either. He was in Burlington."

"Are you sure?"

Malcolm gets to his feet wordlessly and motions for me to follow. He leads me upstairs to his bedroom and shuts the door behind us, then pulls his phone out of his pocket. "He said he had dinner with a guy who used to live here. Mr. Coates. He was my Scout troop leader. I've got his number in here somewhere." He scrolls for a few minutes and presses the screen. I'm standing close enough to him that I can hear a faint ringing sound, then a man's voice. "Hey, Mr. Coates. This is, um, Malcolm Kelly." He laughs self-consciously. "Sorry about the blast from the past, but I had a question for you."

I can't hear what Mr. Coates is saying, but his tone is welcoming. "Yeah, so," Malcolm continues, swallowing hard. "I was just talking to my brother, you know, Declan? Right, of course you do. He's majoring in political science and he's interested in doing, like, an internship or something. I'm probably not supposed to be doing this, but Peter mentioned he had dinner with you last month and there was a chance you might have some kind of opening in your new firm." He pauses and waits for Mr. Coates to speak, his cheeks staining a deep red. "You didn't? On Labor Day weekend?" Another pause. "Oh, sorry. I must've heard wrong. I was just, you know, trying to help my brother out."

Mr. Coates talks for a minute. Malcolm nods mechanically, like Mr. Coates can see him. "Yeah, okay. Thanks a lot. I'll have him call you. It really— That'll be really helpful. Thanks again." He lowers the phone and meets my eyes. "You hear that?"

"Enough."

"Peter wasn't there," Malcolm says. "He lied."

Neither of us says anything for a beat. When I raise a hand to tug at my necklace, it's trembling so hard that my fingers knock against my chest.

"Let's think about this," I say, in a voice I have to fight to keep steady. "It sounds like Peter was probably here, driving

Katrin's car the night of the hailstorm. But if Katrin wasn't in the car when it hit something—or *someone*—why would Brooke be involved? Why would she help get the car fixed if she . . . *Oh*." I grab hold of Malcolm's arm. The pieces are falling into place, and this time I might actually be right. "Oh my God, Mal. Katrin said Brooke took off during a sleepover once, remember? She thought Brooke was slipping out to hook up with you. What if she was with *Peter*?"

"That's impossible," Malcolm says, with no conviction whatsoever. His eyes are like glass.

"Think about it, though. If Brooke and your stepfather were having an affair—which, *ew*, but I guess that's the least of our problems right now—we've been looking at everything wrong. It's not just about the hit-and-run. It's about keeping *everything* quiet." I pull my own phone out of my pocket. "We need to tell Ryan about this. He'll know what do to."

I've just opened a new text window when the door flies open. It's like watching some alt-version of my life to see Peter standing there with a gun pointed straight at us. "Your poker face needs work, Malcolm," he says calmly. His pale hair glints silvery gold in the dim lighting, and he smiles so normally that I almost smile back. "Anyone ever tell you that?"

CHAPTER THIRTY-FIVE

MALCOLM
THURSDAY, OCTOBER 10

All these weeks of wondering what the hell was happening around town, it somehow never occurred to me that the guy I trust least of anyone might be involved.

I'm an idiot. And Ellery sucks at solving true crime. But none of that matters right now.

"I'm going to need your phones," Peter says. He's still in his polo and khakis, but he's slipped on a pair of gloves, too. Somehow that's more chilling than the gun. "This isn't a drill, kids. Put them on the side table next to the bed. One at a time, please. You first, Ellery." We both comply, and Peter waves the gun toward the hallway. "Thank you. Now come with me."

"Where?" I ask, glancing over at Ellery. She's frozen in place, her eyes trained on Peter's right hand.

His nostrils flare. "You're not really in a position to ask questions, Malcolm."

Jesus. This is bad, colossally bad. I'm only just starting to grasp how much shit we're in, but I know this much: Peter would never let any of this unfold if he planned on leaving us alive to talk about it. "Wait," I say. "You can't— Look, it's too late, all right? We found the receipt from Dailey's Auto and gave it to the police. They know something sketchy is going on with Katrin's car and they'll figure out you're involved."

Peter's expression flickers with a second's worth of doubt, then relaxes again. "There's nothing on that receipt that points toward me."

"There's the fact that you're the only family member who was at home to drive," I say.

Peter raises his shoulders in a careless shrug. "Brooke borrowed the car and had an accident. Simple enough."

I keep talking. "I just spoke to Mr. Coates. I asked him about meeting up with you that weekend and he said you never did. He knows you lied."

"I listened to every word you said, Malcolm. You told him you must have heard wrong."

"Mom was there when we talked about it," I say, hating the desperate edge that's crept into my voice. "She'll remember. She'll know something is fishy."

"Your mother will remember whatever I tell her. She's a remarkably compliant woman. It's her greatest asset."

I want to kill him then, and I think he knows it. He takes a step back and lifts the gun so it's pointed directly at my chest. I strain to keep my expression neutral as my brain cycles through every possible reason why it's too late for Peter to get away with another murder. "Officer McNulty was there when Katrin said

Brooke snuck out during a sleepover to meet up with somebody in this house. If she wasn't coming to me, it had to be you."

"If you're not here, there's no reason for anyone to think it wasn't you," Peter points out.

Shit. I wish Ellery would snap out of whatever trance she's in. I could use another brain working right now. "People are going to question another murder. Another couple of murders. Especially if your stepson is involved. First your daughter's best friend, and now me? This is going to come back on you, Peter, and it'll be ten times worse when it does."

"I agree," Peter says. He looks completely relaxed, like we're chatting about baseball scores or the latest Netflix series. Not that we've ever done either of these things. "Now is absolutely not the time for anything even remotely resembling a homicide. I have to insist you come along, though. Downstairs. You first, Ellery."

Hope pulses through me, even though the coldness in Peter's eyes tells me it shouldn't. I contemplate lunging for him, but Ellery's already moving toward the hallway and he has the gun trained on her back. I can't see any choice except to follow, so I do.

"All the way to the basement," Peter says.

He keeps his distance as we troop down two sets of stairs. The Nilssons' basement is huge, and Peter tersely directs us through the laundry room and the finished space my mother uses to exercise. The past week flashes in front of my eyes as I walk, torturing me with everything we missed. There's so much to regret that I scarcely notice where we're headed until the biggest revelation of all hits me. When it does, I halt in my tracks.

"I didn't tell you to stop, Malcolm," Peter says. Beside me, Ellery pauses. I turn slowly, and she does too.

Cold sweat coats my face. "Declan's class ring," I say. "You had it. You dropped it near Brooke's body in Huntsburg."

"And?" Peter asks.

"Declan never got the ring back from Lacey. She still had it when she died. She hadn't stopped wearing it. You took it from her. Because you—" I hesitate, waiting for some sort of signal that he's affected by what I'm about to say. But there's nothing on his face except polite attentiveness. "You killed Lacey, too."

Ellery draws in a sharp, shocked breath, but Peter just shrugs. "Your brother is a useful fall guy, Malcolm. Always has been."

"Did you . . ." Ellery's eyes are locked on Peter's face. She tugs at the silver pendant around her neck, so hard I think she might break it. "Did you do something to my aunt, too?"

Peter's calm expression doesn't change. He leans forward and whispers something in her ear, so faint I can't catch it. When she lifts her head to look at him, her hair tumbles across her face, and all I can see is curls. Then Peter raises the gun again so it's pointed directly at her heart.

"Is this a thing with you, Peter?" I'm so desperate to get his attention off Ellery that my voice bounces off the basement walls. "You hook up with girls your daughter's age, and kill them when there's a chance they might expose you? What did Lacey do, huh? Was she going to tell?" A sudden thought strikes me. "Was she pregnant?"

Peter snorts. "This isn't a soap opera, Malcolm. It's not your business what happened between Lacey and me. She overstepped. Let's leave it at that." The gun swings toward me. "Move a few steps backward, please. Both of you."

I do it automatically, my thoughts tumbling and swirling so much that I barely notice we're standing inside a room. It's in the farthest corner of the Nilssons' basement, piled high with sealed cardboard boxes.

"This is the only room in the house that locks from the outside," Peter says, one hand gripping the edge of the door. "Convenient." He slams the door shut before I can react, plunging the room into darkness.

I'm at the door seconds later, first twisting the doorknob, then pounding so hard that my bruised ribs flare with sharp pain. "You can't just leave us!" I yell against the thick wood. "People know Ellery is here. Her grandmother dropped her off!"

"I'm aware," Peter says. There's a sound of something heavy being dragged across the floor, and I stop pounding so I can hear better. "Are you familiar with how a portable electric generator works, Malcolm?" I don't answer, and he continues, "It should never be turned on inside a house on account of the carbon monoxide it emits. It kills quickly in a concentrated area like this. I'm not sure how this got switched on, but oh well. Maybe you and Ellery knocked against it accidentally while you were down here doing who knows what. We may never know."

My heart plummets to my feet as I twist the knob again. "You locked us in here, Peter! They'll know it was you!"

"I'll be back in a little bit to open the door," Peter says casually. "I'm afraid I won't be able to stay long, though. Wouldn't want to meet the same fate. Plus, I need to head to the grocery store. We ran out of popcorn." A humming noise starts outside the door, and Peter raises his voice. "I'd say it was nice knowing you, Malcolm, but quite honestly you've been a nuisance from the start. All things considered, this has worked out fairly well. So long."

His footsteps recede quickly as I stand at the door, my head reeling and my heart pounding. How did I let it get to this point? Declan wouldn't have gone into the basement like a lemming. He would have tackled Peter in the bedroom, or—

Light blazes behind me. I turn to see Ellery standing by the far wall with her hand on a switch, blinking like she just woke up. She goes back to the center of the room and kneels down in front of a box, ripping a thick strand of tape from its top. She turns the box upside down and dumps its contents on the floor. "There has to be something in here I can use to pick the lock."

"Right," I say, relief flooding through me. I join her in tearing through the boxes. The first few are full of books, stuffed animals, and wrapping paper. "I'm sorry, Ellery," I say as we tear open more boxes. "I'm sorry I invited you over here, and that I let this happen. I wasn't quick enough."

"Don't talk," she says shortly. "Save your breath."

"Right." My head is starting to pound and my stomach rolls, but I don't know whether that's stress or deadly gas. How long has Peter been gone? How much time do we have?

"Ah-ha!" Ellery says triumphantly, seizing a box of Christmas ornaments. "Hooks." She yanks a couple free and heads for the door. "I just need to straighten it and . . ." She's silent for a few seconds, then lets out a grunt of frustration. "These aren't strong enough. They just bend up. We need something else. Do you see any paper clips?"

"Not yet." I open more boxes and root through their contents, but my head is pounding in earnest now and I'm so dizzy that my vision is starting to fuzz around the edges. I struggle to stand up, and look around the room. There are no windows to break, nothing heavy enough to use as a battering ram against

300

the door. I upend more boxes, scattering their contents across the floor. At least we can make a mess, I think hazily. If nothing else, people might question what the hell happened in here.

But my movements are sluggish, and slowing by the second. All I want to do is lie down and go to sleep.

I can't believe I'm thinking that already.

I can't believe I finally learned what happened to Lacey and Brooke, too late to give any kind of closure to their parents.

I can't believe I won't get a chance to apologize to my brother.

My eyes are drooping, so heavy that I nearly miss it glinting on the floor. One small, solitary paper clip. I dive for it with a strangled cry of triumph, but it's almost impossible to pick up. My hands feel rubbery and unwieldy, like I'm wearing giant Mickey Mouse gloves. When I finally get hold of it, I turn toward Ellery and the door.

She's slumped in front of it, motionless.

"Ellery!" I grab her by the shoulders and pull her into a sitting position, cupping her cheeks in my hands until I see her release a breath. I shake her as hard as I dare, until her hair spills across her face. "Ellery, come on. Wake up. Please." She doesn't respond. I lay her carefully on the floor and turn my attention to the paper clip.

I can do this without her. I just need to unfold the clip and get to work. If only my hands hadn't turned into inflatable gloves, it would be a lot easier.

If only my brain wasn't about to pound out of my head.

If only I didn't have to stop to throw up.

If only I could see.

If only.

CHAPTER THIRTY-SIX

ELLERY

FRIDAY, OCTOBER 11

I want to open my eyes, but the light is too bright and painful. It's quiet except for a soft beeping sound, and the air smells faintly of bleach. I try to raise one hand to the agony that's my head, but it won't move properly. Something's stuck in it, or to it.

"Can you hear me?" asks a low voice. A cool, dry hand presses against my cheek. "Ellery? Can you hear me?"

I try to say yes, but it comes out more like a groan. My throat hurts almost as much as my head.

"I'm sorry. Don't talk." The hand leaves my face and curls around mine. "Squeeze if you understand me." I do, weakly, and something wet drips on my arm. "Thank God. You'll be all right. They've used hyperbaric oxygen on you and— Well, I guess the details don't matter right now, but things look good. You look good. Oh, my poor girl."

My arm is getting wetter. I crack my eyes open a slit and see the faint outline of a room. Walls and a ceiling, blending into one another with clean white lines, lit by the pale-blue glow of fluorescent lighting. A gray head is bent in front of me, framed by shaking shoulders. "How?" I ask, but it doesn't sound like a word. My throat is as dry and rough as sandpaper. I try to swallow, but it's impossible without saliva. "How?" I rasp again. It's still unintelligible, even to my own ears, but my grandmother seems to understand.

"Your brother saved you," she says.

I feel like Sadie's robot character in *The Defender*. *That does not compute.* How did Ezra wind up in the Nilssons' basement? But before I can ask another question, everything fades again.

The next time I wake, pale sunlight is streaming into the room. I try to sit up, until a figure in scrubs covered with sailboats gently forces me back down. "Not yet," a familiar voice says.

I blink until Melanie Kilduff's face comes into focus. I want to talk to her, but my throat is on fire. "I'm thirsty," I croak.

"I'll bet," she says sympathetically. "Just a few sips of water for now though, okay?" She raises my head and puts a plastic cup to my lips. I drink greedily until she pulls it away. "Let's see how you do with that before you have any more."

I'd protest, but my stomach is already rolling. At least it's a little easier to talk now, though. "Malcolm?" I manage.

She places a comforting hand on my arm. "In a room down the hall. He'll be all right. And your mother is on her way."

"Sadie? But she's not supposed to leave Hamilton House."

"Oh, honey. Nobody cares about that right now."

Everything about me feels as dry as dust, so it's surprising when tears start rolling down my cheeks. Melanie perches on the side of my bed and snakes her arms around me, folding me into a hug. My fingers curl onto her scrubs and clutch tight, pulling her closer. "I'm sorry," I rasp. "I'm so sorry about everything. Is Mr. Nilsson . . ." I trail off as my stomach lurches and I gag.

Melanie raises me into more of a sitting position. "Throw up if you need to," she says soothingly. "Right here is fine." But the moment passes, leaving me exhausted and coated in clammy sweat. I don't say anything else for a long while, concentrating on getting my breathing under control.

When I finally do, I ask again. "Where is he?"

Melanie's voice is pure ice. "Peter's in jail, where he belongs."

It's such an enormous relief that I don't even mind when I feel myself slipping into unconsciousness again.

By the time Ryan visits, I almost feel like myself again. I've been awake for more than thirty minutes, anyway, and I've managed to keep down an entire cupful of water.

"You just missed Ezra," I tell him. "Nana made him leave. He'd been here for seven hours straight."

Ryan lowers himself into the chair beside my bed. "I believe it," he says. He's not in uniform but wearing faded jeans and a flannel shirt instead. He gives me a nervous, lopsided smile that reminds me of Ezra's and I wish, for one irrational second, that he'd hug me like Melanie did.

Your brother saved you, Nana had said.

She was right. I just didn't realize which one.

"Thank you," I say. "Nana told me you came looking for us at the Nilssons'. But nobody told me why." I search his open, friendly face, wondering how I ever could have imagined that it harbored dark secrets. My Spidey sense is officially crap, which I'm sure Malcolm will tell me as soon as I'm allowed to see him.

"I don't want to tire you out," Ryan starts tentatively, but I cut him off.

"No, please. You won't, I promise. I need to know what happened."

"Well." He hunches his shoulders and leans forward. "I can't get into everything, but I'll tell you as much as I can. It's hard to know where to start, but it was probably with the bracelet Daisy gave me. She says she told you about that."

"The bracelet? Really?" I sit up so fast that I wince from the headache that suddenly hits me, and Ryan shoots me a worried look. I settle back into the pillows with pretend nonchalance. "I mean, okay. Sure. How so?"

He regards me in silence for a few seconds, and I press my lips together so I won't accidentally vomit. "I didn't think much of it at the time," he finally says. "I followed up with the jeweler and she had no paper trail. She'd sold a bunch of bracelets around the same time and kept lousy records. Dead end, I thought. But I asked her to contact me if any similar sales took place, and last month, she did. A guy bought the exact same bracelet and paid cash. When I asked her to describe him, he fit Peter to a T. Not that I realized it at the time. I didn't start connecting dots until you guys brought me that repair receipt. That made me question the whole Nilsson family. Then I asked Brooke's parents if I could look through her jewelry box."

I have to make myself remember how to breathe. "And?"

"She had a bracelet exactly like Lacey's. Her mother didn't know when she'd gotten it, or from whom. But we had our own theories. Obviously."

"Right, right," I say sagely. Like that had ever occurred to me, even once.

"At the same time, we were scouring Brooke's house for clues. Her phone had gone missing when she did, but we were able to seize her computer. There was a diary on it, buried among a bunch of school files and password protected. It took us a while to get it open, but once we did we had most of the story. Brooke's side, anyway. She was cagey about names and details, but we knew she'd had an affair with someone older, that she'd been with him the night something terrible happened, and that she wanted to make things right. We had the car repair receipt, so we were starting to piece things together. But it was all still circumstantial. Then the Huntsburg police found Declan's ring at the crime scene."

Ryan grimaces, burrowing his neck into his shoulders. "I screwed up there, when I questioned Declan. I was trying to rule him out while confirming that the ring was his, because at that point I was pretty sure he was getting framed. But . . . I don't know. Declan and I have never had a great dynamic. I pushed too hard, and raised doubts in Malcolm's head that didn't need to be there. If I could take anything back, it would be that."

The machine next to me beeps quietly. "Okay," I say. "But . . . how did you show up in the nick of time? *Why* did you show up?"

"Your text," Ryan says. I stare blankly at him, and his brows rise. "You didn't know? You managed to get one letter off before

Peter took your phone. All it said was 'P.' I texted back a few times, but you didn't answer. I got worried with everything going on, so I checked in with your grandmother. When she said you were hanging out with Malcolm at the Nilssons' house, I freaked. I'd done my best to get Mrs. Nilsson to leave the house with Malcolm while we were investigating, but she wouldn't leave. And then *you* show up there? I know how you are—always asking questions people don't want to answer. I headed over, thinking I'd make up some excuse to bring you back to Nora's. And I found . . ." He trails off, swallowing visibly. "I found you."

"Where was Peter?"

Ryan's expression darkens. "Heading out of the house just as I was heading in. I guess he'd gone back to the basement to drag you guys into the hallway so we wouldn't know you'd ever been locked in. He didn't say a word when he saw me, just got into his car and took off. Which was enough to make me start tearing through the house. Thank God I heard the hum of the generator when I got into the kitchen, because you were nearly out of time." His mouth sets in a grim line. "Peter almost made it to Canada before someone caught up with him. I can't talk about what we found in his car, but it was enough to tie him to Brooke's murder."

"So this is just . . . a thing with him? Sleeping with teenage girls and killing them when they get in his way?" Malcolm had said that in the Nilssons' house, while I stood silently beside him. Frozen and useless, like I hadn't spent nearly half my life preparing for the moment when I'd be lured into a killer's basement.

"Looks like it. Mind you, he hasn't confessed to anything,

and we don't have hard evidence when it comes to Lacey. Not yet. We don't know what the tipping point was with her. Profilers are analyzing Peter now, and they suspect that she likely wanted to take their affair public. That she threatened to tell his wife or something."

"His second wife, right?"

"Yeah. She doesn't live in Echo Ridge anymore, but she lost her husband and son in a car accident before she married Peter. I think that's his particular brand of evil—acting like some kind of hero figure to vulnerable women while preying on young girls behind their backs." Ryan's face twists with disgust. "I don't know how else to explain why he'd marry the mother of Lacey's boyfriend. It's like he wanted to stay involved with Lacey, or something."

I shudder, thinking back to Peter and Malcolm's mom in their kitchen the first time I'd gone to Malcolm's house. How charming he'd been, but also—now that I have the benefit of hindsight—how controlling. Not letting his wife talk and maneuvering her out of the room, but doing it all with a smile. He'd fooled me as much as anyone. "What a twisted creep. The only thing that would've been worse is if Melanie's husband wasn't around and he'd tried to hook up with *her*."

"Agreed," Ryan says. "Although Melanie never would've gone for it. She's tough. Alicia—not so much."

My heart aches for Malcolm, and what this is going to mean for his family. Declan is finally in the clear, at least, and maybe once people realize Lacey was under Peter's influence, they won't judge him and Daisy too harshly. On the other hand—his *mom*. I can't even begin to imagine how she must feel, and how she's going to pick up the pieces from being married to somebody like Peter.

Ryan inches forward in his chair, his elbows on his knees and his hands clasped together. "There's something I wanted to check in with you about. When I spoke to Malcolm, he said you asked Peter if he'd done anything to Sarah, and that Peter whispered something he couldn't hear. What did Peter say?"

My fingers find the worn edge of my blanket and pluck its loose threads. "I don't know. I couldn't hear him either."

His face falls. "Ah, okay. He's not answering any of our questions, including the ones about Sarah, but don't worry. We'll keep at it."

"What about Katrin?" I ask abruptly. "Why was she doing all that anonymous threat stuff? Was she trying to point people away from her dad or something?"

"No. That's another long story," Ryan says. I lift my brows, and he adds, "Katrin wasn't involved in the threats, at first. It was Vivian Cantrell who started them."

"*Viv?* Why? What does she have to do with Peter? Were they having an affair too?" I almost gag at the thought.

Ryan huffs out a humorless laugh. "No. It was completely unrelated. She's applying to journalism programs this fall, and I guess some high-profile alumni told her that her portfolio wasn't strong enough to stand out. So she decided to manufacture a story she could report on."

I'm not sure I've heard him correctly. I *almost* have my head wrapped around Mr. Nilsson's warped psyche, but Viv's calculated plotting shocks me. "You have *got* to be kidding. She did all that crap—freaked people out, brought up horrible memories, and totally traumatized Lacey's parents—so she could *write* about it?"

"Yep," Ryan says grimly. "And that's why you got dragged into it. Viv fixed the homecoming court election. She thought it'd be more newsworthy to have Sarah Corcoran's niece involved."

"Newsworthy?" The word tastes bitter in my mouth. "Wow. She's a special kind of horrible, isn't she?"

Ryan looks like he fully agrees, but all he says is, "We traced the pep rally stunt back to her, and were about to talk with her parents when Brooke disappeared. Then we couldn't give the situation as much attention as we wanted, although we did let her know she was busted. She was terrified, and swore up and down that she'd stop immediately. So I was surprised as hell when Malcolm turned up with that video."

"Why would Katrin get involved, though?"

Ryan hesitates. "I'm sorry, but I can't tell you that. We're in discussions with Katrin's lawyer about what kind of role she's going to play in the investigation. Her reasons are part of those discussions, and they're confidential."

"Did she know what her father was doing?" I press. Ryan folds his arms across his chest without answering. "Blink once for yes."

He snorts, but more in a fond sort of way than in annoyance. I think. "New subject."

I twist the blanket between my hands. "So you had the whole thing figured out, and all this time I've just been getting in your way. Does that about sum it up?"

"Not entirely. The repair receipt was genuinely useful, especially knowing how much Brooke wanted to find it. When we added it to the bracelet and her diary, we knew who we were dealing with." He gives me a half smile. "Plus, you almost getting killed gave us probable cause to search Peter's car, so . . . thanks for that."

"Any time." My eyelids are getting heavy, and I have to blink fast to keep them from drooping. Ryan notices and gets to his feet.

"I should go. Let you get some rest."

"Will you come by again?"

He looks flattered at the hopeful tone in my voice. "Yeah, sure. If you want me to."

"I do." I let my eyes close for a second, then force them open again as he stands. "Thanks again. For everything."

"You're welcome," he says, shoving his hands in his pockets awkwardly. For that moment he reminds me of the old Officer Rodriguez—the skittish, subpar cop, instead of the crack investigator he turned out to be. "Hey, so, this is maybe not the time or the place," he adds, hesitantly, "but . . . if you're feeling well enough, my sister's having a fall open house in a couple of weeks. She does it every year. She wants to meet you and Ezra. If you're up for it."

"She does?" I ask, surprised. I'd almost forgotten that Ryan has siblings.

"Yeah, but no pressure or anything. Just think about it. You can let me know later if you're interested." He smiles warmly and lifts one hand in a wave. Then he turns, disappearing into the hallway.

I sink back onto the thin pillow, my haze of tiredness suspended. I've almost gotten used to Ryan, but I'm not sure how to feel about even more strangers that I'm related to. Going from a family of three—four, with Nana—to this sudden influx of half siblings, their spouses, and their kids seems like a lot.

I kind of like the idea of a sister, though. Maybe a half one wouldn't be bad.

There's a rustling sound at the door, and the scent of jasmine. I half twist on the bed, and spy a cloud of dark curls framed in the doorway.

"Ellery," Sadie breathes, her blue eyes sparkling with tears. Before I can remember that I'm mad at her, I'm returning her hug with every ounce of strength I have left.

CHAPTER THIRTY-SEVEN

MALCOLM
SATURDAY, OCTOBER 26

"This kid hates me," Declan says.

I don't think he's wrong. The six-month-old baby he's holding is sitting stiff as a board on his knee, red-faced and screaming. Everybody at this party feels sorry for the kid, except Daisy. She's beaming like she's never seen anything so adorable.

"I can practically see her ovaries exploding," Mia murmurs beside me.

"You're holding him wrong," Ezra says. He scoops the baby up in one deft motion, cradling him in the crook of his arm. "Just relax. They can tell when you're nervous." The kid stops crying and gives Ezra a giant, toothless grin. Ezra tickles his stomach before holding him out toward Declan. "Try again."

"No thanks," Declan mutters, getting to his feet. "I need a drink."

A pretty, dark-haired woman climbs the porch stairs, squeezing Ezra's arm as she passes. "You're so good with him!" She's the baby's mother, Ryan Rodriguez's sister, and we're all hanging out at her house two weeks after Peter Nilsson's murder attempt like everything's back to normal.

I don't know. Maybe it is, or maybe we're finally figuring out that we haven't been normal for years and it's time to redefine the word.

Declan heads for a cooler in the backyard, and Mia nudges my arm. "No time like the present," she says.

I glare at my brother's back. "Why is it even my responsibility? He's older. He should extend the olive branch first."

Mia adjusts her cat's-eye sunglasses. "You thought he was guilty of murder."

"Yeah, well, Ellery suspected me at one point. I got over it."

"Ellery had known you for less than a month then. She wasn't your *brother*."

"He didn't even visit me in the hospital!"

She enunciates every word carefully. "You. Thought. He. Was. Guilty. Of. *Murder*."

"I almost *got* murdered."

"You could do this all day, *or* you could be the bigger person." Mia waits a beat, then punches me in the arm. "At least he showed up."

"All right, fine," I grumble, and take off after Declan.

I wasn't sure he'd be here. We've only spoken a couple of times since I was released from the hospital, mostly to sort stuff out related to Mom. That's a mess; all of Peter's assets are frozen, so she's got nothing to her name except a bank account that won't cover more than a couple months' worth of expenses. We'll be moving to Solsbury soon, and while I can't get out of the Nilssons' house fast enough, I don't know what happens after that. Mom hasn't worked in over a year, and my dad's harder to reach than ever.

We got a semilucrative offer to tell our side of the story to a tabloid, but we're not desperate enough to take it. Yet.

Declan's at the far corner of the yard, pulling a frosted brown bottle from a blue cooler. He twists the cap off and takes a long sip, then catches sight of me and lowers the bottle. I'm a few feet away when I notice how white his knuckles are. "What's up, little brother?"

"Can I have one?" I ask.

He snorts. "You don't drink."

"I might need to start."

Declan reopens the cooler and plunges his hand into its depths, extracting a bottle identical to the one he's holding. He hands it to me, expressionless, and I manage to get the top off without wincing when the sharp edges cut into my palm. I take a tentative sip, waiting for bitterness to explode in my mouth, but it's not half bad. Smooth and almost honey flavored. I'm nervous and thirsty, and a quarter of the bottle is gone before Declan grabs my arm.

"Slow down."

I meet his eyes, and force out the words I've been practicing for two weeks. "I'm sorry."

Seconds pass that feel like minutes. I'm ready for just about any response; for him to yell at me, to walk away without saying anything, even to sock me in the jaw. The bruises from Kyle's attack are almost gone, just in time for some new ones.

But Declan doesn't do any of those things. He sips his beer, then clinks his bottle against mine. "Me too," he says.

The bottle almost slips out of my hand. "What?"

"You heard me."

"So you're not . . ." I trail off. *You're not mad* still seems impossible.

Declan looks back at the porch we left, squinting in the bright sun. It's one of those incredible late-October days we get sometimes in Vermont, upper seventies with an almost cloudless blue sky, the trees around us exploding with color. Daisy is holding the baby now, talking earnestly with Ryan's sister. Mia and Ezra are sitting side by side on the wooden railing, legs dangling and their heads bent close together. The sliding door to the house opens and a girl steps outside, dark curls bouncing around her shoulders.

I've been waiting for her to show up, but I guess I can wait to talk a little longer.

"I've been a shit brother to you, Mal," Declan says finally. "For years. I just— I'm not gonna lie, I didn't give a crap about you when we were kids. Too caught up in my own stuff. And you weren't . . . I don't know. Enough like me for me to pay attention." A muscle in his cheek jumps, his eyes still on the porch. "Then everything went to hell and I took off. I didn't think about you then, either. Not for years. So I'm not sure why I expected you to be on my side when somebody found my class ring at a murder site."

My throat's uncomfortably dry, but I don't want any more beer. "I should've realized you didn't have anything to do with that."

Declan shrugs. "Why? We barely know each other. And I'm

316

the adult, or so they tell me. So that's on me." He opens the cooler again and pulls out a ginger ale, holding it out to me. I hesitate, and he takes the beer from my hand, setting it down on a nearby table. "Come on, Mal. That's not you."

I take the ginger ale. "I don't know what's going to happen with Mom."

"I don't either. That shit's not great. We'll figure it out, though. You guys can get a place near Daisy and me. Solsbury's all right." He grins and takes a sip of beer. "The regulars at Bukowski's Tavern aren't half bad when you get to know them."

The tightness in my chest loosens. "Good to know."

A wisp of a cloud passes over the sun, briefly shading Declan's face. "You talk to Katrin?" he asks.

"No," I say. She ended up cooperating fully with the DA's office, handing off one final piece of evidence: Brooke's cell phone case. Katrin had found it the day Peter organized the search party, after she'd gone digging through his office looking for a phone charger. Apparently Peter destroyed Brooke's phone but kept the case—as though it were some kind of sick trophy. Just like he had with Lacey's ring.

It wasn't something you'd find in a store—Brooke had made it herself with a clear case, dried flowers, and nail polish. It was one of a kind, and when Katrin saw it tucked away like that, she knew her father was involved. Instead of turning him in, she'd re-created one of Viv's anonymous threats to try to deflect attention.

Katrin's lawyer painted as sympathetic a picture of her as he could. He claimed Peter had methodically estranged Katrin from her mother for years so he could control and manipulate her, to the point where she was totally dependent on him and unable to distinguish right from wrong. A different type of victim from Lacey and Brooke—but still a victim.

And maybe she was. Is. I don't know, because I haven't answered the one text she sent me since she was released into her aunt's custody. Katrin isn't allowed out of the country, and her mother's not willing to move here.

He's all I have.

I didn't answer. Not only because it wasn't true—she'd had me and my mom, at the very least, plus her aunt and even Theo and Viv—but because I can't think about my stepsister without remembering the last time I saw Brooke in her driveway, glancing back at me over her shoulder before she went inside. Soon after, according to police, she slipped out again to meet up with Peter.

I don't think I can ever accept the fact that Katrin knew Peter was involved in her best friend's disappearance, and stood by him anyway. Maybe one of these days, when everything is less raw, I can try to understand what it was like to grow up with that toxic sewer for a father. But two weeks after he tried to kill me isn't that time.

"Probably a good thing. That whole family's rotten to the core," Declan says, taking another long pull at his bottle. "Anyway, you and Mom should come over for dinner this week. Daisy and I bought a grill."

I start laughing. "Holy hell. You bought a *grill*. You're holding *babies*. What's next, suburban dad? You gonna start talking about your lawn?"

Declan narrows his eyes, and for a second I think I've gone too far. Then he grins. "There are worse fates, little brother. Much worse fates." He turns toward the porch again, shading his eyes against the sun. Ellery has her hands clasped stiffly in front of her as she talks to Ryan's sister. "Why are you still over here yapping at me? Go get your girl."

"She's not my—" I start, and Declan shoves me. Only a little too hard.

"Don't be such a wuss, Mal," he instructs, pulling the ginger ale from my hand. But he smiles when he says it.

So I leave him, crossing the yard toward the porch. Ellery spots me when I'm about halfway there and waves. She says something to her half sister, then bounds down the stairs with an energy that sets my nerves jumping. I've seen her only a couple of times since we left the hospital, always with some combination of Ezra, Mia, or her grandmother around. I even saw Sadie briefly before she went back to rehab. Ellery and I aren't alone here either, but for a few seconds in the middle of the backyard, everybody else fades away and it feels like it.

"Hey," she says, stopping within a foot of me. "I was hoping you'd be here." Her eyes flick over my shoulder to Declan. "How'd that go?"

"Better than expected. How are things with your new half siblings?"

"Same," she says. "Better than expected. They're nice. I'm not as comfortable with the other two as I am with Ryan, though. Ezra's fitting in more easily than I am. As usual." She brushes a stray curl off her temple. "How are you feeling?"

"Other than the headaches? Not too bad. No permanent effects. That's what the doctors say, anyway."

"Me too." She hesitates. "I mean . . . I guess the nightmares will go away eventually."

"I hope so." I wait a beat, then add, "Listen, I'm really sorry you didn't get any closure about your aunt. I know that would have meant a lot to your family. If it's any consolation . . . even if you didn't hear him say it, I'm pretty sure we *know*. You know?"

"I know. I just wish—" Her eyes get bright with tears, and before I can think too much about what I'm doing I pull her into my arms. She leans her head on my chest and I bury my face in her hair. For a few seconds I feel something I haven't experienced since I was a little kid, before my parents started fighting and my brother either ignored or taunted me. Hope.

"It'll be all right," I say into her hair.

Her voice is muffled against my shirt. "How? How are we supposed to get past something like this?"

I look over her head at the porch, where Declan's rejoined Daisy and they're talking with Ryan and Mrs. Corcoran. Ezra's gotten off the porch railing to hold the baby again, and Mia's making faces at it. The Kilduffs arrived at some point, and even though my mother's not here, I can almost picture her venturing into something like this one day. Forgiving herself for believing a monster's lies. We all have to figure out a way to do that. "Just living, I guess," I finally say.

Ellery pulls away from me with a small smile, swiping the back of her palm against her wet cheeks. Her dark lashes are spiky with tears. "Seriously? That's it? That's all you've got?"

"No. I have an ace in the hole I've been saving to cheer you up." Her brows rise, and I pause for dramatic effect. "Would you like to visit a clown museum with me?"

She starts to laugh. "What, now? In the middle of a party?"

"Can you think of a better time?"

"*After* the party?" Ellery suggests.

"It's right down the street. We could be there and back in half an hour. Forty-five minutes, tops. There's free popcorn, and dogs. And clowns, obviously."

"It does sound tempting."

"Then let's go." I link my fingers through hers and we start for the driveway. "Good thing it's walking distance. I've had almost half a bottle of beer."

"You rebel." She smiles at me. "But you did say *living,* after all."

I squeeze her hand and bend my head toward hers. "I'm working on it."

CHAPTER THIRTY-EIGHT

ELLERY

SATURDAY, OCTOBER 26

Malcolm's hand feels warm and solid in mine. Leaves swirl around us like oversized confetti, and the sky is a bright, brilliant blue. It's a beautiful day, the kind that makes you think maybe everything will be okay after all.

Despite all the trauma of the past two weeks, good things have happened, too. While Sadie was in town, she and Nana talked—*really* talked. They still don't understand one another much, but it finally felt like they both want to try. Since she's been back at Hamilton House, Sadie hasn't made a single random phone call.

It's only been eight days, but still. Baby steps.

Nana and Sadie agreed that Ezra and I should finish our senior year at Echo Ridge High, even if Sadie gets a clean bill of health in January. Which is all right by me. I'm making my bedroom a little homier; I bought some framed prints at an art fair last weekend, and put up pictures of Ezra and me with Mia and Malcolm. Plus I have the SATs to take, colleges to visit, half siblings to get to know, and, maybe, more dates with Malcolm.

I almost told him, just now. I wanted to.

But once I say it, I can't take it back. And even though I spent almost six weeks trying to unravel the lies in Echo Ridge, all I've been able to think about since that day in the Nilssons' basement is that some secrets shouldn't be told.

It nearly killed Sadie to believe she'd abandoned her twin on the night Sarah disappeared. There's no way she'd be able to handle this. It's hard enough for me, with no regrets or guilt weighing me down, to watch my brother smile and joke at a party and to know the truth.

We're not supposed to be here.

I grip Malcolm's hand tighter to ward off the chill that runs down my spine every time I remember Peter's voice hissing in my ear, so faint I almost missed it. I wish I had, because I'll spend the rest of my life hoping he never repeats the words he thought I'd take to my grave.

I thought she was your mother.

ACKNOWLEDGMENTS

If writing a first book is an act of faith—that someday, some-body other than your family and friends might want to read your words—writing a second book is an act of will. And boy, does it take a village. I won the literary lottery with the team I got to work with on my debut *One of Us Is Lying,* and their in-credible talent and dedication are the reason that *Two Can Keep a Secret* exists.

I'll never be able to thank my agent, Rosemary Stimola, enough. Not only are you the reason I get to do what I love for a living, but you're a tireless champion, a wise counselor, and the calm in every storm. I'm deeply grateful to Allison Remcheck for your unflinching honesty, your faith in me, and the fact that you woke up in the middle of the night thinking about these characters almost as much as I did.

To my editor extraordinaire, Krista Marino: I'm in awe of your uncanny ability to see directly into the heart of a book and know exactly what it needs. You've made every step of this process a pleasure, and thanks to your insight this story is, finally, the one I wanted to tell all along.

To my publisher, Beverly Horowitz, and to Barbara Marcus and Judith Haut, thank you for welcoming me to Delacorte Press and for your guidance and support through both of my books. Thank you to Monica Jean for your endless patience and keen insight, to Alison Impey for the incredible cover design, to Heather Hughes and Colleen Fellingham for your eagle eyes, and to Aisha Cloud for the stellar promotion (and for answering my emails and texts at all hours). As a former marketer, I'm awed by the sales and marketing team that I'm fortunate enough to work with at Random House Children's Books, including Felicia Frazier, John Adamo, Jules Kelly, Kelly McGauley, Kate Keating, Elizabeth Ward, and Cayla Rasi.

Thank you to Penguin Random House UK, including managing director Francesca Dow, publishing director Amanda Punter, editorial director Holly Harris, and the marketing, publicity, and sales dream team of Gemma Rostill, Harriet Venn, and Kat Baker for taking such meticulous care of my books in the United Kingdom. Thank you also to Clementine Gaisman and Alice Natali of ILA for helping my characters travel the globe.

I couldn't have made it through my debut year or second book without my writing buddies Erin Hahn and Meredith Ireland. Thank you for your friendship, for celebrating all the ups and commiserating with all the downs, and for reading countless drafts of this book until I got it right. Thanks also to Kit Frick for your insight and thoughtful commentary at a critical juncture in the book's development.

I'm grateful to the Boston kidlit group for our community, and for all the contemporary and thriller writers I've gotten to know who inspire me, motivate me, and make this often solitary career more fun, including Kathleen Glasgow, Kristen Orlando, Tiffany D. Jackson, Caleb Roehrig, Sandhya Menon, Phil Stamper, and Kara Thomas.

A profound thank-you to my family (both Medailleu and McManus) for supporting this surprising turn my life took and telling everyone you've ever met to buy my books. A special debt of gratitude to Mom and Dad for helping out when travel calls, to Lynne for being my rock, and to Jack, who inspires me to keep dreaming big.

Finally, thanks always to my readers for caring about stories, and for choosing to spend your time with mine.

ABOUT THE AUTHOR

Karen M. McManus earned her BA in English from the
College of the Holy Cross and her MA in journalism from
Northeastern University. When she isn't working or writing in
Cambridge, Massachusetts, McManus loves to travel with her
son. She is the author of the *New York Times* bestseller *One of
Us Is Lying* and *Two Can Keep a Secret*. To learn more about her,
visit karenmcmanus.com or follow @writerkmc on Twitter or
Instagram.

AN INTERNATIONAL BESTSELLER

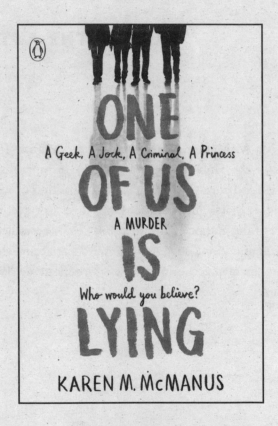

ONE

OF US

IS

LYING

A Geek, A Jock, A Criminal, A Princess

A MURDER

Who would you believe?

KAREN M. McMANUS

'Tightly plotted and brilliantly
written, with sharp, believable
characters, this whodunit is utterly
irresistible'
Heat

"The last novel in the **gripping trilogy** that
encompassed *Alex* and *Irène*"
MARCEL BERLINS, *The Times*

"**Superbly constructed and executed,** it puts Lemaitre very close to Ellroy's class. If you pick it up, you **won't be able to put it down**"
GEOFFREY WANSELL, *Daily Mail*

"Last year, I was not alone in hailing Pierre Lemaitre's *Alex* as **one of my top crime books of 2013** . . . *Irène* is just as **gripping, frightening, intelligent and brilliant** . . ."
MARCEL BERLINS, *The Times*

"Moves from **read-as-fast-as-you-can** horror to an intricately plotted race to a dark truth"
ALISON FLOOD, *Observer*

"**Grippingly original** . . . It enthrals at every stage of its unpredictability"
MARCEL BERLINS, *The Times*

"An **invigoratingly scary,** one-sitting read"
LAURA WILSON, *Guardian*

CAMILLE

Pierre
LEMAITRE

Translated from the French by
Frank Wynne

MACLEHOSE PRESS
QUERCUS · LONDON

First published in the French language as *Sacrifices*
by Editions Albin Michel in 2012
First published in Great Britain in 2015 by MacLehose Press
This paperback edition published in 2015 by

MacLehose Press
an imprint of Quercus Publishing Ltd
Carmelite House
50 Victoria Embankment
London EC4Y 0DZ

An Hachette UK Company

INSTITUT
FRANÇAIS
ROYAUME-UNI

This book is supported by the Institut francais (Royaume-Uni)
as part of the Burgess Programme
(www.frenchbooknew.com)

ISBN (MMP) 978 0 85705 414 2
ISBN (EBOOK) 978 1 78206 811 2

1 3 5 7 9 10 8 6 4 2

Designed and typeset in Minion by James Nunn
Printed and bound in Great Britain by Clays Ltd, St Ives plc

For Pascaline

To Cathy Bourdeau, for her support.
With my affection

We only know about one per cent of what's happening to us.
We don't know how little heaven is paying for how much hell.

William Gaddis, *The Recognitions*

Translator's Note

The judicial system in France is fundamentally different to that in the United Kingdom and the U.S.A. Rather than the adversarial system, where police investigate, and the role of the courts is to act as an impartial referee between prosecution and defence, in the French inquisitorial system the judiciary work with the police on the investigation, appointing an independent *juge d'instruction* entitled to question witnesses, interrogate suspects, and oversee the police investigation, gathering evidence, whether incriminating or otherwise. If there is sufficient evidence, the case is referred to the *procureur* – the public prosecutor, who decides whether to bring charges. The *juge d'instruction* plays no role in the eventual trial and is prohibited from adjudicating future cases involving the same defendant.

The French have two national police forces: the *police nationale* (formerly called the *Sûreté*), a civilian police force with jurisdiction in cities and large urban areas, and the *gendarmerie nationale*, a branch of the French Armed Forces, responsible both for public safety and for policing the towns with populations of fewer than 20,000. Since the *gendarme*rie rarely has the resources to conduct complex investigations, the *police nationale* maintains regional criminal investigations services (*police judiciaire*) analogous to the British C.I.D, they also oversee armed response units (*R.A.I.D.*).

Glossary

Brigade criminelle: equivalent to the Homicide and Serious Crime Squad, the brigade handles murders, kidnappings and assassinations, the equivalent of the British C.I.D.

Commandant: Detective Chief Inspector

Commissaire divisionnaire: Chief Superintendent (U.K.)/Police Chief (U.S.) has though he has both an administrative and an investigative role

Contrôleur général: Assistant Chief Constable (U.K.)/Police Commissioner (U.S.)

G.I.G.N.: "Groupe d'intervention de la *Gendarmerie* nationale": a special operations unit of the French Armed Forces trained to perform counter-terrorist and hostage rescue missions

Identité judiciare: the forensics department of the national police

Inspection générale des services (I.G.S.): the French police monitoring service equivalent to Internal Affairs (U.S.) or the Police Complaints Authority (U.K.)

Juge d'instruction: the "investigating judge" has a role somewhat similar to that of an American District Attorney. He is addressed as *monsieur le juge*

Préfecture de Police: the local police headquarters overseeing a district or arrondissement.

Procureur: similar to a Crown Prosecutor in the U.K. He is addressed as *magistrat* in the same way one might say "sir", or "your honour"

The Périphérique is the inner ring-road circumscribing central Paris, linking the old city gates or *portes*, e.g. porte d'Italie, porte d'Orleans

DAY 1

An event may be considered decisive when it utterly destabilises your life. This is something Camille Verhœven read some months ago in an article entitled "The Acceleration of History". This decisive, disorientating event which sends a jolt of electricity through your nervous system is readily distinguishable from life's other misfortunes because it has a particular force, a specific density: as soon as it occurs, you realise that it will have overwhelming consequences, that what is happening in that moment is irreparable.

To take an example, three blasts from a pump-action shotgun fired at the woman you love.

This is what is going to happen to Camille.

And it does not matter whether, like him, you are attending your best friend's funeral on the day in question, or whether you feel that you have already had your fill for one day. Fate does not concern itself with such trivialities; it is quite capable, in spite of them of taking the form of a killer armed with a sawn-off shotgun a 12-gauge Mossberg 500.

All that remains to be seen is how you will react. This is all that matters.

Because in that instant you will be so devastated that, more often than not, you will react out of pure reflex. If, for example, before she is shot three times, the woman you love has been beaten to a pulp and if, after that, you clearly see the killer shoulder his weapon having chambered a round with a dull clack.

It is probably in such a moment that truly exceptional men reveal themselves, those capable of making the best decisions under the worst of circumstances.

If you are an ordinary man, you get by as best you can. All

too often, in the face of such a cataclysmic event, your decision is likely to be flawed or mistaken, always assuming you have not been rendered utterly helpless.

When you have reached a certain age, or when a similar event has already destroyed your life, you suppose that you are immune. This is the case with Camille. His first wife was murdered, a tragedy from which he took years to recover. When you have faced such an ordeal, you assume that nothing more can happen to you.

This is the trap.

You have lowered your guard.

For fate, which has a keen eye, this is the ideal moment to catch you unawares.

And remind you of the unfailing timeliness of chance.

Anne Forestier steps into the Galerie Monier immediately after it opens. The shopping centre is almost empty, the heady smell of bleach heavy in the air as shop owners open their doors, setting out stalls of books, display cases of jewellery.

Built in the late nineteenth century towards the lower end of the Champs-Elysées, the Galerie is made up of small luxury boutiques selling stationery, leather goods, antiques. Gazing up at the vaulted glass roof, a knowledgeable visitor will notice a host of Art Deco details: tiles, cornices, small stained glass windows. Features Anne, too, could admire if she chose, but, as she would be the first to admit, she is not a morning person. At this hour ceilings, mouldings, details are the least of her concerns.

More than anything, she needs coffee. Strong and black.

Because this morning, almost as if it were destined to be, Camille wanted her to linger in bed. Unlike her, Camille is very much a morning person. But Anne did not feel up to it. Having gently fended off Camille's advances – he has warm hands; it is not always easy to resist – and forgetting that she had poured herself some coffee, she rushed to take a shower and so by the time she emerged and padded into the kitchen towelling her hair, she discovered that the coffee was cold, and rescued a contact lens that was about to be washed down the drain . . .

By then it was time for her to leave. On an empty stomach.

Arriving at the Galerie Monier at a few minutes past ten, she takes a table on the terrace of the little brasserie at the entrance; she is their first customer. The coffee machine is still warming up and she is forced to wait to be served, but though she repeatedly checks her watch, it is not because she is in a hurry. It is an attempt to ward off the waiter. Since he has nothing to do while he waits for the coffee machine to warm up, he is trying to engage her in conversation. He wipes down the tables, glancing at her over his shoulder, and, moving in concentric circles, edges towards her. He is a tall, thin, chatty guy with lank blond hair, the type often found in tourist areas. When he has finished with the last table, he takes up a position close to her and, hands on hips, gives a contented sigh as he stares out the window and launches into pathetically mediocre meteorological musings.

The waiter may be a moron, but he has good taste because, at forty, Anne is still stunning. Dark-haired and delicate, she has pale green eyes and a dazzling smile . . . She is luminously beautiful, with exceptional bone structure. Her slow, graceful movements make you want to touch her because everything about her seems curved and firm: her breasts, her buttocks, her belly, her thighs . . . indeed everything so exquisitely shaped, so perfect it would unsettle any man.

Every time he thinks about her, Camille cannot help but wonder what she sees in him. He is fifty years old, almost bald and, most importantly, he is barely four foot eleven. The height of an eleven-year-old boy. To avoid speculation, it is probably best to mention that, although Anne is not particularly tall, she is almost a whole head taller than Camille.

Anne responds to the waiter's flirtation with a charming smile that eloquently says "fuck off" (the waiter acquiesces and returns to his work) and she, having hastily drunk her coffee, heads through the Galerie towards the rue Georges-Flandrin. She has nearly reached the exit when, slipping a hand into her bag to get her purse, she feels something damp. Her fingers are covered in ink. Her pen has leaked.

For Camille, it is with the pen that the story really begins. Or with Anne deciding to go to a café in the Galerie Monier rather than somewhere else, on that particular morning rather than another one . . . The dizzying number of coincidences that can lead to tragedy is bewildering. But it seems churlish to complain since it was a dizzying series of coincidences that led to Camille first meeting Anne.

The pen is a small dark-blue fountain pen and the cartridge is leaking. Camille can still picture it. Anne is left-handed and holds her pen in a tortuous grip, writing quickly in a large, loping hand so that it looks as if she is furiously dashing off a series of signatures yet, curiously, she always buys small pens which makes the sight the more astonishing.

Seeing the ink stains on her hand, Anne immediately worries about what damage has been done. She glances around for some way to deal with the problem and sees a large plant stand, sets the handbag down on the wooden rim, and begins to take everything out.

She is quite upset, but her fears prove unjustified. Besides, those who know Anne would find it hard to see what she might be afraid of since Anne does not have much. Not in her bag, nor in her life. The clothes she is wearing are inexpensive. She has never owned an apartment or a car, she spends what she earns, no more, but never less. She does not save because it is not in her nature: her father was a shopkeeper. When he was about to go bankrupt, he disappeared with funds belonging to some forty associations to which he had recently had himself elected treasurer; he was never heard of again. This may explain why Anne has a rather detached relationship to money. The last time she had money worries was when she was single-handedly raising her daughter Agathe, and that was a long time ago. Anne tosses the pen into a rubbish bin and shoves her mobile phone into her jacket pocket. Her purse is stained and will probably have to be discarded, but the contents are unaffected. As for the handbag, although the lining is damp, the ink did not bleed through. Perhaps Anne decides to buy a new one, after all an upmarket shopping arcade is the perfect place, but it is impossible to know since what happens next will make any plans superfluous. For now, she dabs at the inside of the bag with some wadded Kleenex and when she has done so sees that both her hands are now ink-stained.

She could go back to the brasserie, but the prospect of having to deal with the same waiter is depressing. Even so, she is steeling herself to do so when she spots a sign indicating a public toilet, an unusual facility in a small shopping arcade. The sign points to a narrow passageway just beyond Pâtisserie Cardon and Desfossés Jewellers.

At this point, things begin to move faster.

Anne crosses the thirty metres to the toilets, pushes open the door and finds herself face to face with two men.

They have come in through the emergency exit on the rue Damiani and are heading towards the Galerie.

A few seconds later . . . it seems ridiculous, and yet it is true: if Anne had gone in five seconds later, the men would have already pulled on their balaclavas and things would have turned out very differently.

Instead what happens is this: Anne pushes open the door and she and the two men suddenly freeze.

She looks from one man to the other, startled by their presence, their behaviour, by their black balaclavas.

And by their guns. Pump-action shotguns. Even to someone who knows nothing about firearms, they look daunting.

One of the men, the shorter one, lets out a moan or perhaps it is a cry. Anne looks at him; he is stunned. She turns to the other man whose face is harsh and angular. The scene lasts only a few seconds during which the three players stand, shocked and speechless, all of them caught unawares. The two men quickly pull down their balaclavas, the taller one raises his weapon, half turns and, like an axeman preparing to fell an oak tree, hits Anne full in the face with the butt of his rifle.

With all his strength.

He literally shatters her cheekbone. He even gives a low grunt like a tennis player making a first serve.

Anne reels back, her hand reaching out for something to break her fall only to find empty air. The blow was so sudden, so brutal, she feels as though her head has been severed from her body. She is thrown almost a metre, the back of her skull slams against the door and she flings her arms wide and slumps to the ground.

The wooden rifle butt has smashed her face from jaw to temple, breaking her left cheekbone, leaving a ten-centimetre gash as her cheek splits like a ripe fruit, blood spurts everywhere. From outside, it would have sounded like a boxing glove hitting a punchbag. To Anne, it is like a sledgehammer swung with both hands.

The other man screams furiously. Anne only dimly hears him as she struggles to get her bearings.

The taller man calmly steps forward, aims the barrel of the shotgun at her head, chambers a round with a loud clack and is about to fire when his accomplice screams again. Louder this time. Perhaps even grabs the tall man's sleeve. Anne is too stunned to open her eyes, only her hands move, flailing in an unconscious reflex.

The man holding the pump-action shotgun stops, turns, wavers: firing a gun is a sure way to bring the police running, any career criminal would tell you that. For a split second, he hesitates over the best course of action and, having made his decision, turns back to Anne and aims a series of kicks to her face and her stomach. She tries to dodge the blows, but she is trapped. There is no way out. On one side is the door against which she is huddled, on the other, the tall man balancing on his left foot as he lashes out with his right. Between salvoes, Anne briefly manages to catch her breath; the man stops for a moment, and perhaps because he is not getting the desired result, decides on a more radical approach: he spins the shotgun, raises it high and starts to hit her with the rifle butt as hard and as fast as he can.

He looks like a man trying to pound a stake into a patch of frozen ground.

Anne writhes and twists as she tries to protect herself, she slithers on the pool of her own blood, clasps her hands behind her neck. The first blow goes awry and lands on the back of her head, the second shatters her interlaced fingers.

This change of tactic does not go down well with the accomplice, since the smaller man now grabs his arm, preventing him from continuing. The tall man, unfazed, goes back to the more traditional method, aiming brutal kicks at her head with his heavy military-style boots. Curled into a ball, Anne tries to shield herself with her arms as blows rain on her head, her neck, her arms, her back; it is impossible to know how many, the doctors will say at least eight, the pathologist says nine.

It is at this point that Anne loses consciousness.

As far as the two men are concerned, the matter has been dealt with. But Anne's body is now blocking the door leading to the arcade. Without a word, they bend down; the smaller man takes her arms and drags her towards him, her head thumping against the tiles. Once there is space to open the door, he drops her arms which fall back heavily, her languid, broken hands coming to rest in the oddly graceful pose of a painted Madonna. Had Camille witnessed the scene, he would immediately have noticed the curious resemblance between the position of Anne's arms, her abandon, and a painting by Fernand Pelez called "The Victim", something he would have found devastating.

The story could end here. The story of an ill-fated incident. But the taller of the two men does not see it like that. He is clearly the leader and he quickly weighs up the situation.

What is going to happen to this woman? What if she regains consciousness and starts to scream? What if she runs back into the Galerie? Worse, what if she manages to get out through the emergency exit and calls for help? Or crawls into a toilet cubicle and phones the police?

He puts his foot against the door to hold it open, bends down and, grabbing her by the right ankle, he leaves the toilets, dragging her behind him with the same ease, the same casual indifference with which a child might drag a toy.

Anne's body is bruised and battered, her shoulder slams against the toilet door, her hip against the wall of the corridor, her head lolls as she is dragged along, banging into a skirting board or one of the plant pots in the Galerie. Anne is no more than a rag now, a sack, a lifeless doll leaving a scarlet trail that quickly clots. Blood dries fast.

She seems dead. The man drops her leg, abandoning her dislocated body without a second glance; he has no more use for her. He loads the pump-action shotgun with swift sure movements that emphasise his determination. The two men burst into Desfossés Jewellers yelling orders. The shop has only just opened. A witness, had there been one, would be struck by the disparity between their fury and the empty shop. The two men bark orders at the staff (two petrified women), and immediately lash out, punching them in the stomach, the face. The Galerie echoes with the sound of smashing glass, screams, whimpers, gasps of fear.

Perhaps it due to being dragged along the ground, to her head being bumped and jolted, but there is a sudden pulse of life and in that moment, Anne struggles to reconnect with reality.

Her brain, like a defective radar, tries desperately to make sense of what is happening, but it is futile, she is in shock, her mind literally numbed by the blows and the speed of events. Her body is racked with pain, she cannot move a muscle.

The spectacle of Anne's body being dragged through the Galerie and abandoned in a pool of blood in the doorway of the jeweller's has one positive effect: it lends a sense of urgency to the events.

The only people in the shop are the owner and a trainee assistant, a girl of about sixteen, thin as a leaf, who wears her hair pinned up in a chignon to give herself some gravitas. The moment she sees the two armed men in balaclavas, she knows it is a hold-up; hypnotised, sacrificed, passive as a victim about to be burned at the stake, she stands, her mouth opening and closing like a goldfish. Her legs can barely hold her up; she clutches the edge of the counter for support. Before her knees finally give way, the barrel of the shotgun is slammed into her face. Slowly, like a soufflé, she sinks to the ground. She will lie here as events play out, counting her heartbeats, shielding her head with her arms as though expecting a shower of stones.

The owner of the jeweller's stifles a scream when she first sees Anne being dragged along the ground, skirt rucked up to her waist, leaving a wide, crimson wake. She tries to say something, but the words die in her throat. The taller of the two men is stationed at the entrance to the shop, keeping lookout, while the shorter man rushes her, aiming the barrel of his shotgun. He jabs it viciously into her belly and she only just manages not to vomit. He does not say a word; no words are necessary. Already she is working on automatic pilot. She clumsily disarms the alarm system, fumbles for the keys to the display cases only to realise she does not have them on her, she needs to fetch them from the back room; it is as she takes her first step that she realises she has wet herself. Her hand trembling, she holds out the bunch of keys. Though she will not mention this in her witness statement, at this moment she whispers to the man "Don't kill me . . ." She would trade the whole world for another twenty seconds of life. As she says this, and without having to be asked, she lies down on the floor, hands behind her head, whispering fervently to herself: she is praying.

Given the viciousness of these thugs, one cannot help but wonder whether prayers, however fervent, serve any practical purpose. It hardly matters: while she prays, the two men quickly open the display cases and tip the contents into canvas bags.

The hold-up has been efficiently planned; it takes less than four minutes. The timing is perfectly judged, the decision to enter the arcade through the toilets is astute, the division of roles between the men is professional: while the first man ransacks the cabinets, the second, standing squarely in the doorway, keeps one eye on the shop and another on the rest of the arcade.

The C.C.T.V. camera inside the shop will show the first robber rifling through cases and drawers and grabbing anything of value. Outside, a second camera films the doorway and a narrow section of the arcade. It is on this footage that Anne's sprawled body can be seen.

This is the point at which the meticulously planned robbery begins to go wrong; this is the moment on the camera footage when Anne appears to move. It is an almost imperceptible movement, a reflex. At first, Camille is hesitant, unsure what he has seen but, studying it with care, there can be no doubt . . . Anne moves her head from right to left, very slowly. It is a gesture Camille recognises: at certain times of the day when she needs to relax, she arches her neck, working the vertebrae and the muscles – the "sternocleidomastoid", she says, a muscle Camille did not know existed. Obviously, on the video the gesture does not have the tranquil grace of a relaxation exercise. Anne is lying on her side, her right leg is drawn up so the knee touches her chest, her left leg is extended, her upper body is twisted as though she is trying to turn onto her back, her skirt is hiked up to reveal her white panties. Blood is streaming down her face.

She is not lying there; she was thrown there.

When the robbery began, the man in the doorway shot several quick glances at Anne, but since she was not moving, he focused his attention on watching the arcade. Now he ignores her, his back is turned, he has not even noticed the blood trickling under the heel of his right shoe.

Emerging from her nightmare, Anne struggles to make sense of what is going on around her. As she looks up, the camera briefly captures an image of her face. It is heartrending.

When he comes to this moment on the tape, Camille is so shocked he twice fumbles with the remote control before he manages to stop, rewind and pause: he does not recognise her. He can see nothing of Anne's luminous features, her laughing eyes in this bruised, bloody face swollen already to twice its size, in these vacant eyes.

Camille grips the edge of the table, he feels an overwhelming urge to weep because Anne is staring straight into the lens, gazing directly at him as though she might speak, might beg him to come to her rescue; he cannot help but imagine this, and imagination can be devastating. Imagine someone you love, someone who relies on you for protection, imagine watching them suffer, watching them die and feel yourself break out in a cold sweat. Now, go one step further and imagine in that moment of excruciating terror, this person crying out to you for help and you will wish you could die too. This is how Camille feels, staring at the video monitor, utterly helpless. There is nothing he can do save watch, because it is all over . . .

It is unendurable, literally unendurable.

He will watch this footage dozens of times.

Anne behaves as though her surroundings do not exist. She would not react if the tall man were to stand over her and aim the barrel at the back of her head. It is a powerful survival instinct even if, watching it on the screen, it seems more like suicide: scarcely two metres away from a man with a shotgun who only minutes earlier made it clear that he was perfectly prepared to put a bullet in her head, Anne is about to do something that no-one in her position would wish to do. She is going to try to stand up. With no thought for the consequences. She is going to try to escape. Anne is a woman of great courage, but confronting a man with a sawn-off shotgun goes beyond bravery.

What is about to happen arises almost automatically from the situation: two opposing forces are about to collide and one or other must prevail. Both forces are caught up in the moment. The difference being that one is backed up by a 12-bore shotgun, which unquestionably gives him the upper hand. But Anne cannot gauge the balance of power, cannot rationally calculate the odds against her, she is behaving as though she were alone. She musters every ounce of strength – and from the flickering images, it is clear she has little left – draws up her leg, hoists herself laboriously with her arms, her hands slipping in a pool of her own blood. She almost falls back, but tries a second time; the slowness of her movements lends the scene a surreal quality. She feels heavy, numb, you can almost hear her gasping for breath, you want to heave her up, to drag her away, to help her to her feet.

Camille wants only to tell her not to move. Even if it takes a minute before the tall man turns and notices, Anne is so dazed, so out of it that she will not make it three metres before the first shotgun blast all but cuts her in two. But several hours have passed, Camille is staring at a video monitor, what he thinks now is of no importance: it is too late.

Anne's actions are not governed by thought but by sheer determination which knows no logic. It is obvious from the video that her resolution is simply a survival instinct. She does not look like someone being threatened by a shotgun at point-blank range, she looks like a woman who has had too much to drink and is about to pick up her handbag – Anne has clung to the bag from the beginning – stagger to the door and make her way home. It seems as though what is stopping her is not a 12-bore shotgun, but her befuddled state.

What transpires next takes barely a second: Anne does not stop to think, she has struggled painfully to her feet. She manages to stay standing, her skirt is still hiked around her waist. She is scarcely upright before she begins to run.

At this point, everything goes wrong and what follows is a series of miscalculations, accidents and errors. It is as though, overwhelmed by events, God does not know how to play out the scene and so leaves the actors to improvise, which, ineptly, they do.

Anne does not know where she is, she cannot get her bearings, in fact in attempting to escape, she heads the wrong way. If she reached out a hand, she would touch the tall man's shoulder, he would turn and . . .

She hesitates for a long moment, disorientated. It is a miracle that she manages to stay upright. She wipes her bloody face with her sleeve, tilts her head as though listening to something, she cannot seem to take that first step . . . Then, suddenly, she tries to run. As he watches the video, Camille falls apart as the last pillars of his stoic courage crumble.

Anne's instinct is fine in theory; it is in practice that things go wrong. She skids in the pool of blood. She is skating. In a cartoon, it would be funny; in reality it is agonising because she is slipping in her own blood, struggling to stay on her feet, trying desperately to run and succeeding only in flapping and flailing dangerously. It looks as though she is running in slow motion. It is heart-stopping.

The tall man does not immediately realise what is happening. Anne is about to fall on top of him when her feet finally reach a patch of dry ground, she regains her balance and, as though powered by a spring, she begins to lurch.

In the wrong direction.

Initially, she follows a curious trajectory, spinning around like a broken doll. She makes a quarter turn, takes a step forward, stops, turns again like a disorientated walker trying to get her bearings, and eventually manages to stumble off in the vague direction of the exit. Several seconds pass before the robber realises that his prey is attempting to escape. The moment he does, he turns and fires.

Camille plays the video over and over: there is no doubt that the killer is surprised. He is gripping his gun next to his hip, the sort of stance a gunman takes when trying to hit anything within a radius of four or five metres. Perhaps he has not had time to regain his composure. Or perhaps he is too sure of himself – it often happens: give a nervous man a 12-bore shotgun and the freedom to use it and he immediately thinks he is a crack shot. Perhaps it is simply surprise, or perhaps it is a mixture of all these things. The fact remains that the barrel is aimed high, much too high. It is an impulsive shot. He does not even try to aim.

Anne does not see anything. She is still stumbling forward through a black hole when a deafening hail of glass rains down on her as the ornamental fanlight above her head is blown to smithereens. In the light of Anne's fate, it seems cruel to mention that the stained-glass panel depicted a hunting scene: two dashing riders galloping towards a baying pack of hounds that have cornered a stag; the hounds are slavering, their teeth bared, the stag is already dead meat . . . It seems strange that the fanlight in the Galerie Monier, which survived two world wars, was finally destroyed by a ham-fisted thug . . . Some things are difficult to accept.

The whole Galerie trembles: the windows, the plate glass, the floor; people protect themselves as best they can.

"I hunched my shoulders," an antiques dealer will later tell Camille, miming the action.

He is thirty-four (he is precise on this point; he is not thirty-five). The stubby moustache that curls at the ends looks a little too small for his large nose. His right eye remains almost entirely closed, like the figure in the helmet in Giotto's painting "Idolatry". Even thinking about the noise of the gunshot, he seems dumbfounded.

"Well, obviously, I assumed it was a terrorist attack. [He apparently thinks this explains matters.] But then I thought, that's ridiculous, why would terrorists attack the Galerie, there's no obvious target," and so on . . .

The sort of witness who revises reality as fast as his memory will allow. But not someone to forget his priorities. Before going out into the arcade to see what was happening, he looked around to check whether there was any damage to his stock.

"Not so much as a scratch!" he says, flicking his thumb against his front tooth.

The Galerie is higher than it is wide; it is a corridor some fifty metres across lined by shops with plate-glass windows. In such a confined space the blast is colossal. After the explosion, the vibrations ripple out at the speed of sound, ricochet off every obstacle sending back wave upon wave of echoes.

The gunshot and the hail of glass stopped Anne in her tracks. She raises her arms to shield her head, tucks her chin into her chest, stumbles, falls onto her side and rolls across the glittering shards, but it takes more than a single shot and a shattered window to stop a woman like Anne. It seems incredible, but once more she gets to her feet.

The tall man's first shot missed its mark, but he has learned his lesson: he takes the time to aim. On the C.C.T.V. footage, he can be seen reloading the shotgun, staring down the barrel; if the video were sufficiently high resolution, it would be possible to see his finger squeezing the trigger.

A black-gloved hand suddenly appears; the shorter man jostles his shoulder just as he fires . . .

The window of the nearby bookshop explodes, splinters of glass, some large as dinner plates, sharp and jagged as razors, fall and shatter on the tiles.

"I was in the little office at the back of the bookshop . . ."

The woman is about fifty, an archetypal businesswoman: short, plump, self-confident, expensive make-up, twice-weekly trips to the beautician, tinkling with bracelets, necklaces, chains, rings, brooches, earrings (it is a wonder the robbers did not take her with the rest of their loot), a gravelly voice – too many cigarettes and probably too much booze, Camille does not take the time to find out. The incident took place only a few hours earlier, he is in shock, impatient, he needs to know.

"I rushed out . . ." she gestures towards the arcade. She pauses, clearly happy to be the centre of attention. She wants to make the most of her little performance. With Camille, it will be short-lived.

"Get on with it," he growls.

Not very polite for a policeman, she thinks, must be his height, it's the kind of thing that must make you bitter, resentful. Moments after the gunshot, she witnessed Anne being hurled against a display case as though pushed by a giant hand, bouncing back against the plate-glass window and then crumpling on the floor. The image is still so powerful that the woman forgets her affectations.

"She was thrown against the window, but she was hardly on the ground before she was trying to get up again! [The woman sounds amazed, impressed.] She was bleeding and disorientated, flapping her arms around, slipping and sliding, you get the picture . . ."

On the C.C.T.V. footage, the two men seem to freeze for a moment. The shorter one shoves the shotgun aside and drops the bags on the floor. He squares up, it is as though they are about to come to blows. Tight-lipped beneath his balaclava, he seems to spit his words.

The tall man lowers the gun, one hand gripping the barrel, he hesitates for a moment, then reality takes hold. Reluctantly he watches Anne as she struggles to her feet and staggers towards the exit; but time is short, an alarm goes off inside his head, the raid has taken far too long.

His accomplice grabs the bags and tosses one to him; the decision is made. The two men run off and disappear from the screen. A split second later, the tall man turns back and reappears on the right-hand side of the image, grabs the handbag Anne abandoned when she fled, then disappears again. This time he will not be back. We know that the two men went through the toilets and out onto the rue Damiani, where a third man was waiting with a car.

Anne barely knows where she is. She falls, gets up and, somehow, manages to make it out of the arcade and onto the street.

"There was so much blood, and she was walking . . . she looked like a zombie." A South American girl, dark hair, copper skin, about twenty. She works in the hairdressing salon on the corner and had just stepped out to get some coffees.

"Our machine is broken and someone has to go out and get coffee for the customers," the manageress, Janine Guénot, explains. Standing, staring at Verhœven, she looks like a brothel madam, she has the same qualities. And the same sense of responsibility: she is not about to let one of her girls talk to some man on the street without keeping an eye open. The reason the girl went out – the coffee, the malfunctioning machine – hardly matters, Camille brushes it aside with a wave. Though not entirely.

Because at the moment Anne stumbled out into the street, the hairdresser was rushing back with five cups of coffee balanced on a tray. Clients in this neighbourhood are particularly annoying, being well heeled they feel entitled to be demanding, as though exercising some ancestral right.

"Serving lukewarm coffee would be a disaster," the manageress explains with a pained expression.

Hence the young hairdresser's haste.

Surprised and intrigued by the two gunshots she hears coming from the Galerie Monier, she is trotting along with her tray when she runs straight into a crazed woman, covered in blood, staggering out of the arcade. It is a shock. The two women collide, the tray goes flying and with it the cups, the saucers, the glasses of water, the coffee spills all over the blue trouser suit the hairdressers in the salon wear as a uniform. The gunshots, the coffee, the delay, she can deal with, but trouser suits are expensive. The voice of the manageress is shrill now, she wants to show Camille the damage. "It's fine," he waves away her concerns. She demands to know who is going to pay for the dry cleaning, the law must surely provide for such eventualities. "It'll be fine," Camille says again.

"And she didn't even stop," the woman insists, as though this were a prang with a moped.

By now, she is telling the story as though it happened to her. She imperiously takes over because, when all is said and done, this was one of "her girls", and having coffee spilled all over her uniform means she has rights. Customers are all alike. Camille grabs her arm, she looks down at him curiously, as though observing a piece of dog shit on the pavement.

"Madame," Camille says with a snarl, "stop pissing me about."

The woman cannot believe her ears. And a dwarf at that! Now she's seen it all. But Verhœven stares her down; it is unsettling. In the awkward silence, the young hairdresser tries to prove how anxious she is to keep her job.

"She was moaning . . ." the girl says, to distract Camille's attention.

He turns to her, wants to know more. "What do you mean, moaning?"

"She was making these little cries, it was like . . . I don't know how to explain it."

"Try," says the manageress, eager to redeem herself in the eyes of the policeman, you never know when it might be useful. She nudges the girl. Come on, tell the gentleman, what did they sound like, these cries? The girl stares at them, eyelashes fluttering, she is not sure what she is being asked to do and so, rather than describing Anne's cries, she tries to mimic them. She begins to mouth little moans and whimpers, trying to find the right tone – *aah, aah* or maybe *uhh, uhh*, yes, that's it, she says, concentrating now, *uhh, uhh*, and having found the right tone the moans grow louder, she closes her eyes then opens them wide and seconds later *uhh, uhh*, it sounds as though she is about to come.

They are standing in the street, a crowd begins to gather on the spot where street cleaners have carelessly hosed away Anne's blood, which is still trickling into the gutter, they step on the fading scarlet blotches leaving Camille distraught . . . The crowd sees a diminutive police officer and, opposite him, the young hairdresser with the sallow tan who is staring at him strangely and making shrill, orgasmic sounds under the approving gaze of a brothel madam. Good heavens, it's is hardly the sort of thing one expects to see in this neighbourhood. The other shopkeepers stand in their doorways, looking on appalled. The gunshots were bad enough – not the sort of publicity that's going to attract customers – but now the whole street seems to have descended into a grotesque farce.

Camille goes on taking witness statements, comparing one to the other, trying to piece together what finally happened.

Utterly disoriented, Anne emerges from Galerie Monier onto the rue Georges-Flandrin next to number 34, turns right and staggers up towards the junction. A few metres on, she bumps into the hairdresser, but she does not stop, she hobbles on, leaning on the parked cars for support. Her bloody handprint is found on the roof and doors of several vehicles. To those on the street who heard the gunshots from the Galerie, this woman covered from head to foot in blood seems like an apparition. She seems to float, swaying this way and that but never stopping, she no longer knows what she is doing, she simply staggers on, groaning like a drunk, but moving forward. People stand aside to let her pass. One man dares to venture a concerned "Madame?", but he is traumatised by so much blood.

"I can tell you, monsieur, I was truly terrified at the sight of the poor woman . . . I didn't know what to do."

He is clearly distraught, this elderly man with his calm face and his pitifully scrawny neck, his eyes are misted over. Cataracts, Camille thinks, his father suffered from cataracts before he died. After each phrase, the old man seems to slip into a dream. His eyes are fixed on Camille and there is a long pause before he picks up his story. He is overcome and he opens his frail arms wide; Camille swallows hard, assailed by conflicting emotions.

The old man calls out "Madame!", but he dares not touch her, she is like a sleepwalker; he lets her pass, Anne stumbles on.

At this point, she turns right again.

There is no point wondering why. No-one knows. Because in doing so she turns into the rue Damiani. And two or three seconds after Anne turns into the street, the robbers' car appears, driving at breakneck speed.

Heading straight towards her.

Seeing his victim within range, the tall man who smashed her head in and twice failed to shoot her cannot resist reaching for his shotgun. To finish the job. As the car comes alongside, the window winds down and the barrel of the gun is levelled at her. Everything happens quickly: Anne sees the gun, but is incapable of even the slightest movement.

"She stared at the car . . ." said the man, "I don't know how to put it . . . it was like she was expecting it."

He realises the enormity of what he is saying. Camille

understands. What the old man means is that he senses a terrible weariness in Anne. After everything she has been through, she is ready to die. On this point everyone seems to agree: Anne, the shooter, the old man, fate, everyone.

Even the young hairdresser: "I saw the barrel of the gun poking out the window. And the lady, she saw it too. Neither of us could look away, but this lady, she was right there, right in the firing line, you understand?"

Camille holds his breath. Everyone, then, is in agreement. Everyone except the driver of the car. According to Camille – who has given the matter long and careful thought – at the time, the driver did not know about the carnage in the Galerie. Sitting in the getaway car, he probably hears the gunshots, knows too that the robbery was taking longer than planned. Panicked and impatient, he drums nervously on the steering wheel, he may even be thinking about driving away but then he sees the two men appear, one of them pushing the other towards the car . . . "Was anyone killed?" he wonders. "How many?" Finally, the robbers climb into the car. Under pressure, the driver starts the car and drives away, but as they come to the corner of the street – they have travelled scarcely two hundred metres since the car had to slow down at the traffic lights – he sees a woman lurching along the pavement, covered in blood. At that moment, the shooter probably shouts at him to slow down, rolls down his window, maybe even gives a howl of victory: one last chance, he cannot pass it up, it is as though fate itself is calling, as though he had found his soul mate, just when he had given up all hope she appears. He grabs the shotgun, brings it to his shoulder and aims. In the split second that follows, the driver suddenly imagines himself being held as an accomplice to cold-blooded murder in front of at least a dozen witnesses, to say nothing of whatever may have happened in the Galerie in which he is already implicated. The robbery has gone horribly wrong. He had not expected things to turn out like this . . .

"The car screeched to a halt," says the hairdresser. "Just like that! The scream of the brakes . . ."

Traces of rubber on the street will make it possible to determine that the getaway car was a Porsche Cayenne.

Everyone in the vehicle pitches forward, including the gunman. His bullet shatters the doors and the side windows of the parked car next to which Anne stands, frozen, waiting to die. Everyone nearby drops to the ground, everyone except the elderly man who does not have time to move. Anne collapses just as the driver floors the accelerator, the car lurches forward and the tyres squeal. As the hairdresser gets to her feet she sees the old man, one hand leaning against a wall for support, the other clutching his heart.

Anne is lying on the pavement, one arm dangling in the gutter, one leg beneath a parked car.

"Glittering," according to the old man, which is not surprising since she is covered with shards of glass from the shattered windscreen.

"It looked like a fall of snow . . ."

10.40 a.m.
The Turks are not happy.

Not happy at all.

The big man with his dogged expression is driving carefully, but as he negotiates the roundabout at the place de l'Étoile and heads down the avenue de la Grande-Armée, his knuckles on the steering wheel are white. He is scowling. He is naturally demonstrative. Or perhaps it is part of his culture to readily show emotion.

The younger brother is excitable. Volatile. He is swarthy with a brutish face, he is obviously thin-skinned. He too is demonstrative, he jabs the air with his finger, it's exhausting. I don't understand a word he's saying – I'm Spanish – but it's not hard to guess: we were hired to pull off a quick, lucrative robbery, and find ourselves caught up in the Gunfight at the O.K. Corral. He flings his arms wide: what if I hadn't stopped you, what then? There is an awkward silence in the car. He spits the question, he's obviously demanding to know what would have happened if the girl had died. Then, suddenly, he snaps, he loses his rag: we were supposed to be raiding a jeweller's, not committing mass murder!

Like I said, it gets a bit wearing. Good thing I'm a peaceable man because if I'd got angry, things might have got out of hand.

Not that it really matters, but it's frustrating. The kid is wasting his breath dishing out the blame when he'd be better off saving his strength, he's going to need all his energy.

Things didn't go exactly as planned, but we got a result, that's all I care about. There are two big bags on the floor. Enough to be going on with for a while. And this is just the beginning, because I've got big plans, and there are more bags where those ones came from. The Turk is eyeing the bags too as he jabbers away to his brother, it sounds like they're planning something, the driver is nodding. They carry on like I'm not here, they're probably calculating the compensation they think they're entitled to. *Entitled* . . . that's a fucking laugh. From time to time, the little guy turns to me and yells something. I catch a couple of slang terms: "dosh", "divvy up". Where the fuck they learned them, I've no idea, they've hardly been in the country twenty-four hours. Who knows, maybe the Turks have a gift for languages. Not that I give a shit. Right now, the best thing I can do is look confused, play it cool, nod my head and give them an apologetic smile. We're coming in to Saint-Ouen, traffic is light, we're in the clear.

The *banlieue* flashes past. Jesus, the big Turk has got some pair of lungs on him. With all the shouting, by the time we get to the lock-up, the air in the car is unbreathable, it feels like he's just getting to his Unified Theory of Everything. The little guy yells at me, asking the same question over and over, he's demanding an answer, and to show he's serious he flashes an index finger and taps it against his closed fist. Maybe it's an offensive gesture back in Izmir, but here in Saint-Ouen it's a different matter. The gist is obvious enough, it's intended as a threat, the best course of action is to nod my head and agree. I don't feel I'm being dishonest, because things are going to be sorted out soon enough.

Meanwhile, the driver has got out of the car and he's struggling to open the padlock on the metal shutters of the garage. He twists the key this way and that, comes back to the car looking puzzled, he's obviously thinking back: when he locked up, the key was working fine. He turns back towards the car and stands there sweating while the engine runs. There's not much chance of us being spotted on this dead-end road in the middle of nowhere, but even so I don't fancy hanging around for ever.

As far as they're concerned, the padlock is just one more unexpected hitch. One too many. By now, the little guy is almost apoplectic. Nothing has gone according to plan, he feels conned, betrayed – "fucking French bastard" – the best thing I can do is look baffled, this whole thing about the lock not working is bizarre, we tried it yesterday and the garage door opened. I calmly step out of the car, looking surprised and confused.

The magazine of a Mossberg 500 holds seven rounds. Instead

of yelling and screaming like a pack of hyenas, these arseholes would have been better off counting the spent rounds. They're about to find out that if you don't know shit about locks, you'd better know a thing or two about arithmetic. Because once I'm out of the car, all I have to do is walk slowly as far as the door to the lock-up, gently push the driver to one side – "Here, let me give it a go" – and when I turn, I'm perfectly positioned. There are just enough bullets to quickly aim at the driver and put a 70mm shell in his chest that flings him back against the concrete wall. Now for the little guy. I turn slightly and feel a sense of relief as I blast his brains out through the windshield. See the blood spurting. The shattered windscreen, the side windows dripping blood, I can't see anything else. I step closer to inspect the damage: his head has been blown to pieces, all that's left is his scrawny neck and his body, which is twitching still. Chickens run around after they've had their heads chopped off. Turks are much the same.

The Mossberg makes a hell of a racket, but the silence afterwards.

There's no time to lose now. Unload the two bags, dig out the right key to open the lock-up, drag the big brother into the garage, roll the car in with the kid inside in two neat pieces – I have to roll it over the other guy, but it doesn't matter, he's not going to make a fuss now – pull down the metal shutters, lock it and it's done and dusted.

All I need to do now is pick up the bags, walk to the far end of the cul-de-sac and get into the rental car. Actually, we're not quite done yet. You might say this is just the beginning. Time to settle the scores. Take out the mobile phone, punch in the number that will set off the bomb. I can feel the shock wave from here. I'm a fair distance away, but even at forty metres I feel the rental car shake from the force of the blast. Now that's an explosion. For the Turks, it's a one-way ticket to the Gardens of Delight. They'll be able to feel up a few virgins. A plume of black smoke rises over the roofs of the workshops – most of them are boarded up, the local municipality has the land earmarked for redevelopment. I've just given them a helping hand with the demolition. It's possible to be an armed robber and still have a sense of civic duty. Within thirty seconds, the fire brigade will be on their way. There's no time to lose.

Stash the bags of jewellery in a left-luggage locker at the Gare du Nord. Drop the key into a letterbox on the boulevard Magenta.

My fence will send someone to pick up the haul.

Finally, assess the situation. They say killers always return to the scene of the crime. I like to respect tradition.

11.45 a.m.

Two hours before going to Armand's funeral, Camille receives a phone call asking whether he knows a certain Anne Forestier. His number is the first entry in the contacts list on her mobile and the last number that she dialled. The call sends a cold shiver down his spine: this is how you learn that someone is dead.

But Anne is not dead. "She has been the victim of an assault. She has been taken to hospital." From the tone of the woman's voice, Camille immediately knows that Anne is in a bad way.

In fact, Anne is in a *very* bad way. She is much too weak to be questioned. The officers in charge of the investigation have said they will call round as soon as possible. It took several minutes of heated negotiation with the ward sister – a thirty-year-old woman with bee-stung lips and a nervous tic affecting her right eye – for

Camille to get permission to go into Anne's room. And then only on condition that he not stay too long.

He pushes open the door and stands for a moment on the threshold. Seeing her like this is devastating.

At first he can only make out her bandaged head. She looks as though she might have been run over by a truck. The right side of her face is a single, blue-black bruise so swollen that her eyes, barely visible, seem to have withdrawn into her skull. The left side is marked by a gash at least ten centimetres long, the edges where the wound has been sutured are a sallow red. Her lips are split and inflamed, her eyelids blue and puffy. Her nose has been broken and has swollen up to three times its normal size. Anne keeps her mouth slightly open, her bottom gums are bleeding, and a thread of spittle trickles onto the pillow. She looks like an old woman. Her arms, bandaged from her shoulders to her splinted fingers, lie on top on the sheets. The dressing on the right hand is smaller and it is possible to make out a deep wound that has been stitched.

When she becomes aware of Camille's presence, she tries to reach out her hand, her eyes fill with tears, then her energy seems to drain away. She closes her eyes then opens them again. They are glassy and expressionless; even her beautiful green irises seem colourless.

Her head lolls to one side, her voice is hoarse. Her tongue seems heavy and clearly painful where unconsciously she bit into it; it is difficult to make out what she is saying, the labial consonants are inaudible.

"I feel sore . . ."

Camille cannot utter a word. Anne tries to speak, he lays a hand on the sheet to calm her, he does not dare to touch her. She suddenly seems nervous, agitated; he wants to do something to help, but what? Call a nurse? Anne's eyes are shining, there is something she urgently needs to say.

"... graaa' ... 'eet ... ard .."

She is still dazed by the suddenness of what has happened, as though it has just happened now.

Bending down, Camille listens carefully, he pretends to understand, he tries to smile. Anne sounds as though she is talking through a mouthful of scalding soup. Camille can hear only mangled syllables, but he concentrates and after a minute he begins to decipher words, to guess at meaning ... Mentally, he translates. It is amazing how quickly we can adapt. To anything. Amazing, and a little sad.

"Grabbed," he hears, "beat ... hard."

Anne's eyebrows, her eyes grow wide with terror as though the man were once more standing in front of her, about to club her with the rifle butt. Camille gently reaches out and rests a hand on her shoulder, Anne flinches and gives a strangled cry.

"Camille ..." she says.

She turns her head, it is difficult to make out what she says. The words are a sibilant hiss through three shattered teeth – the upper and lower incisors on the left hand side – that make her look like she is thirty years older, like Fantine in a crude production of "*Les Misérables*". Though she has begged the nurses, no-one has dared to give her a mirror.

In fact, though she can barely move, she tries to cover her mouth with the back of her hand when she speaks. More often than not she fails and her mouth looks like a gaping wound, the lips bruised and bluish.

"... going to operate ... ?"

This is what Camille thinks he hears. She starts to cry again; her tears seem to come independently of her words, with no apparent logic they suddenly well up and course down her cheeks. Anne's face is a mask of mute astonishment.

'"We don't know yet . . ." Camille says, his voice low. "Try to relax. Everything is going to be fine . . ."

But already Anne's mind is elsewhere. She turns her head away, as though she were ashamed. Her voice is barely audible now. Camille thinks he can make out the words "Not like this . . ." She does not want anyone to see her in this state. She manages to turn onto her stomach. Camille lays a hand on her shoulder, but Anne does not react, she stubbornly looks away, her body shaken by ragged sobs.

"Do you want me to stay?"

There is no answer. Not knowing what to do, Camille stays. After a long moment, Anne shakes her head at something though it is impossible to know what – at what is happening, at what has happened, at the grotesque farce that can engulf our lives without warning, at the injustice victims cannot help but see as personal. It is impossible to ask her. It is too soon. They are not in the same moment. There is nothing they can say.

It is impossible to tell whether she is asleep. Slowly, she turns onto her back, eyes closed. And does not move again.

There.

Camille gazes at her, listening intently, comparing her breathing to that when she is asleep, a sound he knows better than anyone in the world. He has spent hours watching her sleep. In the early days, he would get up in the middle of the night to sketch her features that looked like a swimmer's, because during the day he could never quite capture the subtle magic of her face. He has made hundreds of drawings, spent countless hours attempting to reproduce

41

the purity of her lips, her eyelids. Or sketched her body silhouetted in the shower. His magnificent failures had taught him just how important she is: though he can draw an almost photographic likeness of anyone in a few scant minutes, there is something inexpressible, something indefinable about Anne that eludes his gaze, his senses, his powers of observation. The woman who lies swollen and bandaged before him now has nothing of the magic, all that remains is the outer shell, and ugly, terribly prosaic body.

It is this that, as the minutes pass, fuels Camille's anger.

From time to time, Anne wakes with a start, gives a little cry, glances round wildly and in those moments Camille sees a new and utterly unfamiliar expression, one he saw on Armand's face in the weeks before he died: the incredulous shock that things have come to this. Incomprehension. Injustice.

Hardly has he recovered from the upset than the nurse comes to tell him visiting hours are over. She is self-effacing, but she waits for him to leave. She wears a name-tag that reads "FLORENCE". She keeps her hands clasped behind her back, at once determined and respectful, her compassionate smile rendered utterly artificial by collagen or hyaluronic acid. Camille wants to stay until Anne can tell him everything, he is frantic to know what happened. But all he can do is wait. Leave. Anne needs to rest. Camille leaves.

It will be twenty-four hours before he begins to understand.

And twenty-four hours is much more time than a man like Camille might need to lay to waste the whole earth.

Emerging from the hospital, Camille knows only those few details given him over the telephone and later, here, at the hospital. In fact, aside from broad strokes, no-one knows anything; it has so far been impossible to retrace the precise sequence of events. Camille's only piece of evidence is Anne's disfigured face, a harrowing image that merely serves to fuel the anger of a man inclined to strong emotions.

By the time he has reached the exit, Camille is seething.

He wants to know everything, to know it now, to know it before everyone else, he wants . . .

Camille is not a vengeful man by nature, although, like anyone, there have been moments when he was tempted. But Philippe Buisson, the man who killed his first wife, is still very much alive, despite the fact that, given his contacts, it would have been a simple matter for Camille to have ordered a hit on him in prison.

And this time, seeing the attack on Anne, he is not motivated by a desire for revenge. It is as though what has happened threatens his own life. He needs to act, to do *something,* because he cannot grasp the magnitude of this incident that has almost destroyed his relationship with Anne, the only thing since Irène's death that has given it meaning.

What to others might seem like pompous platitudes sound very different to someone who already feels responsible for the death of a loved one. Such things change a man.

As he dashes down the steps of the hospital, he sees Anne's face again, the yellow rings around her eyes, the livid bruising, the swollen flesh.

He has just pictured her dead.

He does not yet know how or why, but someone has tried to kill her.

It is this sense of *déjà vu* that panics him. After Irène was murdered . . . The circumstances are completely different. Irène was personally targeted by her killer whereas Anne simply ran into the wrong man at the wrong time, but in the moment, Camille is incapable of untangling his emotions.

But he is also incapable of letting things take their course without doing something.

Without trying to do something.

In fact, though he does not realise it, he instinctively began to act from the moment he received the telephone call. Anne had "sustained injuries", he was told by the woman from the Préfecture de Police, having been involved in an "altercation" during an armed robbery in the 8th arrondissement. "Altercation" is one of Camille's favourite words. Everyone on the force loves it. Police officers are also fond of "perpetrator" and "stipulate", but "altercation" is particularly practical since in four syllables it covers everything from a heated argument to a vicious beating, leaving the other party to infer whatever they please.

"What kind of 'altercation'?"

The officer did not know, she was probably reading from a report, Camille could not help but wonder whether she even understood what she was saying.

"Armed robbery. Shots fired. Madame Forestier did not sustain gunshot wounds, but she was injured during an altercation. She has been taken to the nearest casualty department."

Shots fired? At Anne? During a hold-up? It is difficult to make sense of the words, impossible to imagine the scene. Anne and "armed robbery" are concepts that have nothing in common . . .

The woman on the telephone explained that, when she was found, Anne did not have a bag or any form of identification; officers had discovered her name and address from the mobile telephone lying nearby.

"We called her home number, but there was no reply."

So they had dialled the number Anne had called the most frequently – Camille's number.

The woman asked his surname for her report. She pronounced it "Veronε". Camille corrected her: "Verhœven". There was a brief silence and then she asked him to spell it.

This triggered something in Camille's mind.

Verhœven is hardly a common surname, and in the police force it is very unusual. And, frankly, Camille is not the sort of policeman people forget. It is not simply the matter of his uncommonly small stature, every officer knows his history, his reputation, they know about Irène, about the Alex Prévost case. To most people, Camille might as well have a tattoo reading "As seen on TV". He has made a number of high-profile appearances on television; cameramen favour an angled shot of his hawk-like features, his balding pate. But the assistant had clearly never heard about Verhœven, the renowned *commandant de police*, the T.V. appearances: she asked him to spell his name.

In hindsight, Camille decides that this is the first piece of good news in a day that bodes no others.

"Ferroven, did you say?" the girl said.

"That's right," Camille replied, "Ferroven."

And he spelled it for her.

2.00 p.m.

Such is the nature of the human animal: give them an accident and people immediately hang out of their windows. As long as there's a flashing police light or a smear of blood, there will be a rubbernecker there to pry. And right now, there are lots of them. I mean, an armed robbery in the middle of Paris, shots fired . . . Disneyland has nothing on this.

In theory the street is cordoned off, but that doesn't stop pedestrians strolling past. The order has been given that only residents are allowed through the barrier, but it's a waste of time – everyone claims to be a resident because everyone wants to know what the hell is going on. Things have calmed down a little, but from what people are saying, it was chaos this morning. With all the police cars, police vans, forensics teams and motorcycles clogging up the Champs-Élysées, the city was gridlocked from Place de la Concorde to l'Étoile and from the boulevard Malesherbes to the Palais de Tokyo. I have to say that just knowing I'm responsible for all that chaos is kind of exhilarating.

When you've fired a shotgun at a woman covered in blood and made off, tyres shrieking, in a four-by-four with fifty grand's worth of jewels, coming back to the crime scene gives you a little thrill, like Proust and his madeleine. It's quite pleasant, actually. It's not hard to be cheerful when your plans work out. There's a little café on Georges-Flandrin right next to the Monier. The perfect location. It's called Le Brasseur. The noise is deafening. Everyone babbling and arguing. It's very simple: everyone saw everything, heard everything, knows everything.

I stand at the far end of the bar, keeping a low profile, away from the people milling in the doorway, I blend in, I listen.

Fuckwits, the lot of them.

2.15 p.m.

The autumn sky looks as though it has been painted especially for this cemetery. There are lots of people. This is the advantage of serving officers, they turn up to funerals *en masse* so you are guaranteed a crowd.

From a distance, Camille spots Armand's family, his wife, his children, his brothers and sisters. Well groomed, ramrod straight, desolate, serious. He does not know what they are like in reality, but they look like a family of Quakers.

Armand's death four days earlier devastated Camille. It also liberated him. For weeks and weeks he had been visiting the hospital, holding Armand's hand, talking to him even when the doctors could no longer tell whether he could hear or understand. And so now he simply nods to Armand's widow from afar. After the longs months of agony, after all the words he has said to Armand's wife, his children, Camille has nothing left. He did not even need to come today: he has given everything he had to give.

Camille and Armand had a number of things in common. They had started out together at the police academy, a youthful connection made all the more precious by the fact that neither of them had ever truly been young.

Then there was Armand's pathological tight-fistedness. He waged a battle to the death against expense and, ultimately, against money. Camille cannot help but think of his death as a victory for capitalism. It was not this meanness that united them but the fact that, in their different ways, they were small men with an overwhelming need to compensate. It was a kind of solidarity for the differently abled.

Moreover his long, slow death had confirmed that Armand thought of Camille as his best friend.

What we mean to others can be a powerful bond.

Of the four original members of his team, Camille is the only one now standing in the cemetery, something he finds difficult to accept.

His assistant, Louis Mariani, has not yet arrived. Camille is not worried, Louis is a man with a strong sense of duty, he will be here – for someone of Louis' social class, missing a funeral, like farting at the dinner table, is unimaginable.

Cancer of the oesophagus gives Armand the perfect excuse for absence.

That leaves Maleval, whom Camille has not seen for several years. Maleval was a brilliant young officer before he was dismissed from the force. Despite their differences, he and Louis were good friends, they were roughly the same age and they complemented each other. Until it was discovered that Maleval had been feeding information to the man who murdered Irène. He had not done so deliberately, but he had done it all the same. At the time, Camille could happily have killed him with his bare hands, the *brigade criminelle* came very close to suffering a tragedy worthy of the House of Atreus. But after Irène's death, Camille was a broken man; he spent years ravaged by depression and afterwards his life seemed meaningless.

He misses Armand more than anyone. With his death, Verhœven's team has been wiped off the face of the earth. This funeral is the beginning of a new chapter in which Camille will try to rebuild his life. Nothing could be more fragile.

Armand's family are just going into the crematorium when Louis arrives. Pale cream Hugo Boss suit, very elegant. "Hi, Louis." Louis does not say "Hello, guv." Camille has forbidden the expression, they're not in some T.V. police series.

The question that sometimes nags Camille about himself is even more relevant to his assistant: what the hell is this guy doing on the force? He was born into a wealthy family and, as if that were not enough, is gifted with an intellect that saw him accepted into the finest schools a dilettante can attend. Then, inexplicably, he joined the police to work for a schoolteacher's salary. At heart, Louis is a romantic.

"You O.K. ?"

Camille nods, he is fine, in fact he's not really here at all. Most of him is still back at the hospital where Anne, doped up on painkillers, is waiting to be taken for X-rays and a C.A.T. scan.

Louis stares at his boss for just a second too long, nods, then gives a low *hmm*. Louis is man of great tact for whom *hmm*, like the tic of pushing his hair back with the left or right hand, is a private language. This particular *hmm* clearly translates: that long face isn't just about the funeral, is there something else going on? And for that something else to intrude on Armand's funeral, it must be pretty serious . . .

"The team is going to be assigned to deal with an armed robbery up in the 8th this morning . . ."

Louis cannot help but wonder whether this is the answer to his question.

"Many casualties?"

Camille nods, shrugs, yes, no.

"A woman . . ."

"Dead?"

Yes, no, not really, Camille frowns, staring straight ahead as though through dense fog.

"No . . . Well, not yet . . ."

Louis is rather surprised. This is not the kind of case the team usually work on, Commandant Verhœven has no experience in armed robbery. Then again, why not? Louis thinks, but he has known Camille long enough to realise that something is wrong. He manifests his surprise by looking down at his shoes, a pair of impeccably polished Crockett & Joneses, and coughs briefly, almost inaudibly. For Louis, this is the height of expressible emotion.

Camille jerks his chin towards the cemetery, the crematorium.

"As soon as this is over, I'd like to fill you in. Unofficially . . . The team hasn't been called in yet . . . [Camille finally dares to look at his assistant.] I just want us to be ahead of the game."

He glances around for Le Guen and quickly spots him. It would be difficult to miss him, the man is a colossus.

"O.K., we should go . . ."

Back when Le Guen was *commissaire* and his direct superior, Camille had only to lift a finger to get whatever he wanted; these days, things are more complicated.

Next to Contrôleur Général Le Guen, Commissaire Michard waddles along like a goose.

2.20 p.m.

This is one of the greatest moments in the Café Le Brasseur's history. The regulars unanimously concur that an armed robbery on this scale happens just once a century. Even those who saw nothing are agreed. The witness statements are piling up. People variously saw a girl, or two girls, or a woman, with a gun, with no gun, empty-handed, screaming. This was the owner of the jeweller's? No, it was her daughter. Really? Do you remember her mentioning a daughter? There was a getaway car. Make and model? The answers cover pretty much the entire range of imported cars currently available in France.

I slowly sip my coffee, this is the first moment I've had to relax in what has already been rather a long day.

The *patron* – who has a face just begging to be slapped – has decided that the haul from the robbery was five million euros. Not a cent less. I've no idea where he came by the figure, but he sounds convincing. I feel like handing him a loaded Mossberg and steering him towards the nearest jeweller's. Let him rob the place, scuttle back to his little café and fence the loot – if the dumb fuck gets a third of the sort of figure he's expecting, he can retire, because he won't do any better.

And that car they fired into! What car? The one over there – it looks like it stopped a charging rhino. Did they launch a mortar at it? And so begin the ballistic speculations and, as with the make and model of the car, there are advocates for every possible calibre. Makes a man want to fire a warning shot to shut them up, or shoot into the crowd to get a bit of peace.

Strutting and swaggering, the *patron* peremptorily announces, ".22 long rifle."

He closes his eyes as he says the words as though to confirm his expertise.

I cheer myself up by imagining him headless, like the Turk, from a blast with the 12-bore. Whether it was a .22 Long Rifle rimfire or a blunderbuss, the crowd are impressed; these idiots don't know shit. With witnesses like this, the cops are in for a treat.

2.45 p.m.
"Wha . . . why would you want to do that?" asks the *commissaire divisionnaire*, wheeling around, making a sweeping revolution on her major axis: a titanic, positively Babylonian arse that is preposterously disproportionate. Commissaire Michard is a woman of between forty and fifty. Hers is a face that promised much and failed to deliver; she has a shock of jet-black hair, probably dyed, buck teeth and a pair of heavy, square-rimmed glasses that proclaim her as a woman of authority, a safe pair of hands. She is gifted with a personality usually described as "forceful" (she is a pain in the

neck), a keen intelligence (this exponentially increases her ability to infuriate) but, most of all, she is blessed with an arse with a capital A. It is incredible. It seems a wonder she can keep her balance. Curiously, Commissaire Michard has a rather placid face at odds with everything one knows about her: her undeniable competence, her exceptional strategic sense, her mastery of firearms; the sort of boss who works ten times harder than everyone else and is proud of her leadership skills. When she was promoted to *commissaire*, Camille resigned himself to the fact that in addition to dealing with an overbearing female at home (Doudouche, his beloved cat, is emotionally unstable and borderline hysterical), he would now have to deal with one at work.

Hence her question: "Why would you want to do that?"

There are some people with whom it is difficult to remain calm. Commissaire Michard comes over and stands very close to Camille. She always does this when she speaks to him. Between her well-upholstered physique and Camille's slight, scrawny frame, they look like characters from an American sit-com, but this woman has no sense of the ridiculous.

They stand facing each other, blocking the entrance to the crematorium; they are among the last to go in. Camille has carefully orchestrated things so that at the moment he makes his request, they are overtaken by Contrôleur Général Le Guen – Camille's old friend and Michard's predecessor as *commissaire divisionnaire*. Now, everyone knows that Camille and Le Guen are more than simply friends; Camille has been best man at Le Guen's weddings – a time-consuming responsibility given that Le Guen has just got hitched for the sixth time, remarrying his second wife.

Since she was only recently appointed, Commissaire Michard

still needs to "run with the hare and hunt with the hounds" (she loves such clichés, which she strives to inject with a certain freshness), she needs to "hit the ground running" before she can afford to "rock the boat". So when the best friend of her direct superior makes a request, she falters. Especially as they are the last members of the cortège. Though she would like time to mull it over, she has a reputation for thinking on her feet and prides herself on making quick decisions. The service is about to begin. The funeral director glances anxiously towards them. Wearing a double-breasted suit, with a shock of bleached blond hair, he looks like a footballer – clearly undertakers are not what they used to be.

This question – why would Verhœven want his team to take on the case? – is the only one to which Camille has prepared an answer, because it is the only pertinent question.

The robbery took place at 10.00 this morning, it is not yet 3.00 p.m. Back at the Galerie, the forensics officers are completing their examination of the crime scene, various officers are taking witness statements, but the case has not yet been assigned to a squad.

"I've got an informant," says Camille. "Someone on the inside ..."

"You had information about the robbery before it happened?"

Michard's eyes widen dramatically, reminding Camille of the furious glares of samurai warriors in Japanese lithographs. This is the sort of stock expression Michard loves; the look means: you're either telling me too much or not enough.

"Of course I didn't," Camille snaps. (He plays this scene very convincingly; he sounds genuinely affronted.) "I knew nothing about it, though I'm not sure about my source ... I'm telling you this guy's prepared to spill his guts, he's desperate to cut a deal. [Verhœven is convinced this is the sort of cliché that appeals to

Michard.] Right now, he's prepared to cooperate . . . it would be a pity to not use him."

A single glance is all it takes to shift the conversation from matters of protocol to simple tactics. Camille's brief glance towards the man at the far end of the cemetery is enough for the tutelary figure of the *contrôleur général* to loom over the conversation. Silence. The *commissaire* smiles to indicate that she understands: O.K.

"Besides, it's not just an armed robbery," Camille adds for the sake of form. "There's the attempted murder . . ."

The *commissaire* nods slowly and shoots Camille a quizzical look as though she has seen beyond the *commandant*'s somewhat heavy-handed ploy some faint glimmer, as though she is trying to understand. Or has just understood. Or is about to understand. Camille knows how perceptive the woman is: the slightest false step triggers her highly sensitive seismograph.

So he takes the initiative, speaking quickly, using his most persuasive tone: "Let me explain. This informant of mine is connected to another guy, a member of a gang involved in a different job – that was last year, and it's not directly connected to this case, but the thing is . . ."

Commissaire Michard cuts him short with a weary wave that says she has problems enough of her own. That she understands. That she realises she is too new to her post to intervene between her superior and her subordinate.

"It's fine, *commandant*. I'll talk to the examining magistrate, Juge Pereira."

This is exactly what Camille was hoping would happen, though he is careful not to show it.

Because had Michard not given up so quickly, he has not the first idea how he would have finished his sentence.

Louis left quickly. Camille, given his rank, was forced to wait around until the bitter end. The service was long, very long, and everyone wanted a chance to speak. Camille slipped away as soon as was decently possible.

As he walks back to his car, he listens to the voicemail he has just received from Louis, who has already managed to put in several calls and has come up with a lead.

"I've been through the files and the only incidence of a Mossberg 500 being used in an armed robbery was on January 17 last. The similarity between the jobs is unquestionable. And the last case was pretty grim . . . Can you call me back?"

Camille calls him back.

"The incident last January was a lot more vicious," Louis explains. "The gang held up four separate outlets. One person was killed. The leader of the gang was identified. Vincent Hafner. There's been no sign of him since the January robberies, but today's comeback stunt was clearly designed to attract attention . . ."

There's a sudden flurry of excitement at Le Brasseur.

The babble of conversation is interrupted by a wail of sirens and the customers hurry out onto the terrace to gawk as the sirens seem to rise in pitch. The *patron* peremptorily announces it is the *ministre de l'Intérieur*. People vainly rack their brains trying to remember the minister's name. They'd remember if it was a game-show host. The chattering starts up again. A few pundits decide there has been some new development, maybe they've found a body or something; the *patron* closes his eyes and adopts a self-important air. The customers' conflicting theories are a testament to his erudition.

"It's the *ministre de l'Intérieur*, I'm telling you."

With a little smile he calmly goes on polishing glasses, he does not even trouble to glance towards the terrace, thereby demonstrating his faith in his own prognostication.

The customers wait feverishly, holding their breath, as though expecting the arrival of the Tour de France.

3.30 p.m.

It feels as though her brain is filled with cotton wool surrounded by veins thick as arms that hammer and throb.

Anne opens her eyes. The room. The hospital.

She stiffly tries to move her legs, like an old woman plagued by rheumatism. It is agonising, but she succeeds in lifting one knee, then the other. Drawing up her legs gives her a brief moment of relief. Tentatively, she moves her head to see how it feels. Her head seems to weigh a ton, her bandaged fingers look like the claws of a crab. There comes a rush of blurred images: the toilets in Galerie Monier, a pool of blood, gunshots, the skull-splitting howl of the ambulance, the face of the radiologist and, from behind him, the faint voice of a nurse saying "What on God's earth did they do to her?" She feels a wave of emotion, she blinks back tears, takes a deep breath; she needs to keep her self-control, she cannot afford to give in, to give up.

She has to stand up if she is to stay alive.

She throws back the sheet – despite the excruciating pain in her hand – and manages to slide first one leg and then the other over the side. She feels a dizzying rush and waits for a moment, balanced precariously on the edge of the bed, then plants her feet firmly on the ground, hauls herself upright and is immediately forced to sit down again; only now does she truly feel pain rack her

56

body, savage, specific, shooting through her back, her shoulders, her collarbone, she feels crushed, she struggles to catch her breath, hauls herself up again and finally she manages to stand, though she is clutching the nightstand for support.

The toilet is directly opposite. Like a climber, she gropes for handholds – the headboard, the bedside table, the door handle, the washbasin – until finally she is staring into the mirror. Dear God, can this be her?

This time, she can do nothing to stop the sobs welling in her. The blue-black bruises, the broken teeth, the gash along her left cheek where the bone has been shattered, the trail of sutures . . .

What on God's earth did they do to her?

Anne grips the sink to stop herself from falling.

"What are you doing out of bed?"

As she turns, Anne suddenly faints, the nurse only just has time to catch her as she falls and lay her carefully on the floor. The nurse gets to her feet and pops her head out into the corridor.

"Florence, could you give me a hand?"

3.40 p.m.

Camille strides along fretfully. Louis walks beside him, half a pace behind; the precise distance he maintains from his boss is a calculated mixture of respect and familiarity. Only Louis would come up with such nuanced permutations.

Though Camille is anxious and harried, he nonetheless glances up at the buildings that line the rue Georges-Flandrin – typical exponents of Hausmann architecture blackened by years of grime and soot, buildings so commonplace in this part of the city that one hardly notices them. His eye is caught by a line of balconies supported at either end by twin Atlases with loincloths distended by large bulges, each balcony is supported by a caryatid with preposterously large breasts that stare into the heavens. It is the breasts that point heavenward; the caryatids' eyes are demurely lowered in that coy expression of supremely confident women. Camille gives an admiring nod and strides on.

"René Parrain would be my guess," he says.

Silence. Camille closes his eyes and waits to be corrected.

"More likely to be Chassavieux, don't you think?"

It was ever thus. Louis may be twenty years younger, but he knows twenty thousand times more than Camille. What is most irritating is that he is never wrong. Almost never. Camille has tried to trap him, has tried and tried but to no avail; the guy is a walking Wikipedia.

"Yeah," he mutters grudgingly, "maybe."

As they come to the Galerie Monier, Camille stumbles past the wreckage of the car blasted by the 12-bore just as a tow truck is hoisting it onto the flatbed.

Later, he will find out that Anne was standing on the other side of the car when the shots were aimed directly at her.

The little guy is the one in charge. Police officers these days are like politicians, their rank is inversely proportional to their size. Everyone recognises the little one, obviously, given his height. Once seen, never forgotten. But his name is another matter. The café customers come up with a range of suggestions. They know it's a foreign surname, but what? German, Danish, Flemish? One of the regulars thinks it might be Russian, then another triumphantly shouts "Verhœven." "That's it." Everyone laughs. "You see? I told you it was something foreign."

He appears at the corner of the passage. He does not flash his warrant card – when you're less than five foot shit, you get special dispensation. The people peer through the café windows, waiting with bated breath, when they are distracted by something even more miraculous: a tanned, dark-haired girl has just walked into the bar. The *patron* greets her loudly and everyone turns to look. It is the hairdresser from the salon next door. She orders four espressos – the coffee machine in the salon is not working.

She knows everything, she smiles modestly as she waits to be served. To be quizzed. She pretends that she does not have time for questions, but her blushes speak volumes.

They want to know everything.

3.50 p.m.

Louis shakes hands with the officers already on the scene. Camille demands to see the C.C.T.V. footage. Right now. Louis is shocked. He knows only too well that Camille has little respect for etiquette and protocol, but such a gross disregard for procedure is shocking in a man of his rank and experience. Louis delicately pushes his fringe back with his left hand, then follows his boss into the shop's back room which has been temporarily requisitioned as an incident room. Camille absently shakes hands with the owner, a woman decked out like a Christmas tree who is smoking a Gauloise set in a long, ivory cigarette-holder of the sort that went out of fashion a century ago. Camille does nothing to stop her. The first officers on the scene have already tracked down the footage from the two C.C.T.V. cameras.

As soon as the laptop computer is set up in front of him, Camille turns to Louis.

"Right. I'll go through the videos. You go and find out what we've got so far."

He jerks his chin towards the front of the shop, which amounts to showing Louis the door. Without waiting for a reply, he sits at the desk and stares at everyone. He looks for all the world as though he wants to be alone to watch a porn film.

Louis acts as though his boss's behaviour is perfectly logical. There is something of the gentleman's gentleman about him.

"Go on," he says, ushering everyone out, "we'll set up the incident room in here."

The footage Camille is interested in is from the camera position just outside the jeweller's.

Twenty minutes later, while Louis is watching the video, comparing details of the footage with the first witness statements, Camille goes out into the arcade and stands on the spot where the gunman stood.

The forensics team has finished collecting evidence, the shards of glass have all been picked up and collected, the crime scene has been taped off. Once the insurance assessors and structural surveyors arrive, the last officers will slink away and two months from now, the arcade will have been completely refurbished, new shops will open up ready for the next crazed gunman to turn up during opening hours and target their customers or their staff.

The scene is being guarded by a *gendarme*, a tall, thin officer with a jaded expression, a jutting chin, and bags under his eyes. Like a supporting actor whose name no-one can ever remember, Camille dimly recognises the man as someone he has seen at a hundred other crime scenes. They nod vaguely to each other.

Camille gazes at the looted shop, the smashed display cases. Though he knows little or nothing about jewellery, he cannot but wonder if this is the sort of place he himself would have chosen for a hold-up. But he also knows that appearances are deceptive.

A bank might not be much to look at, but steal everything inside one and you would have enough to come back and buy the place.

Camille does what he can to stay calm; his hands are stuffed into the pockets of his overcoat because ever since he watched the video – replaying the harrowing, horrifying images over and over – his hands have not stopped trembling.

He brusquely shakes his head as though he had water in his ears, as though were trying to dispel this excess of emotion, to regain a sense of composure. But it is impossible. The crimson halos on the tiled floor are Anne's blood; she lay exactly there, curled into a ball, while the man with the gun stood over there. Camille takes a step back and the tall *gendarme* watches him uneasily. Suddenly, Camille turns, holding an imaginary shotgun by his side; the *gendarme* makes to reach for his police radio. Camille takes three more steps, glances from where the shooter was standing towards the exit and then suddenly, without warning, he starts to run. This time, the *gendarme* grabs his radio but seeing Camille stop abruptly he does not press the button. Camille anxiously touches a finger to his lips and retraces his steps, he looks up at the *gendarme* and they smile warily at one another like two men with no common language eager to be friends.

What exactly happened here?

Camille glances to left and right, he looks up towards the shattered fanlight blasted by the shotgun, he walks forward again and comes to the exit that leads onto the rue Georges-Flandrin. He is not sure what he is looking for, some clue, some detail, some pointer – his near eidetic memory for places and people stores information differently.

Inexplicably, he somehow knows he is on the wrong track.

That there is nothing to see here. That he is approaching the case from the wrong angle.

And so he leaves the arcade and goes back to questioning the bystanders. He tells the first officers on the scene who have already taken witness statements that he wants "his own sense of things"; he interviews the bookseller, the antiques dealer, out on the pavement he questions the hairdresser. The woman who owns the jeweller's has already been taken to hospital. Her assistant saw nothing, having spent the raid with her face pressed to the floor and her arms over her head. He cannot help feeling sorry for this shy, insignificant girl, hardly more than a child. Camille tells her to go home, asks whether she would like someone to drive her, she tells him she is waiting for a friend at Le Brasseur, nodding towards the far side of the road where the café terrace is thronged with rubberneckers staring back at them. "Go on," Camille says, "get out of here."

He has listened to the witnesses, studied the C.C.T.V. footage.

As the raid began to unravel, the unbearable tension might account for Anne's attempted murder as events spiralled out of control.

But there is something about the gunman's fury, his relentless determination to slaughter her . . .

The examining magistrate has been appointed, he is expected to arrive any minute now. In the meantime, Camille goes over everything that has been said. Every detail of this robbery matches a hold-up that took place in January.

"That's what you said, right?"

"Absolutely," Louis says. "The difference is one of scale. The raid today targeted a single jeweller's, whereas in January there were four separate incidents. Four jeweller's held up in the space of six hours . . ."

Camille gives a low whistle.

"The M.O. is identical. A team of three men, one breaking open the display cases and taking the jewellery, one standing guard with a sawn-off shotgun, and the third waiting in the getaway car."

"You said someone died during the January robberies?"

Louis flicks through his notes.

"The first target was in the 15th. They stormed the place first thing in the morning, right after it opened, and they were in and out in less than ten minutes. This was the only raid that went to plan. At 10.30, they burst into a jeweller's on the rue de Rennes, and this time they clubbed one of the staff who had been slow to open the safe. They left him unconscious – blunt force trauma to the head – and the guy spent four days in a coma. He pulled through, but he has suffered serious after-effects and he's suing the company for a disability pension."

Camille is listening anxiously. Anne clearly had a narrow escape. Camille's nerves are frayed, he forces himself to breathe deeply, to relax his muscles – what was it again? – the sterno-claudio . . . fuck.

"Just after lunch, at about 2.00, the gang turn up in a jeweller's in the Louvre des Antiquaires. By now, they're using brute force, they're in and out within minutes again, leaving a customer lying on the pavement . . . He's not as badly injured as the guy on the rue de Rennes, but his condition is considered critical."

"Things are escalating," Camille says, reading between the lines.

"Yes and no," Louis says. "The gang are not out of control, they're savagely, single-mindedly doing their job . . ."

"Still, it's already a great deal to do in one day . . ."

"True."

Even for an experienced gang with the means and the motivation, four hold-ups in the space of six hours requires extraordinary efficiency and discipline. After a while, fatigue is bound to take over. A hold-up is like skiing; accidents always happen at the end of the day, it is the last effort that causes the greatest damage.

"The manager of the jeweller's on the rue de Sèvres fights back," Louis picks up the story again. "Just as the gang are about to leave he tries to stall them, he grabs the sleeve of the man who has been rifling the display cases and tries to shove him to the ground. Before the lookout has time to aim his Mossberg, the other guy has pulled a 9mm and put two bullets in the manager's chest."

There is no knowing whether this was the last raid they had planned or whether the manager's death forced them to get the hell away.

"Aside from the number of heists they pulled off, the M.O. for the robberies is classic. Most kids who pull this sort of heist bark orders, wave their guns around, fire warning shots, jump over the counter; they carry the sort of massive weaponry they've seen in video games, you can tell that they're scared witless. But these guys are organised, they're single-minded, they don't put a foot wrong. If they hadn't happened on some have-a-go hero, they would have left only minor collateral damage."

"So what was the haul?" Camille asks.

"Six hundred and eighty thousand euros," Louis says. "That's what was declared."

Camille raises a quizzical eyebrow, not because he is surprised that the jeweller's would minimise the value of what was stolen – they would have undeclared valuables in stock – he simply wants to know the true amount.

"The probable value is significantly upwards of a million. Resale, probably six hundred, six hundred and fifty thousand. A good day's work."

"Any idea where they might have offloaded the stuff?"

Given the nature of the haul – high-end, one-off pieces – resale would bring in a fraction of the real value, and few fences in Paris would be prepared to take it.

"We're assuming it was trafficked through Neuilly, but who knows . . ."

Obvious. It would be the ideal solution. Rumour has it the fence in Neuilly is a defrocked priest. Camille has never bothered to check, but he does not find the idea so strange: to him, the two professions have much in common.

"Send someone out to nose around."

Louis makes a note. In most of their cases, it is he who assigns tasks to the team.

At this point Juge Pereira, the examining magistrate, arrives. His eyes are a dazzling blue, his nose a little too long for his face, his ears droop like a spaniel's. Nervous and harried, he shakes Camille's hand – *bonjour, commandant* – as he passes. Strutting behind him comes the court clerk, a stunning woman with a plunging neckline that reveals too much cleavage and with preposterously high heels that click-clack across the tiled floor; someone should have a quiet word with her about appropriate work attire. The magistrate is well aware that she is causing a stir, but despite her revealing dress it's clear that she wears the trousers. If she felt so inclined, she could parade around chewing gum and blowing bubbles. Camille cannot help but think that, at thirty or so, the Lolita look is rather sluttish.

Everyone gathers around: Camille, Louis and the two other members of the squad who have just arrived. Louis takes charge. Analytical, precise, methodical and intelligent (in his day, he was awarded a scholarship to the elite *École nationale d'administration* but chose to study at Sciences Po). The *juge* listens thoughtfully. There is talk of the fact that witnesses identified Eastern European accents, the possibility that they are dealing with a gang of violent Serbs or Bosnians; much is made of the fact that they fired shots when they could have avoided doing so. Someone mentions Vincent Hafner and his string of convictions for gun-related offences. The magistrate nods. Hafner teaming up with a Bosnian gang would be a dangerous combination; it's surprising there were not more casualties. Those guys are animals, the *juge* says, and he is right.

Juge Pereira moves on to enquire about the witnesses. Usually, there are three members of staff in the jeweller's to open up: the manageress, her assistant, and another girl, but she was late this morning. She showed up just in time to hear the last gunshot. When staff in a shop or a bank are miraculously absent during a hold-up, the police are immediately suspicious.

"We've taken her in for questioning," says one of the officers (though he does not seem altogether sure). "We'll look into it, but right now she seems clean."

The court clerk is plainly bored. She squirms on her high heels, shifting her weight from one foot to the other, staring pointedly towards the exit. Her nails are painted blood red, the top two buttons on her figure-hugging blouse have popped open to reveal the pale, cavernously deep furrow of her cleavage while all eyes are drawn to the third button, precariously held in place by straining fabric drawn out like a predatory smile. Camille glances at her, mentally sketching a portrait. She is certainly striking, but only taken as a whole. Because the details tell a different story: her feet are too big, her nose too short, her features are a little crude, her buttocks are amply proportioned but too high. An arse worthy of an alpine climber. And the perfume exudes . . . salt water and sea air. She could be a fishwife.

"Right," the *juge* whispers, taking Camille to one side. "*Madame la commissaire* tells me you have an informant . . . ?" The phrase "*madame la commissaire*" is said in the obsequious tone of someone preparing for the day when he gets to say "*monsieur le ministre*". The clerk is vexed by their *tête-à-tête*. She heaves a long, loud sigh.

"I do," Camille confirms. "I'll know more tomorrow."

"So in theory we should be able to wrap the case up quickly?"

"In theory . . ."

The magistrate seems satisfied. He may not be a *commissaire*, but he appreciates favourable statistics. He decides it is time to leave. He shoots an angry glance at the clerk.

"Mademoiselle?"

His tone is curt, imperious.

From the look on Lolita's face, it is clear he will pay a heavy price.

4.00 p.m.

The little hairdresser proves to be an effective witness. She runs through the statement she gave to the police earlier, eyes coyly lowered like a blushing bride. It's by far the most accurate account I've heard. The girl's got a keen eye. With witnesses like her, it's a good job we were wearing balaclavas. Given the hustle and bustle outside, I stay next to the bar, as far as possible from the terrace. I order another coffee.

The woman involved in the incident is not dead. The parked car took most of the force of the blast. She was taken away in an ambulance.

Time to head for the hospital. The casualty department. Before she's discharged or transferred to another ward.

But first, I need to reload. Seven cartridges in the Mossberg.

The fireworks display is only just beginning.

I'm planning to paint the walls red.

6.00 p.m.

Despite his agitation, Camille cannot drum his fingers on the steering wheel. He drives a specially adapted car with centrally located controls – he has no alternative given that his arms are short and his feet dangle off the ground. And in a vehicle designed or adapted for handicapped persons, you have to be careful where you place your fingers on the steering wheel; one wrong move and the car could go off the road. To make matters worse, Camille is not particularly good with his hands; aside from artistic ability, he is downright clumsy.

He pulls up outside the hospital and walks across the car park, mentally rehearsing what he plans to say to the doctor – the sort of pithy phrases you spend hours polishing only to forget as soon as the moment arrives. When he came here this morning, reception had been crowded so he had immediately gone up to Anne's room. This time he stops. The desk is at eye level (about one metre forty, Camille estimates). He goes around and, without a second thought, pushes open the door marked "AUTHORISED PERSONNEL ONLY. NO ENTRY".

"What the hell?" the receptionist yells. "Can't you read?"

"Can't *you*?" Camille retorts, holding out his warrant card.

The woman bursts out laughing and give him a thumbs-up.

"Good one!"

She is a slim black woman of about forty, sharp-eyed, with a flat chest and bony shoulders. From the Antilles. Her name-tag reads "OPHÉLIA". She is wearing an ugly frilly blouse, a pair of huge, white movie-star glasses shaped like butterfly wings and she stinks of cigarettes. She holds up a fleshy hand telling Camille to wait a moment while she answers the phone, patches the call through, hangs up, then turns and looks at him admiringly.

"Well, ain't you a little thing? For a policeman, I mean ... Don't they have some kind of height requirement?"

Though Camille is in no mood to deal with this, the woman makes him smile.

"I got a special dispensation," he says.

"You got someone to pull some strings, is what you did!"

Within five minutes, their banter has become a friendly conversation. She seems unfazed by the fact that he is a police officer. Camille cuts it short and asks to speak to the consultant dealing with Anne Forestier.

"At this time of night, you'd need to talk to the on-call doctor up on the ward."

Camille nods and heads towards the lifts, only to come back again.

"Were there any phone calls for her?"

"Not that I know ..."

"You sure?"

"Take my word for it. It's not like the patients in that wing are up to taking calls."

Camille walks away again.

"Hey, hey!"

The woman is fluttering a sheet of yellow paper, as though fanning someone taller than her. Camille traipses back to the desk. Ophélia gives him a smouldering look.

"A little love letter from me to you . . ."

It is a bureaucratic form. Camille stuffs it into his pocket, takes the lift up to the intensive care unit and asks to see the registrar. He will have to wait.

The car park outside A. & E. is full to bursting. It's the perfect place to hide in plain sight: as long as you don't park here for too long, no-one is going to notice one more car. All you have to do is be alert, discreet. Ready to act.

It helps if you have a loaded Mossberg under a newspaper on the passenger seat. Just in case.

Now all I need to do is think; plan for the future.

One option is just to wait until the woman is being transferred from the hospital. Probably the simplest solution. Shooting up an ambulance is a breach of the Geneva Convention – unless, that is, you don't give a flying fuck. The C.C.T.V. cameras over the entrance are useless: they're there to deter any prospective criminals, but there's nothing to stop someone from shooting them out before getting down to serious business. Morally, it's a no-brainer. Technically, it's not exactly rocket science.

No, the only snag with his option is logistical: the security barrier at the ambulance bay creates a bottleneck. Obviously it would be possible to put a bullet in the security guard, break through the security barrier – there's no mention of security guards in the Geneva Convention – but it's hardly an elegant solution.

The second possibility is to wait until the ambulance clears the security area. There's a brief window of opportunity here, since it will be forced to turn right and wait for the traffic light on the filter lane to turn green. Though it might arrive with sirens blaring and tyres squealing – after all, it has urgent deliveries to make – the ambulance will be a little less pressurised when it leaves. While it's waiting at the lights, a determined shooter could step up behind, and in three seconds – one second to open the tailgate, one to aim and one to fire – leave the paramedic and any bystanders shitting themselves so much he'd have more than enough time to jump back in his car, floor the accelerator, drive forty metres against one-way traffic before reaching the dual carriageway and the Périphérique. Piece of piss. Job done. Everything back on track. I can almost smell the money.

Both options mean waiting for her to leave, either to be discharged or transferred to another hospital. If that window of opportunity doesn't open up, I'd need to look at other possibilities.

There's always the option of making a home delivery. Like a postman. Like a florist. Just go up to the room, knock politely, enter, deliver my bouquet and leave. It would mean a precisely timed operation. Or alternatively, going in with all guns blazing. Each strategy has its advantages. Option one, the clean kill, would require more skill and be more satisfying, but it smacks of narcissism, it's more about the killer than the victim, it shows a lack of generosity. Firing at random on the other hand is much more generous, more magnanimous, it's almost philanthropic.

In the end, events usually make the decision for us. Hence the need to assess the situation. To plan ahead. That was the Turks' big mistake – they were well organised, but when it came to planning for all eventualities, they screwed up. When you leave some god-forsaken country to go and commit a crime in a major European capital, you plan ahead. Not them. They just showed up at Rois-sy airport, scowling and knitting their bushy eyebrows so I would think I was dealing with big-time gangsters. Jesus Christ! They were cousins of some whore at Porte de la Chapelle, the biggest heists they'd been involved in were robbing some shop in Ankara and knocking over a petrol station in Keskin . . . Given what I need-ed them to do, it's not like I had to recruit top-flight specialists, but even so, hiring dumb fucks like them was almost humiliating.

Forget about them. At least they got to see Paris before they died. They could have said thanks.

It seems good things come to those who wait. I've just spotted the little policeman scuttling through the car park on his way into the hospital. I'm three steps ahead of him, and I plan to keep it that way. I can see him standing at the reception desk. Whoever is behind the desk probably only sees his bald patch looming over the surface, like the shark in "Jaws". He's tapping his foot, he's clearly on edge. He's gone around the back of the desk.

Short but sure of himself.

It doesn't matter, I'll take him on his home turf.

I get out of the car and go for a scout around. The key thing is to act fast, get it over and done with.

6.15 p.m.
Anne is asleep. The bandages around her head are stained a dirty yellow by haemostatic agents, giving her skin a milky whiteness, her eyelids are swollen shut and her lips . . . Camille is committing

every detail to memory, every line he would need to sketch this ruined face, when he is interrupted by someone popping their head around the door and asking to speak to him. Camille steps out into the corridor.

The on-call doctor is a solemn-faced young Indian with small, round glasses and a name-tag bearing an impossibly long surname. Camille flashes his warrant card again and the young man studies it carefully, probably trying to work out how to react. Although it is not unusual to have cops in A. & E., it's rare to get a visit from the *brigade criminelle*.

"I need to know the extent of Madame Forestier's injuries," Camille explains, nodding towards Anne's room. "The examining magistrate will want to question her . . ."

The on-call doctor tells him this is a matter for the consultant, only he can decide when she will be fit to be questioned.

"I see . . ." Camille nods. "But, will she . . . How is she?"

The doctor is carrying a file containing Anne's X-rays and her notes, but does not need to consult it, he knows it by heart: her nose is broken ("a clean break that will not require surgery," he stresses), a fractured collarbone, two broken ribs, sprains to her left wrist and ankle, two broken fingers (also clean breaks) and numerous cuts and contusions to her arms, her legs and her stomach, her right hand suffered a deep cut and although there is no nerve damage, she may need physiotherapy; the long gash down her face is a little more problematic and may leave a permanent scar, she has also sustained serious bruising. Even so, the results of the preliminary scan are encouraging.

"It's amazing, but there's no sign of any damage to the neurophysiological or autonomic systems. There are no fractures to the skull, though she will require dental surgery. She may need

73

a plaster cast . . . but we can't be sure. We'll know more tomorrow when we do the M.R.I. scan."

"Is she in pain?" Camille says and quickly adds, "The reason I'm asking is because if the magistrate needs to question her . . ."

"She's suffering as little as is possible. We have a lot of experience with pain relief."

Camille manages to smile, stammers his thanks. The doctor gives him a curious look, his eyes are piercing. "He seems unusually emotional for a policeman," he seems to be thinking. He seems about to question Camille's professionalism, to ask to see his warrant card again. In the end, he draws on his reserve of compassion.

"It will take time for her to heal," he says, "the bruises will fade, she may have a couple of minor scars, but Madame . . . [he glances down at his file] Madame Forestier is out of danger and she has suffered no permanent damage. I'd say the main problem now is not dealing with her physical injuries, but dealing with the trauma she will have suffered. We'll keep her under observation for a day or two. After that . . . well, she may need some support."

Camille thanks the man again. He should go, there is nothing more for him to do here. But it is out of the question. He is physically incapable of leaving.

The right wing of the hospital offers no possible entry, but things are much better on the left-hand side. There is an emergency exit. This is familiar territory. It's a door like the one in the Monier, a fire-door with a horizontal crash bar that is easily jimmied with a length of flexible metal.

I stand and listen for a minute – which is pointless, since the door is too thick. Never mind. A quick glance around me, slide the metal between the door and the jamb, open it and find myself in a corridor. At the far end is another corridor. I take a few steps, walking boldly, deliberately making noise in case I should bump into someone and seconds later I come to the end of the hallway and emerge behind the reception desk. It's like hospitals are designed with killers in mind.

On the wall to my right is an emergency evacuation plan. The building is complicated, sections have been remodelled, new wings added – it must be a nightmare for security guards. Especially since people never bother to look at official signs. The hospital should organise an impromptu fire drill some day. To visitors, the sight of an evacuation plan, especially in a hospital, is reassuring . . . It gives the feeling that, however overworked the staff might be, you're in safe hands. But an intimate knowledge of the emergency evacuation plan is even more useful when you're faced with a single-minded killer carrying a sawn-off shotgun.

Who cares?

I take out my mobile and snap a picture. The floors are all laid out the same way, since they have to take into account the position of the lift shafts, the conduits and the outflow pipes.

Go back out to the car. Think carefully. Failing to assess the risks is precisely the sort of thing that can mean snatching defeat from the jaws of victory.

6.45 p.m.

Camille does not turn on the light in Anne's room, he sits in the half-light on one of the high hospital chairs trying to collect his thoughts. Everything seems to be moving so quickly.

Anne is snoring softly. She has always snored a little, depending on her position. Whenever she becomes aware of it, she feels embarrassed. Today, her face is a mass of bruises, but usually when she blushes, she looks even more beautiful. She has the complexion of a redhead, with tiny, pale freckles visible only when she is embarrassed.

"You don't snore, you just breathe heavily," Camille invariably reassures her. "It's not the same at all."

She flushes pink, fiddling with her hair to hide her self-consciousness.

"The day you finally recognise my faults as faults," she smiles, "it'll be time to call it a day."

She often casually refers to the time when they will break up. She talks of those moments when they are a couple and those that will occur after they separate as though any difference between them is inconsequential. Camille finds this reassuring. It is the reflexive reaction of a widower, a depressive. He does not know whether he is still a depressive, but he is still a widower. Everything seems less straightforward, less clear-cut since Anne came into his life. They move together towards a future in which time is unknowable, uncertain, endlessly renewed.

"Camille, I'm so sorry . . ."

Anne has just opened her eyes. She articulates each word very deliberately. Despite the leaden vowels, the sibilant consonants, the hand shielding her mouth, Camille understands every word.

"What on earth do you have to be sorry for, darling?"

She gestures towards her mutilated body, it is a gesture that encompasses the hospital bed, the room, Camille, their life together, the world entire.

"Everything . . ."

Her vacant eyes recall the thousand-yard stare of victims who survive a tragedy. Camille reaches for her hand, but he can feel only the splints on her fingers. "You need to get some rest.

You're safe now. I'm here." As though that means anything. Even overwhelmed by private anguish, he finds himself resorting to the platitudes of his profession. Still he cannot shake off the nagging question of why the man at the Galerie Monier was so intent on killing her. So determined that he has made four separate attempts. There would have been the terrible pressure of the hold-up, things spiralled out of control, but even so . . .

"At the jeweller's, during the raid . . . did you see or hear anything else?" Camille says.

"Anything else . . . what do you mean?"

No. Nothing. He attempts a smile, but it is less than convincing, he lays his hand on her arm. Let her sleep for now. But she needs to talk to him as soon as possible. Needs to tell him everything, every last detail; there may be something she does not realise she knows. The crucial thing is to find out what.

"Camille . . ."

He bends down towards her.

"I'm so sorry . . ."

"Come on now," he gently chides her, "that's enough of that."

In the half-light of the hospital room, swathed in bandages, her swollen face black with bruises, her ruined mouth, Anne looks terribly ugly. Already Camille can see time pass, see the black, swollen bruises fade to blue, to purplish yellow. He will have to leave, whether he wants to or not. What pains him most are Anne's tears. They course down her cheeks even when she is asleep.

Camille gets to his feet. This time, he is resolved to go. Besides, there is nothing he can do here. As he leaves, he very carefully closes the door, quietly, as he might the door to a child's bedroom.

6.50 p.m.

Most of the time, the receptionist is snowed under with casualties, but whenever the flood of new patients slows to a trickle, she pops out for a cigarette or two. It's hardly surprising: to hospital workers, cancer is like a colleague. She stands outside, arms folded, smoking miserably.

This is the perfect opportunity. I dash to the side of the building, open the emergency exit, check the switchboard operator hasn't come back from her break. I can see her standing outside the glass doors. Three more steps, reach out and there it is, the admissions file. Ask and it shall be given to you.

They keep all medications in the cabinet under lock and key, but patient files are right there for the taking. It's logical: as a nurse, you assume that danger lies in infection and intoxicants; you're not expecting an armed robber.

Pickup: Galerie Monier, 8th arrondissement, Paris
Ambulance Crew: LR-453
Time of arrival: 10.44 a.m.
Full Name: Forestier, Anne
Room: 244
D.O.B.: unknown
Address: 26, rue de la Fontaine-au-Roi
Discharge/Transfer: decision pending
Ongoing Treatment: X-Rays, C.T. Scan
Consultant: T.B.A.

Back out to the car park. The receptionist is lighting another cigarette – I could have taken my time and photocopied the whole patient file.

Room 224. Second floor.

Back in the car, I lay the Mossberg across my lap and stroke it like a pet. I had hoped to find out if and when the patient was being discharged or transferred to a different unit, but no. It's been a waste of time.

There's a lot at stake here, a hell of a lot. And given all the planning I've had to do to get this far, I'm not about to blow this deal by taking my eye off the ball.

I take out my mobile, study the picture of the floor plan and realise no-one really knows the warren of passageways and corridors in the hospital. It's like one of those "Magic Eye" pictures – turn it one way and it looks a little like a folded star, turn it around again and it's a polygon, turn it again and it's a skull. Not exactly subtle for a hospital.

It doesn't matter. I reckon I should be able to take the emergency stairs to the second floor and from there, room 224 is only about ten metres away. I'll need to be a bit more creative about my getaway – up one floor, down the hall, take the stairs to the fourth floor, past neurosurgery, through three sets of double doors, take the lift down to the reception desk, twenty paces from the emergency exit, then a long route through the car park to the car. I don't mind making a big entrance, but when I leave, I like to make a discreet exit.

There's still the possibility that she'll be transferred. If so I'd be better off sitting tight. Now I know her name, I can just call for any news.

I look up the number for the hospital and dial.

Press 1, press 2, it's all so laborious. The Mossberg is altogether more efficient.

Having not set foot in the office all day, Camille calls Louis for an update. Right now, the team are dealing with a transvestite who has been strangled, a dead German tourist, probably a suicide, a driver stabbed in a road-rage incident, a homeless man who bled to death in the basement of a gym, a teenage junkie fished out of the sewer in the 13th and a crime of passion to which a suspect has confessed – the suspect is seventy-one. Camille listens, he gives instructions, authorises tactics, but he is not really there. Thankfully, Louis can take care of the day-to-day running of the squad.

By the time he hangs up, Camille can barely remember a word that was said. The only thing that seems clear is the terrible damage inflicted.

Pausing to take stock, he assesses his own situation. He has put himself in a difficult position: he has lied to the *commissaire* about a non-existent informant, lied to his superior officers, even given a false name at the Préfecture de Police, all so that this case would be assigned to him.

To make matters worse, he is involved in a relationship with the primary victim, who also happens to be the key witness in an armed robbery which is directly linked to an earlier heist in which a man was murdered.

Coldly considering the sequence of events, this series of rash decisions unworthy of an officer of his experience, he is appalled. He feels like a prisoner of his choices, his impulses. He has been a complete idiot: he is behaving as though he has no faith in his colleagues, a dangerous thing for a man with precious little faith in himself. He is incapable of outstripping himself and so is forced to do what he can do. In this case he has allowed his intuition, usually his greatest asset, to turn to emotion, to recklessness, to blind anger.

His behaviour seems all the more ludicrous given that the case is not all that complicated. A gang of thugs about to commit an armed robbery bump into Anne, she sees their faces, they beat her senseless and drag her with them to the jeweller's in case she gets any silly ideas about making a run for it – which, in the end, is precisely what she tries to do. The man acting as lookout fires his shotgun, misses, and when he tries to fire again his accomplice intervenes. They decide to take their haul and get out. Driving along the rue Georges-Flandrin, the man with the shotgun has one last unexpected opportunity, but there is an argument between him and his accomplices and it is this which saves Anne's life.

The man's savage determination seems terrifying, but he was caught up in the fury of the moment, he targeted Anne simply because she was there.

Now, the die is cast.

The robbers will be far away by now – they are hardly likely to hang around. With the haul they took, they can go anywhere they like, they are spoiled for choice.

The only chance of their being caught depends on Anne being able to identify at least one of her attackers. Given the meagre resources of the *brigade criminelle* and the number of cases they are currently working on – a number that steadily increases every day – there is only a one-in-thirty chance that they will be caught immediately, one in a hundred that they will be tracked down within a reasonable period and one in a thousand that – by pure chance or by a miracle – they will be tracked down one day in the future. However you look at it, it is already a cold case. So many robberies are committed daily that if the suspects are not arrested at the scene, if they are professionals, they have every chance of disappearing without trace.

So, the best thing he can do, Camille thinks, is to stop this charade before it involves someone more senior than Le Guen. Right now, his friend can make all this go away. One more white lie is not likely to faze him, after all he is the *contrôleur général*, but if it goes any further, it will be too late. If Camille comes clean now, Le Guen can have a quiet word with Commissaire Michard, who will be only too happy to have her superior officer owe her a favour – one she will doubtless need some day. She would probably see it as an investment of sorts. Camille has to put a stop to things before Juge Pereira sticks his nose in.

Camille can rationalise things, say that he was angry, that he was tempted, that he was blinded by emotion; no-one would have much trouble recognising such qualities in him.

He is relieved by his decision.

He will give up the case.

Let someone else look for the robbers, his fellow officers are more than capable. He should spend his time with Anne, taking care of her, that is what she will need most.

Besides, what can he do that his colleagues cannot?

"Excuse me . . ."

Camille walks over to the receptionist.

"A couple of things," she says. "The admissions form, you stuffed it in your pocket earlier. I know, I know, you don't give a tinker's damn, but the pen-pushers in this place, they're a little pernickety about these things."

Camille digs out the form. With no social security number, it has been impossible to process Anne's admission. The woman behind the desk points to a faded, tatty poster Sellotaped to the glass partition and recites the slogan in a sing-song voice.

"*In hospital, there is no social contract without social security.* They even make us take courses in this bullcrap, that should tell you how important it is . . . They lose millions every year, that's what they tell us."

Camille shrugs, he will have to go to Anne's apartment. He nods to the woman behind the desk. He hates this sort of red tape.

"One more thing." The receptionist gives him what she hopes is a seductive smile that fails miserably. "I don't suppose you can do anything about parking tickets – or is that too much to ask?"

He hates this fucking job.

Camille wearily holds out his hand. In a split second, the woman has opened the top desk of her drawer. There are at least forty parking fines. She gives a broad smile, as though handing him a trophy. Her teeth are crooked.

"Thing is," she says in a wheedling tone, "today I'm working the night shift, but not every day . . ."

"I get it," Camille says.

He hates this fucking job.

There are too many parking tickets to fit in one pocket and so he has to divide them up between left and right. Every time the automatic glass doors open, a blast of icy air whips at his face but does little to wake him up.

He is exhausted.

No plans to transfer or discharge her. Nothing is likely to happen for at least a couple of days, according to the girl on the phone. And I have no intention of hanging around this car park for two days. I've waited long enough already.

It's nearly eight. He seems to keep odd hours, this cop. He was about to leave and then he suddenly stopped, absorbed in thought, staring out through the glass doors as though he doesn't see them. Give it a minute or two and he will leave.

And then it's show time!

I turn the key in the ignition, drive to the far side of the car park, a deserted area, being so far from the entrance, next to the perimeter wall and the emergency exit I plan to use as my getaway, God willing. And He better be willing, because I'm in no mood to be crossed . . .

I slide out of the car, head back the way I came, keeping in the shadow of the parked cars and come to the fire-door.

Inside. No-one around.

As I pad down the hallway I spot the little cop, standing with his back to me, brooding.

He'll have a fuck of a lot more to brood about soon enough, I plan to launch him into the stratosphere.

7.45 p.m.

As he pushes the glass door leading into the car park, Camille remembers the call he got this morning at the police station and suddenly he realises that providence has anointed him Anne's next of kin. Obviously he is not, but even so he was the first person contacted by the hospital, it is his responsibility to contact everyone else.

Everyone else? he thinks. Though he has racked his brain, he does not know anyone else in Anne's life. He has met one or two of her colleagues, he recalls seeing a woman in her forties with thinning hair and huge, tired eyes walking down the street, she seemed to be shivering. "One of my colleagues . . ." Anne told him. Camille tries to remember her name. Charras? Charron? Charroi, that's it. They were crossing a boulevard, she was wearing a blue coat, she and Anne nodded to each other, exchanged a conspiratorial smile. Camille found it touching. Anne turned back to him. "A complete bitch . . ." she whispered, still smiling.

He always calls Anne on her mobile. Before leaving the hospital, he tracks down her office number. It is eight o'clock, but you never know, there might still be someone.

"Hello, you've reached Wertig and Schwindel. Our offices . . ."

Camille feels a rush of adrenaline. For a second, he could have sworn it was Anne's voice. He feels suddenly distraught because precisely the same thing happened with Irène. One month after she died, he accidentally called his home number to be greeted by Irène's voice: "Hello, you've reached Camille and Irène Verhœven. We're not able to take your call . . ." Dumbfounded, he had burst into tears.

Leave a message. He stammers: "Hi, I'm calling about Anne Forestier. She is in hospital and she won't be able to . . . [what?] to come back to work . . . I mean not straight away, she's been in an accident . . . it's not serious, well, actually it is [how to put this?], she'll call you as soon as she can . . . if she can." A rambling, incoherent message. He hangs up.

He feels self-loathing rising in him like a raging tide.

He turns round, the receptionist is staring at him, she looks as if she is laughing.

8.00 p.m.
Up to the second floor.

To the right, the stairs. Everyone takes the lift, no-one takes the stairs. Especially not in hospitals; people don't need the hassle.

The barrel of the Mossberg is just over forty-five centimetres long. It has a pistol grip and fits easily into the large, inside pocket of a raincoat. You have to walk a little stiffly, a little stilted, lumbering like a robot, trying to keep the barrel pressed against your thigh, but it's the only way. At any moment, you have to be ready to fire or fuck off. Or both. Whatever you do, you need to be accurate. And driven.

The little cop has gone downstairs, she's alone in her room. If he hasn't left the building yet, he'll hear the blast, at which point he'd better get his arse in gear or he'll be charged with professional misconduct. I wouldn't bet much on his future in the force.

I come to the first floor. A long corridor. I go all the way across the building and take the opposite stairwell. Up to the second.

The great thing about the public sector is everyone is so overworked, no-one gives you a second look. The corridors are full of distraught families or anxious friends tiptoeing in and out of rooms as though they're in church, while harried nurses scurry past.

The second-floor corridor is deserted. Wide as a boulevard.

Room 224 is right at the other end, ideally situated for those who need a long rest. And speaking of a long rest, I think I can make it permanent.

I take a few steps towards the room.

I need to be careful as I open the door, a sawn-off shotgun clattering on the floor of a hospital is likely to panic people, they just aren't very understanding. The handle turns as quietly as an angel, I take a step across the threshold, shift the Mossberg from one hand to the other, opening the raincoat wide. She is lying on the bed, from the doorway I can see her feet, lifeless, unresponsive, like the feet of a dead woman. I lean a little to the side and now I can see her whole body . . .

Jesus, the face on her!

I did a bang-up job.

She's lying on her side, asleep, a trickle of drool hanging from her lips, her eyelids swollen shut – she's no oil painting. Instinctively I remember the expression "to rearrange someone's face". It seems appropriate. She looks like a mid-period Picasso. The bandages probably help, but even the mottled colours of her skin. Her skin looks like parchment. Or canvas. Her head is grotesquely bloated. If she was planning a night on the town, she'll need to take a rain check.

Stand in the doorway. Make sure the shotgun is visible.

Let her know I didn't come empty-handed.

The door is now wide open to the corridor, but she doesn't wake up. I go to all this trouble and this is the kind of welcome I get? Usually wounded people are like animals, they sense things. She's bound to wake up; just give her a couple of seconds. Survival instinct. She'll see the gun – she and the Mossberg know each other well, they're practically friends.

When she sees me with the shotgun, she'll be terrified. Obviously. She'll toss and turn, try to sit up against the pillows, her head thrashing about.

And she'll howl.

Given the serious damage I did to her jaw, she won't be up to much in the way of intelligible conversation. The best she'll probably manage is "Heeeeehhh" or "Heeeeeppp", something like that, but to compensate for her lack of clarity she'll go for volume, a full-throated scream to bring everyone running. If this happens, then before we get down to business, I'll signal for her to be quiet – *shhhh* – bring my finger to my lips. *Shhh.* She will carry on screaming the place down. *Shhhh,* this is a hospital for fuck's sake!

"Monsieur?"

In the corridor, just behind me.

A distant voice.

Don't turn round, stand stock-still.

"Are you looking for someone . . . ?"

Usually it's impossible to get anyone's attention in a hospital, but show up with a sawn-off shotgun and suddenly you've got some nurse eager to help you.

Glance up at the number on the door like someone who has just realised their mistake. The nurse is closer now. Without turning, stammer awkwardly:

"Sorry, got the wrong room . . ."

Keep a cool head, that's the most important thing. Whether you're pulling off a heist or paying a visit to a friend in hospital, a cool head is crucial. Mentally, I picture the evacuation plan. Go to the stairwell, up one floor, turn left. Better get a move on, because if I'm forced to turn round now, I'll have to pull out the Mossberg and open fire, thereby depriving a public hospital of a fine nurse when they're short-staffed already. I lengthen my stride. But first, lock and load. You never know.

Loading a round into the chamber takes both hands. And the pump action makes a distinct metallic click. Which echoes ominously down hospital corridors.

"The lifts aren't that way . . ."

A dry clack and the voice suddenly breaks off, giving way to a nervous silence. A young voice, at once pure and troubled, shot down in mid-flight.

"Monsieur!"

With the shotgun loaded, all I need to do is take my time and be meticulous. Keep my back to her at all times. The rigid line of the barrel is visible through the fabric of my trench coat; it looks as though I have a wooden leg. I take three steps. The flap of the coat flicks open for a fraction of a second revealing the end of the barrel. A brief glimmer like a beam of light, like the sun glinting on a shard of glass. Barely noticeable, barely recognisable, and if you've only seen guns in the movies you're unlikely to realise what it is. Still, you know that you've seen something, you hesitate, thinking it might be . . . No, it's too preposterous . . .

In the time it takes for the penny to drop . . . the man turns, head bowed, apologises for his mistake, closes the flap of his coat and goes into the stairwell. But he does not go down, he goes up. He's not running away, otherwise surely he would have gone downstairs. But that stilted way he was walking . . . Very weird. What was that thing under his coat? From a distance, it looked just like a gun. Here? In a hospital? No – she can't bring herself to believe it. Just time to run up the stairs . . .

"Monsieur . . . monsieur?"

8.10 p.m.
Time to leave. As a police officer, Camille cannot afford the luxury of behaving like some star-crossed lover. Detectives don't spend the night at the victim's bedside. He has already made enough blunders for one day.

And at precisely that moment his mobile vibrates, he checks the screen: Commissaire Michard. He stuffs the phone back into his pocket, turns back to the receptionist and waves goodbye. She winks and crooks her finger, gesturing to him. Camille hesitates, pretends he does not understand, but too weary to resist he trudges back. He already has the parking tickets, what more can she want?

"You finally off, then? Don't get much sleep on the force, do you?"

This is meant as an innuendo, because she smiles, showing off her crooked teeth. To think he wasted his time for this. He sighs heavily, gives a half-hearted smile. He desperately needs to sleep. He has taken three steps when she calls after him.

"Oh, there was a phone call, I thought you'd like to know."

"When was this?"

"A while ago . . . around seven o'clock."

And before Camille has time to ask . . .

"Her brother."

Nathan. Camille has never met Anne's brother, but he has heard him on her voicemail. Nervous, excitable and young. He is fifteen years younger than his sister, a researcher in some incomprehensible subject – photons, nanotechnology, some field whose very name is meaningless to Camille.

"And for a brother, he's not exactly polite. Listening to him, I'm glad I'm an only child."

A sudden realisation explodes inside Camille's head: how would Nathan have known Anne was in hospital?

Suddenly wide awake, he races round to the other side of the desk. The receptionist does not even wait for him to formulate the question.

"A man's voice, he was . . . [Ophélia rolls her eyes] well, he was ignorant and rude. 'Forestier . . . Yeah, with an F, how else would you spell it, with two Fs? [She mimics his curt, arrogant tone.] What exactly is wrong with her? And what did the doctors say? [Her imitation is beginning to verge on caricature.] What do you mean, they don't know?' [Her tone now is shocked, outraged.] . . ."

Did he have an accent?

The receptionist shakes her head. Camille glances around. The conclusion will come to him, he knows that, he is simply waiting for the neural pathways to connect, it is only a matter of seconds.

"Did he sound young?"

"Not *young*-young. Forty-something, I'd guess. Personally, I thought he . . ."

Camille is no longer listening, he is running, jostling anyone in his way. He wrenches open the door to the stairs which slams behind him. Already, he is taking the stairs as fast as his dumpy legs can manage.

8:15 p.m.

As soon as he heard my footsteps, he went upstairs, the nurse is thinking. About twenty-two, she has her hair in a skinhead crop and a ring through her bottom lip. On the outside she is all provocation, but inside is a different matter; if anything, she is too soft, too sensitive. She heard the stairwell door bang, but during those few seconds she spent hesitating the man could have gone anywhere – up to the fourth floor, down to reception, through the neurosurgical ward – there is no way of knowing where he went after that.

What was she supposed to do? She wasn't sure what she had seen and you don't go setting off the alarm in a hospital when you're not sure . . . She heads back to the nurses' station. The whole idea is ridiculous. Who would bring a shotgun into a hospital? But if it wasn't a gun, what was it? Some sort of prosthesis? There are visitors who bring giant bunches of gladioli – are gladioli in season now? He got the wrong room, that's what he said.

Still, she has her doubts. She did a course on battered women at nursing college, she knows how brutal men can be, she knows they're quite capable of attacking their wives even in a hospital. She retraces her steps and pops her head around the door of room 224. The woman in the room cries all the time; every time the nurse comes in she is in tears, running her fingers over her face, following the line of her lips. She covers her mouth when she speaks. Twice, the nurse found her in front of the bathroom mirror, though she barely has the strength to stand.

But still, she thinks as she leaves the room, worried now, what could the man have had under his raincoat? It looked like a broom handle, in the split second when his coat fell open, there was a glint of metal, of cold steel. She tries to think of something else, something that might be mistaken for a shotgun barrel. A crutch?

This is what she is thinking as the policeman bursts through the doors at the far end of the corridor, the little officer who spent all afternoon sitting with the patient – no more than five feet tall, his handsome face is grave, unsmiling. He rushes past like a lunatic, almost knocking her over, jerks open the door to room 224 and dashes inside. He looks as though he is about to throw himself on the bed.

"Anne, Anne . . ." he yells.

The way he's acting makes no sense, thinks the nurse, he's a policeman, but you'd think he was her husband. The patient seems very agitated. She shakes her head wildly, raises her hand to ward off the torrent of questions: stop yelling.

"Are you O.K. ?" the policeman whispers over and over. "Are you O.K. ?"

I talk to him, try to keep him calm. The patient lets her arm fall limply by her side, she looks at me. "I'm fine . . ."

92

"Did you see anyone?" the policeman turns back to me. "Did someone come into this room? Did you see him?"

His voice is grim, anxious.

"Did someone come into the room?"

Yes, I mean not really, I mean no . . .

"There was a man . . . he said he'd got the wrong floor, he opened the door . . ."

The policeman doesn't even wait for me to finish. He turns back to the patient, looks at her intently, she shakes her head, she seems confused, bewildered. She doesn't say anything, she simply shakes her head. She didn't see anyone. She slumps back on the bed, pulls the sheets up to her chin and starts to sob quietly. All these questions are frightening her. The little cop is hopping around like a flea. I need to say something.

"Monsieur, I'll thank you to remember that this is a hospital!"

He nods, but you can tell he's thinking about something else.

"And besides, visiting hours are over."

He turns back to me.

"Which way did he go?"

I pause for a split second and before I can answer he's shouting.

"This guy you saw, the one who said he'd got the wrong room, which way did he go?"

I reach down, take the patient's wrist and take her pulse. This is none of my business, what matters is the patient's welfare. I'm not in the business of reassuring jealous lovers.

"He took the stairs, over by . . ."

Before I've even finished the sentence, he's off like a shot, racing towards the emergency door, I hear his feet on the stairs, but it's impossible to tell whether he is going up or down.

But the shotgun . . . Did I just imagine it?

The concrete stairwell echoes like a cathedral. Camille grabs the banister, hurtles down the first few steps. Then stops.

No. If he were the killer, he would go up.

He does a U-turn. The treads are not standard size, the steps are about half a centimetre taller than expected; ten steps and you're tired, twenty and you're exhausted. Especially Camille with his short legs.

Panting, he arrives on the third floor, where he hesitates, racking his brain, trying to decide what he would do. Keep going up? No – he would go back into the maze of corridors. Bursting through the doors, Camille crashes into a doctor.

"What the . . . ? Look where you're going, can't you!"

A quick glance reveals a man of indeterminate age, his white coat freshly ironed (the pleats are still visible), his hair quite grey, he is standing frozen, hands in his pockets, flustered by Camille's frantic appearance . . .

"Did you see a man go past just now?"

The doctor takes a deep breath, struggles to recover his dignity and is about to stalk off.

"Are you fucking deaf?" Camille roars. "Did you see a man go past or didn't you?"

"No . . . I, um . . ."

This is answer enough for Camille, he turns on his heel, jerks the door as though trying to rip it off its hinges, tears back downstairs and into the corridor, he goes right, then left, gasping for breath, there is no-one. He retraces his steps, breaks into a run when he suddenly has a nagging hunch (doubtless fuelled by exhaustion) that tells him he is going the wrong way: the moment such doubts creep in, your pace begins to slacken, in fact it becomes impossible to run faster. As he reaches the end of the corridor where it turns at a right angle, Camille crashes into an electrical cupboard. The door is seven feet high and plastered with lightning bolts and other symbols, all of which mean "Danger of Death". Thanks for the tip.

The true art of a job like this is to leave as unobtrusively as you arrived.

This is no easy feat, it requires determination, concentration, vigilance and a cool head – qualities rarely found in one man. It's like a hold-up: when things go wrong, it's usually at the end. You show up with non-violent intentions, encounter a little resistance and unless you can keep calm, you find yourself spraying bullets and leaving carnage in your wake, all for want of a little self-control.

This time, I had a clear run. I didn't encounter anyone, apart from some doctor loitering inexplicably in the stairwell, and I managed to dodge him.

I get to the ground floor, I walk quickly towards the exit. In hospitals, everyone is always in a hurry, but no-one ever runs, so when you walk quickly it attracts attention, but I'm gone before anyone has time to react. Besides, what is there to react to?

On my right, the car park. The cold air feels good. Under my coat, I keep the Mossberg clamped against my leg; no point scaring the patients now – if they're in A. & E., they're already in a bad way. Down here, everything seems calm, but I'm guessing that things are kicking off upstairs. That pipsqueak fucking cop is probably sniffing around like a prairie dog, trying to work out what happened. The little nurse isn't really sure what she saw. And, O.K., maybe she talks to the other nurses. A gun? Are you kidding? You sure it wasn't a heat-seeking missile? Maybe they tease her. You know you shouldn't be drinking on the job! You been smoking crack again, girl? But then one of them says: all the same, you should maybe say something to the ward sister . . .

But by then, I've had more than enough time to get back to the car, start her up and join the queue of other vehicles leaving the hospital; three minutes later, I reach the street, I turn right and stop at the traffic light.

Now, this is a spot that might offer a window of opportunity.

And if not here, then somewhere close by.

All it takes is a little determination . . .

Camille feels beaten, but he forces himself to run faster. He takes the lift, tries to catch his breath. If there were no-one else in it, he would pound in the walls, instead he simply takes a deep breath. Arriving back in reception, he calmly assesses the situation. The casualty department is teeming with patients and nurses, paramedics are constantly coming and going, a corridor on the right leads to an emergency exit and another on the left leads out to the car park.

There must be at least half a dozen routes by which a man could leave the hospital without being noticed.

Protocol would suggest questioning witnesses, taking statements. But who would he question? Who is there to give a statement? By the time his team arrived at the scene, two-thirds of these people would have been discharged and their places taken by others.

He could kick himself.

Calmly, he goes back up to the second floor and over to the nurses' station. Florence, the girl with the bee-stung lips, is poring over patient files. Her colleague? She doesn't know, she says without looking up. Camille is insistent.

"We're overworked here on the ward," she says.

"In that case, she can't have gone very far . . ."

She is about to say something, but Camille is already gone. He paces up and down the corridor, popping his head around every door that opens, he is about to check the women's toilets – in the mood he is in, nothing would stop him – when the nurse finally reappears.

She seems annoyed, she runs a hand over her skinhead crop. Mentally, Camille sketches her, her features are regular and the cropped hair makes her look fragile. She looks intimidated, but in fact she is sensible and pragmatic. Her immediate reaction confirms this. She does not break her step and Camille is forced to run to keep up with her.

"The guy got the wrong room. It happens. He apologised."

"You heard his voice?"

"Not really . . . I heard him say sorry, that's about it."

Hurrying along a hospital corridor, trying to wheedle information out of this woman, information he needs if he is to save the life of the woman he loves. He grabs the nurse's arm, forcing her to stop, to look down; she is struck by the single-mindedness she can read in his face, by the determination in his calm, measured growl as he says, "I need to you to pay attention . . ."

Camille glances at her name-tag: Cynthia. Her parents clearly watched too many soap operas.

"I need you to tell me everything, 'CYNTHIA'. I need every last detail . . ."

She tells him, the man standing in the open doorway, the way he kept his head down when he turned around – embarrassed probably – the raincoat he was wearing, O.K., so he had a rather stiff way of walking . . . He headed straight for the stairs and a man who is running away would go down, not up, it's only logical, isn't it?

Camille sighs and nods; of course, it's only logical.

9.30 p.m.
"It'll be here any minute . . ."

The head of hospital security is not best pleased. It is late, he had to get dressed and come back to work when he could be at home watching the match. A former *gendarme*, self-important, big-bellied, no-necked, red-faced, the product of a staple diet of beef and red wine. To watch the C.C.T.V. footage, he needs a warrant. Signed by the examining magistrate. In triplicate.

"On the phone, you told me you had a warrant . . ."

"No," Camille states categorically, "I told you I was *getting* one."

"Well, I wasn't aware of that."

Pig-headed. As a rule, Camille favours negotiation, but on this occasion he has neither the time nor the inclination.

"And what exactly are you aware of?" he barks.

"I don't know . . . that you had a sear—"

"No," Camille cuts him off, "I'm not talking about a search warrant. Are you *aware* that a man with a sawn-off shotgun gained access to this hospital? Are you aware that he went up to the second floor intending to kill one of the patients it is your job to protect? And that if anyone got in his way, he would have happily shot them too? Are you aware that if he comes back and butchers people, you're going to be in the dock?"

The conversation is academic since the cameras only cover the front entrance and there is little chance that this man – if he exists – came in that way. He is no fool. If he exists. And indeed, there is nothing on the footage during the period when he would have been in the hospital. Camille checks and double-checks. The head of security is hopping from one foot to the other, puffing and panting to signal his frustration. Camille peers at the screen, staring at the steady stream of ambulances, emergency vehicles and private cars, the people trudging in and out, the injured, the healthy, walking, running. Nothing of any relevance strikes him.

He gets up and leaves the security room, then comes back, presses the EJECT button on the machine, takes the D.V.D. and leaves.

"Do you take me for an idiot?" the security guard roars. "Where's my warrant?"

Camille gives a shrug that says: We'll deal with that later.

Back out in the car park, Camille surveys the area. If it were me, he thinks, I'd go around the side, use the emergency exit. He studies the fire-door closely. He takes out his glasses. There is no sign of forced entry.

When you go outside for a cigarette, who takes over?

It is the obvious question. Camille goes back into the reception area and, at the far end, he discovers the narrow corridor behind the desk that leads to the emergency exit.

Ophélia smiles, showing her yellow teeth.

"Listen, honey, they don't provide maternity cover in this place, so they're hardly likely to cover for cigarette breaks!"

Was he here?

As he walks back to the car, Camille listens to his voicemail messages.

"Commissaire Michard! [Her voice is grating.] Call me back. Doesn't matter what time it is. I need to know where things stand. And I'll have that report on my desk first thing tomorrow morning yes?"

Camille feels alone. Terribly alone.

Night time in a hospital is unlike anywhere else. Silence itself seems suspended. Stretchers and trolleys continue to rattle along the corridors, there are distant cries, intermittent voices, the sound of running footsteps, the bleeping of alarms.

Anne manages to drift off, but her sleep is fitful, filled with pain and blood, she feels the tiled floor of the Galerie Monier beneath her hands, feels with eerie exactness the glass rain down on her; she sees herself crashing into the shop window, hears the gunshots behind her. Her breath now comes in halting gasps. The little nurse with the ring through her bottom lip is reluctant to wake her. But there is no need, since every time this loop of dream plays out, Anne wakes with a scream, jolting upright in bed. She can see the man, towering over her, pulling a balaclava over his face and then a close-up of the shotgun butt about to shatter her cheekbone.

In her sleep, Anne brings her fingers up to touch her face, she strokes the sutures, then her lips, feels for her teeth and finds bare gums and jagged stumps.

He wanted to kill her.

He will come back. He wants to kill her.

DAY 2

6.00 a.m.

Not a wink of sleep. When it comes to Camille's emotions, Doudouche has a sixth sense.

Last night, Camille went back to the station to sort out all the things he had not had the chance to deal with during the day; when he came home exhausted and dossed down fully dressed on the sofa, Doudouche crept up beside him and there they lay, motionless, all night. Camille did not feed her, but she did not mewl, she knows when he is anxious. She purrs. Camille knows by heart every nuanced register of her purring.

Not long ago, nights such as this – sleepless, tense, anxious, desolate – were spent for Irène. With Irène. Camille would think about their life together, go over every painful image. He could think of nothing more important than the death of Irène.

Camille is not sure whether what has pained him most today has been his fears for Anne, the sight of her ravaged face, her terrible suffering or the realisation that gradually, over the days and weeks, she has come to occupy his every thought. There is a sort of crassness about moving on from one woman to another, he feels like the victim of a cliché. He had never even thought about making a new life for himself, and yet a new life has appeared almost in spite of him. Yet for all that, the harrowing images of Irène still continue to haunt him and probably always will. They are immune to everything, to passing time, to encounters with other women. Or rather, encounter; there has only been one woman.

Camille was able to accept Anne since she insisted that she was only passing through. Like him, she has her dead to mourn; she is not looking to plan a future. And yet, without intending to, she has become a permanent part of his life. And in the age-old distinction between the one who loves and the one who is loved, Camille does not know which he is.

They met in spring. Early March. It had been four years since he lost Irène, two years since he re-emerged from grief, insensible but alive. An existence stripped of all risk, all desire that is the lot of men condemned to solitude. It is not easy for a man like Camille to meet women, but he no longer cared, he did not miss it.

To meet anybody is something of a miracle.

Anne is not given to anger, once and only once in her life did she throw a tantrum in a restaurant (she swore as much to him, hand on heart). It so happened that Camille was having dinner two tables away at Chez Fernand when a heated argument turned into a row. Insults are hurled, plates smashed, dishes overturned, cutlery is strewn across the floor, customers get to their feet and demand their coats, the police are called and all the while the owner, Fernand, is shouting at the top of his voice, calculating the damage in astronomical figures. Anne suddenly stops screaming and, surveying the destruction, she bursts out laughing.

She glances over at Camille.

He closes his eyes for a split second, takes a breath, slowly gets to his feet and shows his warrant card.

He introduces himself. Commandant Verhœven, *brigade criminelle*.

He seems to have appeared from nowhere. Anne stops laughing and looks at him worriedly.

"Lucky you were here!" roars the owner, then hesitates. "*Brigade criminelle*, you said?"

Camille nods wearily. He grabs the *patron* by the arm and takes him aside.

Two minutes later, he leaves the restaurant accompanied by

Anne, who is unsure whether to be amused, relieved, grateful or worried. She is free and, like most people, does not know what to do with her freedom. Camille is aware that, like any woman, at this moment she is wondering about the nature of the debt she has taken on. And how she might repay it.

"What did you say to him?" she says.

"I told him I was arresting you."

This is a lie. In fact, Camille threatened to have the place raided every week until the restaurant was left with no customers. A blatant abuse of authority. He feels a little ashamed, but then again a restaurant should be able to serve decent profiteroles!

Anne knows it is a lie, but she finds it funny.

As they reach the corner of the street and a police car screeches past on its way to Chez Fernand, she gives Camille her most devastating smile – her cheeks dimple, there are delicate laughter lines around her green eyes . . . Suddenly, the thought that she feels she owes him something begins to weigh on Camille.

"Are you taking the *métro*?" he says as they reach the station.

Anne thinks for a moment.

"I'll probably take a taxi."

This sounds good to Camille, although regardless of what she chose he would have taken the alternative. He gives her a little wave and trips down the stairs with affected composure, though actually he goes as fast as he can. He disappears.

They slept together the following night.

When Camille left the *brigade* at the end of his shift, Anne was waiting outside on the pavement. He pretended not to notice her and walked on towards the *métro*, but when he turned, she was still serenely standing there. The ploy made him smile. He was cornered.

They had dinner. An utterly routine evening. Indeed it would have been disappointing, but the lingering uncertainty about the debt she owes makes for a charged and gloomy atmosphere. As for the rest, what do a middle-aged man and a woman say when they first meet? They try to play down their failures without suppressing them altogether, allude to their wounds without revealing them, saying more than is necessary. Camille told Anne the essential in a few short words, about his mother, Maud . . .

"I thought as much . . ." Anne said, and seeing Camille's quizzical gaze she added, "I've seen some of her paintings." She hesitated. "Montreal?"

Camille was surprised she knew his mother's work.

Anne talked about her life in Lyons, about her divorce, about how she had left everything behind and it was clear just from looking at her that it was far from over. Camille would have liked to know more about this man, this husband, this relationship. The boundless curiosity men have for the innermost lives of women.

He asked if she would like to slap the restaurant manager now, or wait until after he had paid. Anne's bright, girlish laugh changed everything.

Camille, who had not been with a woman for longer than he could remember, did not have to do anything. Anne lay on top of him and after that it all followed naturally, not a word was said. It was both infinitely sad and extraordinarily happy. It was love.

They made no plans to see each other again. And yet from time to time, they did. As though touching only with their fingertips. Anne is a financial consultant, she spends most of her time visiting travel agencies, overseeing management structures, accounts, all those things of which Camille understands nothing. She is rarely in Paris more than two days a week. Her regular absences and her comings and goings lent a chaotic confusion to their encounters, as though they were constantly meeting by chance. From the beginning they did not understand the nature of their relationship. They met, they went out, they had dinner, they went to bed together, and steadily it grew.

Camille racks his brain, trying to recall the moment he first realised how much it took over in his life. He cannot remember.

All he knows is that with Anne's arrival, the white-hot memory of Irène's death has receded. He wonders whether some new being capable of living without Irène has finally appeared within him. Forgetting is inexorable. But to forget is not to heal.

Today he is devastated by what has happened to Anne. He feels responsible. Not for what has happened – there is nothing he can do about that – but for what is yet to happen, since that will depend on him, on his strength, his determination, his skill. It is overwhelming.

Doudouche has stopped purring, she is finally asleep. Camille slips off the sofa and the cat whimpers resentfully and turns onto her side. He pads over to the desk and picks up one of the Irène sketchpads. There once were countless notebooks, but this is all that remains. The others he destroyed one night when anger and despair got the better of him. The pad is filled with sketches of Irène: sitting at a table raising her glass and smiling, drawings of Irène here and there, sleeping, pensive. Camille puts the book down again. The past four years without her have been the most gruelling, the most miserable of his life and yet he cannot help but think they have been the most interesting, the most emotional. He has not left his past behind. It is the past that has become more . . . he struggles for a word. Subdued? More bearable? More muted? Like the remainder in a Euclidean division he never did, Anne is utterly unlike Irène, they are different galaxies light-years apart, converging on a single point. What distinguishes them is that Anne is still here while Irène has left.

Camille remembers Anne almost leaving him, but she came back. It is August. Standing by the window with her arms folded, naked, thoughtful, she says, "It's over, Camille," without turning to look at him. Then she dresses without a word. In a novel, this would take a minute; in real life it takes an age for a naked woman to get dressed. Camille sits, motionless; he looks like a man suddenly overtaken by a storm, resigned to his fate.

And she leaves.

Camille does nothing to stop her; he understands. Her leaving is not a tragedy, it is a fathomless gulf, a dull, gnawing pain. He is sorry that she is leaving, but he accepts it because he always felt it was inevitable. He is long accustomed to feeling unworthy. For a long time he sits there, frozen, then finally he lies back on the sofa. It is close to midnight.

He will never know what happens in that moment.

It has been more than an hour since Anne left, but suddenly he gets to his feet, goes to the door and, driven by some inexplicable conviction, he opens it. Anne is sitting at the top of the stairs, her back to him, her arms wrapped around her knees.

After a few seconds, she gets up, steps around him and goes into the apartment, lies down on the bed fully dressed and turns her face to the wall.

She is crying. It is something Camille remembers from his time with Irène.

6.45 a.m.
From the outside, the building does not look too bad, but inside the extent of the dilapidation is clear. A bank of battered

aluminium letterboxes has been half corroded by neglect. On the last box in the row, the label reads "6th Floor: Anne Forestier" in her spidery scrawl; at the right-hand edge where she ran out of space, the E and R are so close together they are all but illegible.

Camille ignores the tiny lift.

It is not yet seven o'clock when he taps lightly on the door to the apartment opposite Anne's.

The door immediately opens, as though the neighbour were expecting him. Madame Roman, who owns Anne's apartment, recognises Camille. It is one of the advantages of his height; people do not forget him. He delivers the lie.

"Anne has been called away urgently . . . [He feigns the benevolent smile of a patient, long-suffering friend in search of an ally.] She had to leave quickly and she forgot half the things she needed, obviously."

The macho, casually sexist "obviously" appeals to Madame Roman. She is a single woman, close to retirement age; her chubby, doll-like face makes her look like a child who has aged prematurely. She has a slight limp; some problem with her hip. From what little Camille has seen, she is terrifyingly methodical, with every last detail arranged and classified.

She screws up her eyes and gives Camille a knowing look, turns and hands him the spare key . . .

"Nothing serious, I hope?"

"No, no. [Camille gives her a broad smile.] Nothing serious. [He nods towards the key.] I'll keep this until she gets back . . ."

It is impossible to say whether this is a statement, a question or a request; Madame Roman hesitates. Camille makes the most of this brief pause to give her a grateful smile.

*

The kitchenette is immaculate. Everything in the little apartment is carefully arranged. Women and their obsession with neatness, thinks Camille. The large living room is partitioned and one half serves as a bedroom. The sofa converts into a double bed with a huge dip in the middle, a yawning chasm that draws them in so they end up sleeping on top of each other. It has its advantages. And a bookcase is lined with a hundred paperbacks – a selection that defies logic – and a few knick-knacks that, when he first visited, struck Camille as rather tawdry. He told her he found the place a little sad.

"I had very little money," Anne had said, suddenly tight-lipped. "Besides, I can't really complain."

Camille tries to apologise, but Anne cuts him dead.

"This is the price of divorce."

When she has something serious to say, Anne stares at you defiantly, as though prepared for a confrontation.

"When I left Lyons, I left behind everything I owned. This furniture, these ornaments, I bought second-hand here in Paris. I didn't want things anymore. I don't want things anymore. Maybe one day, but right now this place suits me."

This place is provisional – this is Anne's word. The apartment is provisional, their relationship is provisional. This is clearly why they go so well together.

"The thing that really takes time after a divorce is the clear-out," she says.

That nagging obsession with neatness.

Her blue hospital gown looks like a straitjacket, so Camille has decided to bring her some clothes. He thinks it might cheer her up. He even thinks that, if all goes well, she might go for short walks along the corridor, or downstairs to the little shop on the ground floor.

He made a mental list, but now that he is here, he cannot remember a single thing. Oh, yes: the dark-purple tracksuit. By association of ideas, he suddenly remembers a pair of trainers, the ones she uses for jogging, well worn, the soles still caked with sand. After that it's more difficult. What else?

Camille opens the small wardrobe. For a woman, Anne has very few clothes. A pair of jeans, he thinks, but which? He takes a pair. A T-shirt, a thick jumper. After that it all seems too complicated. He gives up and stuffs what he has into a sports bag with a random assortment of underwear.

He remembers her papers.

Camille goes over to the bureau. Above it a tarnished mirror that probably dates from when the apartment was built. Into one corner of the frame, Anne has slipped a picture of Nathan, her brother. He looks about twenty-five in the photo, an unprepossessing boy, smiling and withdrawn. Perhaps because he knows a little about him, Camille finds that there is something otherworldly about the face. Nathan is a scientist. From what Camille knows, he is pretty disorganised and tends to run up debts. Anne is forever bailing him out. Like a mother. "Actually, that's what I've always been to him," she says. She has always been there for him. She smiles, as though amused, but in fact it is worry. The studio flat, the university fees, the holidays, Anne has financed everything; it is hard to tell whether she is proud or dismayed. In the photograph, Nathan is standing in a little square that could be in Italy, the sun is shining, everyone is in shirtsleeves.

Camille goes through the bureau. The right-hand drawer is empty, in the one on the left are a number of creased envelopes, a couple of receipts from clothes shops, restaurants and a pile of brochures bearing the logo of her travel agency, but there is no sign of what he is looking for: her *carte vitale*, and her mutual insurance policy. They must have been in her handbag. Under the travel brochures he finds her sports clothes. He goes through the pile again. He expected to find pay slips, bank statements, utility bills for the water, the electricity, the telephone. Nothing. He turns around. His eyes are drawn to the small statue, a copy of an Egyptian cosmetic spoon in the Louvre, the dark wooden handle carved into the naked figure of a young woman swimming, with hair and eyes outlined in black paint. And a perfect arse. Camille gave it to Anne as a present. He bought it in the Louvre. They had been to see the Leonardo exhibition, Camille had spent the whole time explaining the paintings, his knowledge of the subject is encyclopaedic, he could talk for ever about them. In the gift shop, they had seen the carved copy of this girl from the late Eighteenth Dynasty, with her perfectly curved *derrière*.

"I swear, Anne, it's just like yours."

Anne had smiled as though to say "I wish! But thank you for saying so . . ." Camille was adamant. She wondered whether he was being serious. He leaned towards her and whispered insistently.

"Honest to God."

Before she had time to say anything, he had bought it, and that night he had undertaken a professional comparison of the two arses. At first, Anne had laughed a lot, then she moaned and gradually one thing led to another. Afterwards, she had cried; she sometimes cries after they make love. Camille thinks this probably has something to do with clearing out.

Just now, the carved figure looks lonely on the shelf; there is a broad space between it and the collection of D.V.D.s at the other end. Camille spins around, surveying the room. His talent as an artist comes from his unerring sense of observation and he quickly arrives at a conclusion.

Someone has been in the apartment.

He goes back and peers into the right-hand drawer of the bureau: it is empty because her personal papers have been taken. Camille goes back to the front door and examines the lock. Nothing. So it can only have been one of the gang who found Anne's address and her keys in the handbag he picked up as he left the Galerie Monier.

Is this the same man who was in the hospital last night, or have they divided up the work?

Their determination to hunt her down seems absurd and out of all proportion to the situation. We're missing something, Camille thinks, not for the first time; there is something about the case we don't understand.

From the sheaf of personal documents they have, the gang probably know everything about Anne: they know where they are going to find her in Paris and in Lyons, they know where she works, they know every place she might go to hide.

With all this information, tracking her, finding her, becomes child's play.

Killing her becomes an exercise in style.

The moment Anne sets foot outside the hospital, she is dead.

He cannot tell the *commissaire* that the apartment was searched without admitting that he knows Anne intimately and that he has lied to her from the start. Yesterday, it was no more than a slight misgiving. Today, no more than a suspicion. To his superiors, it would be indefensible. A forensics team could be sent in, but given the sort of men they are dealing with, they would find nothing. Not a trace.

There is more: Camille entered the apartment without authorisation, without a search warrant, he gained admittance because he lied to get the key, because Anne sent him to pick up her social security documents, Madame Roman would be able to testify that he has regularly been in the apartment . . .

The catalogue of his lies is becoming dangerously long. But it is not this that terrifies Camille. It is knowing that Anne's life is hanging by a thread. And he is utterly powerless.

7.20 a.m.

"No, it's not a bad time."

If a co-worker says this when you phone at 7.00 a.m., ask no questions. Especially when that co-worker is the *commissaire*.

Camille starts to fill her in on what has been happening.

"Where's your report . . ." the *commissaire* interrupts.

"I'm working on it."

"And . . . ?"

Camille starts again from the beginning, groping for words, trying to remain professional. The witness was hospitalised and, from the available evidence, it would appear that one of the armed gang infiltrated the premises, made his way to her private room and attempted to kill her.

"Hold on a minute, *commandant*, I'm not sure I follow you. [She enunciates each word as though her formidable intellect were banging against a brick wall.] The witness in question, Madame Foresti, she . . ."

"Madame Forestier."

114

"If you prefer. The witness maintains she saw no-one come into her room, am I right? [She does not give him time to answer.] And the nurse claims that she saw someone, but in the end she's not sure, is that it? So, first off, who is this 'someone'? And even if it is one of the gang, did he go into the room or didn't he?"

There is no point wishing Le Guen were still in charge. If he were still *commissaire*, he would be asking the same questions. Ever since Camille requested that this case be assigned to him, everything has gone wrong.

"I'm telling you he was there!" Camille is insistent. "The nurse glimpsed the barrel of a shotgun . . ."

"Oh, well that's just perfect!" the *commissaire* says admiringly. "She 'glimpsed', did she . . . ? So, enlighten me, has the hospital filed a report?"

From the moment the conversation began, Camille knew how it would end. He tries his best, but he does not want to cross swords with his superior officer. She earned her promotion. And if Camille's friendship with Le Guen made it possible for him to be assigned the case, it will not protect him for long – in fact, it will probably work against him.

Camille feels a prickling in his temples, a wave of heat.

"No, there's no official police report. [Don't let yourself get riled, be patient and calm, polite and persuasive.] But I am telling you the guy was there. He didn't think twice about going into a hospital carrying a loaded weapon. From the nurse's description, it could possibly be the pump-action shotgun used in the armed robbery."

"'It could possibly be' . . ."

"Why won't you believe me?"

"Because in the absence of an official complaint, a witness, a shred of proof or a single scrap of tangible evidence, I'm having a little trouble imagining a common-or-garden robber going into a hospital to murder a witness, that's why!"

"A 'common-or-garden robber'?" Camille chokes on the words.

"O.K., I'll grant you the raid was pretty violent, but . . ."

"'Pretty' violent?"

"*Commandant*, are you going to repeat everything I say with quote marks? You are requesting police protection for this witness as though she were a supergrass in a mafia trial!"

Camille opens his mouth. Too late.

"I'll let you have one uniformed officer. Two days."

It is a despicable response. If she had refused to assign anyone, she would have been held responsible if anything happened. Assigning a single unarmed *gendarme* to stop a determined killer is like offering someone a beach windbreak to stop a tsunami.

"What possible threat can Madame Forestier be to these men, Monsieur Verhœven? From what I've heard, she witnessed an armed robbery, not a mass murder! By now they'll know that, although she was injured, they didn't kill her – I'm inclined to think they're relieved."

This seemed logical at the beginning. But there is something not quite right about the case.

"So, this informant of yours, what does he have to say?"

Precisely how we make our decisions is one of life's mysteries. At what point do we become aware that we have decided? It is impossible to know what role the subconscious plays in Camille's response, but it comes without a flicker of hesitation.

"Mouloud Faraoui."

Even Camille flinches when he hears himself say the name.

He feels a sickening lurch, the almost physical sensation of a moving rollercoaster, knowing the trajectory he has put himself on by mentioning this name is a blazing arc headed straight for a brick wall.

"So Faraoui is out on parole?"

And before Camille has time to respond:

"And while we're at it, what the hell has he got to do with this thing?"

Good question. Like doctors, criminals tend to specialise: armed robbers, fences, burglars, forgers, con men, racketeers, they all live in their separate worlds. Mouloud Faraoui is a pimp, so it would be astonishing for his name to crop up in an armed robbery.

Camille knows him vaguely, their paths have crossed once or twice, and Mouloud is a little too high-profile to be a snitch. Mouloud Faraoui is a sadistic thug, he controls his turf with brute violence and has been implicated in several murders. He is cunning, vicious and for a long time it proved impossible to make any charges stick. Until he found himself on a trumped-up charge for something he did not do: thirty kilos of ecstasy in a holdall in the boot of his car with his prints all over the bag. A textbook stitch-up. Though he swore blind that the holdall was one he used at the gym, he found himself banged up in a cell nursing a frenzied rage.

"Sorry?"

"Faraoui! What the hell has he got to do with this case of yours? And you said he's your cousin? Well, that's news to me . . ."

"No, he's not my cousin . . . Look, it's complicated, it's a six-degrees-of-separation thing, if you know what I mean . . ."

"No, I'm afraid I don't know."

"Look, I'll deal with it and I'll get back to you."

"You . . . you'll 'deal with it'?"

"Are you going to repeat everything I say with quote marks?"

"Don't fuck with me, *commandant*!" Michard roars, then quickly puts her hand over the receiver. Camille hears a faint, stammered "Excuse my language, darling" that plunges him into confusion. Does this woman have children? How old would they be? A daughter maybe, though from her tone it does not sound as though she is talking to a child. When the *commissaire* comes back on the line, her voice is calm but her fury is still palpable. From the sound of her breathing, Camille can tell she is going into another room. Up until this moment, she has treated Camille as a minor irritation, but now, though given the circumstances she is forced to whisper, her long-suppressed hostility boils over in seething rage.

"What the hell is your problem, *commandant*?"

"Well, first, it's not 'my' problem. And secondly, it's seven in the morning, so while I'd be happy to try and explain, I need time to . . ."

"*Commandant* . . . [Silence.] I don't know what you're doing. I don't understand what you're doing. [All the anger has drained from her voice, as though she has changed the subject. Which, in a sense, she has.] But I want your report on my desk by the end of the day, is that clear?"

"No problem."

The day is mild, but Camille is dripping with perspiration. A slick, cold sweat he recognises as it trickles down his back, the sort of sweat he has not felt since his race to find Irène the day she died. He had been blinkered that day, he had thought he could go it alone . . . No: he hadn't been thinking at all. He had behaved as though he were the only person who could do what needed to be done and he had been wrong: by the time he found her, Irène was dead.

And what about Anne now?

They say men who lose women always lose them in the same way; this is what terrifies him.

8.00 a.m.

They don't know what they're missing, the Turks. Two fat holdalls full of bling. If it was half the weight, it would still be a good haul, even allowing for the fence's cut. Everything's going according to plan. And, with a bit of luck, I plan to make a killing from this stuff.

If all goes well.

And if it doesn't, then there'll be some real killing.

To be sure, to be clear, you have to be methodical. You have to be determined.

In the meantime, bring up the lights, it's show time!

Le Parisien. Page 3.

Fire in Saint-Ouen.

Perfect! Cross the road. Le Balto. A dingy little café. Cigarette. Coffee and cigarettes, that's what it's all about. The coffee in this place is like dishwater, but it's eight o'clock in the morning, so . . .

Open the newspaper. Drum-roll, please.

SAINT-OUEN
TWO DEAD IN MYSTERY BLAZE

The emergency services were called to a major incident in Chartriers shortly after noon yesterday when a serious fire broke out following a fierce explosion. Fire officers quickly contained the blaze which destroyed a number of workshops and lock-up garages. The fire is all the more mysterious since the area, which is scheduled for urban redevelopment, is currently derelict.

In the rubble of one of the lock-ups destroyed by the blaze, police officers discovered the burned-out wreck of a Porsche Cayenne and the charred bodies of two individuals. This has been determined as the locus of the blast, and forensic evidence indicates the presence of Semtex. From fragments of electronic equipment found at the scene, forensics officers have suggested the explosion could have been triggered remotely.

Given the intensity of the blaze, it may prove difficult to identify the bodies of the victims. All available evidence points to a carefully premeditated killing intended to make such identification impossible. Investigators are hoping to determine whether the victims were alive or dead at the time of the explosion . . .

Done and dusted.

"Investigators are hoping to determine . . ." Don't make me laugh! I'm happy to take bets. And if the cops somehow manage to trace this back to a couple of Turkish brothers with no record, I'll donate their half to the Police Orphan Fund.

Nearly there. I'm on the Périphérique, I take the exit ramp at Porte Maillot and into Neuilly-sur-Seine.

It's nice to see how the other half lives. If they weren't so fucking dumb, you'd almost want to join them. I park outside a school where thirteen-year-old girls are trooping out wearing clothes that cost thirteen times the minimum wage. Almost makes me sorry that the Mossberg is not an acceptable social leveller.

I walk past the school and turn right. The house is smaller

than those on either side, the grounds are not as extensive despite the fact that every year enough loot from burglaries and armed robberies passes through to build a new skyscraper at La Défense. The fence is wary, a smooth operator, constantly changing the protocol. By now, he'll have had one of his delivery boys pick up the holdalls from the locker at the Gare du Nord.

One location for the pickup, a second to evaluate the merchandise, a third to deal with negotiations.

He takes a hefty cut to ensure the deal is secure.

9.30 a.m.

Camille would like to be able to question her. What exactly did she see in the Galerie? But letting her see how worried he is would mean letting her know that her life is in danger, it would terrify her and only add anguish to her suffering.

And yet, he has no choice but to ask again.

"What?" Anne howls. "See what? What do you want me to say?"

The night has done her no good, she woke more exhausted than she had been yesterday. She is fretful, constantly on the verge of tears, Camille can hear it in the quaver in her voice, but she is a little more articulate today, she is managing to enunciate more clearly.

"I don't know," Camille says. "It could be anything."

"What?"

Camille spreads his hands helplessly.

"I just need to be sure, don't you see?"

Anne does not see. But she struggles to rack her memory, tilts her head and stares at Camille. He closes his eyes: try to keep calm, try to help me.

"Did you overhear them talking?"

Anne does not move, it is impossible to know whether she understood the question. Then she makes an evasive gesture that is difficult to interpret.

"Serbian, maybe . . ."

Camille jolts upright.

"What do you mean, Serbian? Do you know any words of Serbian?"

He is sceptical. These days, he has more dealings with Slovenians, Serbians, Bosnians, Croats, Kosovars, waves of them are arriving in Paris, but despite all the time he has spent with them he still cannot tell the languages apart.

"No, I'm not sure . . ."

Anne gives up and slumps back on the pillow.

"Wait, wait," Camille says. "This is important."

Anne opens her eyes again and struggles to speak.

"*Kpaj* . . . I think."

Camille cannot believe it, it is like suddenly discovering that Juge Pereira's clerk speaks fluent Japanese.

"*Kpaj*? Is that Serbian?"

Anne nods, though she does not seem completely sure.

"It means 'stop."

"How . . . how do you know this?"

Anne closes her eyes again as though she is exhausted by having to tell him the same things over and over.

"I spent three years organising tours in Eastern Europe . . ."

It's unforgivable. She has told him a thousand times. She has been in the travel industry for fifteen years, and before moving into management, spent a long time organising trips all over the world. She dealt with all of the Eastern Bloc countries except Russia. From Poland all the way south to Albania.

"Did all of them speak Serbian?"

Anne simply shakes her head, but she needs to explain; with Camille, everything has to be explained.

"I only heard one of them . . . In the toilets. The other guy, I'm not sure . . . [Her speech is a garbled, but completely intelligible.] I'm not sure . . ."

But to Camille, this confirms his suspicions: the guy doing the shouting, rifling the display cases, jostling his accomplice, he is Serbian. The man acting as lookout is Vincent Hafner.

He is the one who beat Anne, he is the one who sneaked into the hospital and went up to her room, he is probably the one who broke into Anne's apartment. And he does not have an accent.

The receptionist was categorical.

Vincent Hafner.

When the time comes for her to go for the M.R.I. scan, Anne asks for a pair of crutches. It can be difficult to understand what she wants. Camille translates. She insists on walking. The nurses roll their eyes and are about to manhandle her into a wheelchair and cart her off, but she screams, pulls away from them, sits on the bed with her arms folded. No.

This time, there can be no doubt. Florence, the charge nurse with the bee-stung lips is called, she is peremptory – "This is ridiculous, Madame Forestier, we'll take you upstairs for your scan, it won't take long." She turns on her heel without waiting for a response, her brusque manner clearly signalling that she is up to her eyes this morning and is in no mood to deal with petulant demands . . . But before she can reach the door, she hears Anne's voice ring out clearly, her pronunciation is a little indistinct but the meaning is crystal clear: Absolutely not: either I go on foot, or I'm going nowhere.

Florence comes back, Camille tries to plead Anne's case, but the nurse looks daggers at him – who the hell is this guy, anyway? He steps aside, leans against a wall, he suspects that the charge nurse has just blown her only chance of finding a peaceful solution. Time will tell.

The whole floor of the hospital starts to shake, heads appear in the hallway, the nurses try to restore order – Go back to your rooms, there's nothing to see! Inevitably, the house doctor shows up, the Indian with the interminable name, who seems to be here from morning to night, working shifts as long as his name, and he is probably paid no better than the cleaners. He comes over, and while he bends down to listen to what Anne is saying, he surveys the cuts and contusions; she looks terrible, but it is nothing compared to how she will look in a few days as the bruises develop. Gently, he tries to reason with her. Then, he listens to her chest. The nursing staff are confused, they do not understand what he is doing, M.R.I. appointments are set in stone, they cannot afford to be late. But the doctor takes his time . . .

The charge nurse becomes impatient, the porters are champing at the bit. The doctor calmly concludes his examination, he smiles at Anne and requests a pair of crutches. His colleagues glare at him, they feel betrayed.

Camille looks at the frail figure slumped over the crutches, two porters walk on either side of Anne, supporting her.

She shuffles slowly, but she is moving. She is on her feet.

10.00 a.m.
"This is not an extension of the commissariat . . ."

The office is an indescribable mess. The man is a surgeon, one can only hope things are more organised inside his head.

Hubert Dainville, head of the Trauma Unit. They met in the stairwell the previous night while Camille was chasing a ghost. In that fleeting glance, he looked ageless. Today he looks fifty. He is obviously proud of his shock of curly grey hair, it is the symbol of his ageing masculinity, this is not a hairstyle, it is a world view. His hands are carefully manicured. He is the sort of man who wears blue shirts with white collars and a handkerchief in the breast pocket of his suits. An ageing beau. He has probably tried to screw half of his staff and doubtless attributes to his charm the few successes that are simply statistical anomalies. His white coat is still immaculately ironed, but he no longer has the befuddled air he had in the stairwell. On the contrary, he is brusque and overbearing. He carries on working while he talks to Camille, as though the matter were already settled and he does not have time to waste.

"Nor do I," Camille says.

"Pardon?"

Dr Dainville looks up, frowning. It pains him when he does not understand. He is unaccustomed to the feeling. He pauses in his rummage through the pile of papers.

"I said, nor do I . . . I don't have time to waste," Camille says. "I can see that you're busy, but as it happens I'm rather busy myself. You have your responsibilities; I have mine."

Dainville pulls a face, unconvinced by this line of reasoning, and returns to his paperwork. But still the officer hovers in the doorway, clearly unaware that the interview is at an end.

"The patient needs rest," Dainville mutters finally. "She has suffered severe trauma." He glares at Camille. "Her present condition is little short of a miracle, she could have been left in a coma. She could be dead."

"She could also be at home. Or at work. She could even have finished her little shopping trip. The problem is that she ran into a man with no time to waste. A man like you. A man who thinks that his concerns are more important than those of other people."

The doctor looks up and glowers at Verhœven. To a man like Dainville, the most innocuous conversation involves a confrontation, he is a shock of snowy locks atop a fighting cock. Tiresome. And pugnacious. He looks Camille up and down.

"I realise that the police consider themselves entitled to go anywhere, but a hospital room is not an interrogation suite, *commandant*. This is a hospital, not an assault course. I will not have you tearing around the corridors, upsetting my staff . . ."

"You think I'm running up and down the corridors to keep in shape?"

Dainville brushes the comment aside.

"If this patient does indeed represent a danger to herself or to this institution, then have her transferred to a secure unit. If not, leave us in peace to get on with our work."

"Do you have much free space in the mortuary?"

A startled Dainville gives a little jerk of his head. The cock.

"I only ask," Camille goes on, "because until we can question the witness, the examining magistrate will not authorise a transfer. You would not operate unless you were certain of your facts; the police likewise. And we have very similar problems, you and I. The later we intervene, the greater the potential damage."

"I'm afraid I don't understand your metaphors, *commandant*."

"Then let me be clearer. It is possible that a killer is targeting this witness. If you prevent me from doing my job and he wreaks havoc in your hospital, you will have two problems. You will not have space enough in your mortuary and, given that the patient is fit to answer questions, you will be charged with obstructing a police investigation."

Dainville is a curious man; he seems to operate like a light switch – there is either a current or there is none. Nothing in between. Now, suddenly, there is a current. He looks at Camille, amused, and gives him a genuine smile, revealing a mouthful of perfect, straight teeth. Dr Dainville thrives on confrontation, he may be surly, arrogant and boorish, but he likes complications. He is aggressive and argumentative, but deep down he likes to be beaten. Camille has met his fair share of such men. They beat you to a pulp and then give you a Band-Aid.

There is something feminine about him, which may explain why he is a doctor.

The two men look at each other. Dainville is an intelligent man, he is sensitive.

"O.K.," Camille says calmly. "Now let's talk about how we make this work in practice."

10.45 a.m.
"They don't need to operate."

It takes a second or two for Camille to absorb what Anne has said. He would like to whoop with joy, but instead he decides to be circumspect.

"That's good . . ." he says encouragingly.

The X-rays and the M.R.I. scan have confirmed what the young house doctor told him. Anne will need reconstructive dental surgery, but her other injuries will heal with time. She may be left with some scarring around her lips and on her left cheek. What does he mean, "some scarring"? Will there be several scars, will they be conspicuous? Anne has studied her face in the mirror; her lips are so badly split that it is too early to tell what will permanently scar and what will fade. As for the gash on her cheek, until the stitches are removed, it is impossible to assess the long-term damage.

"We need to give it time," the house doctor said.

From Anne's face, it is clear she does not believe this. And time is precisely what Camille does not have.

He has come this morning to deliver a message. The two of them are alone. He pauses for a second and then says:

"I'm hoping you'll be able to recognise the men . . ."

Anne gives a vague shrug that could mean many things.

"The man who fired the shots, you said he was tall . . . What did he look like?"

It is ridiculous to try to get her to answer questions. The investigating officers will have to start again from scratch; for Camille to persist now may even be counter-productive.

"Handsome." She enunciates carefully.

"What . . . ? What do you mean, 'handsome'?" Camille splutters.

Anne looks around. Camille cannot believe his eyes as she gives what can only be called a faint smile, her lips curling back to reveal three broken teeth.

"Handsome . . . like you . . ."

In the long months while he watched Armand dying, Camille experienced something like this many times: the least flicker of improvement turned the dial to unbridled optimism. Anne has made a joke. Camille almost feels like rushing down to reception to insist that she be discharged. Hope is a dirty trick.

He would like to laugh too, but she has caught him unawares. He stammers. Anne has already let her eyes close again. At least he knows that she is lucid, that she understands what he is saying. He is about to try again when he is interrupted by Anne's mobile phone vibrating on the nightstand. Camille passes it to her. It is Nathan.

"I don't want you to worry . . ." she tells her brother, squeezing her eyes shut. She immediately takes on the role of the long-suffering elder sister, weary yet forbearing. Camille can just make out Nathan's voice, panicked and insistent.

"I said all there was to say in my message . . ." Anne is making a much greater effort to speak normally than she has with Camille. She needs to make herself understood, but mostly she needs to calm her brother, to reassure him.

"No, there's no news," she says, her tone almost cheerful. "And I'm not on my own, so you don't need to worry."

She rolls her eyes and looks at Camille. Nathan sounds a little tiresome.

"No, of course not! Listen, I have to go for an X-ray, I'll call you. Yes, love you too . . ."

With a sigh, she turns her mobile off and hands it back to Camille. He makes the most of this moment of intimacy, he does not have long. He has one thing he needs to say.

"Anne . . . I shouldn't be involved with your case, you understand what I'm saying?"

She understands. She nods and gives a soft "Uh-huh".

"You sure you understand?"

Uh-huh. Uh-huh. Camille lets out a breath, releases the pressure, for himself, for her, for them both.

"I got a bit ahead of myself. And then . . ."

He holds her hand, strokes her fingers. His hand, though smaller, is manly and with pronounced veins. Camille has always had warm hands. He fumbles frantically for words, any words that will not leave her terrified.

Avoid saying: the scumbag who beat you is a vicious thug called Vincent Hafner, he tried to kill you and I'm sure he'll try again.

Say rather: I'm here, you'll be safe now.

Don't say: my superior officers don't believe me, but I know I'm right, the guy's a madman, he's utterly fearless.

Better to say: we'll have this guy in custody soon and this will all be over. But we need you to help us identify him. If you can.

Don't say: they're putting a uniformed officer outside the door for the day, but I can tell you now it's a waste of time because as long as this guy is on the loose, you're in danger. He'll stop at nothing.

Make no mention of the guys who broke into her apartment, the stolen papers, the determined efforts they have made to track her down. Or the fact that the resources at Camille's disposal are almost non-existent. Which, in large part, is his fault.

Say: everything will be fine, don't worry.

"I know . . ."

"You will help me, won't you, Anne? You will help?"

She nods.

"And don't tell anyone we know each other, alright?"

Anne agrees, and yet there is a wary look in her eyes. An uneasy silence hangs over them.

"The *gendarme* outside my room, why is he here?"

She spotted him in the corridor as Camille came in. He raises his eyebrows. Camille either lies with consummate ease or he babbles shamefacedly like an eight-year-old. He can shift from best to worst in a breath.

"I . . ."

A single syllable is enough. For someone like Anne, even this syllable is superfluous. From the flicker of hesitation in his eyes, she knows.

"You think he'll come here?"

Camille has no time to react.

"Are you hiding something from me?"

Camille hesitates for a second and by the time he is ready to answer, Anne knows that she is right. She stares intently at him. In this moment when they should be supporting one another, he feels utterly helpless. Anne shakes her head, she seems to be wondering what will happen to her.

"He's already been here?"

"Honestly, I don't know."

This is not the response of a man who honestly does not know. Anne's shoulders begin to shake, and then her arms, blood drains from her face, she looks towards the door, glances around the room as though she has been told that this is the last place she will ever see. Imagine being shown your own death bed. Ham-fisted as ever, Camille adds to the confusion.

"You're safe here."

The words are like an insult.

She turns towards the window and starts to cry.

The most important thing now is that she gets some rest, builds up her strength, it is on this that Camille focuses all of his energy. If she does not recognise anyone in the photographs, the investigation will go off a cliff. But if she can give them a thread, a single thread, Camille feels confident he can find his way through the maze.

And deal with this. Quickly.

He feels dizzy, as though he had been drinking, he feels a crackling in his skin, the world seems to be reeling.

What has he got himself into?

How will it end?

The officer from *identité judiciaire* is Polish; some call him Krystoviak, others Kristowiak; Camille is the only one who can correctly pronounce it: Krysztofiak. He has bushy sideburns and looks like an ageing rockstar. He carries his equipment in an aluminium flight case.

Dr Dainville has given them one hour, assuming it might stretch to two. Camille knows it will take four. Krysztofiak, who has conducted thousands of photo line-ups as a forensic officer, knows it could take six hours. Spread over two days.

In his folder are thousands of mugshots from which he has to make a careful selection. The objective is not to show the witness too many since, after a while, faces begin to merge and the whole process becomes pointless. Buried among hundreds of pictures is Vincent Hafner and three of his known accomplices together with photographs of everyone in the police database of Serbian origin.

He leans over Anne.

"*Bonjour, madame . . .*"

He has a nice voice. Gentle. His movements are slow, precise, reassuring. Her face still swollen, Anne is sitting up in bed, propped up on pillows. She has had one hour's sleep. To show willing, she gives a faint smile, careful not to part her lips and show her shattered teeth. As he opens his aluminium flight case and lays out various files, Krysztofiak reels off the usual pat phrases. He has had lots of time to polish this routine.

"It could be all over quickly. You never know, sometimes we get lucky."

He flashes a broad, encouraging smile. He always tries to bring a light touch to the procedure because when he is called on to present a photo array it is usually because someone has been beaten or has witnessed a sudden, savage attack, the woman may have been raped or may have seen someone being murdered, so the atmosphere, unsurprisingly, is rarely relaxed.

"But sometimes . . ." he goes on, his tone serious and measured, ". . . sometimes it takes time. So if you start to feel tired, just tell me, O.K. ? We're in no rush . . ."

Anne nods. Her troubled eyes seek out Camille; she understands. She nods again.

This is the signal.

"O.K.," Krysztofiak says, "let me explain how this works."

12.15 p.m.
Suddenly, though he is no mood for such things, Camille tries to think of a joke, of one of Commissaire Michard's idiocies, anything but the serious matter at hand. The *gendarme* sent to stand guard is the same one Camille met yesterday at the Galerie Monier, the tall, raw-boned man, his eyes ringed with blue circles like something that has just crawled from the grave. If he were superstitious, Camille would see this as a bad omen. And he is superstitious, he knocks on wood, throws salt over his shoulder, he is petrified by signs and omens and when he sees this hulking zombie standing guard at Anne's door, he finds it hard to remain calm.

The *gendarme* makes to salute, but Camille stops him.

"Verhœven," he introduces himself.

"*Commandant!*" the officer replies, proffering a cold, skeletal hand.

About six foot one, Camille reckons. And organised. He has already commandeered the most comfortable chair from the waiting room and brought it out into the hall. Next to him, against the wall, is a small blue knapsack. His wife probably gives him sandwiches and a flask of coffee. But what Camille notices is the smell of cigarette smoke. If this were 8.00 p.m. rather than noon, Camille would send him packing on the spot. Because the first time he pops downstairs for a crafty cigarette, someone will be watching, timing this little ritual; the second time, the killer will confirm his schedule, the third time he has only to wait until the *gendarme* emerges before he can sneak into Anne's room and blast her. Michard has sent the biggest officer, but he may also be the dumbest. Right now, it is not much of a problem since even Camille cannot imagine the killer coming back so soon, and certainly not in broad daylight.

The night shift will be critical and he will deal with that when the time comes. Even so, Camille issues a warning.

"You don't move from that spot, is that understood?"

"No problem, *commandant!*" the *gendarme* says cheerfully.

The sort of response that makes your blood run cold.

12.45 p.m.

At the far end of the corridor is a small waiting room which is permanently deserted. It is in an impractical location and Camille cannot help but wonder why it is there at all. Florence, the charge nurse who wants to kiss life full on the lips, explains that there were plans to turn it into an office, but they were vetoed. There are regulations, apparently, so the waiting room is still there, useless. Those are the rules. It's something to do with Europe. And so, since there is a shortage of space, the staff use it to store supplies. Whenever there is a security inspection, everything is piled onto trolleys and taken down to the basement only to be brought up again afterwards. The security inspectors are happy and duly rubber-stamp the form.

Camille pushes piles of boxes back against the wall, pulls two chairs up next to the coffee table. Here, he sits down with Louis (charcoal grey suit by Cifonelli, white shirt by Swann & Oscar, shoes by Massaro, everything made to measure. Louis is the only officer at the *brigade criminelle* who wears his annual salary to work). Louis brings Verhœven up to speed on their current cases: the German tourist's death was suicide; the driver in the road-rage incident has been identified, he is on the run, but they will track him down within a day or two; the 71-year-old killer who has confessed, he was jealous. Having dealt with this, Camille comes back to what is really worrying him.

"If Madame Forestier identifies Hafner as—" Louis begins.

"Even if she doesn't identify him," Camille interrupts, "that doesn't mean it's not him."

Louis takes a breath. His boss is not quick-tempered by nature. There is something not right about this case. And it will not be easy to tell him that everyone has worked out what it is . . .

"Of course," Louis agrees, "even if she can't pick him out of the line-up, it could still be Hafner. The fact remains that he has disappeared off the face of the earth. I've been in touch with the officers who dealt with the raid last January – who, by the way, would like to know why this case wasn't assigned to them . . ."

Camille makes a sweeping gesture, he could not give a damn.

"No-one knows where Hafner has been since January. Oh, there are rumours – that he skipped the country or that he's on the Riviera. With a murder charge hanging over him, and given his age, it's hardly surprising that he would go to ground, but even those closest to him don't seem to know anything . . ."

". . . don't seem to know?"

"Yes. That was my first thought. Someone must know something. People don't just disappear overnight. What is really surprising is him doing a job now. You would have thought he'd want to stay in hiding."

"Any potential leaks?"

The question of information is wide open. Small-time crooks holding up shops are two a penny, but genuine professionals only do a job when they have solid information, when the expected haul is worth the effort if things go wrong. And the source of that information provides the first line of inquiry for the police. In the case of the Galerie Monier, the girl who turned up late for work has been eliminated as a suspect. And therefore it stands to reason . . .

"We will have to ask Madame Forestier what she was doing at the Galerie Monier," Camille says.

The question will be asked as a matter of form, knowing he is unlikely to get an answer. Camille will ask the question because he has to, because under normal circumstances, this would be his next question. He knows very little about Anne's timetable, he does not know which days she spends in Paris, he barely registers her trips, her meetings, he is happy just to know that he will see her tonight, or tomorrow night – the day after tomorrow is anybody's guess.

But Louis Mariani is a first-rate officer. Meticulous, intelligent, more cultured than he needs to be, intuitive and . . . and suspicious. Bravo. One of the cardinal virtues of a good officer.

For example, when Commissaire Michard questions whether Hafner was in Anne's hospital room, she is simply sceptical, but when she asks Camille what the hell he is playing at and demands his daily report, she is suspicious. And when Camille wonders whether Anne might have seen something important apart from the faces of the robbers, he is suspicious.

And when Louis is dealing with a case in which a woman was attacked during the course of a robbery, he asks himself why she was in that particular place at that particular time. On a day when she should have been at work. Just as the shops were opening up. When there would have been few passers-by and no customers except her. He could have asked the question himself, but for some unexplained reason Verhœven is the only officer who has questioned the woman. As though she were spoken for.

And so Louis did not question her directly. He found an indirect approach.

Camille has raised the issue, protocol has been respected and he is about to move on to the next point when he is distracted by Louis bending down and rummaging for something in his briefcase. He takes out a piece of paper. For a little while now, Louis has taken to wearing reading glasses. Presbyopia usually doesn't develop until later, Camille thinks. But then again, how old is Louis? It is a little like having a son, he can never quite remember his age, he asks the question at least three times a year.

Louis holds up a photocopy bearing the letterhead of Desfossés Jewellers. Camille puts on his own glasses and reads "Anne Forestier". It is a copy of an order for a luxury watch, eight hundred euros.

"Madame Forestier was there to pick up something she ordered ten days ago."

The jeweller asked for ten days to complete the engraving. The text to be engraved has been noted down in block capitals to avoid making a mistake on such an expensive gift . . . Just imagine the customer's face if a name were misspelled. In fact, Madame Forestier was asked to write it out herself so there could be no arguments if there was a problem later. Camille recognises Anne's large, graceful hand.

The name to be engraved on the watch: *Camille*.

Silence.

Both men take off their glasses and the synchronicity serves only to heighten their embarrassment. Camille does not look up, he gently pushes the photocopy across the table to Louis.

"She . . . she's a friend."

Louis nods. A friend. Fine.

"A close friend."

A close friend. Fine. Louis realises that he is playing catch-up. That he has missed several episodes in Camille Verhœven's life. As quickly as he can, he reviews the extent of his lacuna.

He thinks back to four years ago: he knew Irène, they got along, Irène called him "*mon petit Loulou*" and made him blush by asking questions about his sex life. After Irène's death came the psychiatric clinic, where Louis visited regularly until Camille said he would rather be alone. For a time, they saw each other only from a distance. It took Le Guen's most Machiavellian machinations to force Camille, two years later, to rejoin the serious crime squad investigating murders, kidnappings . . . and Camille asked that Louis be reassigned to his team. Louis has no idea what had been going on in Verhœven's private life since his time in the clinic.

But in the life of a man as punctilious as Camille, the sudden appearance of a woman should be obvious from countless little details, differences in behaviour, changes in routine, precisely the sort of things Louis generally notices. And yet he saw nothing, sensed nothing. Until today, he would have dismissed the notion of there being a woman in Verhœven's life as idle speculation, because in the life of a widower who is by nature a depressive, a serious romantic relationship would be a seismic event. And yet this feverishness, this exaltation today . . . There is something contradictory about it that Louis cannot quite grasp.

Louis stares at his glasses on the coffee table as though somehow they might help him see the situation more clearly: so, Camille has a "close friend", her name is Anne Forestier. Camille clears his throat.

"I'm not asking you to get involved, Louis. I'm up to my neck right now and I don't need anyone to remind me that what I'm doing is against regulations, that's my business and nobody else's. And I wouldn't ask you to take that kind of risk, Louis. [He looks at his assistant.] All I'm asking for is a little time. [Silence.] I need to close this thing down, and fast. Before Michard finds out that I lied in order to have a case involving someone very close to me assigned to my team. If we can arrest these guys quickly, none of that will matter. Or at least it can be dealt with. But if we don't, if the case drags on and this thing comes out . . . well, you know what Michard's like, there'll be hell to pay. And there's no reason for you to have to pay it too." Louis is lost in thought, he does not seem to be here, he glances around him as though expecting a waiter to come and take his order. Finally, he gives a sad smile and nods towards the photocopy.

"Well, this isn't going to help the investigation much, is it?"

he says. His tone is that of a man who thought he had discovered treasure only to be deeply disappointed. "I mean, Camille is a pretty common name. There's no way of even knowing if it refers to a man or a woman . . ."

And when Camille does not respond:

"What do you want us to do with it?"

He fiddles with the knot on his tie.

Pushes his hair back with his left hand.

He gets to his feet, leaving the piece of paper on the table. Camille picks it up, crumples it into a ball and stuffs it into his pocket.

1.15 p.m.

The officer from *identité judiciaire* has just packed away his things and left.

"Thank you, Madame Forestier, I think we did some good work," he said as he went. It is what he always says, regardless of the result.

Despite the fact that it makes her dizzy, Anne got out of bed and went into the bathroom. She cannot resist the temptation to look, to survey the extent of the damage. Now that the bandages around her head have been removed, she can see only her short, lank hair and the twin shaved patches where she needed stitches. Like holes in her head. There are more stitches along her jawline. Her face seems even more swollen today. It's normal, they tell her over and over, the swelling is always worse in the first few days, she knows, she's been told, but no-one told her what it would actually look like. She has swollen up like a balloon, her face has the flushed complexion of an alcoholic. A battered woman looks a little like a bag lady. Anne feels a fierce sense of injustice.

She brings her fingertips to her cheeks, feels a dull, diffuse, insidious pain that seems rooted there for ever.

And her teeth, my God, it gives her a pitiful air, she does not know why; it is like having a mastectomy, she thinks, she feels utterly violated. She is no longer herself, no longer whole, she will have to have dental implants, she will never recover from this ordeal.

Now, here she is. She has just spent hours reviewing dozens of photographs. She did as she was asked, she was meek, obedient, unemotional, when she recognised the man, she pointed with her index finger.

Him.

How will it end?

By himself, Camille cannot protect her. Who else can she count on, given that this man is determined to kill her?

He probably wants this ordeal to be over. Just as she does. They both, in their different ways, want it to end.

Anne wipes away her tears. She looks around for some tissues. Blowing your nose is a delicate affair when it is broken.

1.20 p.m.

Given my experience, I almost always end up getting what I want. Right now, I've had to resort to drastic measures, partly because I'm in a hurry, but partly because it's in my nature. That's just how I am: impatient, impetuous.

I need money, and I don't fancy losing all the loot I've sweated blood to earn. I like to think of it as a pension fund, but a little more secure. And I'm not about to let anyone siphon off my future prospects.

So, I redouble my efforts.

Having reconnoitred every inch of the area on foot, then in the car, then a second time on foot, I spend twenty minutes watching. Not a living soul. I take another ten minutes and survey the area using binoculars. I send a text message confirming my arrival, then walk quickly past the disused factory towards the van, open the rear door, climb in and slam it behind me.

The van is parked in an industrial wasteland. I don't know how the guy always manages to find places like this – he should be a location scout for the movies rather than an arms dealer.

The inside of the van is as well ordered as the mind of a computer analyst: everything is in its place.

My fence subbed me a small advance, pretty much the most he could give under the circumstances. At the sort of interest rate that should earn him a bullet between the eyes, but I don't have a choice, I need this thing settled right now. I have temporarily set aside the Mossberg in favour of .308 calibre M40 semi-automatic sniper rifle that takes six rounds. Everything is in the case: silencer, Schmidt & Bender telescopic sights, two boxes of ammunition for a clean, accurate, long-range kill. As a handgun, I opt for a 10-shot Walther P99 compact equipped with an astonishingly effective silencer. Lastly, I get a 6" Buck Special hunting knife, which is always useful.

That bitch has already had a sneak preview of my talents.

Now, I'm going to shift things up a gear; she could do with a thrill.

1.30 p.m.

It is Vincent Hafner.

"The witness positively identified him." Krysztofiak has joined Louis and Camille in the waiting room. "She has an excellent memory."

"Though there was only a short period when she could see their faces . . ." ventures Louis.

"It can be enough, it depends on the circumstances. Some witnesses can stare at a suspect for minutes at a time and be unable to identify them an hour later. Other people, for reasons we don't understand, can accurately recall every detail of a person's features after one glance."

Camille does not react; it is as if they were talking about him. He can glimpse someone in the *métro* and, a month or two months later, make a detailed sketch of every line, every wrinkle.

"Sometimes, witnesses block out memories," Krysztofiak goes on, "but a guy who savagely beats you and fires at you from a car at point-blank range, that's a face people tend to remember."

Neither Camille nor Louis can tell whether this is somehow intended to be funny.

"We narrowed the selection down by age, physical characteristics and so on. She's absolutely certain that it's Hafner."

On his laptop screen, he pulls up a photograph, a tall man of about sixty, a full-length shot taken during a previous arrest. Five foot eleven, Camille calculates.

"Six foot, actually," Louis says, leafing through the police record. He who knows Camille's every thought, even when he is saying nothing.

Mentally, Camille merges the man in this photograph with the armed robber at the Galerie, picturing him in a balaclava, raising the shotgun, aiming, firing; he pictures him moments earlier, lashing out with the rifle butt at Anne's head, her belly . . . He swallows hard.

The man in the photograph is broad-shouldered, his angular

face framed by salt-and-pepper hair, his thin, grey eyebrows accentuate his vacant, staring eyes. An old-school gangster. A thug. Louis notices that his boss' hands are trembling.

"What about the other two?" Louis asks, ever willing to create a diversion.

On the screen, Krysztofiak brings up another mugshot, a bearded guy with bushy eyebrows and dark eyes.

"Madame Forestier hesitated a little on this one. It's understandable, after a while these people all look the same. She looked through several photographs and came back to this one, asked to see some others, but kept coming back to this one. I'd classify it as a strong possibility. Name's Dušan Ravic. He's a Serb."

Camille looks up. They crowd around Louis' laptop as he keys the search into the police database.

"Moved to France in 1997." He quickly scrolls through the document. "A clever guy." He reads at the speed of sound and still manages to synthesise the data. "Arrested twice and released, the charges didn't stick. It's not impossible to imagine him working with Hafner. There are lots of thugs out there, but real professionals are rare and it's a small world."

"So where is this guy?"

Louis makes a vague gesture. There have been no sightings since January, he has completely disappeared, he is facing a felony murder charge for his part in the quadruple robbery and he has the means and the motive to hide out for a long time. It's astonishing that the same gang should show up again so soon. They already have one murder charge on file and they're upping the ante. It's bizarre.

They come back to the subject of Anne.

"How reliable is her testimony?" Louis asks.

"As always, it's a sliding scale. The first hit I'd say is extremely reliable, the second is fairly reliable, if there'd been a third, it would probably have ranked lower still."

Camille can hardly stand still. Louis is deliberately dragging out the conversation, hoping that his boss will regain his composure, but when the forensics officer finally leaves, he realises it was a waste of time.

"I have to find these guys," Camille says, calmly placing his hands flat on the table. "I have to find them now."

It is an emotional reflex. Louis nods automatically, but he wonders what is fuelling the blind rage.

Camille stares at the two mugshots.

"This guy" – he nods to the picture of Hafner – "we need to track him down first. He's the real danger. I'll take care of it."

He says these words with such single-mindedness that Louis, who knows him all too well, can sense the looming catastrophe.

"Listen . . ." he begins.

"You," Camille cuts him off, "you take care of the Serb. I'll go and see M chard and get the warrants. In the meantime, round up every officer on duty. Put a call in to Jourdan, tell him I'd like him to second the men in his unit. Talk to Hanol too, talk to everyone, I'm going to need a lot of bodies."

Faced with an avalanche of decisions, each more nebulous than the last, Louis pushes back his fringe with his left hand. Camille notices the gesture.

"Just do what I tell you," he says in a low voice. "If there's any flak, I'll take it. You don't have to worry about getti—"

"I'm not worried. It's just that it's easier to carry out orders when you understand them."

"You understand exactly what I'm saying, Louis. What else do you want to know?"

Camille's voice has dropped so low that Louis has to strain to hear. He lays a warm hand on that of his assistant. "I can't fuck this up . . . do you understand?" He is upset, but remains composed. "So we need to shake the tree."

Louis gives a nod that means: O.K., I'm not sure I completely understand, but I'll do what you've asked.

"The informers, the pimps, the whores, everyone – but I want you to start with the illegals."

The "illegals" refers to the undocumented workers on file to whom the police turn a blind eye because they are the best possible source of information about anything and everything. Talk or take a plane home is a particularly productive threat. If the Serb still has any ties to the community – and he would not last long without them – then tracking him down will take a matter of hours, not days. He was involved in a spectacular raid less than forty-eight hours ago . . . If he did not leave France with a murder charge and four robberies hanging over him, he must have very good reasons to be here.

Louis pushes back his fringe – right hand.

"I need you to get the team sorted as a matter of urgency," Camille says. "As soon as I get the green light, I'll call. I'll join you as soon as I can, but in the meantime, you can get me on my mobile."

2.00 p.m.
Camille is sitting in front of his computer screen.

Police file: Vincent Hafner.

Sixty years old. Almost fourteen years behind bars on various charges. As a young man, he dabbles in all sorts of things (burglary, extortion, pimping), but in 1972, at the age of twenty-five, he finds his true vocation. An armed raid on an armoured van in Puteaux. The raid gets a little messy, the police show up, one man is wounded. He is sentenced to eight years, he serves five, and learns from his experience: he has found a profession he really likes. His only mistake was carelessness, he is determined not to be caught again. Things do not quite work out as planned, he is arrested on a number of occasions, but the sentences are minor, two years here, three years there. Overall, a pretty successful career.

Since 1985, there have been no arrests. In his mature years, Hafner is at the peak of his powers. He is a suspect in eleven separate hold-ups, but is never arrested, never even questioned, there is no evidence, in every single case he has a cast-iron alibi and reliable witnesses. An artist.

Hafner is a major crime boss, and as his record confirms, he is not to be trifled with. He is intelligent and informed, his jobs are meticulously planned, but when his team go in, they go in hard. Bystanders are assaulted, beaten, battered, often with lasting consequences. No deaths, but no shortage of walking wounded. Hafner leaves a trail of victims hobbling, shambling, limping, to say nothing of scarred faces and years of physiotherapy. It is a simple technique: you earn respect by beating the shit out of the first person on the scene, the others get the message and after that everything runs like clockwork.

The first person on the scene yesterday was Anne Forestier.

The Galerie Monier raid fits neatly with Hafner's profile. Camille doodles the man's face in the margin of his notebook as he scrolls through the interviews from previous offences.

For several years, Hafner drew his accomplices from a small

pool of about a dozen men, choosing on the basis of their talents and their availability. Camille quickly calculates that at any given point, on average three of them will be in jail, on remand or on parole. Hafner, for his part, manages to emerge unscathed. Crime is like any business: reliable, proficient workers are difficult to come by. But turnover is even higher in the armed robbery business since these are skilled craftsmen. In the space of a few years, at least six former members of Hafner's gang are put out of commission. Two get life sentences for murder, two are shot dead (twins, they stuck with each other to the end), the fifth is in a wheelchair after a motorcycle accident and the sixth is reported missing after a Cessna goes down off the Corsican coast. It is a serious blow for Hafner. For some time afterwards, he is implicated in no new cases. People begin to draw the logical conclusion: Hafner, who must surely have put a lot of money aside, has finally retired and the staff and customers of jeweller's all over France can light a candle to their patron saint.

Consequently, the quadruple raid in January came as a shock. Especially since, in Hafner's career, the size and scale of those raids were an anomaly. Armed robbers rarely indulge in assembly-line work. The physical force and nervous energy required for even a single raid is difficult to imagine, especially given the brutal, strong-arm methods employed by Hafner. Every last detail is planned to allow for all eventualities, so in order to rob four jeweller's in a single day one would have to be certain that each target was primed, that the distances between them were feasible, that . . . So many things needed to go without a hitch that it is hardly surprising that it went as badly wrong as it did.

Camille scrolls through the photographs of the victims.

First, the woman at the second raid in January. The assistant at the jeweller's on the rue de Rennes is a girl of about twenty-five. Her face after her encounter with these consummate professionals is so badly disfigured that . . . Next to her, Anne looks like a blushing bride. The girl spent four days in a coma.

The man injured during the third robbery. A customer. Though it hardly seems so from the photograph. He looks more like a victim of trench warfare than a customer of the Louvre des Antiquaires. His medical file indicates "critical condition". Anyone seeing his mutilated face (like Anne, he was beaten with a rifle butt) would be forced to agree: his condition is critical.

The last victim. He is lying in a pool of blood on the floor of the jeweller's on the rue de Sèvres. Neater, in a way: two bullets in the chest.

This is another anomaly in Hafner's career. Up until now, not one of his victims had died. The difference this time is that he cannot rely on his old gang, he has to put together a team from whoever is available. He went with the Serbs. Not an inspired choice. Serbs are fearless, but they're volatile.

Camille looks down at his notepad. In the middle, Vincent Hafner, a portrait drawn from one of his mugshots and around it, deft sketches of the victims. The most striking is the sketch, drawn from memory, of Anne's face as he saw it when he first came into her hospital room.

Camille tears out the page, crumples it into a ball and tosses it into the wastebasket. He jots down a single word that summarises his analysis of the situation.

"Critical."

Because Hafner does not come out of retirement in January and cobble together a makeshift team unless there is an overwhelming motive. Aside from the need for money, it is difficult to guess what that might be.

Critical, because Hafner does not simply slip back into his old ways. To maximise his profits, he takes the risk of staging a quadruple robbery with uncertain results.

Critical, because despite a huge haul in January – his share would have amounted to €200,000–€300,000 – six months later, he is back at work. The Hafner Comeback Tour. And if the haul this time was less than he expected, he will come back for another encore. There are innocent people out there living on borrowed time. Better to catch him first.

Anybody would realise there is something fishy about this whole affair. Though he cannot put his finger on it, Camille knows there is something amiss, something not quite right. He is hard-headed enough to know that a man like Hafner will be difficult to catch and that, right now, the most sensible approach is to track down his accomplice, Ravic, in the hope that they can flip him and get a lead on Hafner.

And if Anne is to survive, they need it to be a good lead.

2.15 p.m.
"And you feel this is . . . relevant?" Juge Pereira's voice on the other end of the line sounds suspicious. "It sounds to me like you want permission to conduct a mass round-up."

"Absolutely not, *monsieur le juge*, there will be no mass round-up."

Camille is tempted to laugh, but he stops himself: the examining magistrate is too shrewd to fall for such a ruse. But he is also too busy to question the methods of an experienced police officer who claims to have a solution.

"On the contrary," Camille argues, "it will be a carefully

targeted operation, *monsieur le juge*. We have identified three or four known associates that Ravic might have approached for help while he was on the run after the January raid, we just need permission to shake the tree, that's all."

"What does Commissaire Michard have to say?"

"She agrees with me," Camille says with an air of finality.

He has not yet spoken to the *commissaire divisionnaire*, but he can predict how she will react. It is the oldest bureaucratic trick in the book: tell X that Y has already approved a course of action and vice versa. Like so many hackneyed ploys, it is very effective. In fact, when carefully executed, it is almost unassailable.

"Very well then, *commandant*, do as you see fit."

2.40 p.m.

The fat *gendarme* is staring at his mobile, engrossed in his game of solitaire, when he realises the person who just walked past is the woman he is supposed to be guarding. He scrabbles to his feet and runs after her shouting "Madame!" – he has forgotten her name – "Madame!" She does not turn, but pauses as she walks past the nurses' station.

"I'm going now."

It sounds casual, like saying "Bye, see you tomorrow". The big *gendarme* quickens his pace, raises his voice.

"Madame . . . !"

The young nurse with the ring through her lip is on duty. The nurse who thought she might have seen a shotgun but in the end decided that she hadn't, but then again . . . She rushes from behind the desk, past the *gendarme*, determined to take charge. She was taught to be firm in nursing school, but six months working in a hospital and she has learned to cope with anything.

As she draws level with Anne, she gently takes her arm. Anne, who has been expecting something of the sort, turns to face her. For the nurse, it is the patient's single-minded determination that makes this a delicate situation. For Anne, it is the young nurse's calm persuasiveness that complicates matters. She looks at the lip ring, the shaven head, there is a gentleness, a fragility to the girl, her face is utterly ordinary, but her big puppy-dog eyes could melt the hardest heart, and she knows how to use them.

There is no direct refusal, no warning, no lecture; the nurse takes a different tack.

"If you want to discharge yourself, I need to take out your stitches."

Anne brings her hand up to her cheek.

"No," the nurse says, "not those, it's too soon. I meant these two here."

She reaches up and gently runs her fingers over the shaved patch on Anne's head, her expression is professional, but she smiles and, assuming that this is now agreed, she leads Anne back towards her room. The *gendarme* stands aside, wondering whether or not to tell his superiors about this development, then follows the two women.

Just opposite the nurses' station, they step into a small treatment room used for outpatients.

"Take a seat . . ." As she looks around for her instruments, the nurse is gently insistent. "Please, take a seat."

Standing outside in the corridor, the *gendarme* discreetly looks away as though the two women were in the toilets.

"Shhhh . . ."

Anne flinched, though the young nurse's fingertips have barely grazed the wound.

"Is it painful?" She sounds concerned. "That's a little unusual.

What if I press here? And here? I think it might be best to wait before removing the stitches, consult the doctor, he might want to get another X-ray. Are you running a temperature?"

She presses a hand to Anne's forehead.

"No headache?"

Anne realises that she is now precisely where the nurse wanted her to be: sitting meekly in a treatment room, ready to be taken back to her room. And so she bridles.

"No, no doctors, no X-rays, I'm leaving," she says, getting to her feet.

The *gendarme* outside reaches for his police radio; however this plays out, he needs to call in to ask for instructions. If the killer suddenly appeared at the far end of the hallway, armed to the teeth, he would do the same thing.

"That really wouldn't be wise," the nurse is saying, sounding concerned. "If there's an infection . . ."

Anne does not know what to think, whether there genuinely is a problem or whether the nurse is simply saying this to alarm her.

"Oh, that reminds me . . . [The nurse abruptly changes the subject.] We never did get your admission form filled in, did we? You asked someone to bring in your medical papers? I'll make sure a doctor sees you right now, and that the X-ray is done immediately so you can leave as soon as possible."

Her tone is honest, conciliatory, what she is proposing sounds like the best, the most reasonable solution.

Anne, by now exhausted, agrees and slowly trudges back towards her room, feeling as though she is about to faint, she tires so quickly. But she is thinking about something else, something she has just remembered. She stops, turns.

"You're the nurse who saw the man with the gun?"

"I saw a man," the girl snaps back, "not a gun."

She has been expecting this question. The answer is a formality. From the moment negotiations began, she could tell that the patient was scared witless. She is not trying to leave, she is trying to escape.

"If I'd seen a gun, I would have said so. And if I had, I'm guessing you wouldn't be here, right?"

Though young, she is extremely professional. Anne does not believe a word.

"No," she says, staring intently at the nurse as though she can read her mind, "you're just not sure what you saw, that's all."

Even so, she goes back to her room, her head is spinning, she overestimated her strength, she is completely drained, she needs to lie down. To sleep.

The nurse closes the door. Pensive. What could it have been, that long, bulky thing the guy had under his coat?

2.45 p.m.

Commissaire Michard spends most of her time in meetings. Camille has consulted her diary, an uninterrupted series of appointments back-to-back: it is the perfect opportunity. In the space of an hour, he leaves seven messages on her voicemail. Important. Serious. Urgent. Critical. In the messages, he all but exhausts the glossary of emergency-related clichés, piles on as much pressure as he can, when she calls back he is expecting her to be belligerent. Instead, the *commissaire*'s tone is patient and considered. She is even more shrewd than she appears. On the telephone, she whispers, she has clearly stepped into a hallway for a moment. "And the magistrate has signed off on this police round-up?"

"Absolutely," Camille insists, "precisely because it's not a 'round-up' in the strictest sense, we're look—"

"Precisely how many targets *are* you looking at, *commandant*?"

"Three. But you know how it is, one target can lead to another. Strike while the iron is hot and so forth."

When Camille resorts to a proverb, it means he has run out of arguments.

"Ah yes, the 'iron' . . ." the *commissaire* says wistfully.

"I'm going to need a few bodies."

In the end, everything comes down to resources. Michard lets out a long sigh. What is most frequently requested is always what is not available.

"Not for long, three, four hours, max."

"To bring in three targets?"

"No, to . . ."

"Yeah, to strike the proverbial iron, I get it, *commandant*. But aren't you worried about the effects of going in mob-handed?"

Michard knows how these things work, the bigger the operation the greater the chance the target will get wind of it and do a runner, the longer the search goes on, the more the chances of apprehending the suspect diminish.

"That's why I need more men."

The exchange could go on for hours. In fact, the *commissaire* doesn't give a damn if Verhœven wants to stage a round-up. Her strategy is simply to stand her ground long enough so that if the operation goes pear-shaped she can say "I told you so".

"Well, if the *juge* has signed off on it . . ." she says at last. "Sort it out with your colleagues. If you can."

*

Being an armed robber is like being an actor; you spend most of your time hanging around on set and do a day's work in a few minutes.

So here I am, waiting. Scheming, anticipating, calling on all my experience.

If the witness is strong enough to face it, the police are bound to have her do a line-up. If not today, then tomorrow, it's only a matter of hours. They'll go through a raft of mugshots and if she's a solid citizen and has even the vaguest memory, they'll be on the warpath. Right now, their best option would be to hunt down Ravic. That's what I would do in their shoes. Since it's the easiest and often the most effective method, they'll set up traps in corridors, break down a few doors. You make a lot of noise, use a little intimidation – it's the oldest trick in the police handbook.

And the place to start would be Luka's Bistro on the rue de Tanger, the principal stomping ground of the Serbian criminal fraternity. The goons who hang out at Luka's are tacky, low-rent mobsters who spend their time playing cards, betting on horses, from the stifling clouds of Russian cigarette smoke you'd think a beekeeper was smoking a hive. They pride themselves on being informed. If anything serious goes down, word reaches Luka's Bistro.

3.15 p.m.
Verhœven has given orders to loose the dogs. To get all hands on deck. It seems a little excessive.

Camille capitalises on the *commissaire*'s support to commandeer officers from anywhere he can. As Louis anxiously watches, he puts in calls to other units, calls in favours from colleagues, they let him borrow one man, two men, it is all a little chaotic, but gradually the team begins to swell. None of his colleagues is entirely sure what he is up to, but they don't ask too many questions, Camille makes his case with an air of authority and besides, this is fun, they get to put flashing lights on unmarked cars and drive through the city like boy racers, shaking down drug dealers, pickpockets, brothel-keepers, pimps – and, in the end, the opportunity to play cops and robbers was part of the reason they joined the force. Camille says the operation will only last a couple of hours. They'll go in hard and fast, then everyone can go home.

Some of his colleagues are undecided: Camille sounds nervous, he is quick to give justifications but offers little in the way of hard evidence. More worryingly, the operation is beginning to sound rather different from how it had appeared originally. They believed they were being asked to assign officers for a series of simultaneous raids to take down three specific targets. What Camille is describing is just as violent, but on a much larger scale.

"Listen," Camille says, "if we catch the guy we're looking for, everybody wins, the top brass will be chuffed, they'll hand out medals to every senior officer. And besides, it's only a couple of hours, if we work fast, you'll be back at your units before your bosses start wondering where you stopped off for a beer."

This is all it takes for his friends to concede and give him the manpower. The officers pile into squad cars, with Camille leading the convoy. Louis stays behind and mans the telephone.

Operation Verhœven is not exactly a model of discretion. But this is precisely the point. An hour later, there is not a single thug in Paris from Zagreb or from Mostar who does not know about the frantic search for Ravic. He has to be hiding out somewhere. They smoke out tunnels and corridors, intimidate the prostitutes, and round up everyone in sight – especially the undocumented immigrants.

This is shock treatment.

Sirens wail, police lights strobe the buildings, a whole street in the 18th arrondissement is cordoned off, three men make a run for it and are caught. Standing by his car, Camille watches the scene as he talks on his mobile to the team ransacking a fleabag hotel in the 20th.

If he thought about it, Camille might even feel nostalgic. There was a time – back in the days of the Serious Crime Squad, of the Brigade Verhœven – when Armand would hole up in his office with case files, filling page after page with hundreds of names from related cases, and emerge two days later with the only two names that could move the investigation forward. Meanwhile, as soon as Louis' back was turned, Maleval would be kicking the arse of anyone who moved, slapping whores and forcing them to strip, and just when you were about to put him on a disciplinary charge, he would plead exigent circumstances and hand over a crucial witness statement that saved three days' work.

But Camille is not thinking about this. He is focused on the job in hand.

In sleazy hotels, he takes the stairs two at a time, flanked by officers who burst into the rooms catching couples *in flagrante*, dragging sheepish husbands with their shrivelled cocks off the beds so they can question the prostitutes beneath them – Dušan Ravic, we're looking for him, for his family, anyone, a cousin will do – but no, the name doesn't ring a bell; they carry on barking questions while the panicked johns scrabble to pull on their trousers, hoping to get out before they're spotted. The girls – half naked, scrawny, their breasts tiny, their hip bones jutting through their skin – have never heard of Ravic. "Dušan?" one of them says as though she has never heard the name before. But they are obviously terrified. "Take them in," Camille says. He needs to create an atmosphere of fear and he does not have much time. A couple of hours. Three, if all goes well.

Several miles north, outside a house in the suburbs, four officers put in a call to Louis to check they have the right address, then kick the door down and go in, armed and ready, toss the place, and come up with 200 grams of cannabis. No-one here has heard of Dušan Ravic. They take the whole family into custody save for the elderly grandparents.

Riding in a screeching car piloted by a boy racer who never drops below fourth gear, Camille keeps his mobile glued to his ear, in constant contact with Louis. Backed up by a barrage of orders and the persistent pressure on the teams, Verhœven's fury is contagious.

In the 14th, three young Kosovars are hauled into the police station. Dušan Ravic? The three boys look blank. We'll see. Meanwhile, rough them up a little so when they're released they can preach the Good News: the police are looking for Ravic.

Camille gets word that two pick-pockets from Požarevac are being held at the commissariat in the 15th arrondissement; he consults Louis who checks his map of Serbia. Požarevac is in the north-east, Ravic is from Elemir in the far north, but you never know. Camille gives the word: bring them in. The object is to spread fear.

Back at the *brigade criminelle*, Louis, perfectly calm, fields the calls, he has a mental map of Paris, he has categorised the neighbourhoods, prioritised those areas with residents likely to provide information.

Someone asks a question, little more than an idle suggestion, Camille thinks for a moment and says yes, and so officers round up the buskers in the *métro* stations, kick them along the platforms and drag them into the waiting police vans while they keep a tight grip on their little cloth bags jingling with change. Dušan Ravic? Blank stares, an officer grabs one of them by the sleeve. Dušan Ravic. The man shakes his head, blinking rapidly. "I want a home delivery on this guy," says Camille who has just come up for air because there is no signal in that part of the *métro* and he needs to know what is happening. He glances anxiously at his watch but says nothing. He is wondering how long it will take before Commissaire Michard comes down on him like a ton of bricks.

About an hour ago, the force descended on Luka's and carted off one guy in three – who knows on what charge, I doubt they know themselves. The point of the exercise is obviously to spread panic. And this is just the beginning. My calculations were spot on: in less than an hour the whole Serbian community will be turned inside out, and the rats will be deserting the ship.

I'd be happy to settle for one rat. Dušan Ravic.

Now that the operation is in full swing, there's no time to lose. I'm there in the time it takes to drive across Paris.

A narrow street, almost an alleyway, between the rue Charpier and the rue Ferdinand-Conseil in the 13th. A building whose ground-floor windows have been bricked up, the original door was "salvaged" long ago, there's no lock, no handle now, no door, only a sheet of rotting plywood that bangs with every gust of wind until someone comes down and wedges it shut, only for it to start banging again as soon as the next person arrives. There's a steady stream of people in this place, junkies, dealers, illegals, whole families of immigrants. I've spent too many days (and quite a few nights) holed up here for one reason or another, I know this street like the back of my hand. I loathe this shithole, I could happily get a couple of kilos of gelignite and blow the street to kingdom come.

This is where I brought that big lunk Dušan Ravic one night last January, while we were preparing the Heist of the Century. When we got to the building, he smiled with those thick red lips of his.

"When I find chick, I take her here."

A "chick" . . . Jesus. No-one has used that word in decades, you'd have to be a Serb.

"A chick," I said. "What chick?"

As I asked the question, I looked around. It didn't take much imagination to work out the kind of girl you could bring back here, where you'd find her and what you could do with her. Ravic is a class act.

"Not *one* chick," Ravic said. He liked to sound like a player. He liked to give details. The actual story was much simpler: this moron bunked down on a flea-ridden mattress in this hovel so he could fuck whatever skanky whores he could afford.

His sex life has obviously taken a nose-dive lately, because Ravic hasn't been here in an age – I should know, I've hidden out here often enough – and I'm sure he wouldn't come back for choice. Chick or no chick, no-one comes here for fun, they come here when they have nowhere else to run. And right now, if I'm lucky and if the cops do their job properly, he'll have to come here.

With the police shaking down the whole Serbian community, Ravic will quickly realise that this shithole is the only place where no-one will come looking for him.

I've unscrewed the silencer and slipped the Walther P99 into the glove compartment, there's just enough time to pop into a café for a drink, but I need to be back here in half an hour, because if Ravic does show up, I want to be the one to welcome him.

It's the least I can do.

There is a big guy in an interrogation room at the commissariat. According to his papers, he is originally from Bujanovac; Louis checks, it's a small town in southern Serbia. Dušan Ravic, his brother, his sister? The cops don't care, any scrap of information is welcome. The big guy doesn't understand the question, someone smacks him across the face. Dušan Ravic? This time he understands, he shakes his head, he doesn't know anyone by that name, the cop smacks him across the head. "Let it go," Camille says, "he doesn't know anything." Fifteen minutes later, back on the street, three Serbs, two of them sisters. It's heartbreaking: they're barely seventeen, they have no papers, they turn tricks at Porte de la Chapelle – without a condom for twice the price – they're all skin and bone. Dušan Ravic? They shake their heads. It doesn't matter, Camille tells them, he will hold them for as long as the law allows; the girls purse their lips, they know the beating their pimp doles out will be proportional to the length of time they are in custody, he can't afford to lose money, the city never sleeps, they should be out walking the streets, the girls start to tremble. Dušan Ravic? They shake their heads again and stare towards the waiting police car. Standing behind them, Camille gives one of the officers a nod: Let them go.

In police stations across the capital there are raised voices in the corridors, those who speak a little French threaten to call the consulate, the embassy, as if that is likely to help them. They can call the Pope himself, maybe he's a Serb.

Louis, his phone still pressed to his ear, gives instructions, keeps Verhœven up to date, coordinates the teams. There are flashing dots on his mental map of the city, especially in the north and the north-east. Louis consolidates, updates, dispatches. Camille climbs back into his car. No sign of Ravic. Not yet.

Are all the women scrawny? No, not really. In the condemned building somewhere in the 11th arrondissement the woman is seriously overweight, thirty-something, at least eight kids bawling in the background, her husband is a stick insect in a string vest, he has a moustache – all the men have moustaches – and though not particularly tall, he stares down at Camille. He goes over to a dresser to get their papers, the family are from Prokuplje; on the other end of the telephone, Louis says it is a town in central Serbia. Dušan Ravic? The man says nothing, he racks his brain, no, honestly: they cart him off, the kids start tugging at his sleeves, tragedy is their stock in trade, an hour from now they'll be out begging somewhere between Saint-Martin church and the rue Blavière carrying a misspelled cardboard sign scrawled in marker pen.

Where information is concerned, the card players at Luka's are as good a source as it gets. They spend their days chewing the fat while their wives slave away, their older daughters are on the game and the others are minding the babies. Seeing Camille show up with three officers, they wearily toss their cards down onto the table – this is the fourth time in a month the police have interrupted their game, but this time, they've got the dwarf with them. Wrapped up in his coat, hat pulled down over his forehead, Camille looks each of them in the eye, the brute determination in his gaze drilling into their retinas, as though the search is somehow personal. Ravic? Sure, they know him, but only vaguely, they look at each other – "You seen him around?" "No, you?"

They give apologetic smiles, they'd like to be able to help, but . . . "Yeah, right," Camille says, and takes the youngest of them aside, a gangling figure so tall it looks like Camille chose him deliberately, which he did since it means he has only to stretch out his hand to grab the guy by the balls. He looks away as the guy falls to his knees, howling up in pain. Ravic? If he is not saying anything now, it's because he doesn't know anything. "Or because his balls have stopped working," says one of the other officers. The others laugh. Camille, stone-faced, stalks out of the café. "Bring them all in!"

An hour later, bent double, the officers race down a flight of steps into a cellar as wide as an aircraft hangar with a ceiling barely five feet high. Eighty-four sewing machines in serried ranks, eighty-four illegals. It must be thirty degrees down there, they are working stripped to the waist, not one of them older than twenty. Cardboard boxes are stuffed with polo shirts branded Lacoste, the owner tries to explain, but is cut short. Dušan Ravic? This particular instance of local craftsmanship is tolerated, the police turn a blind eye because the owner regularly feeds them information; this time he screws up his eyes, racks his brain – hang on a minute, hang on a minute – someone suggests they call in Commandant Verhœven.

Before Camille arrives, the officers tip out the contents of the boxes, seize the few identity papers they can find and call Louis, spelling out surnames while the workers hug the walls as though trying to disappear into the stone. Twenty minutes later, the heat in the cellar has become intolerable and the officers have hauled everyone outside; lined up in the street, the illegals look either resigned or petrified.

Camille shows up a few minutes later. He is the only one who does not need to crouch to go down the steps. The owner is from

Zrenjanin in northern Serbia not far from Ravic's village, Elemir. Ravic? "Never heard of him," the man says. "You sure?" Camille insists.

You can tell this is eating him up inside.

4.15 p.m.

I wasn't away very long, too worried I might miss my old friend's arrival. I've spent more than my fair share of time on stakeouts, so I'm not about to make the mistake of sparking up a cigarette or cracking a window to let some air into the car, but if Ravic is planning to show his face, he'd better get a move on, because I'm dead on my feet here.

The cops are moving heaven and earth to track him down, so he's bound to turn up any moment.

Speak of the devil and who do I see rounding the corner? If it isn't my old friend Dušan, I'd know him anywhere, no neck, built like a brick shithouse, feet turned out like a clown.

I'm parked about thirty metres from the doorway, about fifty from the corner where he just appeared. I get a good look at him as he shambles towards me, stopping slightly. I don't know whether he's got a chick back at the henhouse, but Ravic isn't looking too good.

Not exactly cock of the walk.

From the clothes (a shabby duffel coat at least ten years old), and the worn-out shoes, it's obvious he's flat broke.

And that's a bad sign.

Because, by rights, given his share of the haul last January, he should be dressed to kill. When he's got some cash, Ravic's the kind of guy who buys shiny suits, Hawaiian shirts and crocodile shoes. Seeing him dressed like a tramp is worrying.

On the run with a murder charge and four armed robberies on his back, he's been reduced to living by his wits. And if he's been holed up here, he must be on his uppers.

In all probability, he was double-crossed. Just like me. Probably should have seen it coming, but it's pretty demoralising. Just have to suck it up.

Ravic shoves open the plywood door and nearly takes it off its hinges. He was never subtle, in fact you might say he's reckless.

It's because he has a short fuse that we're in this mess, if he hadn't put a couple of 9mm slugs into that jeweller in January . . .

I slink out of the car and get to the door a few seconds behind him, I can hear his lumbering footsteps somewhere to my right. There's no bulb in the hall, so the only patches of light come from the open doors off the corridor. I tiptoe up the stairs after him, first floor, second, third, Jesus the stink in this place, stale piss, hamburgers, weed. I hear him knocking and I wait on the landing below. I suspected there would probably be other people here, which might make the job a little difficult, depending on how many of them there are.

Above me, I hear a door open and close, I creep upstairs, there is a lock, but it's an old model, easily picked. I carefully press my ear against the wood, I hear Ravic's hoarse croak – too many cigarettes. It's a strange feeling, hearing his voice again. It took a lot of effort to track him down, to flush him out.

Ravic doesn't sound happy. There's a lot of crashing and banging coming from the apartment. Eventually, I make out a woman's voice, young, soft-spoken, crying, though not very loudly, whimpering more like. I keep listening. Ravic's voice again. I want to be sure there are only two of them, so I stand there for several minutes listening to my heart pounding. O.K., I'm pretty sure there's just two of them. I pull on my cap, carefully tuck my hair under it, slip on a pair of rubber gloves, take out the Walther, rack the slide, shift the gun to my left hand while I pick the lock and shift it back as soon as I hear the last pin click and push the door open. I see the two of them, they have their backs to me, bent over something or other. Sensing someone behind them, they straighten up and turn; the girl is about twenty-five, dark-haired, ugly.

And dead. Because I put a bullet between her eyes, watch them grow wide in surprise as though someone has just offered to pay three times her usual fee, as if she's just seen Santa Claus show up in his underpants.

Ravic immediately reaches for his pocket, I put a bullet in his left ankle, he leaps into the air, hops from one foot to the other like he's on hot bricks, then crumples to the floor with a howl.

Now that we've dealt with the pleasantries, we can get down to more serious discussions.

The apartment is just one room, albeit a very large one, with a kitchenette, a bathroom, but everything about it is dilapidated and the place is filthy.

"Not much of a cleaner, that girl of yours."

At a glance I spotted the coffee table strewn with syringes, spoons, and tinfoil . . . I hope Ravic didn't squander all his cash on smack.

When the 9mm slug hit her, the girl collapsed onto a grubby mattress laid on the floor. The veins in her bony arms are riddled with track marks. I had only to lift her legs and she was laid out on her bier. The jumble of clothes and blankets beneath her was like a patchwork, it looked very original. Her eyes were still open, but her earlier shocked expression is more serene now, she seems to have come to terms with her fate.

Ravic, on the other hand, is still wailing. He is hunkered on the ground, balanced on one buttock, one leg stretched out, reaching towards the shattered ankle pissing blood, babbling "Oh fuck, oh fuck . . ." Nobody gives a shit about noise round here, you can hear T.V.s blaring, couples fighting and probably guys playing the drums at 3 a.m. when they're off their faces . . . But even so, I need my Serbian friend to concentrate, if only so we can talk in peace.

I pistol whip-him with the Walther, one smack straight to the face just to focus his attention on the conversation; he calms down a little, he's still hugging his leg, but he stops yowling and whimpers softly between clenched teeth. It's progress, I suppose, but I'm not sure I can count on him to stay quiet, he's not discreet by nature. I pick a T-shirt off the floor, roll it into a ball and stuff it into his mouth. And to make sure I get some peace, I tie one hand behind his back. With his other hand, he's still trying to staunch his bleeding ankle, but his arm is too short, he bends his leg under him, contorts himself, writhing in pain. Though you wouldn't think it to look at it, the ankle is a very sensitive part of the body, it's full of tiny, fragile bones – simply twisting your ankle on a step can leave you hobbling in pain, but when reduced by a 9mm slug to a bloody pulp of muscle and shattered bone and connected only by a few tendons, it is sheer agony. And seriously incapacitating. In fact, as I put a second bullet into the splintered remains of his ankle, I can tell he is not faking it, he really is in excruciating agony.

"Well, it's probably best that 'chick' of yours is dead, you wouldn't want her seeing you in this state."

Maybe it wasn't true love, but whatever the reason, Ravic doesn't seem bothered about the fate of the girl. He seems to care only about himself. The air in the place is unbreathable, what with the stench of blood and the smell of gunpowder, so I go over and crack open a window. I hope he got a good deal on the rent, the only view is a blank wall.

I come back and crouch over him, the guy is sweating buckets, he can't sit still, he's twisting and turning, clutching his leg with his free hand. His head is bleeding. Despite the gag in his mouth, he manages to drool. I grab him by the hair, it's the only way of getting his attention.

"Now listen up, big boy, I don't plan to spend the whole night here. So I'm going to give you a chance to talk and, for your sake, I hope you're planning to be cooperative because I'm not feeling especially patient right now. I haven't had a wink of sleep in two days, so if you care about me at all, you'll answer my questions and we can all get off to bed, me, you, your chick here, O.K. ?"

Ravic's French was never very good, his conversation is peppered with errors of syntax and vocabulary, so it's important to communicate in a way he understands. Simple words accompanied by persuasive gestures. So, as I carefully choose my words, I plant the hunting knife into the remnants of his ankle, the blade cuts clean through and embeds itself in the floorboard. Probably leaves a hole in the parquet floor, the sort of damage that will cost him when he tries to get his deposit back, but who cares? Ravic manages to scream through the gag, he struggles and squirms like a worm, his free hand fluttering like a butterfly.

I think he understands the seriousness of the situation now, but I give him a moment or two to think about it, to let the information sink in. Then I explain:

"The way I figure it, you and Hafner planned to double-cross me from the start. Like him, you thought that a three-way split was less attractive than sharing the loot between two. And it does make for a bigger share, I'll grant you that."

Ravic looks up at me, his eyes are filled with tears – of pain, rather than sorrow – but I can tell I've hit the nail on the head.

"Jesus, you're thick as pigshit, Dušan! You're a fucking moron. Why do you think Hafner picked you? Because you're a moron. Do you get it now?"

He grimaces, his ankle really is giving him grief.

"So, you help Hafner to double-cross me . . . and then he double-crosses you. Which confirms my initial analysis: you're as thick as two short planks."

Ravic does not seem to be overly preoccupied with his I.Q. right now. He is more worried about his health, about keeping count of his limbs. It's a sensible preoccupation because the more I talk the angrier I feel.

"My guess is you didn't go after Hafner – the guy's too dangerous, you weren't about to settle scores with him, you haven't got the balls and you know it. Besides, you had a murder charge hanging over you, so you decided to lie low. But the thing is, I need to find Hafner, so you're going to help me track him down, you're going to tell me everything you know: every detail of your little agreement and everything that happened afterwards, are we clear?"

It sounds like a reasonable proposition to me. I remove the gag, but Ravic's rather volatile temperament gets the better of him and he starts screaming something I can't understand. With his one good hand, he makes a grab for my collar. The guy has a powerful fist, but by some miracle I manage to dodge him. This is what I get for trusting people.

And he spits at me.

Under the circumstances, it's an understandable reaction, but even so, it's a little uncouth.

I realise that I have been going about things the wrong way. I have tried to behave in a civilised fashion, but Ravic is a peasant, such subtle nuances go right over his head. He is in too much pain to put up any serious resistance so I lay him out with a couple of kicks to the head and, while he struggles to remove the knife pinning his leg to the floor, I go to find what I need.

The girl is sprawled across the bed. Never mind. I grab one corner of the filthy duvet and tug hard, sending her rolling onto her stomach, her skirt rucked up, revealing her thin, pasty legs and needle marks on the backs of her knees. Even if I hadn't hurried things along, she was living on borrowed time.

I turn back just as Ravic manages to prise the knife out of his ankle. The guy is strong as an ox.

I put a bullet in his knee and his reaction, if you'll pardon the expression, is explosive. He literally launches his whole body into the air and howls, but before he has time to get his bearings, I manage to turn him over, throw the duvet over him and sit on it. I try to find the best position: I don't want him to suffocate, I need Ravic, but I need him to focus on my questions. And I need him to stop screaming.

I pull his arm towards me. It feels strange, sitting on him as he bucks and bridles like a fairground ride or a rodeo bull. I grab the hunting knife, force his hand flat on the floor, but he's strong. I'm pitching and reeling like a big-game fisherman reeling in a 200-lb marlin.

I start by cutting his little finger off at the second phalanx. Usually, I would take the trouble to make a clean cut at the joint, but such refinements are wasted on Ravic. I simply hack it off, which is irksome to an aesthete like me.

I'm prepared to bet that within fifteen minutes, Ravic will have told me everything I need to know. I continue to ask questions, but this is simply for form's sake: he is not concentrating yet and besides, what with the duvet and me on top of him, to say nothing of his ankle and his knee, he is having trouble stringing a coherent sentence together.

I continue my work, moving on to the index finger – it's incredible how much he struggles – and I think about my visit to the hospital.

Unless I'm very much mistaken, in a few minutes my Serbian friend is going to break the bad news to me. In which case, the only solution is to put pressure on the woman in the hospital. Logically, by now she should be prepared to be cooperative.

I hope so, for her sake.

5.00 p.m.
"Verhœven?"

Not even a courtesy "*commandant*". The *commissaire* is obviously livid. No pleasantries, no extraneous chit-chat. Commissaire Michard has so much to say she does not know where to begin.

"I'm going to need a detailed report . . ." is her first reflex.

Bureaucracy is the last refuge of the uninspired.

"You assured the judge that this was to be a 'targeted operation', you spin me some story about 'three known suspects', then you turn the whole city upside down. Are you deliberately trying to piss me off?"

On the other end of the telephone, Camille opens his mouth to speak, but Michard cuts him off.

"To tell the truth, I don't give a shit. But you're going to stand down your men right now, *commandant*, call off this little show of force, it's a waste of time."

A clusterfuck. Camille closes his eyes. He was on the final sprint, only to be overtaken a few yards from the finishing post. Next to him, thin-lipped, Louis looks away. Camille jerks his thumb to let him know the operation is dead in the water, and waves for him to round up all the officers. Louis immediately begins punching in the numbers on his telephone. From the look on Verhœven's face, he knows how things stand. All around, the other officers hang their heads, feigning disappointment, they will all be bawled out tomorrow, but at least they had some fun. As they head back to their cars, one or two flash a complicit smile, Camille responds with a fatalistic gesture.

The *commissaire divisionnaire* is giving him time to digest the information, but her pause is expressly melodramatic, insidious, pregnant with menace.

Anne is standing in front of the mirror again when one of the nurses appears. Florence, the older nurse. Though she is not exactly old . . . She is probably younger than Anne, but her desperate attempt to look ten years younger prematurely ages her.

"Everything alright?"

Their eyes meet in the mirror. As she records the time on the clipboard at the end of the bed, the nurse flashes her a broad smile. Even with those lips, I'll never be able to smile like that again, thinks Anne.

"Everything alright?"

What a question. Anne does not feel like talking, especially not to Florence. She should never have let herself be persuaded by the other nurse, the young one. She should have walked out of the hospital, she feels in danger. And yet she cannot quite make up her mind, there seem as many reasons to stay as to go.

And then, there is Camille.

The moment she thinks of him, her whole body starts to tremble, he is alone, helpless, he will never manage to do it. And even if he does, it will be too late.

45, rue Jambier. The *commissaire* is already on her way. Camille will meet her there in fifteen minutes.

The Operation Verhœven raids have produced results, though not the ones anticipated. Desperate to be left in peace – to prosper, to live or simply to survive – the whole Serbian community came together to track down Ravic. The search turned out to be child's play. An anonymous tip-off gives his location as 45, rue Jambier. Camille had hoped to find a live body; he is sorely disappointed.

At the first wail of a police siren, every adult in the building disappeared within seconds: there will be no witnesses, no-one to question, no-one who heard or saw anything. Only the children were left behind – there was nothing to fear and everything to gain, since the children will be able to tell them exactly what happened when they get back. Right now, uniformed officers have them corralled out on the pavement. The kids are eager and excited, laughing and catcalling. For children who do not go to school, a double murder constitutes playtime.

Upstairs, the *commissaire* is standing in the doorway of the apartment, hands clasped in front of her as though she were in church. Until the forensic technicians from *identité judiciaire* get here, she will allow only Verhœven inside, no-one else. It is a perfunctory and probably futile precaution, so many men have traipsed through this hovel that the forensics team will probably come up with at least fifty sets of fingerprints, stray hairs and sundry bodily fluids. The crime scene will be documented, but it is merely a question of protocol.

When Camille arrives, the *commissaire* does not turn, she does not even look at him, she simply takes a step into the room, her movements careful and deliberate. Camille follows her footsteps. Silently, each of them begins to detail the scene, to draw up a list of obvious facts. The girl – an addict and a prostitute – died first. Seeing her lying on her belly, turned towards the wall as though she is sulking, it is apparent that the duvet that discreetly covers Ravic's body was jerked out from under her, hurling her against the partition. Were there only her pallid corpse, stiffening now with rigor mortis, there would be little to be said. They have witnessed this scene a hundred times. So many prostitutes die in circumstances such as these: an overdose, a murder. But there is another body which tells a very different story.

The *commissaire* moves slowly, walking around the pool of blood seeping into the grimy floorboards. The ankle, a mass of splintered bone, is attached to the leg by ragged ribbons of skin. Hacked? Slashed? Camille takes out his glasses and hunkers down for a closer inspection, his eyes move over the floor until he finds the bullet hole, then back at the ankle; there is evidence of knife marks on the bone, a short blade, possibly a dagger. Camille crouches lower, like an Indian listening for an enemy approaching, and sees the deep groove where a blade was buried in the wood. As he gets to his feet, he mentally tries to reconstruct this part of the scene. The ankle first, then the fingers.

The *commissaire* makes an inventory. Five fingers. The right number, but the wrong order: the index is here, the middle finger there, the thumb a little further away, each cut off at the second phalanx. The anaemic stump of the hand lies on the bed, the sheet is saturated with black blood. Cautiously, using a ballpoint pen, the *commissaire* lifts the hand away to reveal Ravic's face. His contorted features speak volumes about the pain he suffered.

The *coup de grâce:* a bullet in the back of the neck.

"Come on then . . ." the *commissaire* says, her tone almost jubilant; she is expecting good news.

"The way I see it," Camille begins, "the guys came in . . ."

"Spare me the bedtime story, *commandant*, anyone can see what happened here. No, what I want to know is what the hell you're doing."

What is Camille doing? Anne wonders.

The nurse has left, they barely spoke. Anne was aggressive, Florence pretended not to notice.

"Can I get you anything?"

No, nothing. Anne gives a curt nod, but already her mind is elsewhere. As every other time, she finds looking in the mirror devastating and yet she cannot help herself. She comes back, goes back to bed, comes back again. Now that she has had the results of the X-rays and the M.R.I. scan, she cannot sit still, this hospital room troubles and depresses her.

She has to run away.

She summons the instincts she had as a little girl for running away and hiding. What she feels has something in common with rape: she feels ashamed. Ashamed of what she has become, this is what she saw when she looked into the mirror.

What is Camille doing? she wonders.

Commissaire Michard steps back and leaves the apartment, carefully setting her feet in precisely the same places as she did when she entered. As in a well-choreographed ballet, their exit coincides with the arrival of the forensics team. The *commissaire* is forced to move along the hall in a crab-like fashion, given the size of her posterior, then comes to a stop in the doorway. She turns back to Camille, folds her arms and gives him a smile that says: so, tell me everything.

"The four robberies in January were the work of a gang led by Vincent Hafner, a gang that Ravic was a member of." He jerks his thumb back towards the room, now lit by a blaze of forensics spotlights. The *commissaire* nods: we know all this, get on with it.

"The gang abruptly reappeared yesterday and robbed the jeweller's in the Galerie Monier. The raid went pretty smoothly, except for one small problem – the presence of a customer, Anne Forestier. I don't know exactly what she saw besides their faces, but something obviously happened. We're still questioning her, insofar as her injuries permit, but we haven't got to the bottom of it. Whatever it was, it was serious enough for Hafner to come after her and try to kill her. He even came to the hospital . . . [He raises a conciliatory hand.] I know, I know! We've got no hard evidence that it was him."

"Has the *juge* ordered a reconstruction of the robbery?"

Camille has not contacted the examining magistrate since his first visit to the Galerie. By now, he has a lot to say. He will have to choose his moment carefully.

"Not yet," Camille says confidently, "but given how fast things have developed, I'm sure that as soon as the witness is able . . ."

"So what happened here? Did he come to relieve Ravic of his share of the haul?"

"Whatever Hafner wanted, he needed to make Ravic talk. Maybe about the haul . . ."

"The case has thrown up a lot of questions, Commandant Verhœven, none of them more serious than the questions it raises about your own behaviour."

Camille tries to smile; he is prepared to try anything.

"Perhaps I have been a little overzealous . . ."

"Overzealous? You've broken every rule in the book, you tell your superiors you're mounting a targeted operation and then turn half the city upside down without so much as a by-your-leave!"

She is making the most of this.

"You clearly exceeded the authorisation given you by the *juge*."

This moment was bound to come, but it is too soon.

"And by your superior officers. I'm still waiting for that report I requested. You're behaving like a free radical. Who exactly do you think you are, Commandant Verhœven?"

"I'm doing my job."

"And what job would that be?"

"*To Protect and to Serve*, isn't that our motto? I'm pro-TEC-ting!"

Camille takes three steps, repressing the urge to grab Michard by the throat. He composes himself.

"You have grossly miscalculated this case," he says. "It is not simply about a woman who was beaten to a pulp. We are dealing with a gang of experienced armed robbers who left one man dead last January. The leader, Vincent Hafner, is a vicious thug, and the Serbians he's working with are certainly no angels. I may not know why, but Hafner is determined to kill this woman and, though I know you don't want to hear this, I firmly believe he went to the hospital armed with a shotgun. And if this witness is killed, someone is going to have to explain how it happened, and you'll be first in line!"

"Alright, you decide that this woman is of some vital strategic importance, so to neutralise a risk you cannot even prove exists, you round up everyone in Paris born between Belgrade and Sarajevo."

"Sarajevo is in Bosnia, not in Serbia."

"Excuse me?"

Camille closes his eyes.

"O.K.," he concedes, "I haven't followed procedure to the letter, I should have written up a report, I should—"

"Oh, we're well past that, *commandant.*"

Verhœven frowns, his internal warning light is flashing faintly, he knows exactly what the *commissaire* can do if she so chooses. She nods towards the room where Ravic's body lies in the glare of spotlights.

"With your little barnstorming operation, you managed to flush Ravic out, *commandant*. In fact, you made things easier for his killer."

"There's nothing to substantiate that."

"Perhaps not, but it's a legitimate question. And a brutal raid targeting a specific immigrant community, conducted without the backing of your superior officers and in breach of the limited authorisation given you by the examining magistrate, that sort of 'operation' has a name, *commandant.*"

This is something that Camille honestly did not see coming; his face grows pale.

"It's called racial profiling."

Camille closes his eyes. This is a clusterfuck.

What is Camille doing? Anne has not touched the food on the tray in front of her. The orderly, a woman from Martinique, clears it away: you got to eat, child, you can't go lettin' yourself waste away, it's a cryin' shame to waste good food. Anne suddenly feels a furious anger towards everyone welling in her.

Earlier one of the nurses told her, "It'll all be fine, you wait and see . . ."

And Anne had snapped "I can *see* perfectly well right now!"

The nurse was simply being kind, she was trying to help, it was wrong to dismiss her desire to do good. But even as she tried the classic device of counting to ten, Anne found herself snarling.

"So, you've been beaten up, have you? You've had people pistol whip you, kick you, try to kill you? I suppose people fire shotguns at you all the time? Come on, tell me all about it, I'm sure it'll help . . ."

As Florence made to leave, Anne called her back, in tears.

"I'm sorry," she said, "I'm so sorry."

The nurse gave a little wave. Don't give it another thought. As though people are entitled to say anything they like to nurses.

"You wanted this case, you demanded it be assigned to you on the pretext that you had an informant who, so far, you have been unable to produce. And, while we're on the subject, *commandant*, exactly how did you hear about the robbery?"

"From Guérin."

The name just slipped out. The first name that came into his mind. Racking his brain, he could think of no other solution and so he trusted to providence. But providence is like homeopathy: if you don't believe . . . it is a stupid mistake. Now, he has to call Guérin, who is not likely to help him if it means putting his own head on the block. The *commissaire* looks thoughtful.

"And how did Guérin hear about it?"

She stops herself.

"I mean, why would he have mentioned it to you?"

Verhœven can see what is coming and has no choice but to raise the stakes, something he has been doing since the start.

"It just happened . . ."

He has run out of ideas. The *commissaire* is visibly now curious about this affair. He could find himself removed from the case. Or worse. The prospect of a report to the public prosecutor or an investigation by the *Inspection générale des services* now looms on the horizon.

For a split second, an image of five severed fingers hovers between him and the *commissaire,* they are Anne's fingers, he would know them anywhere. The killer is on the move.

Commissaire Michard manoeuvres her gargantuan derrière out onto the landing, leaving Camille to his thoughts.

His thoughts are much the same as hers: he cannot exclude the possibility that his operation helped the killer find Ravic, but he had no other choice if he was to move quickly. Hafner is determined to dispose of all witnesses and protagonists involved in the Galerie Monier robbery: Ravic, Anne and probably the other stooge, the getaway driver . . .

Anyway, Hafner is the key to the whole case, he is the man in charge.

The I.G.S., the *commissaire,* the examining magistrate – Camille will deal with them in due course. For him, the most important thing is to protect Anne.

He remembers something he was taught at driving school: when you miss a bend, you have two choices. The wrong reaction is to brake, since there is every chance you will skid off the road. Paradoxically, the most effective solution is to accelerate, but to do so, you have to curb the natural survival instinct screaming at you to stop.

Camille decides to accelerate.

It is his only way out of this dangerous bend. He tries not to think about the fact that accelerating is also what someone would do if they were determined to drive off a cliff.

And, besides, his choices are limited.

6.00 p.m.

Every time he sees the man, Camille cannot help but think that Mouloud Faraoui does not look much like someone called Mouloud Faraoui. Though his Moroccan roots survive in his name, any North African traits have been diluted over three generations of unlikely marriages and unexpected couplings, an incongruous melting pot that has produced surprising results. Mouloud's face is a distillate of history: light-brown hair verging on blond, a long nose, a square jaw slashed by a scar that was obviously painful and gives him a bad-boy look, ice-cold, blue-green eyes. He is between thirty and forty, though his age is difficult to guess. Camille checks the police record, where he finds documentary evidence that Mouloud was an exceptionally precocious career criminal. It turns out that he is thirty-seven.

He is relaxed, almost offhand, a man of few words and subtle gestures. He slides into the seat opposite, never taking his eyes off Camille, he seems tense, as though expecting the *commandant* to pull his gun. Mouloud is wary. Not wary enough, perhaps, given that instead of staying safely in his cell, he is here in the prison visiting room. Facing a twenty-year stretch, he was sentenced to ten, he will serve seven and has been inside for two. Despite his arrogant swagger, one look is enough to tell Camille that time has been dragging.

Surprised by this unexpected visit, Faraoui's natural mistrust is on red alert. He sits ramrod straight, arms folded. Neither man has said a word, but already they have exchanged a staggering number of messages.

Verhœven's very presence here constitutes a complicated message in itself.

In prison, word gets around. Hardly has the prisoner set foot in the visiting room than the news has spread along the landings. What would an officer from the *brigade criminelle* want with a small-time pimp like Faraoui? Ultimately, it does not matter what is said at their meeting, the prison, like a giant pinball machine, is already buzzing with rumours that range from sober speculation to wild conspiracy theories, depending on the vested interests of those involved and the relative power of the prison gangs, creating a complex web of misinformation.

And this is precisely why Camille is here, sitting in the visiting room, arms folded, staring silently at Faraoui. He need do nothing else. The work is already being done, he does not even have to lift his little finger.

But the silence is uncomfortable.

Faraoui, still sitting stiffly, watches and waits in silence. Camille does not move. He is thinking about how this little thug's name popped into his head when the *commissaire* asked her point-blank question. Subconsciously, he already knew what he planned to do, but it took a while for Camille's conscious mind to catch up: this is the quickest route to Vincent Hafner.

If he is to reach the end of the path he has chosen, Camille is going to have to tough it out. He feels a suffocating panic well up inside him. If Faraoui were not staring at him so intently, he would get up and open a window. Just walking into the prison gave him the jitters.

Take a deep breath. Another deep breath. And he will have to come back again . . .

He remembers the way he confidently announced that there were "three known suspects". His brain works faster than he can; he only realises what he has said after the fact. He understands now.

The clock ticks off the seconds, the minutes; in the airless visiting room, unspoken words quiver in the air like vibrations.

At first, Faraoui mistakenly thought this was a test to see which of them would crack first, a silent form of arm-wrestling, a cheap police trick. And it surprised him that an officer of Verhœven's reputation would resort to such a ruse. So it must be something else. Camille watches as he bows his head, thinking as fast as he can. And since Faraoui is a smart guy, he comes to the only possible conclusion. He makes to get to his feet.

Camille is expecting this, he tut-tuts softly without even glancing up. Faraoui, who has a keen sense of his own best interests, decides to play along. Still the time ticks away.

They wait. Ten minutes. Fifteen. Twenty.

Then Camille gives the signal. He uncrosses his arms.

"O.K. Well, I wouldn't want you to think I'm bored or any-thing . . ."

He gets up. Faraoui remains seated. The ghost of a smile plays on his lips, he leans back nonchalantly in his chair.

"What do you take me for, a messenger boy?"

Reaching the door, Camille slaps it with the palm of his hand for someone to come and open. He turns back.

"In a sense, yes."

"And what do I get out of it?"

Camille adopts a shocked expression.

"What the . . . ? You get to ensure that justice is served! What do you want, for fuck's sake?"

The door opens, the guard steps aside to allow Camille to pass, but he stands on the threshold for a moment.

"While we're on the subject, Mouloud, tell me something . . . The guy who grassed you up . . . damn, what was his name again? It's on the tip of my tongue . . ."

Faraoui never knew who squealed on him, he did everything he could to find out, but he came up with nothing; he would give four years inside just to know that name, everyone knows that. But no-one can possibly know what Faraoui would do with the guy if he ever found him.

He smiles and nods. Done deal.

This is Camille's first message.

Meeting Faraoui amounts to saying: I've made a deal with a killer.

If I give him the name of the guy who grassed him up, he'll do anything I ask.

In exchange for that name, I can get him to hunt you down and before you have time to catch your breath he will be right behind you.

From now on, you had better start counting the seconds.

7.30 p.m.

Camille is sitting at his desk, colleagues pop their heads round the door, they give a little wave, everyone has heard about his dressing down, it's all anyone can talk about. With the exception of the officers who took part in the "racial profiling", they have nothing to worry about, but still the word gets round, the *commissaire* has already begun to undermine him. It's a nasty business. But what the fuck is Camille playing at? No-one seems to know. Even Louis has hardly said a word, and so rumours are rife – an officer of his reputation, he must have done something, the *commissaire* is livid – to say nothing of the examining magistrate who is preparing to summon everyone involved. Even Contrôleur Général Le Guen has been like a bear with a sore head all afternoon, but pop your head round the door of his office and there's Verhœven, typing up his report for all the world as if this is a storm in a teacup, he hasn't got a care in the world, like this whole business with the robbery and the gang of killers is some personal beef. I don't get it, what do you think? I haven't a clue, but you've got to admit it's pretty weird. But the officers go about their business, they have already been called away to deal with other matters, there is a commotion downstairs, voices are raised in the corridors. No rest for the wicked.

Camille has to sort out this report, do a little damage limitation on the impending disaster. All he needs is to buy himself some time, even just a day or two, because if his strategy pays off, it won't be long before he tracks down Hafner.

This is the purpose of his report: to buy himself two days' grace.

As soon as Hafner has been caught and taken into custody, everything will become clear, the haze of secrecy swirling around the case will dissipate, Camille will explain himself, the disciplinary letter will arrive from his superiors, he could be suspended, have his prospects of promotion permanently quashed, he may even have to request – or accept – a change of post, it does not bother him: with Hafner under lock and key, Anne will be safe. That is all he cares about . . .

*

As he sits down to compose this difficult and delicate report (Camille is not one for reports at the best of times), he thinks of the piece of paper he tore from his sketchpad earlier and tossed away. He fishes it out of the wastepaper basket. The pencil portrait of Vincent Hafner, a sketch of Anne in her hospital bed. He lays the crumpled page on his desk and smoothes it out, with his free hand he calls Guérin and leaves a message, the third today. If Guérin does not get in touch soon, it means he does not want to talk to Camille. Contrôleur Général Le Guen on the other hand has been trying to get through to Camille for hours. Four messages in a row: "What the fuck are you playing at, Camille? Call me back right now." He is frantic. Understandably so. Hardly has Camille written the first line of his report than his mobile starts to vibrate again. Le Guen. This time, Camille picks up, closes his eyes and prepares himself for the histrionics.

But Le Guen's voice is calm and measured.

"Do you think maybe we should have a chat, Camille?"

Camille could say yes, he could say no. Le Guen is a friend, the one friend who has come through every disaster with him, the one friend capable of changing the course on which he is embarked. But Camille says nothing.

This is one of those decisive moments which may or may not save his life, and yet he says nothing.

Not because he has suddenly become masochistic or suicidal. On the contrary, he feels completely lucid. On a blank corner of the sheet of paper, he sketches Anne's profile in three quick strokes. It is something he used to do with Irène in his idle moments, the way another man might bite his nails.

Adopting his most considerate, his most persuasive tone, Le Guen tries to reason with him.

"You've really stirred up a shitstorm this afternoon, I've got people phoning to ask me if we're tracking international terrorists. This is a complete fuck-up. I've got informants screaming that they've been stabbed in the back. You've fucked over your fellow officers who have to work with these communities day in, day out. In the space of three hours, you've set their work back by a year, and the fact that your man Ravic has been murdered only makes things more complicated. So, right now, I want you to tell me exactly what you're up to."

Still Camille says nothing, he looks down at his drawing. It could have been some other woman, he thinks, but it is Anne. Anne who stepped into his life just as she stepped into the Monier. Why her and not some other woman? Who knows? As he retraces the line of her mouth on the drawing, he can almost feel her soft lips; he accentuates the hollow just below her jawline that he finds so poignant.

"Camille, are you listening?"

"I'm listening, Jean."

"I'm not sure I can bail you out of this one, you do know that? I'm having a hell of a job trying to placate the magistrate. He's a smart guy, so it's not too wise to treat him like an idiot. Needless to say I had a little visit from the top brass less than an hour ago, but I think we can do some damage limitation."

Camille sets his pencil down and bows his head. In trying to perfect Anne's portrait, he has ruined it. It is always the way, a sketch needs to be spontaneous; as soon as you try to change something, it is ruined.

Camille is suddenly stuck by a curious notion, an utterly new thought, a question that, surprising as it seems, he has never asked himself: what is to become of me afterwards? What do I want? And as so often in a dialogue of the deaf, where neither party is prepared to listen or to hear, the two men come to the same conclusion.

"This is personal, isn't it, Camille?" Le Guen says. "You have a relationship with this woman? A personal relationship?"

"Of course not, Jean, what makes you think . . ."

Le Guen lets a painful silence hang over the proceedings. Then he shrugs.

"If this thing blows up in our faces, there are going to be questions . . ."

Camille suddenly realises that this is not simply about love, it is about something else. He has chosen a dark and winding path, not knowing where it will lead, but he knows, he senses that he is not being swept along by his blind passion for Anne.

Something is urging him on, regardless of the cost.

Essentially, he is doing in his life what he has always done in his investigations: doggedly carrying on to the bitter end, so he can understand why things are as they are.

"If you don't come up with something now," Le Guen interrupts the thought, "if you don't give me some kind of explanation, Michard will have no choice but to kick this upstairs to the *procureur*'s office. There'll be no way to avoid an internal investigation . . ."

"What . . . ? An internal investigation into what?"

Le Guen shrugs again.

"O.K. Have it your way."

8.15 p.m.

Camille knocks softly on the door; no answer. He opens it and finds Anne lying on the bed, staring at the ceiling. He sits down next to her.

Neither says a word. Camille reaches out to take her hand and Anne meekly lets him, she is overcome by a crushing sense of resignation, almost a fatalism. But after a few minutes, she says simply:

"I want to leave . . ."

Resting her weight on her elbows, she slowly sits up in bed.

"Well, since they're not going to operate, you should be able to go home soon," Camille says. "In a day or two, maybe."

"No, Camille." She is speaking very slowly. "I want to leave right now, this minute."

He frowns. Anne shakes her head wildly.

"Right now."

"They don't just let people walk out in the middle of the night. A doctor needs to give you the once-over, you'll need to collect your prescriptions, and . . ."

"No! I need to get out of here, Camille, can't you understand?"

Camille gets to his feet, Anne is getting worked up, he needs to think of some way to calm her down. But Anne has already swung her legs over the side of the bed and is struggling to stand.

"I don't want to stay here, and no-one can force me to . . ."

"But no-one is trying to force you to . . ."

Anne suddenly feels dizzy, she has overestimated her strength. She grabs Camille for support, sits back on the bed and bows her head.

"I'm sure he's been here, Camille, he wants to kill me, he'll stop at nothing, I can feel it, I just *know*."

"You don't know anything," Camille says, "you don't know

anything at all!"

It is futile to browbeat her, because the driving force that motivates Anne is a blind terror impervious to reason or to authority. She starts to tremble again.

"There's an officer guarding the door, nothing is going to happen to you . . ."

"Oh, just stop, Camille! When he's not disappearing off to the toilet, he's playing solitaire on his mobile! He doesn't even notice when I leave the room . . ."

"I'll have another officer come and take over. It's just that . . ."

"What? It's just that what?"

Anne tries to blow her nose, but the pain is too great.

"You know how it is . . . Everything seems frightening at night, but I promise you . . ."

"No, Camille, you can't promise. That's just it . . ."

These three simple words are painful to both of them. Anne wants to leave precisely because he cannot promise to keep her safe. It is all his fault. She angrily throws her tissue on the floor. Camille tries to help, but she brushes him off. "Leave me alone, I can manage by myself."

"What do you mean, 'by myself'?"

"Just leave me alone, Camille, I don't need you anymore."

But as she says this, she lies back on the bed exhausted from the simple effort of standing up. Camille pulls up the sheet.

"Leave me alone."

And so he leaves her alone, sits down again, takes her hand in his, but her hand is lifeless, cold. The way she is sprawled across the bed is like an insult.

"You can go now . . ." she says.

She does not look at him. Her face is turned to the window.

DAY 3

Camille has barely slept in two days. Warming his hands on a mug of coffee, he stares out the window of the studio at the forest. It was here in Montfort that his mother painted for years, almost until her death. Afterwards the place lay abandoned, left to squatters and thieves. Camille hardly gave it a thought and yet, for some obscure reason, he never sold it.

Then, some time after Irène's death, he decided not to keep anything of his mother's, not a single canvas, a vestige of an old grudge between them: it is because of her smoking that he is only four foot eleven.

Some of the paintings now hang in foreign museums. Camille had promised himself he would donate all the proceeds of the sale but, of course, he did nothing with the money. Not until some years after Irène's death, when he finally rejoined the world and decided to rebuild and refurbish the little studio on the edge of the forest of Clamart, which had once been the gatekeeper's lodge to a country house that has long since vanished. Back then, the place was more isolated than it is now, when the nearest house is only three hundred metres away. The dirt road goes no further, it stops here.

Camille had the place renovated from top to bottom, replacing every wonky terracotta floor tile, installing a full bathroom and building a mezzanine which became his bedroom. The ground floor is now a huge sitting room with an open-plan kitchen, one entire wall is taken up by a picture window overlooking the edge of the forest.

The forest terrifies him still, just as it did when he spent long afternoons as a child watching his mother work here. These days it is an adult terror, a wistful feeling of mingled pleasure and pain.

The one piece of nostalgia he has allowed himself is the gleaming cast-iron wood-burning stove in the centre of the room which replaced his mother's that was stolen during the years the studio lay derelict.

Unless carefully regulated, all the heat from the stove rises so that the mezzanine is a sauna while downstairs his feet are freezing, but he likes this rustic method of heating because it has to be earned, because it requires as much attentiveness as experience. Camille knows how to stoke and regulate it such that it will run all night. In the depths of winter, there is a chill to the mornings, but he considers this initial hardship – refuelling and relighting the stove – as a little ritual.

He had much of the roof replaced with glass so that the sky is constantly visible and, the moment you look up, the clouds and the rain seem about to tumble on you. When it snows, it is unsettling. This opening onto the sky serves no real purpose. Though it lets in more light, the house had more than enough already. Le Guen, ever the pragmatist, enquired about the skylights on his first visit.

"What do you want?" Camille said. "I might be knee high to a grasshopper, but I can still reach for the stars."

Camille comes as often as he can. He spends days off and weekends here, but he rarely invites guests. Then again, he does not have many people in his life. Louis and Le Guen have visited the studio, as did Armand, but although he made no conscious decision, the studio has become a secret place. Camille spends much of his time here drawing, always from memory. Among the piles of sketches and the hundreds of notepads are portraits of everyone he has ever arrested, of every body whose death he has investigated, of magistrates with whom he has worked and colleagues he barely knows. He has a particular fondness for sketching the witnesses he has questioned, the fleeting shadows who disappear as swiftly as they appeared, troubled bystanders and bewildered onlookers, anguished women, girls overcome by emotion, men distraught by their brush with death, they are all here, there are two, perhaps three thousand sketches, a vast, incomparable gallery of portraits, the daily life of an officer in the *brigade criminelle* as seen by the artist he might have been. Camille's searingly honest portraits reveal a rare talent, he often claims his drawings are more intelligent than he is, and there is something to the idea. Even photographs seem less faithful, less true. Once, at the Hôtel Salé, Anne had seemed so beautiful that he told her not to move and, taking out his mobile, took a snapshot so that he could freeze the moment and have her appear on the screen whenever she called him, though in the end he replaced it with a scan of one of his sketches which seemed to him more true, more expressive.

September has not yet turned cold so when he arrived this evening Camille put only a few logs in the stove to create what he calls a "comfort fire".

He should bring his cat to live here, but Doudouche does not like the countryside; for her it is Paris or nothing. Doudouche has appeared in many of his sketches. As have Louis and Jean, even Maleval once upon a time. Last night, just before going to bed, he dug out all his portraits of Armand, he even found the sketch of Armand in his hospital bed on the day he died, with that placid, peaceful expression that makes all dead bodies look more or less alike.

Outside the cottage, at the far end of what he thinks of as "the yard", is the forest. As night draws in, the humidity rises. This morning he found his car slick with dew.

He has often sketched this forest, has even ventured a watercolour though colour is not his strong suit. He is captivated by emotion, by movement, but he is not a colourist as his mother was.

A 7.15 a.m. precisely, his mobile vibrates. Still cradling his coffee, he picks it up with his free hand. Louis apologises for the early hour.

"Don't worry," Camille says. "So, tell me."

"Madame Forestier, she's left the hospital . . ."

There is a brief silence. If someone should ever write a biography of Camille, much of it would be dedicated to his silences. Louis, who knows this all too well, cannot help but wonder again precisely what role the missing woman plays in Camille's life. Is she the real reason for the curious way he has been behaving? To what extent is his behaviour some sort of exorcism? Whatever the truth, Verhœven's silence is a measure of his distress.

"How long since she left?" he asks.

"We're not sure, sometime during the night. The nurse did her rounds at ten o'clock and talked to her, she seemed calm, but an hour ago the duty nurse found the room empty. She left most of her clothes in the wardrobe which made it seem as though she had just wandered out of the room for a minute, so it took a while before the staff realised she was actually missing."

"What about the guard?"

"He says he has prostate trouble, so when he has to go, it can take a while."

Camille takes a mouthful of coffee.

"I need you to send someone to her apartment immediately."

"I went round myself before I called you," Louis says. "No-one has seen her . . ."

Camille stares out at the forest as though expecting help to arrive.

"Do you know if she has any family?"

No, Camille says, he does not know. Actually, she has a daughter in the States, he remembers. He gropes for a name. Agathe. He decides not to mention her daughter or the brother.

"If she's checked into a hotel, it might take us a while to track her down," Louis says, "but she might have gone to a friend for help. I'll talk to her colleagues."

"No, leave it," Camille sighs. "I'll do it. You focus on Hafner. Is there any news there?"

"Nothing yet, he seems to have completely vanished. There's no-one at his last known address and there's been no sign of him at his usual haunts. His known associates say they haven't seen him since the January . . ."

"Since the robberies?"

"Around that time, yes."

"So he may have left the country?"

"That's what they seem to think. A couple of them even suggested he might be dead, but there's no basis for it. There is talk that he's seriously ill, more than one witness mentioned this, but given his little performance at the Galerie Monier, I'd say he's in fine fettle. We're still looking, but I can't say I'm optimistic . . ."

"The forensics on Ravic's murder, when do we get results?"

"Tomorrow at the earliest."

Louis is silent for a moment, it is a very particular silence – from his own extensive repertoire, one that he observes before broaching the thorniest questions.

"About Madame Forestier . . ." he ventures. "Will you inform the *commissaire* or should I?"

"I'll do it . . ."

The response came unbidden. Too quickly. Camille sets his mug down by the sink. Ever intuitive, Louis waits for the rest of the response.

"Listen, Louis . . . I'd rather look for her myself."

Camille can almost hear Louis nodding cautiously.

"I think I'll be able to find her . . . fairly quickly."

"Understood," Louis concedes.

Camille's message is clear: say nothing to Commissaire Michard.

"I'm heading in now, Louis. I've got a meeting, but I'll be there as soon as I can be."

The razor-sharp rivulet of cold sweat Camille can feel tracing the length of his spine has nothing to do with the temperature of the room.

7.20 a.m.

He quickly pulls on his clothes, but he cannot leave like this, he cannot help but check that everything is locked and bolted, irritated at the thought that somehow everything is down to him.

He creeps up to the mezzanine on tiptoe.

"I'm not asleep. . ."

Reassured, he walks over and sits on the edge of the bed.

"Was I snoring?" Anne asks without turning towards him.

"With a broken nose, it's unavoidable."

He is struck by her position. Even in hospital she turned away from him, lying on her side, staring at the window. *She can't bring herself to look at me, she thinks I can't protect her.*

"You're safe here, nothing can happen to you now."

Anne merely shrugs, and it is difficult to tell whether this means yes or no.

It means no.

"He'll find me. He'll come here."

She rolls onto her back and looks at him. She almost makes him doubt himself.

"That's impossible, Anne. No-one knows you're here."

Anne shrugs again. This time, however, the meaning is clear: say what you like, he's coming here, he's coming to kill me. Her fear is becoming obsessive, becoming hysterical. Camille takes her hand.

"After everything that's happened to you, it's only normal that you should be scared. But I promise you . . ."

Her shrug this time could mean: how can I make you understand? Or it could mean: forget it.

"I have to go," Camille says, checking his watch. "You'll find everything you need downstairs . . ."

She nods. She is still exhausted. Even the half-light of the bedroom can do nothing to hide the ravages of livid bruises and contusions.

He has shown her everything in the studio, the coffeemaker, the bathroom, a veritable pharmacy to deal with her injuries. He was loath for her to leave the hospital – who will look after her, remove her sutures? But there was nothing to be done; frantic and nervous, she could not bear to stay and was threatening to go back to her apartment. He could hardly tell her that someone would be waiting for her, that this was the trap. What could he do? Where could he take her other than here, in the middle of nowhere?

So this is where Anne is.

No woman has ever come here. Camille immediately dismisses this thought, since it was downstairs, by the doorway, that Irène was murdered. In the four years since, everything has changed, everything has been remade and yet everything is the same. He too has been "remade", after a fashion. It never quite works, tattered shreds of a former life still cling; looking around he can see them everywhere.

"I want you to do exactly what I've told you," he tells her, "I want you to shut . . ."

Anne lays her hand on his. Given the splints on her fingers there is nothing romantic about the gesture. It means: you've told me all this already, I've got it, now go.

Camille leaves. He goes down the stairs from the mezzanine, steps out into the yard, locks the door and gets into his car.

If his situation has become much more complicated, Anne's is more secure. All he can do is grin and bear it, take the whole world on his shoulders. If he were of standard height, would he feel such a crushing sense of duty?

8.00 a.m.

Forests are depressing, I've always hated them. This one is worse than most. Clamart, Meudon, welcome to the armpit of the universe. Gloomy as a wet weekend. A sign announces a built-up area. Difficult to know what to call the cluster of houses for the *nouveaux riches*, it's not a part of the city, it's not a suburb, it's not a village. People say "the outskirts", but the outskirts of what? Looking around at the carefully manicured gardens and terraces, I can't decide which is more depressing, the desolate surroundings or the smugness of the inhabitants.

Once past the cluster of houses, there is nothing but forest as far as the eye can see. The G.P.S. system takes an age to find the rue du Pavé-de-Meudon (and, on the left, the rue Morte-Bouteille. Who the fuck comes up with names like Morte-Bouteille?) Obviously, it's impossible to park a car without attracting attention, which means driving deep into the arse-end of nowhere and walking back.

I'm strung out, I haven't been eating properly and I'm exhausted, trying to do too many things at once. And I fucking hate walking. Especially in the forest . . .

The little damsel just needs to sit tight, I'll be there very soon to bring her a little message. And I've got all the tools I need to make myself understood. And when I'm done with her, I plan to take off to where forests are banned, where there's not a single tree within a hundred-kilometre radius. I need sandy beaches, killer cocktails and a few relaxing hands of poker so I can get over all this excitement. I'm getting old. I'd like to make the most of things while there's still time. But if I'm to do that, I need to stay calm, to be cold-blooded as I tramp through this fucking forest, constantly on the alert. It's hard to believe how many people there are traipsing through this desolate wasteland even at this ungodly hour – young people, old people, couples are out rambling, hiking, jogging. I even came across a couple riding horses.

That said, the further I trek, the fewer people I encounter. The shack is set back at least three hundred metres from the road and the dirt track leading there stops abruptly, beyond it there is nothing but forest.

Carrying a sniper rifle – even in its case – is not quite in keeping with the local country attire, so I've stuffed it into a sports bag. Especially as I don't look like some guy out collecting mushrooms.

I haven't seen a soul for several minutes now, the G.P.S. has no reception, but this is the only dirt track around here.

It will just be the two of us. We'll get this little job done.

Every clanging door, every footstep along the hallway, every face peering through the bars, everything weighs on him. Because deep down, Camille is afraid. Long ago, when he first realised that one day he would have to come back here, he dismissed the thought. But it came back to the surface, thrashing like a fish on a riverbank, telling him that sooner or later this meeting would take place. All he needed was some pretext to come here, to give in without shame to this overpowering need.

Before him, behind him, all around, the heavy metal gates of the central prison open and close.

As he moves along the hallways with little, birdlike steps, Camille stifles the urge to vomit, his head is spinning.

The guard escorting him is deferential, almost protective, as though he understands the situation and feels that, given the exceptional circumstances, Camille deserves special consideration. Everywhere Camille looks there are signs.

A hall, another hall and then the waiting room. The door is opened and Camille sits at the metal table bolted to the floor, his heart is hammering fit to burst, his throat is dry. He waits. He lays his hands flat, but seeing them tremble, he hides them under the table.

The second door opens, the one at the far end of the room. At first he can see nothing but a pair of shoes on the footrest of the wheelchair, shiny black leather shoes, then the wheelchair begins to move, infinitely slowly as though wary or suspicious. Two legs appear, fat knees straining at the fabric of the trousers, then the wheelchair comes to a halt halfway across the threshold. Camille can see a pair of fleshy hands, so pale the veins are invisible, gripping the wheels. One metre further, and the man himself appears.

He pauses for an instant. From the moment he enters, his eyes bore into Camille, they never leave him. The guard steps around the table and moves the other metal chair to make room for the wheelchair and then, at Camille's signal, he leaves.

The wheelchair rolls forward, then pivots with unexpected ease.

Finally they are face to face.

For the first time in four years, Camille Verhœven, *commandant* of the *brigade criminelle*, finds himself confronted by the man who butchered his wife.

The man he knew then was tall and lean, with an old-fashioned, almost rakish elegance and a disconcerting sensuality, especially his full lips. The prisoner before him is slovenly and obese. The same physical traits are now half buried in a bloated body. Only his face is the same, like a delicate mask worn by a fat man. His hair is long and lank. His eyes are as sly, as shifty as ever.

"It was written." Buisson's voice is tremulous, too loud, too shrill. "And it is now," he says, as though bringing the interview to an end.

In his glory days, he prided himself on such turns of phrase. In a sense, this was what led him to murder seven times, this taste for the grandiloquent, his ostentatious arrogance. He and Camille despised each other at sight. Later, as so often, history confirmed that their intuitions had been correct. But this is not the time to go over ancient history.

"Yes," Camille says simply. "It is now."

Camille's voice does not tremble. He feels calmer now he is sitting opposite Buisson. He has a lot of experience of face-to-face encounters, he knows he will not rant and rage. The man he so often imagined dead, tortured, suffering in dreams, is not the same, and seeing him now, Camille realises that he feels only a calm, dispassionate animosity. For years, all his hatred, all his rage was heaped on Irène's killer, but that is finished.

Buisson is finished.

But Camille's life, his story, is not.

His culpability in Irène's death is something that will haunt him for ever. He will never be over her, this truth, this simple fact, illuminates everything. Everything else is evasion.

Realising this, Camille looks up, and his eyes well with the tears that instantly bring him closer to Irène as she was, beautifully, eternally young, for him alone. He grows old; she, more radiant than ever, will never change. What Buisson did has no power over his memories, that intimate collection of images, recollections and sensations that comprise his love of Irène.

Something he bears like a scar, imperceptible yet indelible.

Buisson does not move. From the beginning of this encounter he has been afraid.

Camille's brief pang, quickly overcome, creates no awkwardness between the two men. Words will come, but it was necessary that silence be given its due. Camille shakes it off, he does not want Buisson to see this fleeting moment of pain, their mutual silence, as some sort of mute communion. There is nothing he wishes to share with this man. He blows his nose, stuffs the tissue in his pocket, props his elbows on the table, folds his hands under his chin and stares at Buisson.

Buisson has been dreading this moment since yesterday. When he discovered – on the prison grapevine – that Verhœven had paid a visit to Mouloud Faraoui, he knew his time had come. He lay awake all night, tossing and turning, unable to believe it. His death is now a foregone conclusion. Faraoui's gang has spies everywhere in La Centrale, there is not a cockroach that can hide from him. If Camille has found a way of paying for Faraoui's services – by giving up the name of the man who grassed him up, for instance – then an hour from now or two days from now, Buisson will find a shiv embedded in his throat as he comes out of the dining hall or be garrotted from behind while a couple of weight-lifters hold his arms. He may be catapulted in his wheelchair from the third-floor balcony. Or be smothered by his mattress. It will depend on the order given, Verhœven may even insist on a slow, painful death; Buisson might spend a whole night choking on a gag in the fetid toilets, or bleed to death, drop by drop, in the cupboard of one of the workshops . . .

Buisson is scared of dying.

By now, he had convinced himself that Camille would not exact revenge. The fear that he put behind him years ago floods back, all the more violent and terrifying because it feels somehow less justified. The years he has spent in jail, the things he has endured, the respect he has earned, the power he has managed to acquire, instilled in him a sense of impunity that Verhœven has destroyed in a few short hours. Camille had only to visit Faraoui for everyone to realise that the reprieve has been temporary, that Buisson's stay of execution will last only a few hours more. There has been a lot of talk in the corridors, Faraoui was quick to spread the news, part of his deal with Verhœven was to put the fear of God into Buisson. A few of the screws have heard and the inmates have begun to look at Buisson differently.

Why now? That is the question.

"I hear you've become a big shot . . ."

Buisson wonders if this is the answer. But no. Camille is simply stating a fact. Buisson is an exceptionally intelligent man. When he tried to make his escape, Louis lodged the bullet in his spine that put him in this wheelchair, but before that he had been running rings around the police. By the time he arrived in prison, his reputation had preceded him, in fact he became something of a star for having successfully evaded the *brigade criminelle* for so long. With considerable skill, Buisson capitalised on the prisoners' admiration, he managed to remain aloof from the gang wars, he performed small services for other inmates – in prison, an intellectual, a man who knows things, is a rarity. Over the years, he succeeded in forging a small network of contacts, first within the prison and later outside as he continued to do small favours for paroled prisoners, making introductions, arranging meetings, securing interviews. Last year, he successfully intervened in an internecine war between rival gangs in the western suburbs, calmed the situation, proposed terms and expertly negotiated the ceasefire. Within the prison, he does not involve himself in any trafficking, but he knows all the scams. On the outside, Buisson knows all there is to know about high-profile criminals and is remarkably well connected to those who meet his exacting standards; this makes him a powerful man.

But for all that, now that Camille has made his decision, a day from now or perhaps an hour from now, he will be a dead man.

"You look worried . . ." Camille says.

"I'm waiting."

Buisson immediately regrets the phrase which sounds like a challenge and therefore a defeat. Camille raises a hand: no problem, he understands.

"I'll let you explain . . ."

"No," Camille says, "there will be no explanation. I'm simply here to tell you how this is going to go down."

Buisson is deathly pale. Even Verhœven's calmness seems like a threat. He becomes indignant.

"I deserve an explanation!" Buisson roars.

Though physically he is a very different man, inside he has not changed, his titanic ego has survived intact. Camille fumbles in his pocket and lays a photograph on the table.

"Vincent Hafner. He's . . ."

"I know who he is . . ." The remark is curt, as though Buisson feels insulted. But it also betrays his immense relief. In a split second, Buisson realised that he still has a chance.

Camille registers the instinctive exultation in his voice, but he makes no comment. It was to be expected. Buisson immediately goes on the defensive, attempting to confuse the issue.

"I don't know the man personally . . . He's not a major player, but he has his place. He has a reputation for being somewhat . . . savage. A thug."

It would take electrodes attached to his head to record the astonishing speed of firing synapses.

"He disappeared last January," Camille says. "For months, no-one – not even his criminal colleagues – knew where he was. Complete radio silence. Then, suddenly, he reappears and it's like he's got a new lease of life, he's back to his old ways, back on the job, bright as a button."

"And you find this somehow strange?"

"I'm having a little difficulty squaring his sudden disappearance with his spectacular comeback. For a career criminal so close to retirement, it's unusual."

"So, something is not quite right."

Camille's face darkens, he looks worried, almost angry with himself.

"That's one way of putting it: something is not quite right. Something I don't understand."

Seeing the ghost of a smile cross Buisson's face, Camille knows he was right to trust to the man's overweening pride. It was arrogance that led him to kill again and again, even as it led to his arrest. This is the reason that he will die in a prison cell. And still he has learned nothing, his narcissism is like a bottomless well, ever ready to engulf him. "Something I don't understand." Camille's crucial phrase was designed to appeal to that same vanity, because Buisson is convinced that *he* understands. And cannot resist letting Camille know.

"Perhaps he needs money in a hurry . . ."

Camille steels himself, determined not to show how much it pains him to have to stoop to chicanery. He is leading an investigation; the end justifies the means. So he looks up at Buisson as though intrigued.

"Word has it Hafner is seriously ill . . ." Buisson says slowly.

When you choose a stratagem, it is wise to stick with it to the end.

"Good, I hope he dies," Camille says.

"But don't you see?" Buisson triumphantly retorts. "The reason he is acting out of character is *because* he's staring death in the face. He's involved with a slip of a girl . . . A vulgar whore who had copulated with half the city by the time she was nineteen. She obviously likes turning tricks, I can think of no other explanation . . ."

Camille wonders whether Buisson is brave enough – or reckless enough – to see his thought through. And he does.

"But despite her failings, it would appear that Hafner is infatuated with this girl. Love, *commandant*, is a powerful thing, is it not? It is a subject about which you know a thing or two, as I recall . . ."

Though he does not show it, Camille is devastated. He feels utterly broken as he sits here, allowing Buisson to gloat about the murder of Irène. "Love, *commandant* . . ."

Buisson must sense something because a last flicker of self-preservation suddenly extinguishes his exultant smirk.

"If he is terminally ill," he goes on, "perhaps Hafner wants to ensure his paramour is free of financial worries. One comes across the most generous instincts even in the blackest souls . . ."

Louis had already mentioned these rumours to Camille and, though it cost him dearly, the price he paid to confirm them has been worth it. Camille can suddenly see a light at the end of the tunnel. His palpable relief is not lost on Buisson, a man so twisted that he is already trying to work out why this matters so much to Verhœven, why Hafner is so important that the *commandant* has been reduced to coming here. His life has only just been spared and already he is calculating how he might profit from this situation.

Camille does not give him the time.

"I want Hafner, and I want him now. You've got twelve hours."

"Th—that's impossible!" the piteous wail dies in Buisson's throat. As Camille gets to his feet, he sees his last chance of survival disappear. He feverishly pounds his fists on the armrests of his wheelchair. Camille's face is expressionless.

"Twelve hours, not a second more. I find people do their best work when they have a deadline."

He taps on the door. As the guard comes to open it, he turns back to Buisson.

"Even when this is over, I can still have you killed any time I want." It is enough for him to say the words for both men to realise that he needed to say it, but it was not true. That Buisson would already be dead if it were going to happen. That for Camille

Verhœven, ordering a killing is incompatible with who he is.

And now that he knows that his life is no longer in danger, that it was probably never in danger, Buisson decides to find the information Verhœven needs.

As he steps out of the prison, Camille feels both relieved and overwhelmed, like the sole survivor of a shipwreck.

9.00 a.m.

I'm finding the cold almost as tough to cope with as the tiredness. You hardly notice it at first, but unless you keep moving, it seeps into your bones until you're frozen to the marrow. It's not going to make it easy to get a shot. But at least this place is quiet. The studio is a broad, squat building with a high roof, but there's only one storey. There's an unobstructed line of sight in front. I station myself in a tiny lean-to at the far end of the yard that looks like it was once a rabbit hutch or similar.

I stow the sniper rifle, take the Walther and the hunting knife and brave the great outdoors to do a little reconnaissance. It's crucial to know the terrain. Cause only as much collateral damage as necessary. Go for a clean hit. Precise. What do they call it? Oh, yeah, a "surgical strike". Using the Mossberg here would be like using a roller to paint a miniature. Surgical entails making precise holes in very precise places. And since the vast picture window seems resistant to most things, I'm glad I settled on an M40A3 with telescopic sights; it's a very accurate piece of kit. And it takes armour-piercing bullets.

Just to the right of the house there is a sort of hillock. The soil has been partly washed away by the rain, revealing a heap of building rubble, plaster, breeze blocks that builders were probably supposed to clear away but never did. It's not an ideal position for a sniper, but it's the only one I've got. From here, I have a view of most of the main room, though only at an angle. I'll have to stand up at the last minute before I fire.

I've already seen her a couple of times, but she was walking past too quickly. I'm not bothered, no sense rushing things. Better to do it right.

As soon as she got up, Anne went to the door to make sure Camille had double-locked it. The house has been burgled more than once, which is hardly surprising given the isolated location, so he installed reinforced doors. The double-glazed bay window is fitted with toughened glass which could probably take a hammer blow without so much as cracking.

"This is the code for the alarm," Camille had said, handing her a page torn from a notepad. "Press hash, then this number, then hash again. That'll set off the alarm. It's not connected to the local police station and it only lasts a minute, but take my word for it, it's a powerful deterrent."

The numbers are 29091571; Anne did not want to ask what they meant.

"Caravaggio's date of birth . . ." Camille said apologetically. "It seemed like a good idea for a security code. Not many people know it. But as I said, I guarantee you won't need it."

Anne also checked the rear of the building. There is a laundry and a bathroom. The only external door is reinforced with steel, locked and bolted.

Then she went and showered as best she could. It was impossible to wash her hair properly; she considered removing the splints but decided it would be too painful, she had to stop herself crying out merely touching her fingers. She will simply have to make do.

Picking up the slightest thing with these bear paws has become a feat. She does most of the work with her right thumb since the left is sprained.

The shower is a blessed relief after having spent all night feeling grubby and smelling of hospital disinfectant. She allowed the scalding water to enfold her gently for a long moment, then opened a window to feel the delicious, invigorating chill.

Her face seems unchanged. In the mirror, it looks just as it did the previous night, perhaps even uglier, more swollen, the motley blue and yellow bruises, the broken teeth . . .

Camille drives carefully. Too carefully. Too slowly, especially since this stretch of autoroute is short and drivers tend to ignore the speed limits. His mind is elsewhere, he is so preoccupied that even on automatic pilot he slows to a crawl: the car limps towards the Périphérique, dropping from seventy kilometres per hour to sixty, to fifty trailed by the howl of car horns, shouted insults, flashing headlights. His confusion was triggered by a single thought: he has just spent the night with this woman in the most hallowed place in his life, but what does he know about her? What do he and Anne truly know about each other?

He quickly assesses what Anne knows about him. He has told her the most important things: Irène, his mother, his father. His life is a simple one. With Irène's death, he suffered one more tragedy than most people suffer.

He knows little more about Anne: work, marriage, a brother, a divorce, a child.

As he comes to this conclusion, the car veers into the middle lane as Camille takes out his mobile, connects the charger to the dashboard power socket and opens a browser. The screen on the mobile is tiny, and the device slips from his hands as he fumbles for his reading glasses, and he finds himself rummaging for it under the passenger seat – no easy feat for a man who is four foot eleven.

The car drifts into the slow lane, half straddling the hard shoulder and crawls along while Camille recovers the phone, but all the while his brain is working overtime.

What does he know about Anne?

Her daughter. Her brother. Her job at the travel agency.

What else?

His internal alarm manifests itself as a tingling between the shoulder blades.

His mouth is suddenly dry.

Having finally succeeded in retrieving the mobile, Camille keys "Wertig & Schwindel" into the search engine. It is a difficult name to type, but he manages.

He nervously drums his fingers on the steering wheel, waits for the company website to load – a picture of palm trees and beautiful beaches – as an articulated lorry overtakes him with a deafening roar. Camille swerves a little, his eyes still focused on the tiny screen: "ABOUT US, A WORD FROM OUR C.E.O." – who gives a shit? – finally, he comes to a diagram of the company hierarchy. General Manager, Jean-Michel Faye, in his thirties, overweight, balding, but with a typical managerial smugness.

As he joins the Périphérique, Camille is scrolling through the long page of contact details searching for Anne. Thumb pressed firmly on the forward arrow, he flicks through a series of photographs, somehow manages to skip the letter F and by the time he has scrolled back, he can hear a siren behind him. He pulls over as far as he can, the police motorcycle passes and signals for him to turn off the motorway. Camille drops his mobile. Shit.

He pulls over onto the verge. Cops are a fucking pain in the arse.

The studio is a bachelor pad, with none of the accessories a woman might expect: no hairdryer, no mirror. There is no tea, either. Anne finds the mugs and chooses one bearing a Cyrillic inscription:

Мой дядя самых честных правил,
Когда не в шутку занемог

She finds some herbal tea, long past its best-by date and utterly tasteless.

Almost immediately she realises that in this house, she has to rethink every gesture, make a little extra effort in order to do the simplest thing. Because in the home of a man who is four foot eleven, everything is a fraction lower than expected: the door handles, the drawers, the light switches . . . All around her are tools for climbing – stairs, stools, stepladders – because, strangely, nothing is quite at Camille's height either. He has not dismissed the possibility of sharing this space with another person and so everything is positioned midway between what is comfortable for him and what would be acceptable to someone else.

This realisation is like a knife in her heart. She has never pitied Camille – that is not the kind of response he evokes in people – no, she feels moved. She feels guilty, she feels it more here than elsewhere, more now than ever, guilty of monopolising his life, of dragging him into this business. She struggles not to cry; she has decided she is done with tears.

She needs to get a grip. She tips the herbal tea into the sink, angry at herself.

She is wearing her purple tracksuit bottoms and a polo-necked jumper; they are the only things she has here. The blood-stained clothes she was wearing when the paramedics brought her in have been taken away, and Camille decided to leave the things he brought from her apartment in the wardrobe at the hospital so that if anyone noticed her absence, it would look as though she had just popped out for a minute. He had parked next to the emergency exit of the A. & E. department, Anne had slipped out behind the reception desk, got into the car and lay down on the back seat.

He has promised to bring her some clothes tonight. But tonight seems an eternity away. This is the question that must have haunted soldiers who went to war: am I going to die today?

For all Camille's fine promises, she knows the man is coming. The only question is: when? Ever since Camille left, ever since she has been pacing this room, she has been drawn to the looming presence of the forest.

In the dawn light, it looks almost surreal. She turns away, goes into the bathroom, but each time she is drawn back to the forest. A ridiculous image flashes into her mind: Drogo in *The Tartar Steppe*, staring from the remote forward outpost across the desolate wasteland, waiting for the enemy.

How does anyone come out alive?

Cops are not stupid.

When Camille gets out of the car (he has to launch himself, legs extended, like a child getting down from a booster seat), the motorcycle officer immediately recognises him as Commandant

Verhœven. He and his partner are patrolling a specific area but he offers Camille an escort as far as Porte de Saint-Cloud – though not before issuing a warning: "You do realise that using a mobile telephone while driving, regardless of the reason, is extremely dangerous, *commandant*. Being a detective with the *brigade* does not give you licence to endanger other motorists, even in an emergency." The police escort saves Camille almost half an hour. He carries on jabbing at the keypad on his phone, though more discreetly. He is approaching the banks of the Seine when the officer gives him a wave and drives off. Camille immediately puts his glasses on, and though it takes him ten minutes, he discovers that the name Anne Forestier is not on the list of employees at Wertig & Schwindel. Then again, when he looks more closely, he realises that the web page has not been updated since 2005, at which point Anne would still have been living in Lyons.

He pulls into the car park, gets out of the car and is climbing the stairs to his office when his mobile rings

Guérin. Camille turns on his heel and heads back outside to take the call; he does not need anyone overhearing his conversation with Guérin.

"Thanks for getting back to me," he says, trying to sound cheerful.

He is brief and to the point, no need to panic his colleague, but better to be honest: *the reason I called is because I need a favour, let me explain*, but there is no need, Guérin already knows the story, Commissaire Michard has also called and left a message, probably for the same reason. And in a few minutes he will call her back, at which point he will have to tell her that there is no way he could have been the one to tell Camille about the robbery at the Galerie Monier:

"I've been on holiday for the last four days, buddy . . . I'm calling you from Sicily."

Jesus fucking Christ! Camille could kick himself. He says *thanks, no worries, it's nothing serious, yeah, you too*, and hangs up. His mind is already racing ahead, because Guérin's call did nothing to stop the prickling sensation between his shoulder blades or the dry mouth, which in him are clear signs of professional agitation.

"Good morning, *commandant*!" It is the examining magistrate.

Camille comes down to earth with a bump. He feels as though he has spent the past two days inside a giant spinning top whirling at terrifying speed. This morning he is all over the place, the spinning top is behaving like a free electron.

"*Monsieur le juge . . .*"

Camille flashes the broadest smile he can summon. Anyone else in Juge Pereira's shoes might assume that Camille has been desperately trying to get in touch, that he was at this moment coming to find him and that his sudden appearance is a huge relief; flinging his arms wide, Camille nods enthusiastically at this fortuitous meeting of great minds.

The great mind of the judiciary does not seem quite as enthusiastic as Camille. Pereira coldly shakes his hand. Camille is swept along in the wake of the spindle-shanked magistrate, but already it is too late, the *juge* strides solemnly onward and mounts the stairs, it is obvious from his attitude he does not wish to discuss the matter.

"*Monsieur le juge?*"

Pereira stops, turns and feigns surprise.

"Could I speak to you for a moment?" Camille says. "It's about the robbery at the Galerie Monier . . ."

After the balmy heat of the bathroom, the chill air in the living room marks a return to the real world.

Camille reeled off extremely detailed, highly technical instructions about the wood-burning stove which Anne promptly forgot. Picking up a poker, she lifts off the cast-iron lid to toss in more wood, but one of the logs is too big and by the time she has forced it in, the room is filled with acrid smoke. She decides to make a cup of instant coffee.

She cannot seem to get warm, the cold has seeped into her bones. Her eyes are drawn back to the forest as she waits for the water to boil . . .

Then she settles herself on the sofa to leaf through one of Camille's sketchpads – she is spoiled for choice, the room is littered with them. Faces, figures, men in uniform, she is startled to recognise a fat *gendarme* with a bovine expression and dark circles under his eyes, the man who was standing guard outside her hospital room, the one who was snoring loudly as she made her escape. In the drawing, he is on guard duty. With three deft strokes, Camille has captured him perfectly.

The portraits are moving and yet unsentimental. In some, Camille reveals himself to be a gifted caricaturist, sketches that are more cruel than comical and stripped of all illusion.

Suddenly, unexpectedly, in a sketchpad lying on the glass coffee table, she sees herself. Pages and pages of drawings, none of them dated. Her eyes well with tears. For Camille, imagining him alone here, spending whole days recreating from memory the moments they have shared. And for herself. These portraits bear no resemblance to the woman she is now, they are relics of a time when she was beautiful, before the bruises and the broken teeth, before the scars on her cheek and around her mouth, before the vacant eyes. Though Camille merely hints at the setting with a few quick pencil strokes, Anne realises she can remember the circumstances that inspired almost every drawing. Anne having a fit of the giggles at Chez Fernand the day they met; Anne standing on the pavement outside Camille's building: she has only to turn the pages of the sketchbook to retrace the story of their relationship. Here is Anne at Le Verdun, the café where they went that second night. She is wearing a hat and smiling, she looks astonishingly self-assured and – to judge from Camille's thumbnail sketch – she had every reason to be.

Anne sniffles and looks around for a tissue. Here is a full-length portrait, she is walking along a street near the Opéra, coming to meet Camille who has bought tickets for "Madame Butterfly"; she remembers imitating Cio-Cio San in the taxi afterwards. The pages map out their story from the beginning, week by week, month by month. Anne in the shower, or in bed; a series of pages depicts her in tears, she feels ugly, but Camille's glance is loving and gentle. She stretches out her hand to pick up the box of tissues and finds she has to stand to reach them.

Just as she reaches for a tissue, the bullet punctures the picture window and the glass coffee table explodes.

Though she has feared this moment since she woke this morning, still Anne is surprised. Not by the dull crack of the rifle, but by the impact of the bullet which makes a sound as though the whole façade of the house is collapsing. She is petrified as she watches the coffee table shatter beneath her fingers. She lets out a scream and as quickly as her reflexes allow, she curls into a ball like a hedgehog. When she finally glances outside, she sees that the picture window is not shattered. The bullet has made a large, glittering hole from which deep cracks spread. How long can she hold out?

She abruptly realises that she is a sitting target. It is impossible to say where she finds the strength, but with a brutal movement she launches herself over the back of the sofa. The pressure on her fractured ribs as she rolls leaves her winded; she lands heavily, letting out a howl in pain, but her instinct for survival is stronger than the pain and she quickly huddles against the back of the sofa and immediately panics at the thought that a bullet could pass through the upholstery and hit her. Her heart is pounding fit to burst. Her whole body is shivering as though with cold.

The second shot whistles just above her head. The bullet hits the wall and Anne instinctively ducks, feeling fragments of plaster rain down on her face, her neck, her eyes. She lies flat on the ground shielding her head with her hands, almost the same position she adopted in the toilets of the Galerie Monier when he beat her half to death.

A telephone. Call Camille. Right now. Or call the police. She needs someone here. Fast.

Anne knows this is a tricky situation: her mobile is upstairs next to the bed, to get to it she would have to cross the room.

In the open.

A third bullet hits the cast-iron stove with a deafening clang that leaves her half dazed, clapping her hand over her ears as the ricochet shatters one of the pictures on the wall. Anne is so terrified that she cannot seem to focus her thoughts, her mind is swirling with images – the Galerie, her hospital room, Camille's face, his expression grave and reproachful – her whole life flashing past as though she were about to die.

Which she is. The gunman cannot miss for ever. And this time she is utterly alone, with no hope that anyone will come to her rescue.

Anne swallows hard. She cannot stay where she is; the killer will gain entry to the house – she does not know how, but somehow he will. She has to call Camille. He told her to set off the alarm, but the scrap of paper with the scribbled code is next to the control panel on the other side of the living room.

The telephone is up on the mezzanine. She has to get upstairs.

She raises her head and glances around at the floor, at the rug strewn with pieces of plaster, but there is nothing there to help her; she will have to help herself. Her decision is made. She rolls onto her back and, using both hands, pulls off her jumper. The wool becomes caught in the splints on her fingers, she tugs and rips the fabric. She counts to three then sits up, her back against the sofa, clutching the crumpled jumper to her belly. If he fires at the sofa now, she is dead.

There is no time to lose.

Quickly, she looks to her right; the staircase is ten metres away. She looks up and to the left; through the skylight in the roof she can see the branches of a tree – could he climb up there, get in through the skylight? She desperately needs to telephone for help: phone Camille, the police, anyone. She will not get a second chance. She tucks her legs beneath her and throws the rolled-up jumper left, not too hard, she wants it to glide, high and slow, across the room. Hardly has she let it go than she is on her feet and running for the stairs. As she expected, the next bullet explodes behind her.

Alternating fire is a little trick I learned long ago: you have two targets, one on the left, one on the right, and you have to hit them in quick succession. I have the rifle primed and ready. As soon as I see the jumper, I fire – if she plans on wearing it again, she'll need to do some darning because I blew the fucking thing apart. I quickly turn and see her running for the stairs, I aim and my bullet hits the first step just as she reaches the second and disappears into the mezzanine.

Time to up the ante a little. Turns out, it wasn't hard to get her exactly where I wanted her. I thought it would take for ever, but in the end she just needed a little guidance. Now all I need to do is go around. I should probably get a move on though, nothing is ever straightforward, sooner or later she's going to figure things out.

But if everything goes to plan, I'll get there before her.

The first step implodes under her feet.

Anne feels the whole staircase shudder and scrabbles up so fast that she trips and goes flying, hitting her head against the dresser of the cramped bedroom.

Already she is back on her feet. She looks down over the banister to make sure he cannot see her, cannot hit her; she will stay up here. But first she needs to call Camille. He has to come back now, he has to help her. Feverishly, she fumbles for her mobile on the chest of drawers, but it is not there. She tries the nightstand; still nothing. Where the fuck is it? Then she remembers that she plugged it in to recharge before going to bed. She rummages through her discarded clothes, finds the device and turns it on. She is breathless, her heart is hammering so hard in her chest that she feels nauseous, she pounds a fist on her knee, the mobile takes so long to start up. Camille . . . She hits the speed dial.

Come on, Camille, pick up, pick up please . . .

It rings once, twice . . .

Please, Camille, I'm begging you, just tell me what to do . . .

Her hands tremble as they cradle the phone.

"Hello, you've reached Camille Verhœ—"

She hangs up, dials again and gets straight through to voicemail. This time she leaves a message:

"Camille, he's here! Call me back, please . . ."

Pereira is checking his watch. It seems that getting a moment to speak to the magistrate will not be easy. He is a very busy man. To Verhœven, the message is crystal-clear, he is off the case. The *juge* nods his head, exasperated, all these meetings and schedules. Camille finishes his thought: too many irregularities, too much uncertainty, too many doubts, his whole team may have been thrown off the case. To distance herself and cover her arse, Commissaire Michard will file a report with the public prosecutor's office. The looming prospect of an I.G.S. investigation into the actions of Commandant Verhœven is taking shape with an appalling clarity.

Juge Pereira would love to make time, he hesitates, pulls a face, *Let me see*, he checks his watch again, *It's not really a good time, let me think*, he pauses two steps above Camille and stares down, he is faced with a genuine dilemma, avoiding someone is not in his nature. In the end, he capitulates not to Commandant Verhœven, but to a moral imperative.

"Let me get back to you, *commandant*. I'll call you later this morning . . ."

Camille spreads his hands: thank you. Pereira nods gravely: don't mention it.

Camille is very much aware that this is his last chance.

Between Le Guen's friendship and support and the benevolent attitude of the magistrate, there is still a slim chance that he can come through this. He is desperately clinging to this hope, Pereira can see it in his face. And he cannot deny that he is intrigued by what has been going on with Verhœven, the rumours of what has happened over the past two days are so strange that he is curious to know more, to come to his own conclusion.

"Thank you," Camille says.

The words echo like a confession, like an plea, Pereira makes a vague gesture then, embarrassed, he turns and is gone.

Anne suddenly looks up. The man has stopped firing. Where is he?

The back of the house. The window of the ground-floor bathroom is half open. It is far too small for a body to squeeze through, but it is an opening and who knows what this man is capable of. Without considering the risks, and oblivious to the fact he may still be lying in wait outside the picture window, Anne dashes back downstairs, jumps over the shattered bottom step, turns right and almost falls.

By the time she reaches the laundry room he is there, staring at her through the window, his face neatly framed as in a formal portrait. He slips his arm through the opening. A pistol fitted with a silencer is aimed at her. The barrel seems impossibly long.

The moment he sees her, he fires.

After Pereira disappears, Camille rushes upstairs. On the landing he runs into Louis, looking particularly handsome in a Christian Lacroix suit, a pinstripe Savile Row shirt, Forzieri brogues.

"Sorry, Louis, I'll have to catch up with you later . . ."

Louis gives a little wave – *take your time, it can wait* – and steps aside, he will come by later, the guy is diplomacy incarnate.

Camille goes into his office, throws his coat onto a chair, looks up the number for Wertig & Schwindel and as he dials, he checks his watch: 9.15. A voice answers.

"Could I speak to Anne Forestier, please?"

"Hold the line," the voice says. "Let me look . . ."

Deep breath. The vice-like grip constricting his chest loosens. He almost finds himself heaving a sigh of relief.

"I'm sorry . . . what name was that again?" the young woman asks and laughs conspiratorially to get him on side. "I'm really sorry, I'm a temp, so I'm new here."

Camille swallows hard. He feels the noose tighten again, pain shoots through his body and he feels panic rising . . .

"Anne Forestier."

"Do you know which department she's in?"

"Um . . . account management or something like that."

"I'm sorry, I can't see her name in the directory . . . Hold the line, I'll put you through to someone."

Camille can feel his shoulders hunch. A woman's voice comes on the line, probably the one Anne called "a complete bitch", but it can't be her because *No, I'm afraid the name doesn't ring a bell, I've asked around and no-one seems to have heard of her, if you like I can check – are you sure you've got the right name? I can put you through to someone else? Can I ask what you're calling about?*

Camille hangs up.

His throat is dry, he desperately needs a glass of water, but he does not have the time, and besides, his hands are shaking.

He keys in his password, logs on to the system, brings up a search engine: "Anne Forestier." Too many results. Refine the search: "Anne Forestier, date of birth . . ."

He should be able to track down the date, they met early in March and three weeks later, when he found out it was her birthday, he took her to dinner at Chez Nénesse. The invitation had been a spur of the moment thing since he had no time to buy a present; Anne had laughed and said dinner was the perfect gift because she loved desserts. He drew a sketch on the napkin and presented it to her; though he said nothing, he was very pleased with the portrait, it was natural, it was truthful. There are days like that.

He digs out his mobile and brings up the calendar: March 23. Anne is forty-two. 1965. Born in Lyons? Maybe, maybe not. He thinks back to the evening of her birthday, did she say anything about where she was born? He deletes "Lyons" and clicks "submit". The search brings up two Anne Forestiers, which is hardly surprising: type in your date of birth and if you have a common name, you are bound to find you have a twin or even a triplet.

The first Anne Forestier is not his Anne. She died in 1973 at eight years old. Nor is the second. She died two years ago, on 16 October, 2005.

Camille rubs his hands together. He feels the familiar prickle of unease, one of the fundamental tools of a detective, but this is more than merely professional zeal, he has found an anomaly. And as everyone knows, Camille is a past master when it comes to anomalies. Except that in this case, the inconsistency is mirrored by his own inconsistent behaviour, which has been puzzling everyone.

It is beginning to puzzle even him.

Why is he fighting?

Against whom?

Some women lie about their date of birth. It is not Anne's style, but you never know.

Camille gets up and opens the filing cabinet. No-one ever tidies it. He uses his height as a pretext for not doing so – he's happy to exploit his stature when it suits him . . . It takes several minutes for him to find the instruction manual he needs. There is no-one he can ask for help.

"The thing that really takes time after a divorce is the clear-out," Anne said.

Camille lays his hands flat on the table and tries to concentrate. No, it is impossible, he needs a pencil and paper. He sketches. He struggles to remember. They are in Anne's apartment. She is sitting on the sofa bed. "Don't take this the wrong way," he says, "but the place is a little . . . um . . . well, a little dreary." He had tried to come up with a word that was not upsetting, but any sentence that begins "Don't take this the wrong way" and trails off into awkward silence is bound to crash and burn, it is simply a matter of time.

"I don't give a damn," Anne says curtly. "After the divorce, I just wanted to be rid of everything."

The memory becomes clearer. He needs to remember what was said about the divorce. They did not really talk about it, Camille was reluctant to ask questions.

"It was two years ago," Anne says finally.

Camille drops his pencil. He runs a finger down the list of commands in the instruction manual, launches the relevant database and runs a search for information about the marriage and/or divorce of one Anne Forestier in 2005. He goes through the results, filtering out those that do not correspond until he is left with one: "Forestier, Anne, born 20 July, 1970. Age: thirty-seven . . ." Camille clicks on the link: "Arrested for fraud on 27 April, 1998."

Anne has a police record.

This information is so astounding that he cannot quite take it in. Anne has a record. He reads on. Charged with passing fraudulent cheques, with forgery and use of false documents. He is so stunned that it takes several long seconds before he notices that Anne Forestier is incarcerated in the Centre Pénitentiaire de Rennes.

This is not *his* Anne, it is someone else, a different Anne Forestier.

Although . . . The record indicates she was released on parole. When? Is the file up to date? He has to log into a different database to find the official mugshot for the prisoner in question. I'm nervous, he thinks, too nervous. The message onscreen reads: "CTRL+F4 to Submit." A woman appears on the screen, her face front on and also in profile. She is unquestionably of Asian origin.

Place of birth: Da Nang.

He closes the window. Relief. Anne, his Anne, does not have a police record. But she is proving almost impossible to track down.

At last Camille can breathe a little, but his chest still feels constricted, this room is stuffy, he has said it a thousand times.

The moment she saw him staring at her, Anne dropped to the floor. The bullet hits the doorframe a few inches above her head, an almost muffled thud compared to the shriek of the bullet that ricocheted off the cast-iron stove, but the room shudders at the impact.

Crawling on all fours, Anne frantically tries to get out of the room. Terror-stricken. It is madness, but this is precisely the same scene they played out two days ago in the Galerie. Once again, she is scrabbling to escape before he shoots her in the back . . .

She rolls over, the splints on her fingers slipping on the

polished floor, the pain no longer matters, there is no pain now, only instinct.

A bullet grazes her right shoulder and buries itself in the doorframe. Anne scampers wildly like a puppy, manages to roll over the threshold. Suddenly, miraculously, she is safe, sitting with her back against the wall. Can he get into the house? How?

Curiously, she still has her mobile. She rushed down the stairs into the laundry room and crawled out again still clutching it, as a child clutches a teddy bear while bombs and shells rain all around.

What is he doing? She has a desperate urge to take a look, but if he's lying in wait, she would get the next bullet between the eyes.

Think. Fast. She has already redialled Camille. She hangs up; she is alone.

Call the local police? Where's the nearest police station in this godforsaken place? It will take ages to explain, and if they do come how long would it take them to get here? Ten times longer than it will take Anne to die. Because he is there, just on the other side of the wall.

The only person who can help her now is Caravaggio.

Memory is a strange thing. Now that all his senses are sharp as blades, it all comes flooding back. Anne's daughter, Agathe, is studying for an M.B.A. in Boston. Camille is sure of it, he remembers Anne telling him that she visited Boston (she was coming back from Montreal – in fact, it was there that she saw one of his mother's paintings), that the city is very beautiful, very European, "olde worlde" she called it, though Camille did not really know what she meant by the phrase. It vaguely conjured images of Louisiana. Camille does not like travelling.

He needs to consult a different database which requires a different manual. He goes back to the filing cabinet, finds a list of instructions – in principle, nothing he has done so far requires him to request authorisation from a superior. The network connection is fast: Boston University, four thousand professors, thirty thousand students. The list of results is too large. Camille goes through the list of sororities, copies and pastes them into a document where he can do a simple name search.

No-one named Forestier. Maybe Anne's daughter is married? Or maybe she uses her father's surname? Instead he searches by first name. There are several Agathas and a handful of Agatas, but only two Agathes and one Agate. Three C.V.s.

Agathe Thompson, twenty-seven, Canadian. Agathe Lendro, twenty-three, Argentinian. Agathe Jackson, American. No-one from France.

No Anne and now no Agathe.

Camille considers running a search for Anne's father.

"He managed to get himself elected treasurer of about forty different organisations. One day he emptied every one of the accounts, and no-one ever saw him again."

Anne laughed when she told him the story, but it was a strange laugh. With so little information, it would be difficult to track him down. He was a shopkeeper, but what did he sell? Where did he live? When did all this happen? Too many unknowns.

This leaves Anne's brother, Nathan. It is impossible that a researcher (what was his field? – astrophysics, something like that), who by definition has published scientific papers, would not be mentioned somewhere on the internet. Camille struggles to breathe as he waits for the search to complete.

No research scientist named Nathan Forestier, not anywhere. The closest match is Nathan Forest, a New Zealander aged seventy-three.

Camille changes tack again, he scours the travel agencies in Lyons and in Paris . . . By the time he finally runs a trace on Anne's landline number, the tingling between his shoulder blades has stopped. He already knows what he will find. It is a foregone conclusion.

The number is unlisted, he has to circumvent the system, it is time-consuming but not particularly difficult.

The landline is leased to Maryse Roman, 26, rue de la Fontaine-au-roi. In other words, Anne's apartment belongs to her next-door neighbour and everything is in her name, probably because everything belongs to her: the telephone line, the furniture, even the bookcase with its improbable selection of books.

Anne is renting a furnished apartment.

Camille could make further inquiries, he could send a team of officers round, but there is no point. Nothing there belongs to the phantom he knows as Anne Forestier.

Though he considers this fact from every angle, he comes to the same conclusion. Anne Forestier does not exist.

So who is this person Hafner is trying to kill?

Anne sets down her mobile on the tiled floor, she has to crawl, slowly and painfully, using her elbows, longing to be somehow invisible. A grand tour of the living room. Finally she reaches the little sideboard on which Camille left the scrap of paper with the code. The alarm itself is next to the main door.

29091571

As the alarm howls, Anne claps her hands over her ears

and drops to her knees, as though the ear-splitting shriek is a continuation of the murderous attack by other means. She can feel it drilling into her skull.

Where is he? Though everything in her resists, she slowly gets to her feet and peers around the doorframe. No-one. She tries taking away her hands, but the alarm is so deafening she cannot focus, cannot think. Palms pressed to her ears, she crawls towards the window.

Is he gone? Anne's throat is still tight with panic. It cannot be this easy. He cannot have run off. Not just like that.

Camille barely registers Louis' presence when he pops his head round the door of the office – he tried knocking but there was no response.

"Pereira is on his way up . . ."

Camille has still not quite emerged from his daze. To get to the bottom of this will take time, it will take rigorous, rational, dispassionate logic – it will take a whole host of qualities Camille sorely lacks.

"Sorry?"

Louis repeats what he said. "Fine,'" Camille mutters and gets up. He grabs his jacket.

"Are you O.K. ?" Louis says.

Camille is not listening. He digs out his mobile and sees he has a message. Anne called. Quickly, he punches the keypad and calls his voicemail. "Camille, he's here! Call me back, please . . ." By the time he has heard these words, he is already at the door, he pushes past Louis, races along the corridor, hurtles down the stairs, crashing into a woman on the landing below and almost knocking her over. It is Commissaire Michard. She and Juge Pereira were on their way to meet him. When the magistrate opens his mouth to speak, Camille does not pause even for a millisecond, but as he tears down the stairs, he calls back:

"Later, I'll explain everything later."

"Verhœven!" bellows Commissaire Michard.

But Camille has already left the building. Outside, he scrabbles to open his car, slams the door, throws the vehicle into reverse, rolls down the window and reaches out to stick the police light on the roof. Lights flashing, sirens blaring, headlights on full beam, he roars out of the car park. A beat cop blows his whistle, bringing traffic to a standstill so he can pass.

Camille takes the bus lane. He redials Anne's number, puts the call on speakerphone.

Pick up the phone, Anne.

Pick up the phone!

Anne gets to her feet again. She waits. She cannot understand this absence. It could be a ruse, but the seconds tick past and still nothing happens. The alarm stops, giving way to a throbbing silence.

Anne takes another step towards the window, standing to one side, half hidden, ready to retreat. He cannot simply have run away like that. So swiftly. So suddenly.

At that moment, he materialises right in front of her.

Anne shrinks back in terror.

They are less than two metres apart, on either side of the plate-glass window.

He has no weapons, he stares into her eyes and takes a step forward. If he reached out, he could touch the glass. He smiles and nods his head. Unable to tear her eyes from his, Anne takes a step back. He holds his hands palms out, like Jesus in a painting Camille once showed her. Still gazing into her eyes, he raises his hands above his head and slowly turns around as though she has a gun trained on him.

See? I'm not armed.

And as he comes to face her again, his hands are outstretched in welcome.

Anne cannot move. Like a rabbit sitting in headlights, paralysed with fear, waiting for death.

His eyes still fixed on hers, he takes a step, then another, slowly moving towards the sliding door. Gently, he grasps the handle, he seems anxious not to panic her. And it seems to be working: still Anne does not move, she stares at him, her breathing ragged, her heart pounding, each beat heavy, muffled, painful. The man stops, his smile a rictus, he is waiting.

We might as well get this over with, thinks Anne, we've almost reached the end of the road.

She looks down at the terrace outside the window and notices that he has thrown his leather jacket on the ground. The butt of his pistol is clearly visible and the gleaming handle of a hunting knife sticking out of the other pocket. The man puts his hands into his pockets and turns them inside out.

See? Nothing in my hands, nothing in my pockets.

Just two steps. She has already taken so many. The man does not move a muscle.

She comes to her decision suddenly, as though hurling herself into the flames. One step forward, the splints make it difficult for her fingers to release the latch, especially as she can barely grip it.

The moment the latch slides back, the moment the door is open and he has only to step through, Anne scuttles back, clapping a hand over her mouth, as though suddenly realising what she has just done.

She lets her arms fall limply to her sides. The man steps into the room. In the end, she cannot contain herself.

"Bastard!" she shrieks. "Bastard, bastard, bastard . . ."

Slowly edging backwards, she unleashes a torrent of insults mingled with sobs that come from deep within her belly, *bastard, bastard . . .*

"Oh, dear, oh dear . . ."

He clearly finds this tedious. He steps further into the studio, looking around curiously like a visitor or an estate agent – the mezzanine is a nice touch, and there is a lot of light . . . Panting for breath, Anne is cowering next to the stairs.

"All better now?" the man says, finally turning to her. "Feeling a bit calmer?"

"Why are you trying to kill me?" Anne wails.

"What the . . . what on earth makes you think I'm trying to kill you?"

He sounds genuinely upset, almost outraged.

Anne's hand falls away from her mouth and in a sudden frenzy, all her rage, all her fear comes pouring out, her voice is high and shrill, she has lost all self-control, she feels nothing now but pure hatred. But she is still afraid, afraid that he will beat her, she shrinks back . . .

"You're trying to kill me!"

The man sighs . . . This whole situation is tiresome. He listens wearily as Anne rages on.

"That wasn't part of the plan!"

This time he nods his head, disappointed in the face of such naivety.

"Oh, but it was."

Clearly, she needs to have everything spelled out for her. But Anne has not finished.

"No, it wasn't! You were only supposed to push me aside! That's what you said, 'I'll just give you a little push'!"

"But . . ." He is dumbfounded to find he has to explain something so basic. "But it needed to be convincing. Don't you get it? Con-vin-cing!"

"You've been stalking me!"

"Well, yeah, but bear in mind it's all in a good cause . . ."

He laughs, which further fuels Anne's rage.

"That's not what we agreed, you fucking bastard!"

"O.K., so there are a couple of details I didn't fill you in on . . . And don't call me a bastard or I'll give you a fucking slap."

"Right from the start you've been planning to kill me."

This time, he snaps.

"To kill you?" he growls, "No, no, no, darling. Because if I really wanted to kill you, you wouldn't be here to bitch about it now. [He raises his index finger to emphasise the point.] With you, I was just trying to make an impression, there's a difference! And let me tell you it's a lot harder than you think. Even that little performance at the hospital where I had to scare that runty little boyfriend of yours without him calling in an armed response unit took restraint, it took talent."

The argument hits home. Anne is beside herself.

"You ruined my face! You smashed my teeth! You . . ."

"O.K., I'll admit you're no oil painting right now. [He struggles to suppress a smile.] But it can be fixed, plastic surgeons these days can work miracles. Tell you what, I'll pay for two gold teeth out of my share if I hit the jackpot. Or silver if you prefer. You choose. But if you're hoping to find a husband, for the front teeth I'd recommend gold, it's classier . . ."

Slumped on the floor, curled into a ball, Anne has no more tears, only hatred.

"I'll kill you one of these days . . ."

"So, not bitter, then . . ." The man laughs, wandering around the room as though he owns the place. "But you're only saying that because you're angry. No, no, no . . ." he says, his tone deadly serious now. "If all goes well, you'll have your stitches removed, you'll have a couple of plastic teeth fitted and you'll go home like a good little girl."

He stops and looks up at the staircase, the mezzanine.

"It's not bad, this place. I like what he's done with it. [He looks at his watch.] Right, you'll have to excuse me, but I can't hang around."

He steps towards her and she presses herself against the wall.

"I'm not going to touch you!"

"Get the fuck out!" she shrieks.

The man nods, but he is distracted by something else. Standing at the foot of the stairs he looks down at the shattered step, then back at the bullet hole in the window.

"Pretty good, don't you think?" He turns back to Anne, eager to persuade her.

"Get out . . . !"

"Yeah, you're right. [He glances around. Satisfied.] I think we've put in a good day's work. We make a good team, don't we? And now [he gestures to the bullet holes around the room], everything should go smoothly, unless I'm very much mistaken."

He strides over to the windows.

"I have to say, the neighbours aren't exactly fearless! That alarm could have gone on all day and no-one would come over to see what was up. Still, it's hardly surprising. It's the same everywhere these days. Right, better run . . ."

He steps out onto the terrace, picks up his jacket, slips a hand into one of the pockets and comes back.

"There," he says, tossing an envelope towards Anne. "You use this only if everything goes according to plan. And you better hope for your sake that it does. Whatever happens, you don't leave here without my permission, understood? Because otherwise, what you've suffered so far will just be a down payment."

He does not wait for an answer. He disappears.

A few metres from where she is sitting, Anne's mobile starts to ring, vibrating against the tiled floor. After the piercing howl of the alarm, it sounds tinny, like a child's toy telephone.

It is Camille. She has to answer.

"Do exactly what I tell you and everything will be fine."

Anne presses the answer button. She does not need to pretend to be devastated.

"He's gone . . ." she says.

"Anne?" Camille roars. "I can't hear what you're saying. Anne?"

Camille is panicked, his voice is colourless.

"He came to the house," Anne says, "I set off the alarm, he panicked and ran off . . ."

Camille can barely hear her. He turns off his siren.

"Are you alright? I'm on my way there now, just tell me you're alright . . ."

"I'm O.K., Camille," she speaks a little louder. "Everything's fine now."

Camille slows the car, takes a breath. His terror gives way to agitation. He wants to be there now.

"What exactly happened? Tell me everything . . ."

Cradling her knees with her arms, Anne starts to sob.

She wishes she were dead.

10.30 a.m.

Camille feels a little calmer, having turned off the siren. He turns it on again now. There are so many elements of the case to consider, but his mind is still a jumble of emotions and he is incapable of ordering his thoughts . . .

For the past two days, he has been inching forward on a rickety plank with an abyss on either side. Now Anne has dug another chasm right beneath his feet.

Despite the fact that his career is at stake, that three times in the past two days someone has attempted to kill the woman in his life, that this woman he is involved with has been living under a false name, that he no longer knows exactly what her role is in this case, Camille needs to think strategically, to think logically, but his mind is consumed by a single thought that trumps all others: what is Anne doing in his life?

In fact, he has not one question, but two: if it turns out that Anne is not Anne, what does that change?

He goes back over the time they have spent together, the evenings spent finding each other, hardly daring to touch, and the nights they spent between the sheets . . . In August, she dumps him and an hour later he finds her still outside in the stairwell – was this simply a ploy on her part? A clever ruse? The whispered words, the tender embraces, the hours, the days, was it all just deliberate manipulation?

In a few minutes, he will find himself face to face with a woman who calls herself Anne Forestier, a woman he has been sleeping with for months, a woman who has been lying to him since the day they met. He does not know what to think, he is completely drained, put through a wringer.

What is the connection between Anne's false identity and the robbery at the Galerie?

And what exactly is his role in this story?

But the most important thing is that someone is trying to kill this woman.

He no longer knows who she is, but he knows one thing It is his responsibility to protect her.

When he walks into the studio, Anne is still sitting on the floor, her back against the sink, her arms wrapped around her knees.

In all the confusion, Camille had forgotten what she looks like now. On the long drive here, it was the other Anne he was picturing, the pretty, smiling Anne he fell for, with her green eyes and her dimples. Seeing her mutilated face, the yellow bruises, the bandages, the grubby splints, he is shocked – almost as shocked as he was two days ago when he saw her in the casualty department.

Overcome by a wave of compassion, he feels himself founder. Anne does not move, does not look at him, she is staring into the middle distance as though hypnotised.

"Are you alright, darling?" Camille creeps towards her as if attempting to tame an animal. He kneels and clumsily takes her in his arms – not easy given his size. He touches her chin and turns her face towards his. She stares at him as though only now registering his presence.

"Oh, Camille . . ."

She lays her head in the hollow of his shoulder.

The world could end right now.

But the world is not destined to end just yet.

"Tell me."

Anne looks left, then right, it is difficult to tell if she is distraught or if she simply does not know where to begin.

"Was he alone? Was the whole gang here?"

"No, just him . . ."

Her voice is low and resonant.

"Hafner? The man you identified from the photo array?"

Anne simply nods. Yes, it was him.

"Tell me what happened."

As Anne struggles to describe the events (her words come in halting, ragged fragments, never complete sentences), Camille pieces together the scene. The first shot. He turns towards the shards of glass strewn across the floor where the coffee table was, the splintered cherrywood that looks as though it came through a tornado. As he listens, he gets to his feet and walks over to the window, the bullet hole is too high for him to reach, he visualises the trajectory.

"Go on . . ." he says.

He moves to the wall, then back to the cast-iron stove, lays a finger on the spot where the bullet ricocheted then scans the back wall and sees the gaping hole. He walks to the staircase and crouches there for some time, one hand resting on the splintered fragments of the first step, glances thoughtfully towards the top of the stairs, then turns back to the spot from which the shot was fired. He stands on the second stair.

"What happened next?" he says, stepping down.

He walks into the bathroom; from here, Anne's voice is faint, barely audible. Camille continues his reconstruction; this may be his house, but just now it is a crime scene. Conjecture, observation, conclusion.

The window is half open. Anne comes into the room, Hafner is waiting, he pushes his arm through the gap and aims the pistol fitted with a silencer. Camille finds the bullet lodged in the doorframe above his head. He goes back into the living room.

Anne has fallen silent.

Camille fetches a broom from under the stairs and quickly sweeps the remains of the coffee table against the wall, dusts off the sofa, then goes to boil some water.

"Come on . . ." he says at length. "It's over now . . ."

Anne huddles next to him on the sofa and they sip something Camille insists is tea – it tastes horrid, but Anne does not complain.

"I'll take you somewhere else."

Anne shakes her head.

"Why not?"

It little matters why, Anne flatly refuses to leave though the folly of her decision is evidenced by the ruined coffee table, the bullet holes in the window, the door, the staircase, by every object in this room.

"I think th—"

"No," Anne cuts him off.

This settles the matter. Camille decides that if Hafner did not manage to gain access to the house, he is unlikely to try again today. There will be time to think again tomorrow. Over the past three days, whole years have elapsed so tomorrow seems very far away.

Besides, Camille has finally decided on his next move.

It has taken him a little time, just as long as a boxer might need to scrape himself up off the canvas and get back into the fight.

Camille is almost there.

He needs an hour or two. Maybe a little longer. In the meantime, he will lock up the house, check all the exits and leave Anne here.

They sit together in silence, their thoughts interrupted only by the vibrations from Camille's mobile which rings constantly. He does not need to check, he knows who is calling.

It feels strange to sit here holding this unknown woman he knows so well. He knows he should ask questions, but that can wait until after. First he needs to unravel the thread.

Camille feels suddenly exhausted. Lulled by the leaden sky, the shadowy forest, this squat, slow house transformed into a blockhouse, cradling this mystery to his chest, he could sleep all day if he allowed himself. Instead, he listens to Anne, her ragged breathing, to the soft gulp as she drains her tea, to the heavy silence that has come between them.

"Are you going to find him?" Anne whispers after a moment.

"Oh yes."

The answer comes immediately, instinctively; Camille sounds so certain, so convinced, that even Anne is surprised.

"You will let me know as soon as you find him, won't you?"

To Camille, the subtext to Anne's every question could be a whole novel. He frowns quizzically: why?

"I just need to feel safe, you can understand that, can't you?"

Her voice is no longer a whisper, her hand falls away from her mouth and he can see her gums, her broken teeth.

"Of course . . ."

He almost apologises.

Finally, their separate silences merge. Anne has dozed off. Camille can find no words. If he had a pencil, in a few strokes he could sketch their twin solitudes; they are each coming to the end of a story, they are together yet alone. Curiously, Camille has never felt closer to her, a mysterious solidarity binds him to this woman. Gently, he withdraws his arm, lays Anne's head against the back of the sofa and gets to his feet.

Time to go. Time to find out the real story.

He creeps up the stairs like a hunter tracking prey, he moves soundlessly, being intimately familiar with every stair, every creaking board, and besides, he does not weigh much.

The roof upstairs slopes steeply, at its lowest point the room is only a metre or so high. Camille lays down on the floor and crawls to the far side of the bed to a trapdoor that swings open to provide access to the narrow crawlspace. The cubbyhole is filthy with dust and cobwebs. Camille reaches inside and gropes around, finds the plastic bag and pulls it towards him. A black bin-liner containing a thick folder. A file he has not opened since . . .

He cannot help but see that everything about this case has forced him to confront his greatest fears.

He looks around, finds a pillowcase and carefully slips the file inside. With every little movement, the film of dust creates clouds of ash. Camille gets up and steals back downstairs.

Some minutes later, he is writing a note to Anne.

"Get some rest. Call anytime. I'll be back as soon as I can be."

I'll keep you safe – no, this is something he cannot bring himself to write.

When he is finished, he makes a tour of the house, checking all the door handles, ensuring everything is locked. Before he leaves, he stands and stares at the sleeping form of Anne on the sofa. It pains him to think of leaving her alone. It is difficult to leave, but impossible to stay.

Time to go. Carrying the thick folder in the striped pillowcase under one arm, Camille crosses the yard and heads through the forest to where he parked the car.

He stops and looks back. From here, surrounded by the forest, the silent house looks as though it is built on a plinth like a casket or a still-life painting, a *vanitas*. He thinks of Anne asleep inside.

But by the time his car slowly moves away into the forest, Anne's eyes are wide open.

11.30 a.m.

As the car speeds towards Paris, Camille's mental landscape becomes simplified. He may not know what happened, but he knows the questions to ask.

The key thing now is to ask the right questions.

In the course of an armed robbery, a killer assaults a woman who calls herself Anne Forestier. He hunts her down, he is determined to kill her, he tracks her all the way to Camille's isolated studio.

What is the link between the robbery and the fact of Anne's false identity?

Everything would suggest that the woman was simply in the wrong place at the wrong time, having come to collect a watch being engraved for Camille, but though they seem utterly unrelated, the two events are connected. Intimately connected.

Are there any two things that are not connected?

Camille has not been able to find out the truth from Anne, he does not even know who she really is. So now he must look elsewhere. At the other end of the thread.

Three missed calls from Louis who, typically, has not left a voicemail. Instead he sent a text message: "Need help?" Some day, when this is all over, Camille plans to adopt Louis.

Three voicemails from Le Guen. In fact, the message is the same, only the tone changes. With every call, Jean's voice is calmer, his message shorter and more circumspect. "Listen, I really need you to call me b—" *Message deleted.* "Um . . . why haven't you ca—" *Message deleted.* In the third message, Le Guen sounds grim. In fact, he is simply sad. "If you don't help me, I can't help you." *Message deleted.*

Camille empties his mind of every obstacle and pursues his train of thought. He needs to stay focused.

Everything has become more complicated.

He has had to radically rethink the situation after the mayhem at the studio. The damage caused is undeniably dramatic, but though he is not a ballistics expert, Camille cannot help but wonder.

Anne is behind a picture window twenty metres wide. Outside, there is a skilled, determined, heavily armed killer. It is not impossible that missing Anne was sheer misfortune. But failing to put a bullet in her head when he had his arm thrust through an open window and was less than six metres away is suspicious. It is as though, since the Galerie Monier, he has been cursed. Unless this has all been carefully planned from the start. Such a spectacular run of bad luck is scarcely credible . . .

In fact, one might think that to avoid killing Anne, given the number of opportunities there have been, would take an exceptional marksman. Camille has not known many people equal to such a task.

This question inevitably prompts others.

How did he track Anne down to the studio in Montfort?

Last night, Camille drove this same route from Paris. Anne, exhausted, fell asleep almost immediately and did not wake until they arrived.

There is a lot of traffic on the motorway and on the Périphérique even at night, but Camille stopped the car twice and waited for several minutes, watching the traffic, and took a roundabout route on the last leg of the journey, along byroads where the headlights of another would have been visible from a considerable distance.

He has a chilling sense of *déjà vu*: by launching a raid on the Serbian community, he led the killers straight to Ravic; now he has led them to Anne in Montfort.

This is the most plausible hypothesis. It is obviously the one he is supposed to accept. But now that he knows that Anne is not Anne, that everything he assumed about the case until now is in doubt, the most plausible theories become the least likely.

Camille is certain that he was not followed. Which means that someone came looking for Anne in Montfort because they knew she would be there.

He needs to come up with a different theory. And this time, the possibilities are limited.

Each solution is a name, the name of someone close to Camille, someone close enough to know about his mother's studio. To know that he is in a relationship with the woman who was brutally beaten during the raid on the jeweller's.

To know that he was planning to take her there for safety.

Camille racks his brain, but try as he might he can barely come up with a handful of names. If he excludes Armand, who he watched go up in smoke two days ago, the short list is very short indeed.

And it does not include Vincent Hafner, a man he has never met in his life.

The only possible conclusion sends Camille into a tailspin.

He already knows that Anne is not Anne. Now he is convinced that Hafner is not Hafner.

It means starting the investigation over.

It means: back to square one.

And given everything that Camille has done so far, it may mean: *Go to jail. Go directly to jail. Do not pass Go . . .*

There he goes again, the runty little cop, making the trip between Paris and his country estate, like a hamster in a wheel. Like a rat. Always scuttling around. I just hope it pays off. Not for him, obviously, at this point he's up shit creek, he's well and truly screwed as he'll find out very soon. No, I hope it pays off for me.

I'm not about to give up now.

The girl has done what she needed to, you might reckon she paid her pound of flesh, I can't complain. It's going to be a close-run thing, but right now everything seems to be going like clockwork.

Now it's my move. My good friend Ravic and I did a perfect dummy run. If the guy were still alive, he'd testify to that, though with all those missing fingers, he'd have a job swearing on the Bible.

Thinking back, I went easy on him, in fact I think I was pretty lenient. Putting a bullet in his head was almost an act of kindness. I swear, the Serbs are like the Turks, they're a thankless bunch. It's their culture. They have no sense of gratitude. And then they come bitching about how they've got problems.

But it's time to get down to some serious business. I know that wherever he is – I don't know if there's a heaven for Serbian thugs, after all there's definitely one for terrorists – Ravic will be happy. He'll have his revenge served *post mortem* because I have a powerful urge to flay someone alive. I'm going to need a bit of luck. But since I haven't had to call on her so far, I figure the goddess Fortuna owes me a favour.

And if Verhœven does his job, things should move pretty fast.

Right now, I'm heading back to my fortress of solitude to rest up a bit, because when this kicks off, I'm going to have to move fast.

My reflexes might be a little blunted, but my motivation is intact, and that's what counts.

12.00 noon

In the bathroom mirror, Anne examines her gums, stares at the ugly, gaping hole. Since she was admitted to hospital under a false name, she will not be able to access her medical file – the X-rays, the test results – she will have to start over. Start again from scratch – though the word hardly does justice to her injuries.

He says he wasn't trying to kill her because he needs her. But he can say what he likes, she does not believe a word. Dead or alive, Anne would have served her purpose. He beat her so brutally, so savagely . . . He might claim that it had to look authentic, but she knows that he actually enjoyed beating her, that he would have done more damage if he could have.

In the medicine cabinet, she finds nails scissors and a pair of tweezers. The young Indian doctor assured her that the gash on her cheek was not deep. He suggested removing the stitches after ten days. She wants to do it now. In one of the drawers in Camille's desk she finds a magnifying glass. Working with makeshift instruments in a dimly lit bathroom is not ideal. But she cannot bear to wait any longer. And this is not simply about her obsession with neatness. This is what she used to say to Camille when they were together, that she was a neat freak. Not this time. Contrary to what he might think when all this is over, she did not tell him many lies. The bare minimum. Because it is difficult to lie to Camille. Or because it is too easy. It amounts to the same thing.

Anne wipes her eyes with her sleeve. It is hard enough to remove the sutures by herself; with tears in her eyes, it is impossible . . . There are eleven stitches. She holds the magnifying glass in her left hand and the scissors in her right. Close up, the little black threads look like insects. She slides the tip of the scissors under the first knot and immediately she feels a sharp pain as though she has stabbed herself. Under normal circumstances, the procedure would be painless, obviously the wound is not yet healed. Or perhaps it is infected. She has to slide the blade quite far to cut the stitch, she screws up her face and goes for it. The first insect is dead, now all she has to do is pull it out. Her hands are trembling. Still trapped beneath her skin, she has to tug with the tweezers, struggling to keep her hands from shaking. Finally it begins to move, leaving an ugly mark as it emerges. Anne peers at the wound but can see no difference. She is about to start on the next suture, but she feels so tense, so unsteady, that she has to sit down and take a breath . . .

Coming back to the mirror, she presses on the gash and winces, she snips the second suture, and the third. She pulls them out too quickly. Looking through the magnifying glass, the wound is still red, it has not closed up. The fourth stitch is more troublesome, it feels almost welded to her skin. But Anne is determined. She grits her teeth, digs the tip of the scissors into her flesh, tries to cut the thread and fails, the wound gapes and oozes a little blood. Finally the thread snaps, but great drops as big as tears are now trickling from the cut. She deals with the next few sutures quickly, sliding them out and flicking the corpses into the sink, but for the last few Anne has to work blindly because as she wipes away the blood, more gushes to the surface. She does not stop until all the stitches have been removed. Still the blood flows. Without thinking, she rummages in the medicine cabinet for the bottle of surgical spirit and, having no compress, pours some onto her palm and dabs it on.

The pain is excruciating . . . Anne howls and pounds her fist on the washbasin, the splints on her fingers come loose making her scream even louder. But this scream is hers and hers alone, no-one has ripped it from her body.

She dabs more alcohol directly onto the wound, then grips the sink with both hands, she feels as though she might pass out, but she stands firm. When the pain finally subsides, she finds a compress, soaks it in surgical spirit and applies it against her cheek. When finally she looks, the bandage does little to hide the ugly, swollen gash which is still bleeding a little.

There will be a scar. A straight line slashed across her cheek. On a man, people would call it a "war wound". She cannot tell how big the scar will be, but she knows it will never go away.

It is permanent.

And if she had to dig out the wound with a knife she would have done it. Because this is something that she wants to remember. For ever.

12.30 p.m.

The car park at the casualty department is always full. This time, Camille has to flash his warrant card just to get in.

The receptionist is blooming like a rose. A slightly wilted rose, but she lays the concern on thick.

"So, I hear she disappeared?"

She makes a sad pout, as though she understands how difficult this is for Verhœven – *what happened, it must have come as a shock, it doesn't say much for the police, does it?* Camille walks on, desperate to be rid of her, but this is not as easy as he might have expected.

"What about that admission form?"

He retraces his steps.

"I mean, it's not really my department, but when a patient does a runner and we don't even have a social security number, there's ructions upstairs. And the big shots are quick to pass the buck, they don't care who's responsible, they come down on us like a ton of bricks. It's happened to me often enough, that's the only reason I'm asking."

Camille nods – I get the picture – as though he sympathises while the receptionist fields a series of telephone calls. Obviously, since Anne was admitted under a false name, she could not have produced a social security number. This is why he found no papers in her apartment. She has no papers, or none under that name.

Suddenly he feels the urgent need to call, for no reason, as though he is afraid he cannot handle the situation without her, without Anne . . .

And once again he remembers that she is not Anne. Everything that name once signified is meaningless. Camille feels distraught, he has lost everything, even her name.

"You O.K. ?"

"Yes, I'm fine," Camille tries to look preoccupied, it is the best thing to do when you need to throw someone off the scent.

"Her file, her medical file," he says, "where is it?"

Anne disappeared the night before, so all the paperwork is still up on the ward.

Camille thanks the receptionist. When he gets upstairs, he realises he has no idea how to play this, so he takes a moment to think. He stands at one end of the corridor, next to the waiting room that is now a junk room where he and Louis did their first debriefing on the case. He watches as the handle slowly turns and the door reluctantly opens as though a child is afraid to come out.

When he appears, the child turns out to be close to retirement: it is Hubert Dainville, the consultant, the big boss. His grey mane is perfectly blow-dried, it looks as though he has only just removed his curlers. He flushes scarlet when he sees Camille. Usually, there is no-one in the junk room, it has no purpose and leads nowhere.

"What the devil are you doing there?" he snaps officiously, ready to bite.

I could ask the same of you. The retort is on the tip of Camille's tongue, but he knows that is not the way to go about things. He looks around distractedly.

"I'm lost . . . [Then, resigned:] I must have taken the wrong corridor."

The surgeon's blush has faded to pale pink, his awkwardness forgotten, his personality reasserts itself. He strides off as though he has just been summoned to an urgent case.

"You no longer have any business here, *commandant*."

Camille trots after him, having been caught off-guard, his brain is whirring feverishly.

"Your witness absconded from this hospital last night!" Dainville growls as though he blames Verhœven personally.

"So I heard."

Camille can think of no other solution, he thrusts a hand into his pocket, takes out his mobile and drops it. It clatters across the tiled floor.

"Shit!"

Dainville, who has already reached the lifts, turns and sees the *commandant*, his back towards him, scrabbling to pick up the pieces of his mobile. Stupid prick. The lift doors open; Dainville steps inside.

Camille gathers up his mobile, which is actually in one piece, and pretends to put it back together it as he walks back towards the junk room.

Seconds pass. A minute. He cannot bring himself to open the door, something is holding him back. Another few seconds tick by. He must have been mistaken. He waits. Nothing. Oh, well. He is about to turn on his heel, but changes his mind.

The handle turns again, and this time the door is briskly opened.

The woman who bustles out, pretending to be preoccupied, is Florence, the nurse. Now it is her turn to blush as she sees Camille. Her plump lips form a perfect O, he hesitates for a second and by then it is too late to create a diversion. Her embarrassment is clear as she pushes a stray lock of hair behind her ear and, staring at Camille, she closes the door calmly, deliberately – *I'm a busy woman, I'm focused on my job, I have nothing to feel guilty about.* Nobody believes her little performance, not even Florence herself. Camille does not have to press his advantage, it is not really in his nature . . . He hates himself for doing it, but he must. He stares at Florence, tilts his head quizzically, increasing the pressure – *I didn't want to interrupt you during your little tryst, see how tactful I am?* He pretends he has just been standing here fixing his mobile, waiting for her to conclude her *tête-à-tête* with Dr Dainville.

"I need Madame Forestier's medical file," he says.

Florence walks ahead of him, but makes no attempt to lengthen her stride as Dr Dainville did so blatantly. She is not mistrustful. And there is not an spiteful bone in her body.

"I'm not sure . . ." she says.

Camille squeezes his eyes shut, silently imploring her not to make him say it: *maybe I should have word with Dr Dainville, I suspect he . . .*

They have come to the nurses' station

"I'm not sure . . . if the file is still here."

Not once does she turn to look at him, she pulls opens a drawer of patient files and promptly takes out one marked "FORESTIER", a large manila folder containing the C.A.T. scan, the X-rays, the doctor's notes. To hand this over to someone, even a policeman, is a serious breach of nursing protocol . . .

"I'll bring over the warrant from the *juge d'instruction* this afternoon," Camille says. "In the meantime, I can issue a receipt."

"That won't be necessary," she says hurriedly, "I mean, as long as the *juge* . . ."

Camille takes the file. Thank you. They look at each other. Camille feels an almost physical pain, not simply because he has resorted to such an ignoble ploy, extorting information to which he has no right, but because he understands this woman. He knows that her botoxed lips are not an attempt to remain young, but stem from an overpowering need to be loved.

1.00 p.m.

You go through the wrought-iron gates, along the long path. The imposing pink building rises up before you, tall trees tower above your head. You might be forgiven for thinking you have arrived at a mansion; it is difficult to believe that behind the graceful windows, bodies are lined up and dissected. Here, livers and hearts are weighed, skulls are sawn open. Camille knows this building like the back of his hand and cordially loathes it. It is the people he likes, the staff, the assistants, the pathologists, Nguyên above all. The many shared memories, most of them painful, have created a bond between them.

Camille makes his usual entrance, waving to this person or

that. He can tell there is a certain chill in the air, that rumours about the case have preceded him, it is obvious from the awkward smiles, the diffident handshakes.

Nguyên, inscrutable as a sphinx as always. He is not much taller than Camille, thin as a rail and last smiled in 1984. He shakes Camille's hand, listens attentively, takes Anne's medical file and reads it. Guardedly.

"Just a quick once-over," Camille says, "in your spare time."

In this context, "Just a quick once-over" means: *I need your advice, something doesn't feel right, I want your honest opinion, I won't say any more because I don't want to influence your opinion, oh, and if you could do it a.s.a.p.*

"In your spare time" means: *this is not official, it's personal* – implying that the rumours that Verhœven is up shit creek are true. Nguyên nods, he has never been able to refuse Camille. Besides, he is not in any trouble and cannot resist a mystery, he has a nose for inconsistencies, an eye for detail – he is a pathologist.

"Give me a call around five o'clock," Nguyên says and locks the file in his desk drawer; this is personal.

1.30 p.m.

Time to head back to the office. Knowing what awaits him at the *brigade*, Camille is reluctant to go, but he has no choice.

From the way his fellow officers greet him in the hallway, it's obvious the atmosphere is fraught. At the morgue, the tension was muted; here it is palpable. As in any other office, three days is more than enough time for a rumour to circulate widely. And it is a natural law that the more vague the rumour, the more it is blown out of proportion. His colleagues' expressions of sympathy sound more like condolences.

Even if he were asked point-blank, Camille has no desire to explain himself, to anyone; besides, he would not know what to say, where to start. Luckily, only two of his team are there, the other officers are all out working on cases. Camille gives a vague wave. One of his colleagues is busy on the telephone, the other barely has time to turn around before Camille disappears into his office.

Minutes later, Louis appears and, without bothering to knock, steps into the *commandant*'s office. The two men look at each other.

"A lot of people are looking for you . . ."

Camille looks down at his desk. An order to appear before Commissaire Michard.

"I can see that . . ."

The meeting is scheduled for 7.30 p.m. In the meeting room. Neutral territory. The memo does not state who else will be in attendance. It is an unusual request. An officer suspected of misconduct is not generally summoned to explain himself, since this would be tantamount to acknowledging that his actions might warrant investigation by the I.G.S. This means that it does not matter who will be there, it means that Michard has got tangible evidence of misconduct that Camille no longer has time to neutralise.

He does not try to anticipate what might happen. It is not exactly pressing. 7.30 seems a thousand years away.

He hangs up his coat, slips a hand into one of the pockets and extracts a plastic bag which he handles as delicately as if it were nitroglycerine, careful not to touch the contents with his bare fingers. He sets the mug down on his desk. Louis walks over and, bending down, reads the inscription in a low voice: Мой дядя самых честных правил . . .

"It's the first line of 'Eugene Onegin', isn't it?"

For once, Camille knows the answer. Yes. The mug belonged to Irène. He does not say this to Louis.

"I need you to have it dusted for prints. Quickly."

Louis nods and re-seals the plastic bag.

"On the docket, I could say it's evidence in . . . the Pergolin case?"

Claude Pergolin, the transvestite found strangled in his own home.

"That sort of thing."

It is increasingly difficult for him to carry on without explaining the situation to Louis, but Camille is reluctant, partly because it is a long and complicated story, but mostly because if he knows nothing, Louis cannot be accused of misconduct.

"Right," Louis says. "Well, if you want these results immediately, maybe I should take advantage of the fact that Madame Lambert is still in the lab."

Madame Lambert has a little crush on Louis; like Verhœven, if she could, she would adopt him. She is a militant trade unionist committed to fighting mandatory retirement at sixty. Madame Lambert is sixty-eight, and every year she finds some new ruse to carry on working. She will carry on the struggle for another thirty years unless someone defenestrates her.

Despite the urgency of the job, Louis has not moved. Holding the plastic evidence bag, he stands in the doorway brooding, like a young man steeling himself to propose.

"I think I may have missed a few episodes . . ."

"Don't worry," Camille smiles. "So did I . . ."

"You decided to keep me out of the loop . . . [Louis raises his hand in submission.] That's not a criticism."

"Oh, but it is a criticism, Louis. And you're bloody right to point it out. But right now . . ."

"It's too late?"

"Exactly."

"Too late for criticism or too late for explanations?"

"Worse than that, Louis. It's too late for anything. Too late to understand, to react, to explain . . . And probably too late for me to emerge with my honour intact. It's pretty grim."

Louis nods towards the ceiling, towards the powers that be.

"Not everyone seems to have my long-suffering patience."

"I promise you, Louis, you'll get the scoop," Camille says. "I owe you that at least. And if everything goes according to plan, I might have a little surprise for you up my sleeve. The greatest honour any serving officer can dream of: the chance to shine in front of your superiors."

"'Honour is . . .'"

"Oh, come on, Louis! Give me a quote!"

Louis smiles.

"No, don't tell me, let me guess," Camille says. "Saint-John Perse! Or even better, Noam Chomsky!"

Louis turns to leave.

"Oh, by the way . . ." He turns back. "I'm not sure, but I think there's a message for you under your desk blotter."

Yeah, right.

A Post-it note bearing the unmistakable scrawl of Jean Le Guen: "Bastille *métro* station, rue de la Roquette exit, 3.00 p.m.", which is much more than simply a meeting.

When the *contrôleur général* feels obliged to leave an anonymous message under a desk blotter rather than calling him on his mobile, it is a bad sign. Le Guen is unambiguously saying: I'm being careful. He is also saying: As your friend, I care about you enough to take the risk, but meeting with you could put an end to my career, so let's try and be discreet.

Given his height, Camille is well used to being shunned, sometimes he only has to take the *métro* . . . But finding himself under suspicion by his own colleagues – though hardly a surprise, given everything that has happened in the past three days – comes as a bitter blow.

2.00 p.m.

Fernand is a decent guy. He may be a fuckwit, but he's biddable. The restaurant was closed, but he opened up again just for me. I'm hungry, so he whips up an omelette with some wild mushrooms. He's a good cook. He should have stayed in the kitchen, but what can you do, a little guy always dreams of being the big boss. Now he's up to his eyes in debt, and for what? For the pleasure of being "*le patron*". Fucking moron. Not that I'm complaining; morons are very useful. Given the exorbitant interest rate I'm charging him, he owes me more money than he will ever be able to repay. For the first year and a half, I bailed out the business almost every month. I'm not sure that Fernand realises it, but his restaurant belongs to me. I can click my fingers and "*le patron*" will find himself penniless and on the streets. Not that I ever mention this to him. He is much too useful. I use him as an alibi, a mailbox, an office, a witness, a guarantor, a cash machine, I'm slowly drinking his wine cellar and he feeds me when the need arises. Last spring, when we staged Camille Verhœven's brief encounter, Fernand was perfect. In fact everyone was perfect. The scene went off without a hitch. In the nick of time, my favourite *commandant* stepped in, he got up from his dinner and did what he does best. My only worry was that someone else would try to intervene, because she's a very beautiful woman. Well, not anymore, obviously, what with the scars and the broken teeth and her face swollen up like a beach ball. If we staged the scene in the restaurant today, there wouldn't be many men rushing to rescue her, but back then she was pretty enough to make a man want to take on Fernand. Pretty, and cunning, she managed to give just the right looks to just the right person. She reeled Verhœven in without him even knowing.

The reason I'm thinking about all this is because I've got time on my hands. And because this is where it all began.

I've left my mobile on the table, but I can't help checking it every five minutes. Subject to the end results, I'm pretty happy with the way things have gone so far. I'm just hoping the pay-off is big enough, because otherwise I'm liable to get a little angry and to rip the nearest person limb from limb.

In the meantime, I savour the first breather I've had in the past three days. God knows, I deserve it.

Fundamentally, manipulation is a lot like armed robbery. It takes a lot of preparation and a skilled team to carry it off. I don't know how she managed to manipulate Verhœven into letting her leave the hospital and taking her to his little house in the country, but she pulled it off.

She probably went with the hysterical crying routine. That's always a winner with the more sensitive man.

I check my mobile.

When it rings, I'll have my answer.

Either I've done all this work for nothing, in which case we might as well all go home.

Or, I've hit the jackpot, and if that's the case, I don't know how much time I'll have. Not much, certainly, I'll need to act fast. But now I'm so close to the finish line, I have no intention of missing my prey. I ask Fernand for a glass of mineral water, this is no time to piss about.

In the medicine cabinet, Anne found some plasters. She needed to use two to cover the scar. The pain from the wound is still excruciating. But she doesn't regret removing the stitches.

Next, she picks up the envelope he tossed her, the way a keeper might throw a circus animal a hunk of meat. She can feel it burning her fingers. Carefully, she opens it.

Inside is a wad of notes – two hundred euros – a list of phone numbers for local taxi companies, a map of the area and an aerial photograph in which she can make out Camille's house, the path, the outskirts of Montfort village.

In full and final settlement.

She sets her mobile on the sofa next to her.

And waits.

3.00 p.m.

Camille is expecting Le Guen to be foaming at the mouth, instead he finds him shell-shocked. Sitting on a bench outside Bastille *métro*, he is staring at his shoes, looking utterly despondent. There is no bollocking. The only criticism sounds more like a plea.

"You could have asked for my help . . ."

Camille notes the use of the past tense. For Le Guen, some part of this case is already over.

"For an intelligent man," he goes on, "you really know how to pick them."

And he doesn't even know the half of it, Camille thinks.

"Asking for the case to be assigned to you was pretty suspicious. Because I don't believe this story you cooked up about having an informer, it's bullshit . . ."

And that's not all. Le Guen is about to find out that Camille personally helped the key witness in this case to leave the hospital and thereby to evade justice.

Camille does not even know the real identity of the witness, but if it turns out that "Anne" is guilty of a crime, he could well be charged with aiding and abetting . . . If that happens, he could be charged with anything: armed robbery, kidnapping, accessory to murder . . . And he will have a hard time convincing anyone of his innocence.

Camille swallows hard but says nothing.

"As for your dealings with the *juge*," Le Guen goes on, "you've been a bloody idiot: you went over his head, you told me as much, you set up this raid. And the dumb thing is that Pereira is the kind of guy you can talk to."

Very soon, Le Guen will find out that Camille has done much worse since: he has illegally obtained medical documents relating to the witness. A witness he has harboured in his own home.

"Your little raid yesterday has stirred up a shitstorm! You must have known it would! Do you have any idea what you're doing? You've been completely irresponsible."

The *contrôleur général* does not even know that Camille's name appears on an invoice, a crucial piece of evidence that went missing from the jeweller's, and that he gave a false name at the station. And it is too late now to do anything.

"As far as Commissaire Michard is concerned," Le Guen continues, "you manipulated her to get this case because you're trying to protect this woman."

"That's bullshit!" Camille snaps.

"I'm sure it is. But you've spent the past three days behaving like a loose cannon. So, obviously . . ."

"Obviously," Camille acknowledges.

The trains continue to disgorge crowds. Le Guen studies every woman who passes, every single one, there is nothing salacious about his gaze, he admires them all, he owes his many marriages to womankind. Camille has always been his best man.

"But what I want to know is why you're turning this investigation into a personal vendetta!"

"I think it might be the other way round, Jean. This is a personal vendetta that became an investigation."

As he articulates the thought, Camille realises just how true it is. He is plunged into turmoil, it will take some time for him to work out all the ramifications. He tries to engrave the words in his mind: a personal vendetta that became an investigation.

Le Guen is bewildered by what Camille has said.

"A personal vendetta . . . Who exactly do you know in this case?"

A good question. A few hours ago, Camille would have said Anne Forestier. But everything has changed.

"The robber," Camille says unthinkingly, his mind still struggling with what he has just realised.

Le Guen is no longer bewildered, he is panicked.

"You were *in business* with one or more of these thugs? With an armed robber who at the very least was an accomplice to murder? [His tone is concerned, in fact he is utterly hysterical.] You know this Hafner guy *personally*?"

Camille shakes his head. No. It is too complicated to explain.

"I'm not sure," Camille says evasively, "I can't explain it right now . . ."

Le Guen brings his index fingers to his lips, a sign that he is in deep thought.

"You don't really seem to understand what I'm doing here."

"Of course I understand, Jean."

"Michard is going to want to call in the public prosecutor. She's well within her rights, she has to protect herself, she can't turn a blind eye to what you've done, and I don't see how I can possibly object. The very fact that I'm telling you this means that I'm also implicated. Just being here implicates me."

"I know, Jean, and I'm grateful . . ."

"That's not why I came here, Camille! I don't give a fuck about your gratitude! You may not have the I.G.S. breathing down your neck yet, but believe me, they're coming for you. Your phone will be tapped, if it isn't already, you're probably being followed, your every move will be scrutinised . . . And from what you've just told me, Camille, it's not just your job on the line, you could be banged up!"

Le Guen falls silent for a moment, a few brief seconds in which he is hoping against hope that Camille will get a grip. Or explain himself. But he has no ace up his sleeve to force his friend to talk.

"Listen," he says, "I don't think Michard will call in the *procureur* without talking to me. She's just been promoted, she needs my support, but your fuck-up has given her some serious leverage . . . This is why I'm getting in first. I was the one who organised for you to meet with her at 7.30."

When sorrows come, they come not single spies . . . Camille stares at Le Guen questioningly.

"That will be your last chance, Camille. It will be a small, informal meeting. You tell us the whole story and we'll see about damage limitation. I can't promise it will end there. It all depends on what you tell us. So what are you planning to tell us, Camille?"

"I don't know yet, Jean."

He has an idea, but no words to explain it; first he has to set his doubts at rest. Le Guen is annoyed. In fact, he says as much.

"I'm pissed off, Camille. My friendship obviously doesn't mean much to you."

Camille lays a hand on his friend's enormous knee, he pats it as though trying to console Le Guen, to show his support.

It is the world turned upside down.

5.15. p.m.

"What do you want me to say? She was beaten up, that's all there is to it."

Over the telephone, Nguyên's voice has a nasal twang. He sounds as though he is calling from a large, high-ceilinged room, his voice reverberates, he sounds like an oracle. Which, to Camille, he is. Hence his next question:

"Was there any attempt to kill her?"

"No . . . No, I don't think so. The intention was to hurt, to punish, even to scar, but not to kill . . ."

"Are you sure about that?"

"Have you ever known a doctor to be sure about anything? All I can say is that, unless someone physically stopped him, if the guy had really wanted to, he could have burst this woman's skull like a ripe melon."

And since that did not happen, Camille thinks, he had to exercise great self-control. He had to calculate. He pictures the thug raising his shotgun and bringing the butt down on her cheekbone and her jaw, rather than her skull, easing up at the last second. This man is cool-headed.

"Same goes for the kicks," the pathologist says. "The hospital report documented eight separate blows, I found nine, but that's not the most important discrepancy. The guy is aiming to break her ribs or fracture them, he's aiming to cause damage, but given the location of the bruises and the shoes he was wearing, it would have been easy for him to kill the woman had he wanted to. With three swift kicks he could have ruptured her spleen and she would have died of internal bleeding. She could have died, but it would have been an accident: everything points to him intending to leave her alive."

As Nguyên describes it, it sounds like a warning. A sort of punishment beating intended as a show of force. Brutal enough to make the point, but not so brutal that it jeopardises the future.

If her attacker (there's no way that it was Hafner now, he's ancient history) did not intend to kill Anne (there's no way, now, that it was Anne either), this raises the question of her involvement in the robbery, which now seems not just probable, but almost certain.

But in that case, the real target is not Anne, it is Camille.

5.45 p.m.

There is nothing to do now but wait. The deadline of Camille's ultimatum to Buisson expires at 8.00 p.m., but these are just words, a mere fiction. Buisson gave his orders, he made a few telephone calls. He shook down his networks, his contacts, the fences, the middle-men, the traffickers in forged papers, all Hafner's known accomplices. He has to squander all the favours they owe him to get what he wants. He might come through in the next two hours, but it might as easily take him two days and, however long it takes, Camille will just have to wait: he has no other choice.

It is a terrible irony to know that his salvation, when it comes, if it comes, is in the hands of Buisson.

Camille's whole life depends on the success of the man who murdered his wife.

Anne, meanwhile, is sitting on the sofa in Montfort, she has not bothered to turn on the light, the forest shadows have gradually invaded the house. The only light comes from the flickering L.E.D.s on the alarm and on her mobile, as they count off the seconds. Anne sits motionless, silently rehearsing the words that she will say. She worries that she might not have the strength, but she cannot fail, it is a matter of life and death.

If it were simply a question of her own life, she would give up now.

She does not want to die, but she would accept it.

But this is the last step, and she has to succeed.

Fernand plays cards much the way he lives his life in general – scared of his own shadow. He's so terrified, he's deliberately losing to me. The dumb fuck he thinks he's humouring me. He doesn't say anything, but he's scared shitless. In less than an hour, the staff will start turning up and he'll have to sort things before the restaurant opens for dinner. The chef has already arrived – *Bonjour, patron!* – Fernand is so proud to be called *patron*, he's sold his soul for it and he still believes it was bargain.

I'm thinking about other things.

I watch as the hours roll by, I can keep it up all day and all night. I hope Verhœven lives up to his reputation, I've taken a gamble on his ability, so he'd better not disappoint me.

According to my calculations, the cut-off time is noon tomorrow.

If I haven't got what I want by then, I think the deal is dead.
In every sense of the word.

6.00 p.m.
Rue Durestier. The headquarters of Wertig & Schwindel. The ground floor is divided in two. On the right is the lobby and lifts up to the offices, on the left is a travel agency. In old buildings like this, the lobby is vast. To make the reception area seem less forbidding, the ceilings have been lowered and everywhere there are potted plants, comfy chairs, coffee tables and display stands full of colourful travel brochures.

Camille stands in the doorway. He can easily picture Anne sitting in one of those chairs, checking her watch, waiting for the moment when she can leave and be with him.

When she emerged, she was always a little flustered, always a little late and she always give an apologetic shrug – sorry, I did my best to get away – and the smile that accompanied that shrug would have made any man say: don't worry, it's fine.

Seeing a courier suddenly appear by the lifts, a motorcycle helmet tucked under his arm, Camille realises that the plan was even more cunning than he thought. Stepping forward, he sees that there is a separate entrance on the rue Lessard so that, if Anne arrived after he did, she could sneak into the lobby and come out onto the rue Durestier.

Camille would be standing there, thrilled to see her; a win-win situation.

He wanders off the boulevard and finds a table on the covered terrace of La Roseraie at the corner of the rue de Faubourg-Laffite. If he has time to kill, he might as well keep busy; when you feel your life spiralling out of control, doing nothing is a killer.

Camille checks his mobile. Nothing.

The office workers are beginning to head home. Camille sips his coffee, peering at the bustle of people over the rim of his cup, watching as they say their goodbyes, as they smile and wave or hurry towards the *métro*. People of all races, colours, creeds. He spots a boy whose face connects him to another hundred faces imprinted on Camille's memory, the self-satisfied paunch of a middle-aged man, the graceful silhouette of a young girl awkwardly holding a handbag, not because she likes it, nor because she needs it, but because a girl must have a handbag. If he observes it for too long, life pierces Camille to the core.

Then, suddenly, she appears at the corner of the rue Bleue and stops, sensibly standing back from the pedestrian crossing. She is wearing a navy-blue coat. Her face is eerily similar to the woman in Holbein's "The Artist's Family", but without the squint; it is because of this mental association that he remembers her so perfectly. He pushes open the glass door to the street as she crosses and waits by the traffic lights. She hesitates for a moment, looking at him with an expression of mingled concern and curiosity. Camille's height often has this effect on people. He is staring at her, but she goes on her way, walks past as though she has already forgotten him.

"Excuse me . . ."

She turns and looks down at him. Camille calculates she is about five foot seven.

"I'm sorry," he says. "You don't know me . . ."

She seems about to contradict him, but says nothing. Her smile is not as sad as her eyes, but it has that same pained, compassionate air.

"Madame . . . Charroi?"

"No," she says with a smile of relief, "I'm afraid you must be mistaken . . ."

But she does not move, she realises that the conversation is not yet over.

"We bumped into each other here once or twice before . . ." Camille continues, nodding towards the pedestrian crossing. If he carries on like this, he will get bogged down in protracted explanations; he decides it is easier to take out his mobile, he clicks, the woman leans down, curious to see what he is doing, to understand what it is he wants.

He had not noticed that there is a message from Louis. Concise: "Fingerprints: N.O.F."

N.O.F: not on file. Anne does not have a police record. A false lead.

One by one, the doors are closing. An hour and a half from now, the last door will slam, the one he least imagined would ever close, and with it his career.

He will be thrown off the force after a long and humiliating process. It will be up to him to decide how long it takes. He tells himself he has no choice though he knows that whether or not one chooses is in itself a choice. Caught up in a maelstrom, he no longer knows what he wants, this swirling vortex is terrifying.

He looks up, the woman is still standing there, curious, attentive.

"Excuse me . . ."

Camille looks down at his mobile, closes one app and opens another – the wrong one – then manages to open his contacts, scrolls down and holds out a picture of Anne towards the woman.

"You don't work with her, do you?"

It is not really a question. But the woman's face brightens.

"No, but I know her."

Happy to be of help. But the misunderstanding does not last long. She has been working in the area for the past fifteen years, so the number of people with whom she is on nodding acquaintance is vast.

"We waved to each other on the street one day. After that, whenever we ran into each other, we'd say hello, but we never actually spoke."

"A complete bitch," Anne had said.

6.55 p.m.

Anne has decided that she cannot wait much longer. Regardless of the consequences. It's been too long. And the house is beginning to frighten her, as though as the night draws in, the forest has begun to close in around her.

When they were together, she noticed Camille had a number of irrational rituals; they were alike in that they were both prone to superstition. Tonight, for example, in order to ward off misfortune (though it seems scarcely possible that anything worse might befall her), she does not turn on the lights. She moves around by the faint glow of the nightlight at the foot of the stairs above the shattered step where Camille lingered for so long.

How long before he comes back and spits in my face? she wonders.

She cannot bring herself to wait any longer. It seems irrational now that she is so close to the end, but it seems impossible that she will ever achieve her goal. She has to leave. Leave now.

She picks up her mobile and calls for a taxi.

Doudouche is sulking, but she will get over it. The moment she senses that Camille is in no mood to indulge her, she slinks off.

Camille once dreamed of getting a housekeeper, a crabby old biddy who would come in every day, clean the flat from top to bottom and cook him boiled potatoes as flabby as her buttocks. Instead he got himself a cat, which amounted to the same thing. He adores Doudouche. He scratches her back, opens a tin of cat food and sets a bowl on the window ledge so she can sit and watch the comings and going along the canal outside.

Then he goes into the bathroom where he carefully extracts the file from the dusty plastic bag, careful not to get dirt everywhere, comes back into the living room and sets the file down on the coffee table.

From her perch at the window, Doudouche glares at him reproachfully. *You shouldn't be doing that.*

"What else can I do?" Camille says aloud.

He opens the file and reaches immediately for the envelope containing the photographs.

The first is a large, slightly over-exposed colour snapshot showing the remains of an eviscerated corpse, broken ribs protruding through a crimson pouch – probably the stomach – and a woman's severed breast, covered in bite marks. The second photograph shows a woman's head which has been severed from her body and nailed to a wall . . .

Camille gets to his feet, walks to the window to get a breath of air. It is not that these images are more appalling than many of the squalid murders he has seen in the course of his career, it is the fact that, in a sense, these are his murders. Those that are closest to him, those he has constantly struggled to keep at arms' length. He stands for a moment, stroking Doudouche and staring down at the canal.

It has been years since he opened this file.

This, then, was how it began, with the discovery of the bodies of two women in a loft apartment in Courbevoie. It ended with the murder of Irène. Camille goes back to the table.

He needs to skim-read the file, find what he is looking for quickly so that he can close it. And this time he will not stow it in the attic space of the Montfort studio . . . He is startled to realise that he has spent months sleeping in the same room as this file without giving it a second thought, that it was almost within reach last night, while Anne lay next to him and he held her hand, tried to calm her as she tossed and turned.

Camille flips through the sheaf of photographs, stops at random. This one shows the body of a different woman. The lower half of her mutilated body, to be precise. A large section of the left thigh has been ripped away and black clotted blood marks out a long deep gash that extends to her vagina. From the way they are positioned, it is clear that both legs have been broken at the knees. One toe bears a fingerprint, carefully applied using a rubber stamp.

These corpses were Camille's first glimpse into the vicious mind of Philippe Buisson.

Inexorably, this series of sadistic murders led to the murder of Irène, though Camille could not have known that when he first saw the bodies.

Camille remembers Maryse Perrin, the young woman in the next photograph. Buisson clubbed her to death with a hammer. Camille moves on.

The young foreign girl who was strangled. It had taken some time to identify her. The body was discovered by a man called Blanchet or Blanchard, the name escapes him, though, as always, Camille perfectly remembers the face: the grey thinning hair, the rheumy eyes, the mouth thin-lipped as a knife wound, the pink neck beaded with sweat. The girl had been found half buried in mud, her body had been unceremoniously dropped onto the canal bank from the bucket of the dredging machine in which it had been dumped. A dozen people were watching from the pedestrian bridge – among them Buisson, who was determined to see the show – and, in a sudden surge of compassion, Buisson had covered the naked body with his coat. Camille cannot help but linger on the picture. He has sketched the pale, thin hand of the girl emerging from beneath the coat a dozen times.

You need to stop this, he tells himself, just find what it is you're looking for.

He randomly grabs a large sheaf of papers, but fate, though it does not exist, is tenacious: he comes up with the picture of Grace Hobson. Though he has not thought about the case for years, he still remembers almost every word, every comma of the text: "She was partly covered by foliage . . . Her head was skewed at a funny angle on her neck, as if she was listening for something . . . On her left temple he saw a beauty spot, the one she had thought would spoil her chances." A passage from a novel by William McIlvanney. A Scotsman. The young woman had been raped, sodomised. She had been found with every item of clothing intact, except one.

This time, Camille is determined; he picks up the file with both hands, turns it over and, starting at the end, begins to work his way backwards.

What he does not want is to happen on the photographs of Irène. He has never been able to face them. Moments after she died, Camille glimpsed the body of Irène in the blue flash of a police light for one flickering instant before he passed out, he remembers nothing more, this is the one image that has remained with him. The file contains other images, those taken by the forensics team, the photographs taken during the autopsy, but he has never looked at them. Never.

And he is not going to now.

In his long career as a serial murderer, Buisson had needed no help from anyone. He was terrifyingly efficient. But in order to kill Irène, in order to conclude his murderous spree with a grand finale, he had needed reliable information. Information he had obtained from Camille himself, after a fashion. From those closest to him, and from one of the members of his team.

Camille comes back to reality, he glances at his watch, picks up his mobile.

"You still at the office?"

"Of course I am . . ."

It is rare that Louis would say such a thing, it is almost a rebuke. His concern is usually expressed with a half-smile. Camille only has twenty minutes to get to his meeting with Michard and the *contrôleur general*, and from Camille's first words, Louis realises that he is far away. Very far away.

"I don't want to take advantage, Louis."

"What can I do for you?"

"I need Maleval's file."

"Maleval . . . Jean-Claude Maleval?"

"You know another one?"

Camille stares at the photograph on the coffee table.

Jean-Claude Maleval, a big man, heavyset but athletic, a former judoka.

"I need you to send everything we've got on him. To my personal e-mail."

The photograph was taken when Maleval was arrested. His face is sensual, he must be thirty-five, perhaps a little older, Camille finds it hard to tell a person's age.

"Can I ask what Maleval has got to do with any of this?" Louis says.

Dismissed from the police force after Irène's death for feeding information to Buisson, Maleval had been unaware that the man was a murderer and so was not technically an accessory, something that was reflected in the verdict. But that did not change the fact that Irène was dead. Camille has dreamed of killing both Buisson and Maleval, but he has never killed anyone. Not until today.

Maleval is behind all this. Camille is convinced of it. He has studied every detail of the case from the robberies in January to the raid at the Galerie. The only thing he does not know is how Anne fits into it.

"Will it take long for you to pull the stuff together?"

"No, about half an hour. It's all on the system."

"Good . . . Can you keep your mobile on in case I need to get in touch?"

"Of course."

"And take a look at the duty roster, you might be needing back-up."

"Me?"

"Who else, Louis?"

In saying this, Camille is admitting that he is out of the running. Louis is shocked. He has no idea what is going on.

Meanwhile, it is not difficult to imagine the scene in the fourth-floor meeting room. Slumped in an armchair, Le Guen is drumming his fingers on the table and trying not to look at his watch. On his right, half hidden behind a vast pile of paperwork, Commissaire Michard is hurriedly reading files, signing, initialling, underlining, annotating, her whole attitude declares that she is a very busy woman, that every second counts, that she is utterly in control of her . . . Shit!

"I'd better go, Louis . . ."

Camille spends the rest of the time sitting on the sofa with Doudouche on his lap. Waiting.

The case file is now closed.

Camille simply snapped a picture of Jean-Claude Maleval with his mobile, then stuffed everything back into the folder and closed it. He even left it by the front door, by the exit.

In Montfort and in Paris, Anne and Camille are both sitting in the gathering dusk, waiting.

Because Anne did not call a taxi; the moment the telephone was answered, she hung up.

She has always known that she would not leave. There is still a faint glow. Anne is stretched out on the sofa, clutching her mobile, every now and then checking the charge left in the battery, checking that she has not missed a call, checking she has a signal.

Nothing.

Le Guen crosses his legs, his right foot idly kicking at the empty air. He seems to recall that Freud believed this nervous tic was merely a substitute for masturbation. What a fucking idiot, thinks Le Guen, who has racked up eleven years on the couch and twenty years of marriage. Surreptitiously, he glances at Michard who is rapidly checking her e-mail. Trapped between Freud and Michard, Le Guen does not rate his chances of surviving the evening.

He feels terribly upset about Camille. There is no-one with whom he can share this feeling. What is the use of six marriages if you have no-one to talk to about such things?

No-one will call Camille to ask whether he is simply running late. No-one will help him now. It is all such a waste.

7.00 p.m.
"Turn it off, for fuck's sake!"

Fernand apologises, runs back and flicks off the light, mutters some excuse, he's obviously relieved I'm letting him go back and help out in the restaurant.

I'm sitting on my own in the little room where we were playing cards earlier. I prefer to sit in the dark. It helps me think.

It's waiting and not being able to do anything that I find exhausting. I need to be in the thick of the action. Idleness just makes me angry. I was like this even as a kid. And it's not something that has improved with age. I guess I'll have to die young.

A shrill *beep* rouses Camille from his thoughts. A flashing message on his computer screen informs him that he has an e-mail from Louis.

The Maleval file.

Camille slips on his glasses, takes a deep breath and opens the attachment.

At first, Jean-Claude Maleval had a distinguished service record. He graduated top of his class from the police academy, rapidly proved to be a promising officer and this led, within a few short years, to him being transferred to the section of the *brigade criminelle* led by Commandant Verhœven.

This was the high point, working on important cases, doing rewarding work.

What Camille remembers is not in the file. Maleval working

relentlessly, constantly on the go, always coming up with ideas, an ambitious, intuitive officer who works hard and plays hard. He goes out a lot, begins to drink a little too much, becomes a womaniser, though it is not the women he loves so much as the act of seduction. Camille has often thought that working on the force, like working in politics, is a form of sexually transmitted disease. Maleval is a player, he is constantly seducing women, a sure sign of a deep-rooted anxiety about which Camille can do nothing; it is not his responsibility, and besides, they do not have that kind of relationship. Maleval is forever chasing women, including witnesses if they are female and under thirty. He begins to show up for his shift looking as though he has not slept a wink. Camille becomes a little worried about his rather dissolute lifestyle. Louis lends him money that is never repaid. Then the rumours start. Maleval is shaking down drug dealers a little more often than necessary and not always turning in all the evidence. A prostitute claims he robbed her, no-one listens, but Camille overhears. He takes Maleval aside, invites him out for dinner, talks to him. But by now it is too late. Maleval swears blind that he's clean, but already he's on the fast track to dismissal. The bars, the late nights, the whisky, the girls, the clubs, the dodgy company, the ecstasy.

Most officers, when they are on this slippery slope, slide slowly and steadily, giving those around them time to adjust, to compensate. Maleval does not do things by half; his descent is meteoric.

He is arrested for aiding and abetting Buisson, who has been charged with seven murders, but the authorities manage to contain the scandal. Buisson's story is so bizarre, so baroque that it completely dominates the press coverage, it burns up all the oxygen, like a forest fire. Maleval's arrest all but disappears behind the curtain of flames.

Immediately after Irène's death, Camille is hospitalised with severe depression. He spends several months in a psychiatric clinic staring out of the window, sketching in silence, refusing to see anyone. Everyone assumes he will never come back to the *brigade.*

At the trial, Maleval is found guilty, but his sentence is covered by the time he has spent on remand, and he is immediately released. Camille does not know this because no-one dares tell him. When he finally does find out, he says nothing, as if too much time has passed, as if Maleval's fate is no longer important, as if it does not concern him personally.

Released on parole and dismissed from the force, Maleval vanishes. And then he begins to reappear, briefly, unremarkably. Camille comes across his name here and there in the dossier that Louis has compiled.

For Maleval, the end of his career in the force coincides with the beginning of his career as a thug, something for which he displays a remarkable aptitude, which is perhaps why he had previously made such a good officer.

As Camille quickly scrolls through the document, a picture begins to take shape. Here are Maleval's first charge sheets: misdemeanours, minor offences. An investigation turns up nothing particularly serious, but it is clear that he has made his choice. Not for him the usual route of parlaying his time on the force into a job with a security firm, working in a shopping centre or driving an armoured van. Three times he is questioned and released without charge. Which takes Camille up to the summer of last year.

This time, Maleval's name crops up in another case.

Nathan Monestier.

Now we're getting there, Camille sighs. Monestier/Forestier, it's not much of a leap. It's an old technique: the best lie is a half-truth. Camille needs to find out whether Anne had the same surname as her brother. Anne Monestier? Maybe. Why not?

Reading on, Camille sees how closely they have stuck to the truth: Anne's brother Nathan is indeed a promising scientist, a child prodigy with a whole alphabet of letters after his name, though he seems to have a nervous disposition.

Nathan's first arrest is for possession with intent to supply. Thirty-three grams of cocaine can hardly be dismissed as personal use. Nathan first denies everything, then he panics, then he claims that Jean-Claude Maleval supplied the drugs or introduced him to the dealer, in a vague and inconsistent statement which he quickly retracts. Pending trial, he is released on bail. And almost immediately turns up in hospital having been beaten to a bloody pulp. Unsurprisingly, he declines to press charges . . . It is obvious that Maleval's solution to his problems is brute force. His penchant for violence foreshadows his taste for armed robbery.

Camille does not have all the details, but he can guess. Maleval and Nathan Monestier are in business together. How does Nathan come to be indebted to Maleval? Does he owe him money? And how does Maleval go about blackmailing the young man?

Other names begin to turn up in Maleval's wake. Among them, a number of vicious thugs. Guido Guarnieri, for example. Camille, like everyone on the force, knows the man by reputation. Guarnieri is a loan shark who buys up debt cheaply and uses strong-arm tactics to recover the money. A year ago, he was questioned about a body discovered on a building site. The pathologist confirmed that the victim had been buried alive, had taken days to die and endured unimaginable suffering. Guarnieri knows how to make himself feared. Did Maleval threaten to sell on Nathan's debt to Guarnieri? It's possible.

It hardly matters since Camille does not care about Nathan, he has never even met the man.

What matters is that all this leads to Anne.

Whatever the nature of her brother's debt to Maleval, it is Anne who pays.

She bails him out. Like a mother. "Actually, that's what I've always been to him," she told Camille.

She has always bailed him out.

Sometimes, just when you most need something, it appears.

"Monsieur Bourgeois?"

Number withheld. Camille had allowed the mobile to ring several times until finally Doudouche looked up at him. On the other end, a woman's voice. Fortyish. Working-class.

"I think you've got the wrong number," Camille says calmly. But he does not even think of hanging up.

"Really?"

She sounds surprised. He almost expects her to ask if he is sure. She reads something from a piece of paper.

"It says here, 'Monsieur Éric Bourgeois, 15, rue Escudier, Gagny.'"

"As I said, you have a wrong number."

"Oh . . ." the woman says. "So sorry."

He hears her mutter something he cannot make out. She hangs up angrily.

It has finally happened. Buisson has done the favour Camille requested. Camille can now have him killed at his leisure.

But right now, this new information has opened a single door. Hafner has changed his name. He is now Monsieur Bourgeois. Not a bad name for a retired crook.

Behind every decision lurks another decision waiting to be made. Camille stares at his mobile.

He could rush to the meeting with Michard and Le Guen, tell them: this is Hafner's address, if he's there we can have him banged up by morning, let me explain the whole thing. Le Guen heaves a sigh of relief, though not too loudly, careful not to make Camille's confession to Commissaire Michard sound like a triumph, he glances at Camille, gives an almost imperceptible nod – *you did well, you had me scared for a minute* – then says testily: "That hardly constitutes a full explanation, Camille, I'm sorry."

But he is not sorry, and no-one present is fooled. Commissaire Michard feels cheated, she was so happy at the prospect of hauling Verhœven over the coals, she paid for her ticket and now the show has been cancelled. Now it is her turn to speak; her tone is poised, disciplined. Sententious. She has a fondness for categorical truths, she did not choose this profession for the good of her health, at heart she is a deeply moral woman. "Whatever your explanations might be, Commandant Verhœven, I should warn you that I am not going to turn a blind eye . . . To anything."

Camille holds up his hands. No problem. He explains the whole story.

The whole scam.

Yes, he is personally connected to the person who was attacked in the raid on the Galerie Monier, that is where it all started. There is a barrage of questions: how exactly do you know this woman? Is she implicated in the robbery? Why did you not immediately . . . ?

The rest is predictable. The most important thing now is to go and pick up Hafner a.k.a. Monsieur Bourgeois from his hideout, and charge him with grievous bodily harm, armed robbery and murder. They cannot spend all night quibbling about the details of Verhœven's story, there will be time for that later. Right now, Michard agrees, they need to be pragmatic – it is one of her favourite words, "pragmatic". In the meantime, Commandant Verhœven, you will remain here.

He will not be involved, he will be merely a spectator. He has already provided the evidence and it is damning. When Le Guen and Michard get back, they will decide whether he is to be sanctioned, suspended or transferred . . . It is all so predictable that it is hardly worth the effort.

This is what he could do. But Camille has long since known that this is not how things are going to play out.

He has already made his decision, though he is not quite sure when.

It relates to Anne, to this case, to his life, to everything. There is nothing anyone else can do.

He thought he was being tossed about by circumstance, but that is not true.

We are masters of our own fate.

7.45 p.m.

France has almost as many rues Escudier as it has inhabitants, all leafy suburban streets lined with stone-clad houses featuring identical gardens, identical railings, and identical patio furniture bought from the same branch of IKEA. Number 15 is no exception: stone cladding, patio furniture, wrought-iron railings, garden, all present and correct.

Camille has driven past two or three times in each direction and at different speeds. The last time he drove past, one of the lights on the first floor is turned off. No point waiting any longer.

He parks at the far end of the street. On the corner is a mini-market, the only shop for miles around in this deserted wasteland. Standing on the doorstep, an Arab man of about thirty who looks as though he has just stepped out of a Hopper painting is chewing a toothpick.

Camille turns off the engine at precisely 7.35 p.m. He slams the car door. The grocer raises a hand in greeting. Camille waves back and heads down the rue Escudier, past identikit houses differentiated only by an occasional dog growling half-heartedly or a cat curled up on the wall. The streetlights cast a yellow glow on the potholed pavement, the dustbins have been put out for collection and other cats – the waifs and strays – are fighting over the spoils.

The steps leading up to number 15 are about fifteen metres from the wrought-iron gate. A garage door on the right is padlocked.

Since he passed, another light on the first floor has been turned out. Only two windows are lit up, both on the ground floor. Camille presses the buzzer to the right of the gate. But for the time of day, he could be a sales rep hoping to find a warm welcome. The door opens a fraction and the figure of a woman appears. With the light behind, it is impossible to tell what she looks like, but her voice sounds young.

"Can I help you?"

As though she does not know, as though the ballet of lights flickering on and off is not clear evidence that he has been spotted, that he is being watched. If this woman were in an interrogation room, he would tell her: you're not very good at lying, you're not going to get very far. She turns back to someone inside, vanishes for a moment, then reappears.

"I'll be right there."

She comes down the steps. She is young, but she has the sagging belly of an old woman and her face is slightly swollen. She opens the gate. "A vulgar whore who had copulated with half the city by the time she was nineteen," was how Buisson described her. To Camille she seems ageless and yet the one thing that is beautiful about her is her fear, he can see it in the way she walks, in the way she keeps her eyes lowered, there is nothing submissive about her, it is pure calculation because her fear is courageous, defiant, almost aggressive, capable of withstanding anything. This woman could stab you in the back without a moment's hesitation.

She walks away without a word, her every movement radiating hostility and determination. Camille crosses the patio, climbs the steps and pushes the door which has begun to close. The hallway is bare, with only an empty coat rack on the wall. In the living room to the right, sitting in an armchair, his back to the window, is a terrifyingly gaunt man, his eyes are sunken, feverish. Even indoors, he wears a woollen cap that accentuates the perfect roundness of his head. His face is pale and drawn. Camille immediately notices how much he looks like Armand.

Between two men of long experience, there are many things that go unsaid, to voice them would almost be an insult. Hafner knows who Verhœven is; there are not many policemen of his height. He also knows that if Camille were coming to arrest him, he would have done it differently. So it must be something else. Something difficult. Best to wait and see.

Behind Camille, the young woman stands wringing her hands, she is accustomed to waiting. "*She must get off on being beaten, I can't see why else she would stay . . ."*

Camille hovers in the hall, caught in a vice between Hafner, sitting, staring at him, and the woman behind. The heavy, pointed silence makes it clear that they will not easily be taken in. But he also knows that to them, the unprepossessing little officer has brought chaos into their midst. And given the lives they lead, chaos means death.

"We need to talk . . ." Hafner says finally in a low voice.

Is he talking to Camille, to the woman, perhaps only to himself?

Camille takes a few steps, never taking his eyes off Hafner. He can see none of the savagery described in the police reports. This is not unusual, Camille has often noticed that, excepting those few minutes when they are intent on their violent activities, robbers, thugs and gangsters are much like everyone else. Murderers are just like you and me. But there is something else too: disease and the looming spectre of death. And this silence, this mute menace.

Camille takes another step into the room, which is lit only by the dim bluish glow of a standard lamp. He is not particularly surprised to find the room tastelessly furnished with a large flat-screen T.V., a sofa covered with a throw, a few knick-knacks and a round table covered with a patterned oilcloth. Organised crime often goes hand in hand with very middle-class tastes.

The woman has disappeared; Camille did not notice her leave the room. For an instant he pictures her sitting on the stairs holding a pump-action shotgun. Hafner does not move from his chair, he is waiting to see how things will go. For the first time, Camille wonders if the man is armed – the thought had not occurred to him before. It doesn't matter, he thinks, but even so, he moves slowly and deliberately. You never know.

He takes his mobile from the pocket of his coat, turns it on, brings up the picture of Maleval and, stepping forward, hands the device to Hafner who simply grimaces, clears his throat and nods – *I get it now* – then gestures to the sofa. Camille chooses a chair instead, pulls it towards him, lays his hat on the table. The two men sit facing each other as though waiting to be served.

"Someone told you I would be coming . . ."

"In a way . . ."

Logical. Whoever Buisson forced to give up Hafner's address and his new identity will have wanted to cover his own back. But this does not change anything.

"Shall I recap?" Camille says.

From another part of the house, he hears a distant, high-pitched wail and then hurried footsteps upstairs and the crooning voice of the woman. Camille wonders whether this new factor will complicate matters or simplify them. He jerks his chin at the ceiling.

"How old?"

"Six months."

"Boy?"

"Girl."

Someone else might have asked the girl's name, but the situation hardly lends itself to such familiarity.

"So, last January, your wife was six months pregnant."

"Seven."

Camille indicates the woollen cap.

"It must make being on the run more difficult. And on that subject, do you mind if I ask where you've been having your chemo?"

Hafner pauses for a moment.

"In Belgium, but I've stopped treatment."

"Too expensive?"

"No. Too late."

"And therefore too expensive."

Hafner gives the ghost of a smile, it is almost imperceptible, just a shadow that plays on his lips.

"So back in January," Camille continues, "you knew you didn't have much time to make sure your family were provided for. And so you organised the Big Stick-Up. Four armed robberies in a single day. The jackpot. Most of your usual partners were out of circulation – and maybe you even had qualms about fucking your old friends over – so you hired Ravic, the Serb, and Maleval, the ex-cop. I have to say, I didn't know armed robbery was Maleval's thing."

Hafner takes his time.

"He spent a long time trying to find his way after your lot tossed him out," he says at length, "He was doing a lot of cocaine."

"So I heard . . ."

"But, actually, he's really taken to armed robbery. It suits his personality."

Ever since the penny finally dropped, Camille has been trying to picture Maleval holding up a shop, but he cannot seem to manage. His powers of imagination are limited. And besides, Maleval and Louis will always be part of his team, he cannot picture them in any other context. Like many men who will never have children, Camille has a paternal instinct. His height has a lot to do with it. And he created two sons for himself: Louis, the perfect son, diligent, faultless, who makes everything worthwhile, and Maleval, violent, generous, sinister, the son who betrayed him, the one who cost him his wife. The son who carried evil in his very name.

Hafner waits for Camille to finish. Upstairs, the woman falls silent, she is probably rocking the baby.

"In January," Camille goes on, "everything goes according to plan – but for the niggling exception of a murder. [Camille is not so naive as to expect a reaction from a man like Hafner.] You planned to double-cross everyone and disappear with the cash. All the cash. [Once again, Camille points to the ceiling.] Hardly surprising, a man with a sense of responsibility would want to ensure his loved ones are provided for. In a sense, the proceeds from the four armed robberies were to be your legacy. I'm no lawyer, so tell me, would that be taxable?"

Hafner does not so much as blink. Nothing will shift him from his planned course. He is not about to vouchsafe a smile, a confession, to the harbinger of doom who has finally flushed him out.

"Morally, I suppose, your position is unassailable. You're doing what any good father would do, making sure that your family don't go without. But for some reason, your partners in crime are unlikely to see it that way. Not that it matters, since you have everything planned. They may try to find you, but you have anticipated their every move, you've bought yourself a new identity, cut all ties with your old life. I'm a little surprised that you didn't decide to go abroad."

At first, Hafner says nothing but, sensing that he may well need Camille's help, he throws him a crumb.

"I stayed for her sake . . ." he mutters.

Camille is not sure whether he is referring to his wife or his child. It comes to the same thing.

Outside, the streetlights suddenly flicker off; they must be on timers, or there has been a power cut. The light in the living room dims a little. Hafner is framed in silhouette like an empty carcass, spectral, menacing. Upstairs the baby begins to cry quietly, there is another patter of footsteps and whispered words and the wailing stops. Camille would be happy to stay here, in this half-light, in this silence. What is there waiting for him elsewhere, after all? He thinks of Anne. *Come on, Camille.*

Hafner crosses and uncrosses his legs, he does so infinitely slowly as though wary of frightening Camille. Or else he is in pain. *Come on.*

"Ravic . . ." As Camille says the name he realises that he has dropped his voice to a muffled whisper, in tune with the atmosphere of the house. "I didn't know Ravic personally, but I'm guessing he didn't much appreciate being double-crossed and left without a red cent. Especially since he came away from the robberies with a murder charge hanging over him. I know, I know, it's his own fault, he should have held his nerve. But even so, he'd earned his share of the loot and you just took off with it. Did you hear what happened to Ravic?"

Camille thinks he sees Hafner stiffen slightly.

"He's dead. His girlfriend – or whatever she was – got off lightly: a bullet to the head. But before he died, Ravic saw his fingers hacked off one by one. With a hunting knife. Personally, I think a guy who would do something like that is a savage. I know Ravic was a Serb, but France has always been a safe haven for refugees. And chopping up foreigners is hardly good for tourism, wouldn't you say?"

"I would say you're a pain in the arse, Verhœven."

Camille inwardly heaves a sigh of relief. Unless he can jolt Hafner out of his self-imposed silence, he will not get any information out of him. He will be forced to listen to his own soliloquy when what he needs is dialogue.

"You're right," he says. "Now is no time for recriminations.

Tourism is one thing, armed robbery is something very different. But then again . . . So let's talk about Maleval. Now he's someone I used to know very well, in the days before he went in for dismemberment."

"If I were you, I'd have killed the fucker."

"That would have suited you, wouldn't it? Because even if Maleval has become a brutal, bloodthirsty bastard, he's still as cunning as he ever was. He didn't appreciate being double-crossed either, and he's been doing his best to hunt you down . . ."

Hafner nods slowly. He has his own informants, he will have been following the progress of Maleval's search from a distance.

"But you managed to change your identity, you cut yourself off completely from everyone and everything, you had a little help from those who still admire you – or fear you – and although Maleval has moved heaven and earth to find you, he doesn't have your contacts, your resources, your reputation. Eventually he was forced to accept that he might never find you. And then he came up with a brilliant idea . . ."

Hafner looks at Camille, puzzled, waiting for the other shoe to drop.

"He got the police to do his searching for him." Camille spread his hands wide. "He entrusted the task to your humble servant. And he was right to, because I'm a pretty decent cop. It would take me less than twenty-four hours to track down someone like you, if I was motivated. And what better to motivate a man than a woman? And a battered woman at that, I mean I'm such a sensitive soul, it was bound to work. And so, a few months ago, he arranged an introduction, and at the time I was flattered."

Hafner nods. Though he realises that his time is up, and senses that very soon he may have to fight for his life, he cannot but admire Maleval's ingenuity. Perhaps, half hidden in the shadows, he is smiling.

"In order to persuade me to track you down, Maleval organised an armed robbery, being sure to give it your M.O., your panache, for want of a better word: a jeweller's, a sawn-off shotgun and a helping of brute force. Everyone at the *brigade criminelle* was convinced that the raid on the Galerie Monier was your work. And I panicked. I was bound to – the woman I cared about was beaten half to death on her way to pick up a present for me, the whole set-up was designed to ensure I would be a loose cannon. I did what I had to do to ensure I was assigned the case, and since I'm not as dumb as I look, I succeeded. My suspicions were confirmed when this woman, the only witness, formally identified you, though she had only ever seen you in a photograph Maleval showed her. You and Ravic. She even claimed to have recognised a few Serbian words. So now we're certain that you were behind the job at the Galerie, there's not a shadow of a doubt."

Hafner slowly nods again, seemingly impressed by the preparation that has gone into the plan. And realising that in Maleval he has found a formidable adversary.

"And so I set out looking for you on Maleval's behalf," Camille says. "Unwittingly, I become his private detective. The more he piles on the pressure, the faster I work. He appears to try to kill the witness, so I redouble my efforts. You have to admit, he made the right choice. I'm a good cop. To find you, I had to make a particularly painful sacrifice, a . . ."

"What sacrifice?" Hafner interrupts.

Camille looks up. How can he put it into words? He thinks for a long moment – Buisson, Irène, Maleval – then gives up.

"I . . ." Camille says almost to himself, "I had no score to settle with anyone."

"That's not true. Everyone has . . ."

"You're right. Because Maleval has an old score to settle with me. In feeding information to Buisson, he was guilty of serious professional misconduct. So he was arrested, humiliated, banished, his name was all over the papers, the scandal, the trial, the verdict. And he spent time in prison. Not long, I'll grant you, but can you imagine what it's like for an officer to be inside? And so this is the perfect opportunity to get his revenge. Two birds with one stone. He gets me to track you down and in doing so he makes sure that I will be fired."

"You did it because you wanted to."

"Partly . . . It's too complicated to explain."

"And I don't give a flying fuck."

"Well, you're wrong there. Because now I've found you, Maleval will be paying you a visit. And he's not just going to want his share. He's going to want everything."

"I've got nothing left."

Camille pretends to weigh up the merits of this answer.

"Yes," he says. "You could try that, I mean, nothing ventured . . . I'm guessing Ravic tried the same spiel: I've nothing left, I spent it all, I might have a little left, but not much . . ." Camille smiles broadly. "But let's be serious. You've put that money aside for the time when you won't be here to provide for your family. You've still got it. The question isn't whether Maleval will find your savings, only how long it will take him to do so. And, incidentally, what methods he's prepared to use to get that information."

Hafner turns towards the window as though expecting Maleval to appear wielding a hunting knife. He says nothing.

"He'll pay you a visit. If and when I decide. All I have to do is give your address to his accomplice and Maleval will be on his way. I'd give it an hour before he blasts your front door open with his Mossberg."

Hafner tilts his head to one side.

"I know what you're thinking," Camille says. "You're thinking that you'll be waiting, that you'll take him down. Well, no offence, but you don't seem in such great shape right now. Maleval has got twenty years on you, he's trained and he's cunning. You made the mistake of underestimating him once before. You might get a lucky shot in, of course, but that's your only hope. And if you want my advice, make sure you don't miss. Because he's not exactly your biggest fan right now. If you do, you'll regret it, because after he's put a bullet between the eyes of that pretty little wife of yours, he's liable to take a knife to your kid, to her little hands, her little feet . . ."

"Don't talk shit, Verhœven, I've dealt with guys like him dozen of times."

"That was the past, Hafner, even your future is behind you now. You could try to send your family into hiding with the cash – assuming I give you enough time – but it won't make any difference. If Maleval tracked you down for all your cunning, finding them will be child's play. [Silence.] I'm you're only hope."

"Go fuck yourself!"

Camille nods, reaches for his hat. His face neatly sums up the paradox, a combination of feigned resignation and frustration – *Oh well, I did what I could*. Reluctantly, he gets to his feet. Hafner does not move.

"O.K.," Camille says, "I'll leave you to spend some time with your family. Make the most of it."

He heads into the hallway.

He has no doubt that this is the right strategy. It will take as long as it takes: he might get to the front door, the steps, the garden, maybe even as far as the gate, but Hafner will call him back. The streetlights come on again, casting a pale-yellow glow over the far end of the garden.

Camille stands for a moment in the doorway, staring out at the tranquil street, then he turns and jerks his chin towards the ceiling.

"What's her name?"

"Ève."

Camille nods. A pretty name.

"It's a good start," he says, turning away again, "I just hope it lasts."

He walks out.

"Verhœven!"

Camille closes his eyes.

He retraces his steps.

9.00 p.m.

Anne is still in the studio. She does not know whether this is bravery or cowardice, but she is still here, waiting. The hours tick by and the exhaustion has become a crushing weight. She feels as though she has survived an ordeal, as though she has come through: she is no longer in control, she is an empty shell, she can do no more.

It was her ghost who, twenty minutes earlier, packed up her few belongings. Her jacket, the money, the piece of paper with the map and the telephone numbers. She heads for the sliding glass door, then turns back.

The taxi driver from Montfort has just called to say he has been driving around but cannot find the lane. He sounds Asian. Anne is forced to turn on the living-room light so she can study the scribbled map and try to guide him, but it is no use. "Just past the rue de la Loge, you said?" "Yes, on the right," she says, though she does not know which direction he is coming from. She will come to meet him, she says, *Park next to the church and wait for me there, alright*? The driver agrees, he is happier with this solution, he apologises but his G.P.S. . . . Anne hangs up. Then goes and sits on the sofa.

Just a few minutes, she promises herself. If the telephone rings in the next five minutes . . . But what if the call does not come?

In the darkness, she runs her finger over her scarred cheek, over her gums, picks up one of Camille's sketchpads. She could do this a hundred times and not happen on the same drawing.

Just a few minutes. The taxi driver calls back, he is impatient, unsure whether to stay or go.

"Wait for me," she says, "I'm on my way."

He tells her the meter is running.

"Give me ten minutes. Just ten minutes . . ."

Ten minutes. Then, whether Camille calls or not, she will leave. All this for nothing?

What then? What will happen then?

At that moment, her mobile rings.

It is Camille.

Jesus, I fucking hate waiting. I opened up the futon, ordered a bottle of Bowmore Mariner and some food, but I know I won't get a wink of sleep.

On the other side of the wall, I can hear the bustle of a busy restaurant. Fernand is raking it in, which will add to my bank balance. That should make me happy, but it's not what I want, what I'm waiting for. After all the effort I've put in . . .

But the more time passes, the less chance I have of pulling this thing off. The biggest risk is that Hafner fucked off to the Bahamas with his tart. Word on the street is that he's terminally ill, but who knows, maybe he's decided to do his convalescing on the beach. With my cash! It really pisses me off to think that right now he could be living it up on the money he owes me.

But if he *is* still in France, then the moment I find out where he's holed up I'll be all over him before the cops even have time to get their boots on, I'll drag him down to his cellar and we'll have a nice little chat, just me, him and a blowtorch.

In the meantime, I sip my fifteen-year-old malt, think about the girl, about Verhœven – I've got the little fucker by the short and curlies – and I think about what I'll do when I find Hafner . . .

Deep breath.

In his car again, Camille sits motionless behind the steering wheel. Is it the fact that it still has not sunk in? That he can finally see light at the end of the tunnel? He feels cold as a snake, prepared for anything. He has everything set up for a finale that will be done by the book. He has only one doubt: will he be strong enough?

Standing in the doorway of his shop, the Arab grocer smiles cordially and goes on chewing his toothpick. In his head, Camille tries to replay the footage of his relationship with Anne, but nothing comes, the film is caught in the sprockets. He is too preoccupied by what is about to happen.

It is not that Camille is incapable of lying, far from it, but he always hesitates when the end is in sight.

Anne needs to get away from Maleval, this is why she agreed to spy on Camille's investigation. She has promised to pass on

Hafner's address.

Camille is the only person who can help her, but his actions will signal the end of their relationship. Just as it has already signalled the end of his career. Camille feels a great weariness.

Let's do this, he thinks. He shakes himself, takes his mobile and calls Anne. She picks up immediately.

"Camille . . . ?"

Silence. Then the words come.

"We've found Hafner. You don't have to worry anymore . . ."

There. It is done.

His calm tone is intended to persuade her that he is completely in control.

"Are you sure?" she says.

"Absolutely." He hears a sound in the background, like a breath. "Where are you?"

"On the terrace."

"I told you not to leave the house!"

Anne does not seem to understand. Her voice is quavering, her words come in a rush.

"Have you arrested him?"

"No, Anne, that's not how it works. We've only just tracked him down, but I wanted to let you know as soon as possible. You asked me to call, you insisted. Look, I can't stay long on the phone. The important thing is th—"

"Where is he, Camille?"

Camille hesitates, for the last time no doubt.

"We found him in a safe house . . ."

The forest around Anne begins to rustle. The wind whips through the treetops, the light on the terrace flickers. She does not move. She should bombard Camille with questions, gather all her strength and say: *I need to know where he is.* This is one of the lines she has been rehearsing. Or: *I'm scared, can't you understand I'm scared?* She needs to make herself shrill, hysterical, she needs to insist, *What safe house? Where?* And if that does not work, she needs to be aggressive: *You say you've found him, but do you even know he's there? Why can't you just tell me?* Or she might try a little emotional blackmail: *I'm still worried, Camille, surely you can understand that?* Or remind him of the facts: *That man beat me half to death, Camille, he tried to kill me, I have a right to know!*

Instead there is silence, she cannot bring herself to say any of these things.

She had precisely the same feeling three days ago as she stood in the street, covered in blood, clinging to a parked car, and saw the robbers' jeep round the corner, saw the man aim the shotgun at her, the barrel only inches away, and yet, drained, exhausted, ready to die, unable to summon a last ounce of strength, she did nothing. And now, once again, she finds she can say nothing.

Camille will come to her rescue one last time.

"We tracked him down to the suburbs, to 15, rue Escudier in Gagny. It's a quiet residential neighbourhood. I've only just found out, I don't know how long he's been there. He's going by the name Éric Bourgeois, that's all I know."

Another silence.

Camille is thinking: That was the last time I will hear her voice, but it is not true because she continues to press him.

"So, what happens now?"

"He's a dangerous man, Anne, you know that. We'll stake out the area, work out exactly where he is, try to find out if there is anyone there with him. There may be several of them. We can't just go storming a Paris suburb as if it's the Alamo, we'll need to bring in a tactical unit. And we'll need to make sure the timing is right. But we know where to find him, and we have the resources to make sure he doesn't do any more harm. [He forces himself to smile.] You feel better?"

"I'm fine."

"Listen, I have to go now. I'll see you later.

Silence.

"See you later."

9.45 p.m.

I'd more or less given up hope, but we got our result! Hafner has been found.

It's not surprising he was impossible to track down if he's going by the name "Monsieur Bourgeois". I knew this man, this ruthless gangster, when he was at the height of his powers, so it's kind of pathetic to discover he's saddled himself with such a name.

But Verhœven is convinced it's him. So I'm convinced.

The reports that he was ill are true, I just hope he hasn't pissed away all of that cash on chemo. There'd better be a decent wad left to compensate me for all my efforts, because otherwise cancer will be nothing compared to what I have in store for him. Logically, he'll need to eke out the money, keep it handy in case he needs it.

Now I just jump in the car, head down the Périphérique, pedal to the metal, and before you know it I'll be in Gagny.

Difficult to picture Vincent Hafner in a dump like that. Have to hand it to him, it's a clever place to hide out, but I can't help thinking that if he's slumming it in a cosy little suburban house, there's probably a woman in the picture. Probably the woman I've heard about on the grapevine, the sort of torrid May-December romance that can persuade a man to become Monsieur Bourgeois to impress the neighbours.

It's the kind of thing that makes you think about life: Hafner spends half his life bumping off his neighbours, then he falls in love and all of a sudden he's totally pussy-whipped.

It suits me. If there's a girl involved, I can use it to my advantage. Women make for good leverage. Break her fingers and he'll hand over his life savings, gouge out her eye and he'll throw in the family silver. I tend to think of a woman as an organ donor, and every piece is worth its weight in gold.

Obviously, nothing beats a kid. If you really need to get your hands on something, the best weapon you can have is a kid.

When I get to Gagny, I drive around for a bit, take a tour of the neighbourhood, steering clear of the rue Escudier. Cordoning off the area won't be a problem, the police just need to set up a couple of roadblocks, but raiding the house will be a lot more complicated. First they have to be sure that Hafner is in there, and that he's alone. That won't be easy because there's nowhere for a G.I.G.N. Special Ops team to park in this neighbourhood, and given there's almost no traffic in the area, a car prowling around would be noticed straight away. Best would be to bring in a couple of plain-clothes to keep a watch on the place, but even that can take half a day.

Right now, the boys at G.I.G.N. are probably devising complicated strategies, poring over aerial maps, marking out zones, sectors, trajectories. They're in no hurry. They've got the whole night to think about it, they can't do anything before about 6 a.m. and even then it's all about surveillance, surveillance, surveillance . . . The operation could take two days, maybe three. And by then, their target will be no threat at all, I'll see to that.

I parked the car two hundred metres from the rue Escudier,

shouldered my bag and walked past the gardens, bludgeoned a few dogs that tried to play the tough guy, crept past the hedges and the railings and here I am, sitting in a garden under a pine tree. The residents are in the living room watching television. On the other side of the railing separating the gardens, I have a perfect view of the back of number 15, thirty metres away.

The only light is a bluish glow from an upstairs window, obviously a T.V. The rest of the house is in darkness. There are only three possibilities: either Hafner is watching T.V. upstairs, or he's out, or he's in bed and the girl is watching educational programmes on T.F.1.

If he's gone out, I'll be the welcome committee when he gets back.

If he's in bed, I'll be his alarm clock.

And if he's watching television, he's going to miss the ad break because I've got my own entertainment planned.

I study the place through my binoculars, then I'll creep over and slip inside. Make the most of the element of surprise. I'm having fun already.

A garden is the ideal place for meditation. I assess the situation. Realising that everything is going smoothly, almost better than I had expected, I force myself to be patient – by nature I tend to be impulsive. When I got here, I felt like firing shots in the air and charging into the house, screaming like a lunatic. But just getting to this point has taken a lot of work, a lot of thought and effort, I'm so close to the money I can almost smell it, so it's important that I keep a cool head. When nothing happens after half an hour, I pack up my things and do a recce of the house. No burglar alarm. Hafner wouldn't have wanted to attract attention by turning his little haven into a bunker. He's a crafty bastard, that Monsieur Bourgeois, he just blends into the background.

I go back to the tree and sit down, zip up my parka and again look through the binoculars.

Finally, at about half past ten, the T.V. upstairs is turned off. The small window in the middle lights up briefly. Narrower than the others, it must be the toilet. I couldn't have wished for a better set-up. I get to my feet. Time for action.

It's a standard '30s house with the kitchen at the rear of the ground floor. The back door leads onto a small flight of steps and down to the garden. I move silently. The lock is so old you could open it with a tin-opener.

On the other side is the great unknown.

I leave my bag by the door, taking only the Walther fitted with a silencer and the hunting knife tucked into a leather sheath on my belt.

Inside, the silence is pounding; there's always something nerve-racking about a house at night. I need to calm my heart rate, otherwise I won't hear a thing.

I stand for a long time, watching, listening.

Not a sound.

I steal across the tiled floor, moving slowly because here and there the tiles creak. I emerge from the kitchen into a narrow hall. The stairs are on my right, the front door straight ahead and on my left is an archway that probably leads to the living or the dining room.

Everyone is upstairs. As a precaution, I hug the walls, gripping the Walther with both hands, the barrel pointed downwards.

As I pad across the hall towards the stairs, something catches my eye: the living room on my left is in pitch darkness, but at the far end, bathed in the faint glow of the streetlights, I see Hafner sitting, staring at me. I'm so shocked that I'm literally rooted to the spot.

I just have time to make out a woollen cap pulled down to his eyebrows, his bulging eyes. Hafner sitting in an armchair, I swear, like Ma Barker in her rocking chair.

He has his Mossberg trained on me.

The moment he sees me, he fires.

The noise fills the whole house, a blast like that is enough to stun anyone. I move fast. In a split second, I throw myself to the ground behind the door. Not fast enough to avoid the buckshot peppering the hallway, I'm hit in the leg, but it feels like a flesh wound.

Hafner has been waiting for me, I've been hit, but I'm not dead. I scrabble to my knees, feeling blood trickling down my shin.

Everything is happening so fast my mind is having trouble processing it. Luckily, my reflexes are focused in the reptilian brain, they come straight from my spinal cord. And I do what no-one would anticipate: even though I'm startled, shot and wounded, I snap into action.

Without taking time to assess the situation, I swing round to face him. From the expression on Hafner's face I can tell he wasn't expecting me to reappear in the doorway where he just shot at me. I am hunkered on the ground, my outstretched arm gripping the Walther.

The first bullet slices through his throat, the second hits him right between the eyes, he doesn't even have time to squeeze the trigger. His body jerks wildly as the last five bullets leave a cavernous crater in his chest.

I have scarcely processed the fact that there's lead in my leg, that Hafner is dead and all my hard work has resulted in an epic failure, when I dimly become aware of something else: I am kneeling in the hall holding an empty gun and the barrel of another gun is pressed against my temple.

I freeze. I set the Walther down on the ground.

The hand holding the pistol is steady. I feel the barrel dig into my flesh. The message is clear: I push the Walther away from me, it skids two metres and comes to a stop.

I've just been well and truly screwed. I spread my arms to indicate that I don't plan to resist, I turn slowly, head down, careful not to make any sudden movements.

It doesn't take long for me to work out who would want to kill me, and my suspicions are confirmed when I see the tiny shoes. My brain is still racing, trying to come up with some way out, but all I can think is: How did he get here before me?

But I don't waste time trying to analyse what went wrong, because before I figure it out, he'll have put a bullet in my brain with complete impunity. In fact I can feel the barrel drag across my skin and stop in the middle of my forehead, precisely where Hafner took the second bullet. I look up.

"Good evening, Maleval," Verhœven says.

He's wearing a hat and has one hand stuffed into the pocket of his overcoat. He looks as though he's about to leave.

More worryingly, I notice that he's wearing a glove on the other hand, the one holding the gun. I can feel the panic rising. No matter how fast I move, if he manages to get a shot off, I'm dead. Especially since there's lead in my calf already, I'm losing a lot of blood and I'm not sure what will happen if I try to put any weight on it.

Verhœven knows this all too well.

Cautiously, he takes a step back, but his arm is steady, his hand doesn't tremble, he's not afraid, he's determined, his bony face is grave, serene.

I'm on my knees, he's standing, our faces aren't quite at the same level, but there's not much in it. This could be my last chance. He's almost within reach. If I can just gain a few centimetres, stall for a few minutes . . .

"I see you've still got the same quick reflexes, son."

"Son" . . . Verhœven has always been protective, paternalistic. Given his height, it's ridiculous. But he's a clever runt, I'll give him that. And I know him well enough to recognise that this hasn't been one of his good days.

"Well, I say 'quick' . . ." he says, "but tonight you're missing something. And you were so close to pulling it off, it must be galling." His eyes never leave mine. "If you came looking for a suitcase full of cash, you'll be thrilled to know that it was right here. Hafner's wife left with it an hour ago. In fact, I even called her a taxi. You know me, I never could resist a damsel in distress, whether she's carrying a heavy suitcase or causing a scene in a restaurant. I'm always willing to step in."

He can't miss, the gun is cocked, and it's not his service revolver . . .

"Well spotted," he says, as though he can read my mind. "The gun is Hafner's. You wouldn't believe the arsenal he's got upstairs. But he recommended this one. Personally, I don't much care, in a situation like this, one gun is as good as the next . . ."

His eyes are still fixed on mine, it's almost hypnotic. It's something I remember from when I worked with him, that icy, razor-sharp stare.

"You're wondering how I got here before you, but mostly you're trying to think of a way out. Because you must know that I'm feeling fucking furious."

From his strange stillness I can tell that any second now . . .

"And insulted," Verhœven says. "Above all, insulted. And for a man like me, that's much worse. Fury is something you live with, sooner or later you calm down, you get things in perspective, but when a man's pride is injured he's capable of terrible things. Especially a man who has nothing left to lose, a man who has nothing left at all. A guy like me, for example. Right now, I'm capable of anything."

I swallow hard and say nothing.

"Any minute now, you're going to try and rush me. I can tell." He smiles. "It's what I would do in your position. Double or quits, that's the way we work. When it comes down to it, we're very alike, don't you think? That's what made this whole thing possible."

He blethers on, but he's still perfectly focused.

I tense.

He takes his left hand from his pocket.

Without moving my eyes, I calculate the angle of attack.

He's gripping the gun with both hands now, pointing it directly between my eyes. I'll take him by surprise, he's expecting me to rush him or to dodge sideways, but I'll dive backwards.

"Tsk tsk tsk . . ."

He takes one hand from the gun and brings it to his ear.

"Listen . . ."

I listen. Sirens. They're approaching fast, Verhœven doesn't smile, he doesn't savour his triumph, he just looks sad.

If I weren't in this fucked-up situation, I'd almost pity him.

I always knew I loved this man.

"Three counts of murder," he whispers, his voice so low I have to strain to hear. "Armed robbery, accessory to murder in the January raid . . . In Ravic's case, malicious wounding and murder, for his girlfriend, you might get off with second-degree. You're going to be banged up for a very long time, and that upsets me, it really does."

He's completely sincere.

The sirens converge on the house, there are at least five cars, maybe more. Through the windows, the flashing lights illuminate the rooms like a blaze of neon at a fairground. Slumped in the armchair at the far end of the living room, Hafner's face flickers blue and red.

I hear running footsteps. The front door seems to explode into splinters. I turn to look.

Louis, my old friend Louis, is the first on the scene. His suit is pressed, not a hair out of place, he looks like an altar boy.

"Hey, Louis . . ."

I'd like to sound indifferent, cynical, to go on playing the role, but seeing Louis again after all this time brings everything flooding back, the terrible waste is heartbreaking.

"Hi, Jean-Claude . . ." Louis steps closer.

I turn back to Verhœven, but he has disappeared.

10.30 p.m.

Every house in the street is lit up, every garden, too. The residents are standing in their doorways, shouting to each other, some have crept out to their railings and a few brave souls are standing in the middle of the road, reluctant to come any closer. Uniformed officers are posted on either side of the house to deter rubberneckers.

Commandant Verhœven, hat pulled down, hands buried in the pockets of his overcoat, stares down the street which is lit up like a Christmas scene.

"I want to apologise, Louis." He speaks slowly, like a man

overcome by fatigue. "I'm sorry for not confiding in you, for giving the impression I didn't trust you. That's not why I did it, you know that, don't you?"

The question requires no answer.

"Of course," Louis says.

He is about to protest, but Verhœven has already turned away. This is how it has always been between them, they start a conversation but rarely finish. But this time is different. Each feels he is seeing the other for the last time.

This thought prompts Louis to be particularly reckless.

"That woman . . ." he says.

For Louis to utter these two words is momentous. Camille quickly turns back.

"No, Louis, please don't think that!" He seems not angry, but indignant. As though he is being unjustly accused. "When you say 'that woman', you make it sound as though I am the injured party in a tragic love story."

For a long moment, he stares down the street again.

"It wasn't love that made me do it, it was the situation."

There is a steady clamour from outside the house, idling engines, sporadic voices, shouted orders. The atmosphere is not frenzied but calm, almost peaceful.

"After all this time," Camille goes on, "I thought I'd got over Irène's death. But actually, though I didn't realise it, the embers were still smouldering. Maleval fuelled the fire at the crucial moment, that's all. In fact 'that woman', as you call her, had very little to do with it."

"But still," Louis says. "The lies, the betrayal . . ."

"Oh, Louis, they're just words . . . When I realised what was happening, I could have stopped it, there would have been no more lies, there would have been no betrayal."

Louis' silence is a deafening: *So?*

"The truth is . . ."

Camille turns back to Louis, he seems to be searching for his words in the young man's face.

". . . I didn't want to stop, I wanted to see it through, I wanted it over with once and for all. I think . . . I think I did it out of loyalty. [Camille himself seems surprised by the word. He smiles.] And this woman . . . I never thought her intentions were evil. If I'd thought that, I would have arrested her on the spot. By the time I realised what was happening, it was a bit late, but I could live with the damage done, I could still do my job. Actually, it's more than that. I knew that she wouldn't have suffered everything she suffered . . . for some selfish reason. [He shakes his head, as though waking from a trance. He smiles again.] And I was right. She was sacrificing herself for her brother. Yes, I realise the word 'sacrifice' is a bit much. People don't use the word so often these days, it's old-fashioned. Look at Hafner, he was no angel, but he sacrificed himself for the woman and her child. Anne did it for her brother . . . People like that still exist."

"And you?"

"And me."

Camille hesitates.

"When I hit rock bottom, I realised that maybe it wasn't so bad to have someone for whom I was prepared to sacrifice something important. [He smiles.] A little luxury in these selfish times, don't you think?"

He turns up the collar of his coat.

"Well, that's that, I'm done for the day. And I've got a resignation letter to write. I haven't slept since . . ."

Still he does not move.

"Hey, Louis!"

Louis turns. One of the forensics officers on the pavement outside Hafner's house is calling him.

Camille waves: go on Louis, don't keep the man waiting.

"I'll just be a minute."

But when he comes back, Camille has already gone.

1.30 a.m.

Camille felt his heart pound when he saw there was a light on in the studio. He stopped the car, switched off the engine and sat in the darkness, considering what to do.

Anne is here.

This is an additional disappointment he could have done without. He needs to be alone.

He sighs, grabs his coat and hat, the package with the thick file held together by elastic bands, then trudges up the path wondering how she will react, wondering what he is going to tell her, *how* he is going to tell her. He pictures her as he last saw her, sitting on the floor next to the sink.

The terrace door is ajar.

The faint glow in the studio comes from the night-light under the stairs, it is too dark to see where Anne might be. Camille sets his package on the terrace, reaches for the handle and slides the door open.

He is alone. He hardly needs to ask, but he does.

"Anne . . . are you there?"

He already knows the answer.

He walks over to the stove, this is what he always does. He

throws in a log. Opens the flue.

He takes off his coat, switches on the kettle as he passes, then immediately turns it off, wanders to the cupboard where he keeps the liquor and hesitates: whisky, cognac?

Let's go for cognac.

Just a snifter.

Then he goes outside and fetches the package from the terrace and closes the patio door.

He will take his time, sip the brandy. He loves this house. Up above, the skylight is darkened by the shifting shadows of the leaves. Inside he cannot hear the wind, but he can see it.

It is strange, but in this moment – though he is a big boy now – he misses his mother. Misses her terribly. He could cry if he let go.

But he resists. There is no point to crying alone.

Then he sets down his glass, kneels next to the coffee table and opens the thick file of papers, photographs, official reports and newspaper clippings; somewhere amongst them are the last pictures ever taken of Irène.

He does not search, he does not look, methodically he takes fistfuls of documents and feeds them into the gaping maw of the stove, which is now humming peacefully, at cruising speed.

Acknowledgements

My thanks to my wife, Pascaline, to Gérald Aubert for his advice and to my friend Sam, a constant presence and a constant help. Thanks also to Pierre Scipion for his care and his kindness, and to all the staff at Albin Michel.

And of course I would like to express my gratitude to those authors from whom I have borrowed (in alphabetical order): Marcel Aymé, Thomas Bernhard, Nicholas Boileau, Heinrich Böll, William Faulkner, Shelby Foote, William Gaddis, John le Carré, Jules Michelet, Antonio Muñoz Molina, Marcel Proust, Olivier Remaud, Jean-Paul Sartre, Thomas Wolfe.

PIERRE LEMAITRE was born in Paris in 1951. He worked for many years as a teacher of literature and now writes novels and screenplays. In 2013 he was awarded the C.W.A. International Dagger for *Alex*, the second in a crime series known as the Commandant Camille Verhœven trilogy that began with *Irène*, and concludes with *Camille*. That year he was also winner of the Prix Goncourt, France's most prestigious literary award, for his novel *The Great Swindle*. In 2015 he was awarded the C.W.A. for a second time, for *Camille*.

FRANK WYNNE is a translator from French and Spanish of works by Michel Houellebecq, Boualem Sansal, Antonin Varenne, Arturo Pérez-Reverte, Carlos Acosta and Hervé le Corre. He was the winner of the *Independent* Foreign Fiction Prize for his translation of Frédéric Beigbeder's *Windows on the World*.

AVAILABLE NOVEMBER 2015

Pierre Lemaitre

THE GREAT SWINDLE

Translated from the French by Frank Wynne

WINNER OF THE PRIX GONCOURT

October 1918: the war on the Western Front is all but over. Desperate for one last chance of promotion, an ambitious lieutenant, Henri d'Aulnay Pradelle, sends two scouts over the top, and shoots them in the back to incite his men to heroic action once more.

Thus is set in motion a series of shocking events that will inextricably bind together the fates and fortunes of Pradelle and the two soldiers who discover his crime: Albert Maillard and Édouard Péricourt.

Set amid the ruins of one of the most brutal conflicts of the modern era, this is a devastating portrait of the darker side of post-war France with all her villains, cowards and clowns, revealing the unbearable tragedy of the lost generation.

MACLEHOSE PRESS

www.maclehosepress.com

Subscribe to our quarterly newsletter

AVAILABLE MARCH 2016

Pierre Lemaitre

BLOOD WEDDING

Translated from the French by Frank Wynne

Sophie is losing her grip, haunted by visions from her past, of her loving husband, who committed suicide after a car accident.

One morning she wakes to find the child in her care strangled in his bed with her own shoelaces. She can remember nothing of the night before. Could she really have killed him? She flees in panic, but this only cements her guilt in the eyes of the law.

Soon afterwards it happens again – she wakes with blood on her hands and no memory of the murder committed. What comes over her when she sleeps? And what else might she be capable of?

Wanted by the police, and desperate to change her identity, Sophie decides to find a man to marry. To have and to hold. For better or for worse. Till death does them part . . .

MACLEHOSE PRESS

www.maclehosepress.com
Subscribe to our quarterly newsletter